Crystet

By

Nicoline Evans

Crystet copyright © 2018

Author: Nicoline Evans – www.nicolineevans.com

Editor: Kate Watts – www.kateedits.com

Cover Design: Julia Iredale – www.juliairedale.com

A special shout-out to my beta readers and a big thank you to everyone who has offered me support (in all ways, shapes, and sizes) during this entire process.

All rights reserved. Without limiting the rights under copyright reserved above, no part of this publication may be reproduced, stored in or introduced into a retrieval system (excluding initial purchase), or transmitted, in any form, or by any means (electronic, mechanical, photocopying, recording, or otherwise) without the prior written permission of the above author of this book.

This is a work of fiction. Names, characters, places, brands, media, institutions, and incidents are either the product of the author's imagination or are used fictitiously. The author acknowledges the trademarked status and trademark owners of various products referenced in this work of fiction, which have been used without permission. The publication/use of these trademarks is not authorized, associated with, or sponsored by the trademark owners.

Dedicated to the promises we keep

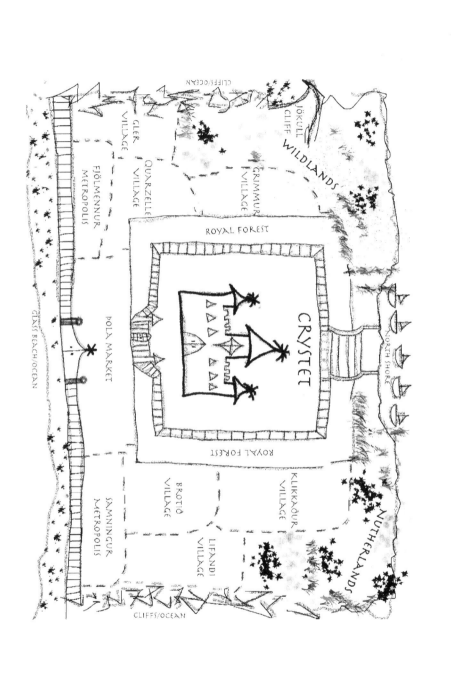

Planet: Namaté of the Avitus Galaxy

Year: Cycle 2008 around the Nebila Sun

Chapter 1

"Come on, Kipp," Gwyn shouted at her mountain dog as she ran through the snow. Spring blossoms had sprouted on the branches overhead, but only a few would fully bloom. Ice plagued Crystet, and though the flowers tried to grow, the nightly frost often thwarted their attempts. Moonrise brought with it an arctic chill.

Her large-pawed puppy barreled after her, barking happily as he chased his beloved owner. When he caught up to her, he knew better than to tackle the little girl. She was fragile, made of glass and breakable. Gwyn giggled and halted, bending to her knees and allowing the dog to snuggle against her.

"I love you," she whispered into Kipp's ear. He licked her face in response.

They were both young; Kipp was given to Gwyn on her sixth birthday. Now he was two and it was her eighth birthday and their bond was unbreakable. Kipp was her best friend.

She fell into the snow and began making snow angels. Kipp collapsed beside her and spastically rolled around.

"You're doing it wrong," she said with a laugh, but the puppy continued his antics.

The castle bells rang, causing Gwyn to pause her revelry. She lay motionless in the snow, counting the chimes till they ceased.

Her energy drained with each bell. Kipp noticed and stopped his playful conduct.

"I don't want to go home," she said in a whisper.

Kipp licked her glass cheek.

The final bell rang and Gwyn rolled over and buried herself in his dark, brown fur. He was warm and his heartbeat thudded against her forehead. He licked the top of her head and nuzzled her hair until she looked up at him.

"You're the only one who cares," she confessed before smothering him in kisses. He accepted her love with happy grunts.

The distant sound of the royal army chanting and blowing their crystal trumpets filled the afternoon sky.

She sighed. "My parents are looking for us."

A few moments later, the sound of glass feet crunching snow emerged. Gwyn lifted her head from Kipp's fur to see that her uncle approached with three soldiers.

"Didn't you hear the horns?" Lorcan asked as he neared. The afternoon sun caught the healed fissures on his face and reflected brightly off of them.

"Yes."

"You know very well what that means. Why didn't you obey?"

"Why should I?"

Lorcan exhaled heavily; forcing himself to be patient with his defiant niece. "For starters, those are the rules. You might be a princess, but you are not above the law." Gwyn rolled her eyes from where she remained sprawled in the snow with her dog. Lorcan continued, "But also, it's your birthday. Cake and presents await your arrival. Your parents organized a party and you are selfishly abstaining."

"I don't like cake. Or parties. They overwhelm me."

"It's time to grow up," Lorcan replied, then signaled his soldiers to intervene. They grabbed her arms with forceful care and yanked her upright.

"You'll break me!" she exclaimed, objecting their firm grip. Kipp growled and the fur along his spine rose.

"Release her," Lorcan instructed, then addressed his niece. "Follow us back or they will constrain you again."

Gwyn obeyed begrudgingly and trudged back to the castle, hopping in and out of her uncle's snowy footsteps. Kipp followed close behind, protecting her every step.

Barefoot, she followed her glassened elders without further objection up the field, through the patches of snow-covered evergreens, and into one of the many side doors of the shimmering castle. The moment the glass door opened, the noise of a large gathering in the main hall echoed down to them.

"Must I?" Gwyn asked her uncle.

"You must."

He took her hand and gently led her forward. Kipp tried to follow, but the soldiers blocked the doorway. Gwyn tugged on her uncle's sleeve in protest.

"No dogs allowed," Lorcan insisted.

She knew better than to press this issue, so she spoke to Kipp instead.

"I'll be with you again soon," she promised as she was tugged away. Kipp whimpered in response. The noise of the party grew louder, drowning out his desperate whines.

Lorcan led her into the enormous, vaulted chamber and the merriment paused. Expressions of disgust and disapproval greeted her wet and dirty appearance. Gwyn wished to retreat within herself, but found she was trapped.

Her mother glided toward them, donning a false but pleasant smile. Her silvery gown flowed and shimmered in the sunlight that poured through the glass ceiling.

"Why does she look a mess?" Dalila hissed at Lorcan.

"I found her near the royal forest, rolling around in the snow with her dog."

"You know better," she scolded, looking down at Gwyn.

"I was having fun."

"You've spoiled your party."

"Everyone is having a fine time without me."

Queen Dalila clicked her tongue at her daughter then summoned Gwyn's handmaiden, Mina.

"Clean her up and return her in time for the blessings," she instructed. "Trista, go with them."

Mina obeyed, as did Dalila's most trusted spiritual adviser, and they led Gwyn to the nearest washroom.

While she was scrubbed clean and dolled up for the ceremony, another handmaiden fetched her dress.

"Can I see Kipp?"

"No," Trista snarled from the far corner of the room.

"Why not?"

"He will soil you again with his dirty paws."

"But I want to see him," she demanded.

Trista was a Valið, chosen by Gaia to be the queen's spiritual adviser. And though Gwyn was young, she understood that she outranked the andlega ráðgjafi in power.

"I demand you let me see him," Gwyn tried again.

"I cannot allow it. Your mother wouldn't approve."

"She doesn't need to know."

"She knows everything," Trista warned. "You know this better than I."

Gwyn sighed in surrender. Her mother was witchy with knowledge, sneaky with eyes and ears everywhere. Though she conceded, her heart still yearned to be with her best friend.

Gwyn was morphed from a messy little girl into a porcelain doll. She sat in a thin, satin slip as her handmaidens brushed her cheekbones with a rosy powder. Her lashes were darkened and elongated until their length enhanced the silver in her eyes, and a light pink gloss was smeared onto her lips as a final touch. When they shifted their focus to her hair, she flinched, anticipating the pain.

"Must we?" she asked.

"We must," Mina replied.

They yanked her long, blonde tresses, combing out the knots with rough strokes. Gwyn tried to stay quiet, but found herself groaning in agony with every tug. When they pulled out the iron, she whimpered, but her pleas went unheard. They twisted her glass-coated hair into a wild bouquet of tight curls. The finished effect looked wonderful, but she knew the nightmare she'd face when trying to untangle them later.

In the mirror, she looked lovely, but she never got used to the mask they made her wear.

"I don't understand why I am forced to look like someone other than myself."

"You look like yourself," Trista objected. "Just a prettier version."

"I think I'm quite pretty without the paint."

"You'll understand what I mean when you're older."

Gwyn didn't think she would.

Mina went to the closet and located the dress Gwyn would wear for her eighth birthday celebration. The bodice was made of white lace with long sleeves and a scoop neck collar. At the waist, a ball gown skirt made of light purple tulle began and extended to the floor. The bottom of the skirt had lace flowers stitched into the hem that ran up the gown from her feet to her knees. Mina wrangled the gown onto Gwyn's little body and tightly tied the ribbons that laced up the back.

"The finishing touch," Mina announced as she removed a diamond tiara from a velvet-cushioned box. She placed it onto Gwyn's head and the entire room sighed at the sight of the young girl's completed look. The tiara wrapped around the back of her head from ear to ear and was made of pure diamond. The precious gem was shaped into a crown of flowers and it sat in her bed of curls with magnificent splendor.

Gwyn examined herself in the mirror, impressed, but also unnerved. Her reflection felt like a trick, like a lie, yet there she was, standing in a stranger's body.

"You are a vision," Mina complimented.

"Perhaps, but I am also not myself."

"Stop saying that," Trista scowled before taking Gwyn's tiny wrist and dragging her out of the room.

Dressed like a proper princess, she was escorted back into the party. But no one paid her any attention until her father stood from his throne of glass daggers and clinked his fork against his crystal chalice.

The room hushed as he spoke.

"Our dear Gwynessa turns eight today, as you are all well aware. This marks the start of her womanhood, the beginning of her journey toward enlightenment."

Almas waved her closer and she obeyed. She stood in front of the long table where her parents and other high-ranking members of their council sat. The afternoon sun beamed through the high windows, creating patches of light on the floor, and her father motioned for her to stand in the square of sunlight directly in front of him. The light traveled through her translucent skin, highlighting her pristine complexion. Not a single crack or break on her body. The veins in her neck and legs were bright through her plush, iridescent flesh, but her dress blocked the onlookers from viewing her tiny organs. Gwyn took a deep breath, uncomfortable in the spotlight, but maintained her composure. This would be over soon.

"Our first child, our pride and joy," her father continued. The people of Crystet greatly admired their king, almost as much as they admired the queen and high priest, Orlan. They soaked in every word as King Almas continued, "is now a woman.

Though my son Calix will eventually become king and take his mother's spot as ruler of Crystet, Gwynessa will undoubtedly be a great leader in her own right one day. I trust the same respect you give to Dalila and I will be offered to her once she fully blooms. She is our seed after all, and through her and her children, Dalila and I live forever." The crowd murmured in awe and understanding. "To her vitality and the blessing of vivacious ovules, we drink." He raised his chalice to the crowd, then drained the remaining frostshine from his cup. The party guests followed his lead, chugging their alcoholic beverages, and the music resumed.

Seven glass flutes, three aquarian marimbas, and one armonica filled the hall with eerie, yet enchanting music. The echoing glass instruments inspired everyone to dance.

Gwyn remained in the patch of blinding sunlight, as beautiful and rigid as a porcelain doll. She heard little of what her father said as the onslaught of unfamiliar glares deafened her mind and smothered her ability to listen. Though she always thought it peculiar that there were never any children at her birthday parties, only adults, it was all she ever knew. Her life was plagued by royal politics and the only other child in the room was her five-year-old brother, Calix.

"You could smile, you know," her mother sneered, stirring Gwyn from her daze.

"Can I leave now?"

"You haven't received your blessings yet."

Gwyn fidgeted. "Can't we get that over with already?"

"No. Be patient until we are ready for you again."

Gwyn hated the blessings. By the time the nobles finished bestowing their hollow words upon her, they were always drunk and reeked of liquor. Their gifts, although disguised as presents for her, were always intended for her parents. The ordeal was long and arduous and she was forced to endure it every year.

Looking around the hall, she spotted Calix on the lap of Chandi, his primary handmaiden. Orlan and Dalila always disapproved of Gwyn spending too much time with him—they feared she would tarnish his perspective and ruin his relationship with the gods—so seeing an opportunity, Gwyn skated toward him.

The floors of the castle were coated with Nearctic whale oil, which was reapplied each quarter of the year when the mammoth sea beasts mated near the shores of Crystet. Despite the already slick and greasy floor, Gwyn produced some of her own traveler's oil, which excreted from the soles of her glass feet.

"Come with me," she ordered, sliding to an abrupt stop and extending her hand to her brother.

Calix's face lit up with a rare smile as he accepted his sister's offer.

"Don't wander too far," Chandi advised.

Gwyn responded with a defiant glare; she hated being told what to do.

Though the handmaiden's suggestion served as inspiration to escape, Gwyn knew better than to succumb to her rebellious desires. Instead, she led her little brother around the perimeter of the large room. Behind the columns that separated the side aisles from the nave, the children found a safe space to talk.

"Are you having fun?" she asked.

"I don't think so," Calix replied, unsure what fun was.

"They've ruined you."

His eyes filled with pearly tears.

"Don't worry," she continued in a softer tone. "You can play hide-and-seek with Kipp and I after the party. We'll remind you what fun feels like."

"Okay," he mumbled through a sniffle. Though his eyes remained wet, his smile returned.

He wore a small crown made of elongated diamonds that were twisted and carved to look like wooden branches. It sat atop his blond hair, resting perfectly in place. He would make a great king one day.

"Promise me you'll never change," she said suddenly.

"I can't stay this way forever," Calix replied, staring down at his tiny, pristine hands, confused. "I will grow."

"Of course you will grow, that's not what I meant. I need you to promise me that you'll remain kind and curious. That you won't accept the truths they try to force upon you."

"Who?"

"Everyone."

"Mamma and Pappa?"

"Mamma and her council." She paused. "Orlan most of all."

"You sound like Trepedene."

"I am not controlled by Trepedene, or any of Gaia's Vorso children."

"Well, you sound mighty suspicious to me."

Gwyn groaned. "The heilög lessons are poisoning your brain. We aren't controlled by the Vorso," she reminded her brother. "No one is controlled by them; those gods and goddesses do not rule our personalities. Don't let Orlan or Mamma scare you into obedience."

"I'm not afraid of the truth."

Gwyn cursed beneath her breath, aggravated with herself. She promised she'd help him decipher truth from propaganda when he was placed into holy lessons with the high priest.

"I'm sorry," she said. "I should've been paying closer attention."

"Why are you sorry?"

"I let you down."

"I don't understand."

"Religion is dangerous," she warned him. "Don't take those lessons too seriously. The only god that matters is Gaia."

"You shouldn't say that," Calix shuddered. "You'll make the others mad."

Gwyn didn't have to wonder why Calix believed that. Using fear to control the Glaziene was a trademark of the vicious æðsti prestur.

"Orlan told you that, didn't he?"

"Yes."

"Forget the æðsti prestur."

"But he is training me to be a holy king."

"His role is fake."

"He was chosen by Gaia; he's the only Glaziene that can speak to Her."

"He's lying to you, trying to scare you into compliance so that he and Mamma can shape you into the man *they* want you to be." Gwyn stopped their progression and knelt to her brother's height. She stared into his eyes imploringly, sending all her love for him through her gaze. "You must resist. You must become the man *you* wish to be."

"What if I don't mind what they are teaching me?"

"Do you love me?"

"I love you a lot."

"Then you must trust me. I'd never lead you astray." Gwyn kissed his forehead and then stood. "I will take care of you, always."

He smiled up at her, bright silver-green eyes gleaming.

Orlan took his place at the pulpit next to the royal table. The æðsti prestur was the only person whose rank matched that of the queen. As high priest, chosen by Gaia centuries ago, his word was divine. He had no authority to enact change, but his words were persuasive and often heeded by those in power. Gwyn hated that everyone took him seriously, that the masses bent and broke at his command, but there was no changing the fear they placed in the heavens. Their creed debilitated them and made them vulnerable to snakes like Orlan. If it wasn't for her father, Gwyn would be just like the rest of them.

"It is time for Princess Gwynessa to receive her birthday blessings," Orlan announced to the party guests. The dancing and carousing ceased at the sound of his monotonous, nasally voice and the party guests formed a line facing the royal throne.

"Guess that's my cue," Gwyn said before letting go of her brother's hand and skating toward the throne. When she reached the enormous chair, she extended her arms and two soldiers lifted her onto the seat. She scanned the room, unimpressed by the large attendance of regally dressed nobles.

"Dearest Princess," the first man in line began, kneeling at the foot of her throne. He wore a white tunic and headband made of vines and pine needles. "To thee, I bestow this painting, made by me under the influence of the god Romanel, in hopes that genuine romance finds you. I pray that love greets you in womanhood. Blessings aplenty, in the name of the Mother, the Vorso, and all of their Spirits, I vow."

Gwyn recognized the painter; Merliando was the most famous in all of Crystet, and the painting was a world map of Namaté with her parents' faces underlaid in the background. Crystet was drawn to be larger than all the other lands in Namaté—a depiction she suspected was inaccurate. Gwyn sighed and waved him forward.

Merliando stood, kissed his palm, and guided the kiss toward her. The guards accepted his painting on her behalf and placed it on the table where they'd pile all the other blessings.

Up next was a lady dressed in silk. She curtsied, then kneeled.

"Princess Gwynessa, fair and clever, I devise this blessing through Clevren, god of logic and reason, to thee in the form of a gilded game of Pikantu." She held up a board game made of gold. "I pray that your life is one guided by reason. Blessings aplenty, in the name of the Mother, the Vorso, and all of their Spirits, I vow."

The woman kissed her hand and then lifted it to guide the invisible kiss toward the throne. Gwyn nodded, accepting the blessing, and the guards retrieved the golden board game. Another gift for her parents, as it would surely find a home in the room dedicated to precious metals from Coppel.

More blessings came, all in the name of Gaia's benign Vorso children. Out of the seventeen gods, only four fell into that category: Romanel, Clevren, Devotene, and Altrudene. The majority were dualist, meaning their intentions could be good or bad, depending on the use and interpretation of their ruling traits, and two of the gods were malignant. A few blessings, presented with careful wording, came in the name of the dualist gods, but no one dared cast a blessing in the name of Vindicene or Deraingla. To do so was considered obscene, and if anyone had, their fate would have fallen to the wrath of the king and queen for cursing their child.

Up last was Jahdo Uveges, owner of the top armor shop in all of Crystet. He was also father to Ario, who was Gwyn's secret foe and the catalyst to the difficult year she just endured. Jahdo was broad in build and covered in fissures, though he wore his battle wounds proudly.

"Princess Gwynessa, brave and wild, I've always sensed your dissidence."

This caught her attention and snapped her out of her bored compliance. She sat up, interest focused, as Jahdo continued.

"I hope it is of no offense to their highnesses or the priesthood that I use this name, but it only seems appropriate after what I have heard about our young princess. In the woods, she talks to the bears, unafraid of their strength or fury. They listen to her, unprovoked, in peaceful serenity. Her words, her songs, soothe the hostile beasts and demand their respect. No Glaziene in the history of our people has been known to offer kindness to the beasts of the wild."

Gwyn was unable to hide her shock. Ario *did* tell his father, and now, Jahdo was revealing her secret for all to hear. She glanced back at her parents. Almas held a sturdy grip on Dalila's arm, preventing her from overreacting.

Jahdo continued, unaware that he said anything that wasn't already common knowledge, or that his words utterly rattled the royal family. "After so many years alive, and as a father to a child of my own, her behavior is peculiar, but quite admirable. I must insist that she is onto something revolutionary. Kindness toward what we fear most might seem foolish, but after seeing the power of such behavior, I am forced to reconsider my long held beliefs. With that explanation, I send my blessing in the name of Rebelene, goddess of mischief and rebellion." Jahdo paused as the crowd gasped in shock. When they settled, he continued. "May you always resist what is learned in examination of more noble paths, may your explorations lead to progress for the greater good, and may your defiance shape our world into a better place. I carved this crystal bear from the shield I used during the Sparks War against Coppel. During times of growth, I hope this gift provides you with luck and courage. During times of sorrow, I hope it acts as a reminder that you are strong enough to endure. Always know that you are capable of achieving your heart's greatest desires."

For the first time, the gift was truly meant for her. Her eyes widened with excitement as Jahdo glided to the throne and handed the gift directly to her. "Blessings aplenty," he continued, "in the name of the Mother, the Vorso, and all of their Spirits, I vow."

This was the first time she did not loathe the thought of being connected to Rebelene.

"Thank you," she whispered with delight as she examined the majestic crystal bear.

"Blessings are over," her mother announced. "Let the merriment commence!"

The band resumed their song. The armonica took the lead, twirling chilling melodies throughout the room.

The queen zeroed in on Jahdo. She snagged him by the arm and pulled him into the side aisle where they could speak in private.

"What kind of blessing was that?" Dalila growled.

"One of sincerity; it came from my heart."

"Unacceptable. You are fortunate that your services are greatly needed, otherwise, I'd banish you to the Nutherlands."

"Rebelene isn't a malignant god."

"She is one of the dualist gods that we avoid! You've filled Gwyn's head with poison and I am left to reverse the damage."

"You ought to leave the girl alone. Like I said, she is on to something far greater than what we've come to know and accept. Her spirit, her soul, they're unlike the rest, and for that, you should be proud."

"Don't tell me how to feel about my daughter," Dalila spat. "You know what we must do tonight and still, you chose to offer her a blessing honoring her infuriating love for animals."

"I recommend you break tradition," Jahdo suggested.

"You're mad. I will not raise a feeble daughter."

"It's not my place to interfere, but I suspect you will come to regret this night. I do not think it will affect her the way you hope it will."

Dalila pursed her lips. "It's time for you to leave the party."

Jahdo did not object and departed with grace.

Dalila returned to her daughter, who stood by her father's side.

"What in the black-sands of Namaté was Jahdo talking about?" she asked in an angry whisper. "You go into the woods? You *tame* the monsters with kindness?"

"It makes me happy," Gwyn replied, unafraid of her mother's wrath.

"It's unnatural."

"Leave her be," Almas interjected.

Dalila answered him with a slap. Glass hand to glass cheek, the crack along his jaw splintered toward his ear. Everyone gasped.

"Look what you've done," Dalila shouted at Gwyn. "All you bring to this family is turmoil."

"I don't mean to," Gwyn stammered.

"You must find other avenues that provide happiness," Dalila insisted. "A princess in the wild is dangerous."

"The animals won't hurt me."

"But the people might. You are a royal, which means there are individuals who inherently despise you."

Tears glistened Gwyn's eyes. "The bears and wolves will protect me."

"Enough," Dalila demanded, her anger enflamed. "Lorcan," she called out to her brother, who was drunkenly teasing a lady in the council. His head lifted at the sound of his sister's authoritative voice. "It's time."

Lorcan took a deep breath and departed from the fun. His merry, inebriated demeanor stiffened as he approached.

"Time for what?" Gwyn asked.

"It would be better if I sobered up a little first," Lorcan said to his sister.

"It's not my fault you overindulge."

"But this is a big moment."

"It is a critical moment, yes," Dalila agreed. "Chug a glass of ginger water and let's go."

Dalila grabbed her daughter's skinny bicep and yanked her through the arched exit. Almas stayed behind with Calix.

"It's time," Dalila said to Trista as they passed.

"Understood." Trista grinned, charging ahead.

"Where are we going?" Gwyn demanded.

"To your sleeping quarters."

"But why? The first moon isn't fully risen!"

"This is the final stage of your transition into womanhood."

Gwyn's eyes widened with fear. "You aren't going to make me have a baby, are you?"

"No more talking," Dalila insisted, but Gwyn didn't listen. She jabbered in panic the entire walk, begging for answers or a clue of what was to come.

She didn't stop talking until they burst through her bedroom door and she saw Kipp, bound, muzzled, and whimpering on the ground. Trista knelt beside him and held a knife made of volcanic glass to his throat.

"No," Gwyn exclaimed, charging toward her dog, but her uncle emerged from the shadows and caught her by the arm. "Leave him alone," she bellowed.

"This is necessary," Lorcan reassured her.

"You're scaring me," she screamed.

"You cannot turn into a fierce woman if you are bogged down by insignificant attachments," her mother droned. "Therefore, we must eliminate those attachments."

"Are you going to kill him?"

"Yes."

"No!" Gwyn fought her uncle's grip, but could not escape. She burst into tears of fury and grave sorrow. Kipp's whimpers grew more desperate. "He's my best friend," she sobbed.

"Don't cry," Dalila demanded.

"But I love him."

"Love is a weakness."

"Please, don't. I beg you. I will do anything you ask, anything you want, just let him live."

"This will make you strong." Dalila extended her hand and Trista handed her the knife. She then plunged the blade into

Kipp's lower abdomen. Blood poured out and the dog howled in pain through the muzzle. Dalila raised the knife to strike again. Her vicious silhouette paused with the blade raised high, her tall shadow looming along the back wall like a demon risen from Kólasi's abyss.

"Stop!" Gwyn pleaded through the tears.

"I told you not to cry." The blade lowered into the innocent creature's body once more.

The whites of Kipp's eyes were now red and tears ran down his fur as he searched for Gwyn, desperate to find his best friend.

"I love you, Kipp," she wept, though nothing she said would eliminate the devastation she felt. "I am so sorry," she sobbed, terrified that he blamed her in his dying thoughts.

When Kipp became silent and still, Dalila took a step back and Lorcan let Gwyn go. She ran to Kipp's side and collapsed onto the floor next to him. Unconcerned by the bloody mess, she placed an arm around her best friend and held him in a final hug.

"I love you, I love you, I love you," she repeated with her face buried in the fur of his neck. Tears dampened his thick coat and he moved his head to look at her one last time.

She adjusted herself so she could look him in the eyes.

Apologetic tears poured down her face. She kissed his nose a hundred times, and then his snout and forehead a hundred more. She buried him in love as the light in his soul faded. He closed his eyes and succumbed to death beneath the onslaught of her love.

When he stopped breathing, Gwyn's tears turned into panicked fury and her bereaved adrenaline induced a fit of rage. The hurt she held inside came out as a deafening shriek. The sound that left her tiny body was so ferocious, it caused the nearest glass window to splinter. Gwyn stood and charged at her mother, arms flailing. Dalila did not flinch and Lorcan caught Gwyn by the waist before she made contact.

"I will kill you!"

"Your dramatics are tiring," her mother proclaimed in a bored tone. She handed the bloody knife to Trista for cleaning.

"Calm down," Lorcan whispered into Gwyn's ear. "Remember what I told you about reacting from a place of reason, not emotion."

Gwyn screamed so loud she ripped the flesh lining inside her throat. Blood coated her tongue, but she was too enraged to care.

The three adults watched her tirade with patience, waiting as she exhausted herself. When her screams turned into sobs, Lorcan released her from his grip and she collapsed to the floor next to Kipp. She wrapped her arms around his lifeless body, refusing to let him go.

"It's over. He's gone. Get up," her mother demanded.

"No!"

"Do as I say."

"I hate you," Gwyn seethed from her hiding place in Kipp's lifeless embrace.

"Your pain will pass."

"Go away!" Gwyn demanded.

Dalila looked to Trista for guidance, who nodded, indicating that Gwyn needed time alone to grieve.

"Fine," Dalila conceded, "but know that this is for the best. Every child loses something they love on their eighth birthday. You are not special. The traditions of Vale Octavum are honored by all across Crystet. This is the way of our culture. Every child must experience loss and grief at a young age."

"You're a monster."

"As are you, you'll see. Embrace who you are designed to be."

The adults left the room and Gwyn curled her little body around Kipp's. She couldn't understand the horror, couldn't understand what murdering her best friend was supposed to teach her. All she felt was grief and rage. Hatred coursed through her bones and she wasn't sure how she'd ever forgive her mother for this crime.

Chapter 2

The soldiers came to clear Kipp's body the next morning. The sound of fists thudding against her bedroom door shook Gwyn from her all-consuming grief.

"Go away," she hollered.

"We have to take the dog's body away," Lorcan explained.

"No. Kipp stays with me."

"That is unacceptable."

"You are a peasant," she shouted back at him.

"Stop your nonsense and let me in."

"I don't answer to peasants," she taunted.

"I am your uncle, brother to the queen, and I hold more power than you."

"Not for long."

"It is Heilög Day. The body must be disposed of before moonrise."

"Disposed of?" Gwyn asked in horror.

"Open the door!"

Gwyn refused, so Lorcan's soldiers kicked in the door, shattering it completely.

"Leave," Gwyn screeched, still sitting on the floor with Kipp's head in her lap, but the soldiers ignored her. They charged forward to rip the body off of her. She kicked and screamed, throwing punches at the guardsmen as they tried to steal Kipp. A swing at one of the soldier's faces came with a loud snap and Gwyn bellowed in pain. A large crack splintered from her knuckles to her elbow. Silvery-red blood seeped from the fracture and dripped all over the party dress still wore.

"Make it stop!" she screeched in agony as the fissure crept up her arm.

Lorcan darted to her side and placed pressure on the end of the crack. Its progression slowed beneath his firm grip until it stopped completely.

The soldiers continued their duty and dragged Kipp's body away.

"No," she sobbed. "Bring him back!"

Her words were disregarded. The soldiers left with Kipp in tow. Frantic, Gwyn grabbed a sharp shard that broke off her forearm and held its tip to the side of her neck.

"Order them to bring him back," she demanded, voice shaking.

"No," Lorcan replied, masking his concern for her mental state. "Put the dagger down."

"I will not!" she sobbed. "I'd rather die."

"Don't be a fool. You will be embarrassed by this behavior in a month from now."

"You're wrong."

"Think of your brother. He needs you."

Her resolve softened, though she kept the glass shard in place.

"They don't let me see him."

"He will always need you."

"Then why do they keep me from him?"

"Do they? Or were you too preoccupied by your friendship with Kipp?"

Gwyn lowered her weapon, unsure if he was right. The possibility that she'd been neglectful of others she loved intensified her grief.

"Perhaps this was for the best," Lorcan said as he sat on the floor beside Gwyn. He gently took the dagger from her grip and placed it out of reach.

"Am I a terrible person?"

"No. This is life. This is what your mother has been trying to prep you for all these years."

"But *she's* the one who killed him! It never needed to happen!"

"You must let this go."

"How?" she cried. "He was my only friend."

"Kipp was an animal. A pet. Grieving his death as you would a person's is unhealthy."

"But I loved him as much as I love any person," she explained. "Calix might be the only person I love more than I loved Kipp."

"Then focus on the love you have for your brother."

"I will not just forget about Kipp."

"Then don't. Keep him alive inside of you, but move on. You must, for your sake and for the sake of everyone else. Your parents need you to be strong."

"Then they shouldn't have killed my dog."

"I also lost my best friend on my eighth birthday. He was a peasant, but I enjoyed his company. He was the only child I would play with. My mother invited him to my birthday party and had him killed in front of everyone."

"They killed a kid on your Vale Octavum?" Gwyn asked, appalled.

"It's not an uncommon practice amongst royals."

"That's terrible."

"Yes. I was devastated at the time, but I couldn't even cry for fear of embarrassment. The attention of the entire party was focused on my reaction. It took a while, but I recovered just fine. You will too."

"I don't want to," she sniffled. "I must suffer just as Kipp did. It's not fair that he died because of me."

"The world is cruel and unfair," Lorcan explained. "That's what the killing was meant to teach you. It was also meant to show you that you can survive the worst of what life deals you, but if you refuse to carry on, then maybe you'll be the first in the history of Crystet to be defeated on your eighth birthday."

"No one defeats me."

"Prove it." Lorcan stood. "Quit the pity party and be strong."

"It's not a pity party for myself, it's for Kipp. I owe him that."

"Fine. Though I advise you not dwell too long in your sorrow. Your parents will not tolerate your melancholy for long."

Gwyn shrugged, unconcerned by what her parents wanted. She owed them nothing.

"I'll send a glazician to tend to your first break."

He left the room, stepping over the shattered pieces of her bedroom door. Handmaidens glided by, gawking through the doorway at the distraught princess. Their glares were critical. Angry that she could not grieve in private, she stood and pushed her tall, diamond armoire to block the opening.

She took off her party dress, which was stained with blood, hung it in her closet where it would remain unwashed, and sat on her bed in her underwear. Her breathing was heavy as she came down from her marathon of hysterics. She ran out of tears to cry; her insides were dehydrated by the trauma. This was the first time she had stopped crying since last night. This was her first moment of clarity amidst the horror. Her throat hurt from screaming, her eyes stung from the onslaught of salty tears, and her chest hurt from the stress. She looked down at her fragile glass body to examine the organs beneath her plush, translucent skin.

Her heart beat with vigor, so much so she wondered if it was working a little too hard. The bones protecting it expanded with each heavy breath. She raised her hand to touch the glass skin that separated her from her heart, aware that there was nothing she could do to soothe its rapid beat.

Her eyes darted to the spot where Kipp had died; it was still covered in his blood. She knelt beside the pool of crimson and placed a finger into the wet blood. Carefully, she dragged the wet liquid over the nearest crack in the floor. The blood seeped into the fissure, staining it forever. She sighed with relief, then continued her unexpected art project. Crack by crack, she filled each fissure with Kipp's blood until the entire room appeared to be covered in red spiderwebs. Lost in the monotony of this therapeutic endeavor, she did not notice the medic entering her room.

"What are you doing?" the glazician asked after a moment of observation.

Her mother stormed in a few seconds later.

"What have you done?" she screeched, appalled by the graffiti. "Those stains will never come out!"

"That's the point," Gwyn replied, unaffected by her mother's anger.

"Why have you done this?"

"So Kipp can stay with me forever."

"You are deranged. Get off the floor and put some clothes on."

Gwyn stood, but she did not find new clothes to wear. Instead, she stared up at her mother with dead hollowness. Her silver-green eyes held nothing in their depths, just emptiness.

"You will be the death of me," Dalila scoffed.

"It's okay," the glazician intervened. "It's better for me to assess the damage this way."

He grabbed Gwyn's arm and lifted it to get a better look. He traced his fissured, glass fingers along the break that ran from her middle knuckle all the way up to her elbow. With a gentle breath, he blew into the crack and Gwyn winced in pain.

"That hurt," she declared.

"Of course it does," he replied. "Sit on your bed and I'll get you patched up."

Gwyn obeyed and Dalila watched from the doorway as he placed his tools on the nightstand.

"Are you ready?" he asked.

"Will it hurt?" Gwyn asked.

"Yes."

"Okay, go ahead."

The glazician dabbed a piece of cloth into a saucer filled with acetone before cleaning her break and the glass around it. He then dipped a glass spoon into a separate bowl and scooped out diamond dust.

"You get the good stuff," he noted before carefully spreading the fine particles throughout her crack. The diamond dust filled the cavity.

"What does everyone else get?" she asked.

"Liquid resin, which is made with artificial chemicals such as epoxy, silicone, polyurethane, and polyester. Very dangerous stuff to put into your body, but it's an accessible method that is affordable and simple to perform."

She nodded in understanding as he leveled the layer of crushed diamonds. The glazician continued, "Those who oppose these inorganic options and cannot afford to buy raw diamond or crystals to make an organic resin take the barbaric route of creating their own resins using pieces of the deceased. They grind up glass fragments from the graveyard and mix it into a liquid resin that they smear into their fissures. It's never as smooth as fire-healed breaks, nor is it as pretty once cooled," he explained.

Dalila chimed in, "It's also rather off-putting to put the pieces of a deceased person inside yourself, don't you agree?"

Gwyn shivered at the thought.

The glazician then lifted a tool obtained from another land: a metal blowtorch. A long, silver cylinder stretched from the nozzle, which he pointed at Gwyn's wound. Without warning, he pulled the trigger, the gadget clicked, and a scorching hot flame hit her skin. She howled in pain and flinched, but the glazician held her arm firmly in place.

"Don't move. If you fidget, your scar will be worse," he advised.

She obeyed as best she could, but kept her eyes closed tightly. Tears rolled down her flushed cheeks. She opened them slightly to witness the procedure, but her vision had gone black from the pain. She saw nothing and her stomach turned.

"I'm going to throw up," she warned.

"I'm almost done."

The fire melting her skin glowed a bright blue. The heat liquefied the glass, which slowly fused with the diamond particles. The glazician ran the flame up and down her fissure with great care, making sure to only hit the broken parts. When the procedure was complete, Gwyn's arm seared with scorching pain.

"It still hurts," she cried.

"That's because we aren't done yet."

"What is left to do?"

"Your wound needs to be annealed. A quick dip into the kiln will suffice for a break this size. Follow me."

"The kiln is scary," she whined.

"Do as he says," her mother insisted, handing her a nightgown to put on.

Gwyn obeyed and the glazician led her to the western medical wing on the third floor. There, countless kilns of different sizes and shapes decorated the large space, each designed to anneal specific body parts. The glazician brought her to an oblong kiln that sat atop a crystal table.

"This will fuse your crack with precision. Place your arm into the hole."

Gwyn obeyed and the doctor clamped the opening around her bicep until the aperture was air-tight. The kiln was preheated and the scorching temperature was searing. Gwyn squeezed her eyes shut, imagined running through the snowy fields with Kipp, and the pain lessened as the warmth decreased. The temperature lowered and once it matched that of the room, the glazician released her arm from the clamp and opened the kiln.

Gwyn yanked her arm out of the hellish machine to see that her arm was fully fused and properly annealed. The diamond dust filled every space of her crack, leaving no air bubbles, and blended into her skin as if it were natural and always there.

"It's pretty," Gwyn noted in a daze.

"It's hideous," the glazician retorted, "and it ought to serve as a reminder to act like a princess."

Gwyn glared up at him with defiance, but said nothing. The scar would act as a reminder of her love for Kipp. Nothing more and nothing less. As she stared at her scar and remembered her friend, sorrow gushed through her. It wasn't fair that she was alive, with only a scar to show for this tragedy, and he was dead.

Blinded by grief, she absentmindedly followed the glazician back to her bedroom where her mother waited.

The queen stood at the foot of Gwyn's bed wearing a severe expression while Mina and Trista used bristled horsehair brushes to clean Kipp's blood out of the foundation cracks. Gwyn examined her work, thoroughly impressed that she covered as much area as she had. The floors and walls were forever decorated in blood.

"You're fixed," Dalila stated without enthusiasm. "Wonderful. Now grab a brush and get to cleaning."

"I'm not cleaning anything."

"Yes, you are. You made this mess and you will help my andlega ráðgjafi and your handmaiden clean this room until it looks the way it did before."

"I like it like this. I don't want it to go back to the way it was."

"I don't care what you want. This is my kingdom and you will do as I say."

Gwyn grabbed a brush and half-heartedly helped the older women scrub the blood from the crevices of her glass floor. As she worked silently, the deep stains remained and she only tinged the tips of her fingers with the blood that sat at the surface of the cracks. She refused to play an active part in erasing his memory. Kipp would remain here, in this room, forever.

When it was time for the midday feast, the agitated women paused their futile efforts to clean the room. Stained and bedraggled, they left without saying anything to Gwyn.

She was alone again, surrounded by the blood of her lost friend. The longer she sat on the floor, wallowing in the memory of Kipp's death and blaming herself for letting it happen, the deeper she sank into despair. The darkness that lived inside her crept back to the surface, casting a shadow over the light she always struggled to find and hold onto. On this occasion, she decided to let the darkness win. It was easier to give in than to fight.

She went to her window and stared at the castle grounds. The tracks she and Kipp made yesterday were already blanketed by a fresh layer of snow, as if they'd never even been there, as if the friendship never happened, as if Kipp never existed at all. Gwyn's thoughts spiraled with grievous gloom when she noticed the bowmen along the roof of the east wing abandoning their stations. The uniformed soldiers marched in synchronicity as the shift changed. She had seen this transition of duty countless times before and there was often a fifteen-minute gap between the switch.

Without any forethought, Gwyn rose and headed toward the roof. She knew what she had to do.

The walk consisted of multiple flights of stairs and minimal passersby. Almost everyone in the castle was attending the weekly Heilög feast, which was hosted in the grand hall for all castle residents—servants to nobles.

Gwyn pushed open the heavy, glass door and exited into the chilly air. Dressed only in her nightgown, the breeze sliced through her freshly fused wound. It appeared even the best remedies weren't infallible. She smiled through the pain; Kipp was with her.

Barefoot, she walked through the snow that collected on the roof and made her way to the edge. The sorrow living inside her multiplied as she climbed atop the parapet. Everything hurt: her heart, her mind, her soul. Across the gray sky and through the snow-swollen clouds flew an emissary owl. It circled overhead before nose-diving into one of the many small windows of the aviary tower.

"Even the spies don't care to know of my pain," she mumbled in self-pity.

Her misery was all-consuming until she reminded herself why she came here: to end her suffering. Relief struck like anesthesia and her vivid pain and reckless thoughts were stunned into paralysis. She was numb to the sorrow, numb to the tragedy, numb to the world. Crystet was a tragic place masked by pristine beauty and false strength. The Glaziene hid wretched souls within their lovely glass-fleshed bodies. This wasn't a place where she wished to live; she couldn't be the person they wanted her to be.

Gwyn extended her arms, as if they were wings, and stepped over the edge. The only sound that came from her was the crack of her broken pieces as she hit the ground.

Chapter 3

Alone and broken, Gwyn stared at the bright afternoon sky. Her head, neck, shoulder, and left arm remained intact, but the rest of her was strewn across the ground. She could feel her newly exposed broken parts crystalizing. The tingling sensation of paralysis washed over her in a calm wave. It wouldn't be long before her entire body turned solid.

From where she lay, she could see her bedroom window, and after a few minutes of solitude, a small head emerged through the frame. It was Calix. He looked down, saw his sister dying, and then disappeared from sight.

Gwyn couldn't process much, the crystallization was slowly creeping into her brain, but in the fading light she hoped that her brother would let her die.

"What have you done?" Calix sobbed as he exited the castle and ran to her. He fell to his knees beside her head.

"Leave me," Gwyn whispered, "like this." Her words came out between struggled breaths.

"No!" He picked up her head and cradled it. "Pappa is on his way. We will fix you."

"I don't… want to… be fixed."

"Don't you love me at all?"

"I love you," Gwyn confessed, "more than anyone."

"Then how could you try to leave me like this?"

"It's not about you." She winced in pain. "You'll be fine without me."

"You are so selfish," Calix spat. His grief was morphing into anger. "Without you, I am all alone."

Tears fell from Gwyn's fading gaze. "They murdered Kipp."

"I heard." Calix's wrath lessened and a wave of profound empathy emanated from his small body. "I am so sorry."

"How can I live… knowing I let him die?" She paused. "He stared into my eyes as he bled out—helpless and betrayed—and I could do nothing to save him."

"It's not your fault."

"I can't live… with the heartache."

"You must. If not for yourself, then for me."

Gwyn looked to her brother, who stared down at her with grave determination. He would not let her die. The outside air was quickly hardening her body, turning her skin rigid and her insides black as it crept through her broken pieces.

"What happened?" Almas declared as he skated along the smooth, glass path toward his children. "Who did this to you?"

"*You* did this to me," Gwyn seethed through thinning breath. "And Mamma… and Uncle Lorcan… and Trista. And everyone else in this stupid castle… I hate our people… I hate this world."

"Darling, what in the realm of Namaté do you mean?"

"Where were you?" she gasped. "Why didn't you stop them?"

Almas knelt next to Calix and looked down at his daughter with sympathy. He did not answer her question, which only increased Gwyn's rage.

"Let me die!" she screamed, summoning the last of her energy.

"You know I won't allow that," Almas said in a calm voice. He lifted her head from Calix's lap and stroked her long, blonde hair as the crystallization reached her face. Bit by bit, her beautiful face was taken over by the process. When her silver-green eyes turned black, the medics arrived and Almas released the breath he held.

He turned to Calix.

"Let's put your sister back together."

Gwyn lay motionless in her bed, unconscious and healing from her self-inflicted trauma. The blackness that consumed her insides receded as her body regained its normal functions and the usual translucency of her skin had returned. Calix and her father stood by her side, along with Dalila, Lorcan, Trista, and Mina.

No one knew for sure when her spirit would locate her body, but since she had not been shattered long—only a few hours of true death passed before her rebuild—they suspected it would be quick. They called to her, hoping she would hear their loving pleas from the other side. What they did not anticipate was her reluctance to return. Gwyn's soul fluttered in limbo, sensing no urgency to reenter its healed vessel.

An entire day passed before Gwyn opened her eyes again. Their bright, silver glow shimmered with tears as she took her first breath from her second life. She looked around the room, confused.

"You put me back together?" she asked, her voice soft from the suffering she endured.

"Of course we did," Almas replied. "How do you feel? Did you hear our calls?"

Since her time spent in purgatory was so brief, her death so short, she remembered nothing that transpired between her death and renewed life.

"I don't remember anything except the fall."

"How dare you insult this family with such reckless selfishness," Dalila proclaimed. "Did you not consider the backlash of your behavior?"

Gwyn took a deep breath and tried to hold back the onslaught of tears, but they fell anyway. Calix grabbed her hand and held it tight.

"Leave her be, Dalila," Almas demanded. "She's endured enough."

"She is weak."

"Almas is right," Lorcan interjected. "Chastising her during this fragile moment will only make matters worse. Give her time to heal."

Dalila clenched her teeth, biting back the words she clearly wished to unleash, then skated with ferocity out of the room.

"Mamma," Gwyn pleaded in a hoarse voice, but Dalila ignored her.

The sight of her mother leaving in anger while she lay in anguish, barely alive with a shattered spirit, left Gwyn feeling more broken than ever. Though she was mended, her mother's harsh reaction broke parts of her she didn't realize could break. The pounding inside her chest intensified, but there was no remedy for an aching heart.

Chapter 4

Gwyn sat in the forest alone, wearing only a thin nightgown. Her translucent skin, blonde curls, and white dress blended with the blinding afternoon snow. She held Jahdo's gift in her hand, staring down at it with a blank heart.

She looked to the sky, which was blocked by a tangled maze of tree branches, and then placed her hand on the nearest tree trunk, willing it to speak.

It responded to her lonesome hope with silence.

"I wish you could talk to me," she confessed.

A reply came from a voice she wasn't expecting to hear.

"You look different." Ario emerged from behind.

She wasn't startled, merely indifferent to his arrival.

"I'm broken now."

"You wear your scars well."

Gwyn finally looked up at Ario, who approached with arms raised. His smile was contagious, infecting her gloom with his confident optimism.

"I didn't bring any weapons," he promised.

She scrutinized his appearance to determine if he was telling the truth and found no evidence of a lie. His silver tunic and cotton drawstring pants lay flat. Not only was he weapon-free, but also armor-free.

"You came here without your gear?" she asked.

"Yes, in an attempt to win your trust." The embroidered collar of his shirt enhanced the shimmering blue in his silvery eyes.

"All you won is my disapproval."

"Why?"

"Because you're a fool not to wear your armor out here."

"*You* don't wear any armor."

"I don't need to. The animals trust me. You on the other hand used to hunt these woods. The animals don't forget. I'm surprised you made it this far without suffering their wrath."

"Do you wish I had?"

"I do," she replied with contempt.

"The reputation you've acquired is quite fitting," he remarked, but she ignored his observation. She did not care what the commoners assumed about her.

Ario was a few years older than her and he tolerated her insult with grace. She was the princess, and though he was part of a noble family, he knew his place.

"Where is your dog?" he finally replied to her insult after a long pause of stubborn silence.

"My mother killed him."

"Why?"

"What does it matter?" Gwyn snapped, fury overtaking her senses. "Why did you come?"

"I thought maybe you'd like a friend."

Gwyn shot him a critical glare. "*You* caused my suffering. Your father announced my guard of the animals to everyone at my birthday party. Later that night, my mom killed my best friend."

"He wasn't supposed to say anything," Ario stammered. "He promised he wouldn't."

"Well, he did."

"I'm sorry. I didn't realize I managed to spoil everything again from afar."

"Why'd you tell him?"

"He believed it was unsafe for me to be in the woods, amongst the animals, and demanded I tell him why I visited so often." Ario paused. "I told him that it was for you. That you changed my views. I told him how you are able to tame the most ferocious creatures with gentleness and love. It took a while to convince him, but eventually, his views about it all changed too. I am certain he did not reveal your secret with malicious intent."

"I know," Gwyn mumbled while twirling the crystal bear between her fingers.

"I'm sorry you had a terrible Vale Octavum."

"Yeah, me too," Gwyn said, her energy somber. "What did you lose on yours?"

Ario hesitated as a look of shame crossed his face.

"A crystal fox."

"That's it?"

"It symbolized my first kill."

"You lost a *toy*?"

Ario's gaze shifted downward. "It was the last thing my mom made for me before she died."

Gwyn's expression softened, but Ario continued before she could ask any more questions.

"I want to be your friend."

"Why?"

"Don't you *want* a friend?"

"I don't need people."

"Aren't you curious what it's like to be a Glaziene outside the castle walls? It's much different than what you're used to in your bubble."

"No," she lied, though her interest was piqued. "I only care to explore the wilderness beyond this one."

"I can help you do that," Ario bribed.

"How?"

"I'll sneak you through the villages and away from the castle. If you already spend this much time away from home, I doubt they'll notice you've wandered beyond the borders of the royal forest."

"If anyone sees me, I'll get into trouble."

"I'll dress you up in armor so no one recognizes you."

Gwyn narrowed her eyes at the boy she despised and considered his offer. It was an opportunity to protect *all* the animals of Glaziene, not just those she could access in the royal forest.

"You won't try to stop me when I scare the children away from the animals?"

"I'll *help* you scare them off." He grinned. "It would be a thrill to be part of your haunting legacy."

Gwyn huffed. "Fine. Just don't get in my way."

"I wouldn't dream of interfering with your reign of terror."

She raised her right brow, unsure what he meant.

"You are a modern-day legend," he explained. "A living, breathing nightmare. All the kids are scared of you. They fear your connection to the Vorso."

"Good, let them be scared."

"Do you talk to them? To the gods?"

"Yes," she lied. "I am their favorite daughter."

Ario smirked, eyes gleaming. "I don't believe you."

"That's unwise."

"Perhaps," he said, lowering his mischievous glare. "Time will tell."

"Do you think it's wise to test my patience?"

Ario grinned—his infuriating, yet charming smile. "Of course not. I don't fight with princesses."

Gwyn didn't argue. She was too sad to fight his stubborn insistence.

"Let me be your friend. Let me help you."

Gwyn sighed. "Fine. Do as you wish. I'm just telling you the facts of the matter as a kindness so you don't waste your time."

"You're not a waste of time," he stated. The depth of his comment struck deeper than intended and they both felt its weight.

Gwyn glared up at him skeptically, startled but appreciative of the pure and unprovoked compliment.

"I mean it," he followed up. "You're far more wonderful than you realize."

"In a terrifying way?"

He smiled. "In the *best* way."

As the seasons changed, Gwyn slowly mended her broken spirit. Trips into the forest were her medicine and nothing else mattered except the healing balm she received from the woods.

"Where are you going?" Calix asked one night after dinner. Family meals were now the only time the two were allowed to be together.

"Into the woods with Ario," Gwyn replied.

"When will you let me join? I want to go on adventures too."

"Soon, I promise." She leaned in and kissed his forehead.

"I don't like it when you leave."

"You know how grateful I am to you, right? For not giving up on me."

"I know."

"I love you to the third moon and back."

"I love you more."

"Impossible." Gwyn smirked, then tossed her carrier bag over her shoulder and raced out of the room.

It was a few hours before nightfall and the setting sun filled the clouds with bright orange light as the first moon crested the horizon. Though Mina, Trista, and Lorcan were tasked to keep a closer eye on Gwyn after her suicidal plight, no one bothered her after she was put to bed and no one checked on her until it was time to wake up. That meant she had the wee hours of morning to do as she pleased.

Her trek through the open field went unnoticed and she made it through the royal forest without any trouble. Upon entering the vacant glass streets of Quarzelle, she lifted the large hood of her rabbit-fur cape to avoid being recognized by any emissary owls or insomniac villagers. A dark shadow blanketed her face, which thoroughly hid her identity, but she managed to cross through the entire village without seeing one Glaziene.

The glass roads and ice-covered pathways between villages were well marked, making it easy for her to find her way. Once over the border and into Gler, she excreted extra traveler's oil so she could skate a little faster. The large lettered sign for Uveges Armor came into sight and she found Ario waiting on the porch. A huge smile crept onto his stern face as he caught sight of her arrival.

"You made it," he called out.

"Of course I did. You have a promise to keep."

"Happily. Come inside."

"Will we wake your dad?"

"No. Nothing can wake him from slumber."

Making as little noise as possible, she followed him to the back of the shop where large cases displayed varying types of protective gear.

"This one holds all the face masks that we offer," Ario explained. "Your cape hides you pretty well, so maybe all we need to get you is a piece to disguise your face in case you're ever caught with your hood off."

Gwyn took a step closer to the glass pane separating her from the beautiful pieces crafted by Jahdo and Ario.

"You designed all of these?" she asked.

"My father made most of those. I'm learning though." He opened the case and pulled a mask from the bottom shelf. "I made this one a few days ago with you in mind."

He held up the thin, tinted piece of chemically tempered glass.

"This mask is called a Volto," he explained. "It's delicate in design and would cover everything but your nose and mouth. I'd adhere two small buttons to your temples and the mask would stay on your face by latching onto those."

He handed the Volto mask to Gwyn, who examined it in awe. The eye slits were decorated with intricate swirling patterns carved into the glass, as was the thin outline bordering the entire shape of the mask. Unlike the other masks, which were functional but rudimentary in design, this one was both practical *and* pretty. Ario had a talent for art, an eye for design that was missing in the pieces made by Jahdo.

"You made this one for me?"

"Yes."

"It's lovely."

"Just like you."

Gwyn looked up at him, embarrassed.

"Can I try it on?"

"Of course."

Ario retrieved a vial of birch wood sap collected from the Wildlands and dabbed a dot onto each of Gwyn's temples. He then attached a glass button to each spot of sticky goo and once they dried, he snapped the mask onto Gwyn's face. It fit her perfectly.

"Let's go," she declared with a mischievous smile. Ario mirrored her look of wild adventure and they took off.

They raced each other through Gler, skating at high speeds atop the glass roads. Northward bound, they darted toward the Wildlands, only slowing their speed when they reached the outer edge of the forest.

"Ready?" Ario asked.

Gwyn nodded and led the way through the tightly spaced trees. They could not glide here, the snow was too deep, so they trudged barefoot through the thick slush instead. As they made their own trail, the dirt soil beneath the glass-fragmented terrain began to show. Out here, the land was not manicured or paved to appear as perfect and groomed as that in the villages or cities.

The early morning shadows cast by the tall trees engulfed their young bodies as they trekked farther into the dense forest. It wasn't long before they encountered their first gathering of animals.

A yoke of musk oxen stood in front of three yellow-leaved aspen trees.

"I've never met an ox before," Gwyn whispered in awe.

"It doesn't matter," Ario replied. "They'll love you just like all the other animals do."

The longer Gwyn stayed still, the more restless the oxen became. They snorted and spat, expelling saliva and snot all over the place.

"Go to them," Ario encouraged.

"They don't know who I am."

"Of course they do." He gave her a slight push and she stumbled forward. Already advancing, she kept her momentum going and took slow and careful steps toward the filthy animals. Dirt matted their long hair and their faces were covered with drool. They made strange noises as she approached, but did not attempt to scare her away. Instead, they controlled their primal outburst and Gwyn realized their aggressive behavior was merely restrained excitement. They were eager to meet her.

Her confidence grew and she approached with an outstretched hand. The oxen rearranged themselves and circled the small princess, bowing their heads after a thorough sniff verified her identity. With an astonished expression, she looked over her shoulder at Ario. He returned her shock with an all-knowing grin.

Gwyn embraced the love these unfamiliar animals gave. Once they had their fill of her, they returned to graze on the tall grass peeking through the trampled snow.

Gwyn hurried back to Ario, thrilled that her reputation preceded her. Little work would need to be done in the Wildlands if all the animals here already heard of her devotion to them.

"Where to next?" Gwyn asked.

Ario paused to think, then replied, "Jökull Cliff."

"Okay. What's there?"

"Beauty, tragedy, history. I suspect your parents won't tell you the significance of that spot until you're older. I can beat them to it." He smirked, then led the way.

They saw many animals along the way, all of which gravitated to Gwyn. She took a moment to dole out love to all, but did her best not to dawdle. She only had a few hours before she needed to be back in her bed at the castle.

The tree line ended and a snowy incline rose to the top of the cliff. Ario and Gwyn hiked the steep hill, dodging naturally formed glass-covered boulders as they went.

When they reached the top, the view was breathtaking. An endless stretch of black ocean glistened beneath the rising sun. Each passing wave shimmered as it crested and fell, making its way toward the shore. The white sky was filled with fluffy, gray snow clouds. The contrast of the black ocean against the stark white backdrop was a sight of pure beauty; a picturesque work of art. Gwyn took a few steps closer to the edge and peered over. The beach was littered with broken pieces of glass, just like every other beach in Crystet, but this one was slightly different. The glass was untouched, never walked upon, so the pieces were slightly bigger. They weren't crushed into tiny, granular specks over time; they were large enough to make out where they came from. Arms, legs, torsos, and faces were visible among the wreckage, as were the blackened, crystalized innards of the deceased.

Gwyn stepped back.

"This is where many come to die," Ario explained.

"What do you mean?"

"The ancients. The quitters. The strong. The tired," Ario explained. "When someone is ready to die, they come here. Just like King Rúnar—his was the first known suicide in Crystet. He deemed this cliff as the death of choice for champions, intending for only the bravest and most resilient to follow his lead, but every type of Glaziene, both weak and strong, has jumped from this cliff since."

"Why'd he do it?"

"After a thousand years of life, I guess he had enough."

"I don't know his story."

"Really?" Ario asked, shocked. "King Rúnar was the first prince of Crystet and the only king in Crystet's history to possess the scepter of alchemy. It's the only time our land ruled all the others. But he was a wicked child with a twisted mind. At the age of eight, he tore his heart out of his body."

"Why?"

"Some say he was testing his mortality, others say he was guided by the Vorso. Either way, this action unveiled the discovery of a new type of magic: heart magic."

"Heart magic?"

"Every Glaziene possesses a heart that can produce magic if removed from the body. Some hearts are more potent and can produce greater magic than others, no one knows why though. Rúnar's heart contained a force like no other."

"How'd he do it?"

"No one knows for sure. Judging by the hole in his chest, it looks like he slammed his fist right through, but my dad says the hole is a decoy. Most people shatter when they try to remove their heart in that way. That's why we see little heart magic rampaging about; those who try often shatter immediately." Ario leaned in and whispered. "My dad thinks that Rúnar shoved his hand down his throat and pulled it out through his mouth."

"Is that even possible?"

"I suppose so. Our throats have multiple pipes connected to them, you'd just have to select the right one to reach the ribcage cavity."

"Gross."

"It gets worse. On the night of his eighth birthday, he used the magic to turn his parents into glass droplets, which he wore around his neck throughout his entire reign."

Gwyn wore a look of disgust.

"It sounds appalling," Ario continued, "but it was an awe-inspiring shift in power. It was also the start of Vale Octavum and the reason every Glaziene child enters adulthood at the age of eight. Rúnar took the throne and ruled with reckless abandon for the next one thousand years. His hardhearted approach to life shaped Crystet into what it is today. He molded our culture and made his ruthless style of ruling the standard for all future leaders to match. The populace revered him. They say he was the greatest king we ever had."

"He sounds miserable."

"Perhaps he was. He did kill himself in the end."

"Was he really the first Glaziene to take their own life?"

"In this manner, yes. If they weren't murdered, people usually broke apart from old age in the streets, their pieces trampled into sand as time passed. No one ever had the courage to take their own life until they saw their beloved leader die by choice with noble valor. The populace was so bereaved by Rúnar's death, they scaled down the cliff and tried to put him back together. Look down the shore," he instructed, pointing to the silhouette perched atop a rocky causeway above the crashing waves. "You can see their attempt. Rúnar stands as a statue, outsides crystalized, insides blackened stone."

"If they put him back together, why is he still dead?" Gwyn asked.

"Because they never found his heart."

Gwyn squinted in an attempt to see farther and noticed the large, gaping hole in the middle of Rúnar's chest. The spot for his heart was vacant; one missing piece kept him from renewed life.

"I don't suspect he wanted to be rebuilt, anyway," Gwyn commented.

"Probably not. Worst part about it is that before he jumped, he gifted the scepter to the Woodlins of Wicker. No one knows why."

"Perhaps they were better balanced to handle such power."

"Well, the Metellyans stole the scepter from them the moment they heard of the transfer of power. Burnt down half of Wicker while searching for it."

Gwyn felt the ancient loss as if it were her own.

"That's a shame," she said with a heavy heart.

"It's a shame that Rúnar gave the power away. He should have gifted it to his daughter, Nikhita."

"I don't think our people can handle that type of power," Gwyn observed. "We are cruel enough as it is. Selfish, too. Having great power would probably bring out the worst in us."

Ario paused. "Maybe you're right. But Rúnar, he was a legend," he expressed with deflated admiration. "I can't fathom why anyone, especially someone so great, would want to end their life."

"I can." Her reply came out as a whisper.

Ario looked over at her, examining her somber gaze, which remained fixed on the statue of the patchwork king. Without his heart to bring him back to life, Rúnar remained alone and half built on the desolate shores of Crystet.

Ario then examined Gwyn's scars—the countless foggy patches that held her together—but decided to swallow his questions. Some secrets were better left buried where no light could give them life.

"Let's go," he said, no longer intrigued by the death that plagued this place.

Gwyn scanned the view from the edge one last time, admiring the tragic beauty this spot possessed, before following Ario down the hill, leaving her dark thoughts behind.

Chapter 5

Gwyn and Ario walked in silence, heads down, shoulders slouched, neither addressing the melancholic gloom that shrouded their return to Gler. Gwyn barely noticed how her dark energy blanketed their entire expedition in sorrow.

Dawn was upon them, as was a storm of snow thunder, and Gwyn was running out of time. She had to be in bed when Mina came to wake her.

"We have to hurry," Gwyn expressed, charging past Ario.

"Why?"

"I won't be able to come again if anyone realizes I left."

"You used to sneak out all the time. What makes this any different?"

"It just is."

They could see the village of Gler through the tree line in the distance and Gwyn marched through the snow with speed.

The sound of jeering children accompanied this new sight.

Gwyn snapped on her facemask and charged toward the noise.

The scene she embarked upon was bloody and savage. Six ragged children, none older than Gwyn, were tearing out chunks of fur from a baby fox they held pinned to the ground.

The animal screeched in protest, wailing in pain, but the children reveled in its agony.

"Stop," Gwyn demanded, but they did not hear her. "I said stop!"

The oldest turned her attention to the cloaked vigilante, her expression ravaged by rage.

"Who are you to tell me to stop?" the girl roared, fueled by adrenaline from the torture and ready to accept the new challenge.

"If you don't stop, you will suffer greatly. Worse than that fox."

The girl laughed and rubbed her nose, leaving a trail of fox blood on her face.

"Prove it."

When Gwyn stalled, the girl kicked the animal, further antagonizing the princess, and Gwyn had no choice but to call upon her reputation.

Gwyn lowered her hood and removed the facemask.

"*You*," the girl gasped. She then looked to Ario. "Why are you with *her*?"

"She's my friend," he replied.

"You're a rotten traitor," she spat. "Think you can get in with the royals by befriending this freak?"

"You should watch what you say," Ario warned.

"Rebelene doesn't like to be taunted," Gwyn added.

"My issue is with *you*, not the Vorso."

"Leave that fox alone or suffer the consequences," Gwyn advised.

"I will not."

Gwyn raised her arms and spoke with confidence.

"May the gods curse your fate!"

Before any of the children could respond, a crack of lighting bolted through the sky and enormous snowflakes began to fall.

Fear from the heavens shook the children to their cores, causing them to scatter in fear.

Gwyn raced to the injured animal to assess the damage. It needed medicine and a safe place to heal. Mostly, it needed someone to nurture it and provide love while it mended.

She cradled the shaking fox in her arms, bloodying her pristine white cape.

"So much for sneaking back in," she muttered to herself.

"How did you do that?" Ario asked in amazement.

"Do what?" she asked, attention now focused on the fox.

"The lightning," Ario exclaimed. "That was brilliant. How'd you do it?"

"Really good luck," Gwyn replied with amused wonder.

"I think you might have Gaia on your side."

Gwyn furrowed her brows, but found that Ario spoke with sincerity.

She sighed. "I think a lot of things would be different if She was really on my side."

"The tough stuff makes us better," he remarked with a shrug. "Maybe She needs you to suffer a bit."

Gwyn scowled, but kept her snarky reply to herself.

They parted ways at the armor shop and Gwyn was on her own with the injured fox. She put on her mask and maneuvered her cloak to hide the small animal from the critical stares of onlookers. They did not know who she was, only that she cared for an animal that would normally be left to die.

Using a lower-level servants' entrance, she made it back into the castle with only the guards witnessing her escapade. A combination of low-trafficked corridors and hiding behind drapes and statues got her back to her bedroom without being caught. There, she placed the Volto mask into the pocket of her cape, which she threw into the closet. She placed the fox in her private bathtub and then jumped into bed. Mina entered the room a moment later, unaware of the ordeal she just missed.

"Time to wake up, Princess," Mina said, gently running her hand over Gwyn's soft, glass-laced curls.

"I'm still tired," Gwyn moaned, managing to yawn as she spoke.

"There is no time to waste. It's Heilög Iðrun. You have obligations."

"Since when?"

"Since the queen decided you'd be placing the bread on every plate."

"I've been demoted to servant?" Gwyn asked, appalled.

"No. It's a gesture to show we are all equal in our search for Gaia's forgiveness."

Gwyn groaned.

"Now, get up."

She obeyed, but as soon as her hands emerged from the covers, Mina let out a loud gasp.

"You are covered in blood! What happened?"

"I can't tell you."

"You must."

A high-pitched cry came from Gwyn's washroom and Mina's gaze darted in the direction of the sound.

"Oh, Gwynessa," Mina groaned. "What have you done now?"

"You cannot tell anyone!"

From the bathroom, Mina shouted, "A fox? Why on Namaté would you bring that thing here? Your mother will kill it if she finds out."

"That's why you can't tell her," Gwyn pleaded as she raced into the bathroom and stood next to her handmaiden.

"I am obligated to tell her everything you do."

"No. You are *my* handmaiden. Your loyalty should be to *me*."

"But you left again. Your safety is jeopardized. I must do what's best for you."

"She doesn't care about my safety. She only cares about her reputation."

"Gwynessa—"

"I am happy again. I am finding new purpose in the day. Isn't *that* what's best for me?"

"You test my honor daily," Mina complained.

"I will release the fox once it's healed."

Mina sighed, but said no more. She opened the closet to retrieve Gwyn's heilög dress, but instead, she found Gwyn's ruined cape.

"I can't fix this," she gasped. "This is blood—blood stains."

"There must be a way," Gwyn suggested.

"Look at your room!" Mina protested. "Look at all the blood we could not erase! Every little crack is filled with the memory of Kipp, despite hours upon hours of trying to clean it up."

"I wanted it this way."

"We know. That doesn't make it right, though. How are you supposed to heal when remnants of your dead dog are visible every time you wake from slumber? And this cape." Mina groaned. "I cannot clean it. No matter what I do, there will always be a pink tint to the white fur."

"Then throw it away. What do I care?"

"This cape is lined with the finest silk imported from Fibril. It costs them much to acquire replacement fibers. Your mother will question my sanity if I discard of this fine cloak like it's garbage."

"Tell her I outgrew it."

"She will want to repurpose the material."

Gwyn snatched the coat from Mina's grip and threw it back into the closet.

"I have other capes I can wear until I grow tall enough to warrant getting a new one. She never needs to know." Gwyn tore off her nightgown and raised her arms into the sky. Her tiny, naked body was no longer pristine, no longer pure and perfect; it was now sullied by the mended cracks of her free fall. Innocence gone, marked by the blemishes she wore. Beneath the foggy scars fused together with diamond dust, her colorful organs were still visible. They pulsated with life, vibrant in shades of red, blue, green, and pink that weren't often seen in the world of Crystet.

It was Heilög Iðrun, the most wretched day of the year, and Gwyn braced herself for countless hours of Orlan's mindless droning.

Heilög Iðrun was a day of remembrance, a day of retribution. Unlike the weekly Heilög feasts, Heilög Iðrun happened once a year and was a sunrise-to-sundown festival of tedious rituals, countless group prayers, chanting to the sun, humming to the moons, and lavish sacrifices meant to prove that the Glaziene were selfless and changed. The Glaziene population spent this celebrated occasion honoring the day Gaia stripped all the lands of their natural magic and confined it within the scepter of alchemy. The day of reckoning happened over an eon ago, during their 750th cycle around the Nebila sun, but the Glaziene believed that if they habitually begged for forgiveness, Gaia would return their magic one day.

Gwyn, however, found the tradition embarrassing. Prayerful pleading was unbecoming and proved that the Glaziene were not worthy of powerful magic. They didn't understand that improving their daily behavior would earn Gaia's forgiveness for their ancient misconduct—not one day each year filled with desperate pleas. But no one cared to hear her views on the holiday. Instead, she was forced to participate, keeping her judgment silent.

Chapter 6

Orlan stood atop the altar in the northern steeple, giving his usual Heilög Iðrun speech. He rambled on about the gods and how they needed everyone's utmost devotion. Calix stood by his side, looking up and smiling with adoration.

Gwyn's rage threatened to explode.

"Let us live in their light," Orlan said, concluding his homily. "Blessings aplenty, in the name of the Mother, the Vorso, and all of their Spirits, I vow."

Gwyn stormed toward the doors of the Grand Hall, only to be thwarted by her uncle.

"Where do you think you're going?" Lorcan asked in a whisper. "We aren't even halfway through the Heilög Iðrun rituals."

"Do you see how Calix is looking at Orlan?"

"With respect?" Lorcan asked.

"With admiration. It's disgusting."

"You are the only Glaziene who doesn't view the æðsti prestur in that light."

"Then I am the only smart one."

"You are setting yourself up for a miserable existence," Lorcan warned.

Gwyn gazed up at him with hurt defiance.

Lorcan softened his approach as he explained. "You are not responsible for the actions of others, but you are responsible for how you *react* to the actions of others. If you continue to use mutiny as your answer to everything bad that happens, you will never find contentment." He exhaled deeply, revealing his waning patience. "This is what killing Kipp was meant to teach you."

"I don't care about any of that. I just want my friend back."

"Kipp is gone forever."

"And now, so is Calix. I am losing everyone I love."

"Calix isn't going anywhere, and he loves you just as much as he always has."

"Orlan will poison his heart. He will mold his thoughts until he turns Calix's love for me into hatred."

"He would never do such a thing."

"Let's bet on it."

"I don't bet with children."

"I am a woman."

"Says the ancient traditions of our people, but you haven't been alive long enough to truly understand what it means to be a woman."

"Yet you kill my dog—my best friend—in the name of my womanhood."

"It's initiation into womanhood. It's the first of many trials you have yet to endure."

"So, you and my mother will be slaughtering more of the things that I love?"

"No. But being an adult comes with many natural hardships. Kipp's death will hopefully be the worst of what you're forced to face, but knowing the nature of our society and how most Glaziene lives go, I suspect it won't be."

Gwyn did not care to hear her uncle's lame reasoning and returned her attention to the spotlight of the ceremony: Orlan casting personal blessings with Calix by his side. They held hands as the high priest visited and spoke with each attendee individually.

Gwyn stormed out of the room, unable to stomach the sight of her innocent little brother trusting a liar.

She raced through the royal forest toward Gler Village. There, she found Ario sweeping diamond dust off the front porch of his family's armor shop.

"My dad said I could go with him to your party tomorrow," Ario revealed with a smile.

"Really?" Gwyn asked in happy amazement, forgetting that her ninth birthday followed Heilög Iðrun this year. "This will be the first time I've ever had a friend at my birthday party."

"Children aren't usually allowed at royal parties, but he got your mom to give her blessing."

Gwyn smiled, excited by the prospect of celebrating her birthday for a change.

"Eight was a bad year," she noted. "Hopefully nine will be better."

"It will be," Ario assured her. "Vale Octavum only happens once."

And he was right.

The party was a success; she even danced with Ario while the adults stumbled around drunk off frostshine and snow ale. She laughed with Ario into the late hours of night, outlasting many of the grownups there. It was the first time she ever enjoyed her birthday.

The year that followed was just as pleasant. After seeing how well she responded to Ario's presence at the party, her parents lifted their watch over her and allowed her more freedom. This gift of time was spent exploring the Wildlands with Ario. He was unaware how significant his friendship with her was and he unknowingly helped her find purpose again. Time spent with Ario filled Gwyn with life. She felt genuinely happy, for the first time ever, and she cherished the newfound feeling. She lost interest in everything else in her life and spent every free moment she had adventuring with Ario. They became fast friends and completely inseparable. No rules or responsibilities could keep them apart.

Their friendship bloomed over the year. They made countless trips into the forest, shared games and private jokes, enjoyed early breakfasts with Jahdo in the armor shop, and reveled in a surplus of moments where they used their confidence and high-ranking social titles to scare the other Glaziene children. By the time Gwyn's tenth birthday approached, she appeared to be a brand new girl.

"I'll race you," Gwyn challenged Ario with a mischievous smirk.

"Again?" Ario teased. "You know I'll win."

Gwyn wasted no time bantering and took off. She skated as fast as she could along the well-worn ice path they made over the months. Ario chased after her, using all his energy to catch up.

Gwyn reached a patch of snow where the trees were spaced far apart and the sun kissed the ground.

"I won," she exclaimed. But Ario did not slow his speed and when he reached her, he wrapped his arm around her waist and took her down into the snow. The fall was soft and she playfully protested his poor sportsmanship.

"What if you broke me?" she asked.

"But I didn't."

"You could've."

Ario repositioned himself so that he hovered over her. He held himself up with his hands near her shoulders and gazed at her with an unfamiliar intent.

"What?" Gwyn asked, feeling uncomfortable and excited simultaneously.

Ario didn't respond. He simply stared down at her with a foreign fire in his eyes. Gwyn's chest felt heavy and the intensity of the moment took her breath away. She couldn't pinpoint why his energy changed, or what it meant, but she felt the shift in her entire body.

Then he leaned in and kissed her. An innocent peck on the lips. He held the contact for a few seconds before lifting and giving Gwyn the giddiest of grins.

When he ended the kiss, Gwyn felt unsure how to react.

"Why'd you do that?" she asked, afraid because she enjoyed the contact. She never thought of Ario like that—she never thought of anyone like that—but Ario was a few years older than her and already interested in exploring more mature activities. His desire came as a shock, one she thought she would have protested but instead, found herself welcoming.

He leaned in and kissed her again. She wanted to fight his affection, but could not bring herself to do so. The connection felt too good.

"Tell me why," Gwyn continued her former line of questioning.

"Because I like you."

Her instincts told her to be mean, to challenge his adoration by telling him she didn't feel the same, but she took a pause and was able to stifle the false reaction before it left her mouth. She didn't need to be defensive with him. His motives were genuine, proven so over the past year, and she did not fear him.

She took a deep breath.

"Okay," she said, then wiggled out from underneath his body.

He smiled. "I'll give you time."

He took her hand and they walked into the shadows of the trees, toward the gelid fox den.

When they found a spot to rest, Gwyn confessed the silent sadness she'd been concealing.

"I've been missing Calix lately."

"Bring him into the woods one day."

"I'm not sure if I can trust him anymore. It's been so long since we've spent time alone together. I only see him at meal times."

"Skip a day with me and spend it with him."

"It would be pointless. Anytime I *am* there he's always locked away in the steeple with Orlan. I hunted down Chandi,

Calix's handmaiden, and asked her when he would have some free time to spend with me, and she told me that there was no room in his itinerary for 'play dates'. That he was deep in the process of being groomed for kinghood and all of his free time was allotted toward food and sleep."

"That sounds miserable. I bet he misses you too."

Gwyn sighed. "I'll find a way."

Later that evening, after Mina blew out the torch in her adjacent sleeping chamber, Gwyn snuck out of bed and crept through the hallways toward Calix's room. When she found the door, she turned the glass knob and pushed it open with slow and quiet care.

"Calix," she whispered, aware that his multiple handmaidens sleeping in their private quarters would be able to hear anything that was said too loud.

She tiptoed to his bed and rustled him awake.

"Calix," she repeated.

He rolled over and rubbed his eyes. When his vision adjusted and he saw that it was his beloved sister, tears welled in his pretty silver-green eyes.

"Why are you crying?" Gwyn asked, startled by his response.

"I miss you," he replied with a sniffle.

"I miss you too. They are keeping us apart."

"They told me you didn't want to see me anymore."

"What?" she asked, appalled. "That's a horrible lie."

"They said you cared more about the forest. And Ario."

"Who told you this?"

"Orlan, mostly."

"Orlan is a dirty liar. You are my brother. You will always be most important to me."

"It didn't feel that way."

"I tried to see you," she informed him. "Multiple times. They always have you locked away in the steeple."

"I'm always with Orlan," he confirmed, his voice sullen.

"Want to journey into the forest with me tomorrow morning?"

"Really?" he asked, eyes aglow with eagerness.

"Yes. I'll get you back before they even realize you're gone."

"Okay," he replied, spirits lifted.

Gwyn kissed his forehead. "Good, now get some sleep. I'll be back in a few hours."

Calix nodded. He wore a huge smile despite the tears in his eyes.

A few hours before dawn, Gwyn snuck back into his room and gently woke him with a push.

"Time to go," she whispered.

As soon as Calix shook himself from his dream and realized it was time for an adventure, he perked up and jumped out of bed.

Gwyn helped him put on his fur-lined cape and then escorted him out of his room.

Only the guards were awake, and they were easy to avoid. Gwyn checked each corner before turning. Whenever royal guards were in sight, they hid behind the long, white curtains that decorated every corridor window.

It didn't take long to sneak into the cellar. They passed the entrance to the dungeon, which was filled with countless vacant prison cells. Her mother had no time for law and order in Crystet when all her attention was focused on rebelling against the Voltains. And until she successfully stole the scepter of alchemy from them, this prison would remain unoccupied.

Gwyn and Calix exited the castle and made their way to the royal forest. The bowmen stationed atop the roof surely saw them leave, but babysitting the royal children was not, and never was, part of their job description, so as always, Gwyn knew their departure would remain a secret. Though she was now allowed to come and go from the forest through the gate, she opted to take Calix through her old spot.

They slipped under the glass-spiked fence and into the woods. The trees cast shadows over the land, making it too dark to see. Gwyn followed her well-worn path to an area that had logs for them to sit on.

"This is a safe spot to stop," she announced when they reached her intended location.

Calix picked the driest log and carefully sat down. He moved slower than Gwyn and with far more care. While she raced about, unconcerned that her speed might cause her harm, he took every precaution to avoid an injury.

"Why do you move so slow?" she asked.

"I have a lot to live for."

Gwyn paused, then nodded. "Fair point."

"You should move a little slower too," he suggested. "You don't want to add any more scars to your collection."

"Maybe I do."

"Really?" Calix asked, taken aback by his sister's reckless attitude. "You look like one of those broken porcelain dolls the poor girls find in the garbage and piece back together."

"Are you saying I look pitiful?"

"No, just broken."

"I wear my scars with pride."

"Why?"

"They are proof that I survived."

Calix paused. He never saw it in that light before. "I suppose that's a positive spin on something so grim."

"It's not a spin, it's the truth. Live a little, let yourself feel the freedom of a breakdown, and you'll understand what I mean."

"I have to keep it together. It would rattle too many people if I fell apart."

"You're still a kid. You're allowed to have a meltdown."

"If I jumped off the roof, Mamma would give up. She'd shatter us both and start over." When he saw his sister's hurt reaction, he abruptly stopped speaking. "I'm sorry."

"It's okay," Gwyn promised. She never considered that her little brother's mental stability was the only thing that kept their mother from losing it completely. If he wasn't so strong during her periods of extreme sorrow, it's likely their mother's impatient wrath during those times would have been much worse. "I never realized how much you've done for me. Thank you for always being rock-solid."

Calix nodded.

"You're safe here with me," Gwyn reminded him. "No one will ever know if you let yourself go for a moment."

"What if I do? What if I let myself feel all the sadness I kept secret these last few years, and then I cannot find it in myself to be strong again?"

"You are hardwired to be strong, even when you feel weak. Unlike me, it's in your genetic makeup to show a brave face. I have no doubt a moment of fragility won't hinder you a bit. If anything, it will help you be stronger. Releasing pent up emotion is often quite healing."

"I'm not sick or broken," Calix countered. "I don't need to heal."

Gwyn shrugged. "If you say so. Just remember that the forest is a safe place."

"Okay," Calix replied, maintaining his stubborn bravado.

Over the next two weeks the siblings made countless trips into the forest together, rekindling their bond and finding their lost happiness.

Obelia, the first boreal bear Gwyn ever healed, sat with the children in the tiny snow-covered clearing. The giant creature ate the winter bugs that crawled up and down the sequoia trees while Gwyn drew in the snow with a stick.

"This is the layout of the land," she explained to Calix, who now appeared far more comfortable in the forest. "And these lines are all the paths Ario and I have established and explored. The vast range of animals hiding in the woods is incredible. I'd love to take you into the Wildlands one day."

"That sounds like a wonderful adventure."

"I used to do it all the time during the early hours of morning before Mamma lifted my guard and let me roam around during the day. We could make it work so that no one ever realizes you left at all."

"Okay," Calix agreed with excitement.

Obelia released a rumbling groan before collapsing into the snow with a thud. Gwyn stood and mimicked the fall, landing atop the bear's fuzzy arm.

"Join me, Calix," she requested with a happy smile.

He hesitated, but eventually crawled into the nook between Obelia's soft body and Gwyn. Mornings with Calix, afternoons with Ario. Gwyn hadn't felt this content in a long time.

Calix quickly became as connected to the forest as his older sister, and after two weeks of exploring as a duo, Ario began joining them on their early morning expeditions.

The young prince leaned against Obelia's large, slumbering body.

"You're a brave little guy," Ario noted.

"Obelia and I are friends," Calix replied. "The first time I met her, I wasn't so sure. But Gwyn showed me that it was okay. Obelia could hurt me, but she doesn't want to."

"None of the animals *want* to hurt us, sometimes it happens on accident," Gwyn commented. "Or it happens out of self-defense."

"True. Some of the animals are predatory though, you can't deny that. They'd eat us if they weren't so afraid of us," Ario countered.

"They won't eat me, or anyone who is with me," Gwyn insisted with confidence.

Ario shrugged. "You *do* have a way with the animals."

"Gwyn is magic," Calix added in a soft voice.

She looked at him with a smile. "So are you. Remember how sad I used to be? You fixed me."

"That wasn't magic, that was love," Calix replied.

"Love *is* magic," Ario informed the young prince. "It's one of the most powerful forces we have access to, matched only by anger and sorrow."

"Still," Calix countered, "it's not *actual* magic."

"Then neither am I," Gwyn responded.

"Of course you are. You tamed the beasts of the Wildlands."

"It wasn't magic that earned me their trust, it was love and respect."

Calix looked perplexed by the ideas running through his mind. After a long pause, he vocalized his thoughts.

"Real magic exists, right?"

"It does, but it costs a lot to possess it," Ario answered. His response captured their attention, as neither knew much about the topic.

"How much?" Gwyn asked.

"Your soul, your safety, your life," Ario replied. "Diamonds won't get you magic."

"Tell us more," Gwyn insisted. Her intrigue was piqued.

"Well, one way to acquire magic is to make a deal with Kólasi. Gaia's brother is gluttonous—his appetite for souls is insatiable. If you promise to give him your soul in the afterlife, he'll provide you with all the dark magic you could possibly need during your mortal life. But this method is the least common because no one wants to doom their fate to Kólasi's abyss. Only the desperate take this route."

"What are the other ways?" Gwyn asked.

"The Vorso sometimes bless their chosen few with small doses of magic. The Valið have been known to possess charmed abilities. Another way is through ancient artifacts. A long time ago, magic ran rampant across all of Namaté. This planet was a very different place when all of its inhabitants were blessed with magical abilities. While it was a gift from the heavens, most did not respect the blessing and abused the power. Thousands were dying every day at the hands of those more powerful. It was a daily bloodbath. Gaia put a stop to that when she harnessed all the voodoo, witchcraft, enchantments, and sorcery from each of the lands and contained it all within the scepter of alchemy. Now, instead of fighting each other with our born-magic, we fight to seize that stupid stick. In the end, it's less bloody than it used to be, but letting one land have all the magic has certainly created divides between cultures."

"All that magic is gone," Calix expressed.

"So they say, but my dad told me it is still possible to discover artifacts from that time that still retain magic."

"Like what?" Calix asked.

"The lost relic of Gaia, Rúnar's heart, Jasvinder's glowing eyeballs, Barzilai's finger coils, the black feathers of Elzaphan, Amezite's stone brain. Those are just a few. Tons are buried, drowned, and hidden—all you have to do is search."

"That sounds like a fun treasure hunt," Gwyn replied, as if this revelation was a challenge she wished to accept.

"These enchanted artifacts are few and scattered all over the globe."

"New motivation to explore Namaté," Gwyn countered.

"If you say so."

"If those are the only ways to get magic, then no wonder it's so rare," Calix said with a huff.

"There's one more way," Ario inserted, his expression shifted with apprehension. "At least one more way that I know of, and I'm pretty sure it only works for the Glaziene. The Metellyans can do it too, but it doesn't result in magic for them."

"What is it?" Calix asked.

"Removing one of your vitals."

"Rúnar," Gwyn whispered in awe.

Calix looked to his sister, confused, then back to Ario. "What does that mean?"

"Heart, brain, lungs, liver, or kidneys. The liver and kidneys provide less power, but those missing pieces are easier to hide—no one notices missing torso organs because the torso is usually hidden under clothes—so those vitals are the most popular choice. They give enough magic to surpass those around you, but not enough to cause significant damage. You've probably encountered many people with this level of magic and didn't even realize it." Ario took a moment, then continued. "Next level up are the lungs and brain. Both of these organs give immense quantities of magic to their possessor, but also have debilitating side effects. Besides the fact that many shatter in their attempt to remove theses pieces, a missing brain leaves the person half as sharp and less likely to be able to use any magic effectively, and missing lungs leave the Glaziene physically weak. Without airflow, they lose their strength. Both of these symptoms leave the person wildly vulnerable to those who wish to thwart their newfound power, and since they are already missing a piece, they are that much easier to shatter."

"What about the heart?" Calix asked.

"The heart has the potential to produce the most powerful vital magic. But every heart is different and there is no guarantee that taking yours out will give you the abilities you desire. Some are thriving with enchantment, while others are no stronger than a liver or kidney. And like the brain and lungs, most people shatter in the attempt to remove their heart. Those that succeed are often murdered shortly after. The fact that there is no guarantee that your heart will be capable of fierce magic, most don't think it's worth the risk. It's safer to stick with the liver and kidneys."

"What are the side effects?" Gwyn asked, thinking of Rúnar.

"Hearts are tricky," Ario replied. "They are the most powerful and deliver fewer negative side effects. In fact, the negative side effects are often viewed as positive. Removing a heart strips the Glaziene of their 'weaker' emotions—love, sorrow, fear, and happiness. Only rage survives the removal, which tends to be a strength in our culture."

"My life would be a whole lot easier if I didn't have a heart plagued by emotion," Gwyn commented.

"Maybe, but over time, you'd also lose all feeling attached to your memories. Eventually, your most important memories would grow fuzzy and unclear, leaving you unsure how you came to be the person you are. Removing a heart results in a morally numb individual with too much power and minimal ties to the past. They are often reactive people who make rash decisions moment by moment, unable to see the big picture or plan for the future."

"Sounds more like something a person would suffer from after removing their brain."

"Emotion is much stronger than thought. A missing heart ultimately destroys the brain. It's also much easier to notice when a person is missing their heart because the black void left in its wake often spreads up to the collar bones. It also warps everything about their personality, so the longer the person carries on without their heart, the more obvious it becomes to those around them. The last known person to remove their heart was Prince Rúnar, and that was centuries ago."

"Looks like we'll be sticking to the hunt for ancient magical artifacts," Gwyn concluded.

"Count me out. I'm not interested," Ario countered.

"Why not?"

"According to history, it never ends well for those who possess magic."

"Fine. More magic for Calix and I then." Though she did not covet magic, the idea of obtaining it seemed to comfort her brother. She glanced over at Calix, who was nuzzled up against Obelia, and gave him a confident nod.

Chapter 7

Early morning arrived and it was time for her usual secret trip into the woods with Calix, but when she arrived at his bedroom, all she saw was blood.

Gwyn ran to his side. His stomach was torn open and his insides were slowly crystalizing.

"What happened?" she sobbed.

"I tried to remove my liver."

"Why?" she demanded, tears cascading down her glass cheeks.

"I think I might feel better with a little bit of magic on my side," he answered, his voice quivering as his body gradually shut down.

"We need to close this wound so you can heal."

"Don't tell Mamma," Calix begged. "She'll think I'm weak."

"If the doctors see this, they'll have to tell her."

"You need to fix me."

"I don't know how."

"Try."

Gwyn exhaled slowly as she assessed her next move.

"We can trust Mina," she finally said. "I'll be right back."

She covered Calix with his enormous, feather-filled comforter to conceal his self-inflicted wound, then ran out of the room. She returned with Mina a few minutes later.

"Don't make a scene," she instructed her handmaiden as they entered.

Gwyn lifted the blanket, revealing Calix's bloody body, and Mina gasped.

"What happened?"

"Night terrors," Gwyn lied. "He gets them real bad sometimes. This is the worst yet."

"We need to tell your mother," she said.

"No," Gwyn insisted. "She cannot know. No one can. That's why I brought you here. I trust you."

"I could be executed for concealing such a secret."

"Not if you *keep* the secret. No one knows but the three of us."

Mina groaned and Gwyn took that as a pact.

"Good," Gwyn continued. "I'm going to raid the medical wing and you will guard Calix. Chandi and his other handmaidens shouldn't be here until after dawn, when they usually wake him up, so we have time."

"Wonderful." Mina's reply was loaded with sarcasm.

Gwyn darted out of the room, skating with speed down the corridor. She hid behind the long window curtains whenever the early morning guards were in sight and made it to the medical wing without being seen. She gathered what she thought she'd need and raced back to Calix.

Back in his room, she arranged her tools on his glass nightstand and then removed his blanket. She remembered how the glazician healed her arm, but was unconscious when they pieced her back together after her fall.

"What if I do it wrong?" she asked while staring hesitantly at his injury. "I don't want to make your pain any worse."

"I watched them put you back together," Calix replied in a whisper. "I can help."

"Stop," Mina interjected, leaving her post near the door and committing herself to this reckless endeavor. "You'll hurt him more."

"Do you know how to heal a break?" Gwyn asked.

"Of course I do. It was part of my training. Step aside," she said, shooing Gwyn, who obeyed. "Did you get the diamond dust?"

"Yes." Gwyn retrieved the glass jar from the nightstand.

Mina pushed her fingers into the break to examine Calix's insides.

"Are they blackened?" he cried.

"Not yet. The exposed organs are gray. We have time."

Calix whimpered.

"Mix the diamond dust with vinegar until it makes a paste," she instructed Gwyn. The princess did as she was told and handed the concoction to Mina, who then slathered the paste onto Calix's exposed organs. Next, she filled the lesion with dry diamond dust until it filled the opening, and finally, she used the blowtorch to seal the wound.

Calix grimaced in pain, but never made a sound.

The extreme heat melted the diamond dust until it fused with Calix's glass-skin. Once it looked decent enough, Mina removed the fire and stepped back to assess her work.

"You need to be annealed." The morning bells began to chime and Mina gasped. "I need to get to the kitchen."

"I will take him to be annealed. I can figure that part out."

"Just make sure the kiln is hot when he enters and the cooling lowers one Celsiuheit degree every thirty seconds."

"Understood."

Mina groaned, fully realizing the extent of the situation she was now in as she looked at Calix's freshly scarred belly.

"His handmaidens will see the wound and ask what happened. And now that we've gone above and beyond to mend him, they will be even more suspicious about how he got injured and healed in secrecy."

"They won't make a big deal out of it if his health is intact. You let me get away with a lot of things when I was younger," Gwyn reminded her.

"Yes, but I was your only handmaiden. Calix has five. It's much easier to keep a secret when only two people know. Also, your mother is far more engaged with Calix's day-to-day schedule than she was with yours. She will find out and seek the truth."

"Well, until she does, this secret remains ours. Understood?"

"Fine. Just promise me you don't include my name in this story when you're forced to tell it one day."

"I will protect you," Gwyn vowed.

Mina pursed her lips and huffed. The young princess held no power amongst her elders and could not uphold such a promise.

Mina hurried to the kitchen to prep Gwyn's breakfast as the children snuck through the halls to the medical wing. The annealing room was unlike any other in all of Crystet. Years of acquiring resources from other lands through trade helped make the room functional. Much of the machinery was made of metal and powered by electricity. Though the equipment was old, it still worked. Gwyn wasn't sure how her parents got the Voltains to agree to give them electricity, but a giant, glowing orb of concentrated energy hovered above a glass pedestal. It's energy naturally replenished itself and never ran out.

Calix's wound was in an awkward location on his torso, so one of the specialized annealing machines wouldn't work—they were designed to anneal a Glaziene's extremities. And Calix could not go into the body chamber, as only his torso needed the slow-cooling heat. Gwyn searched the room and found a table covered in metal wands of varying sizes.

"Lay on that bed," she instructed Calix, pointing to a table topped with a thin mattress in the center of the room. He obeyed and she chose a wand with a wide, flat end. A rubber-coated wire extended from the wand and at its end, a collection of frayed metal wires was exposed.

She walked the long cord to the glowing purple orb of energy, knowing what she had to do. The orb buzzed with electricity and when she was in reach, its power radiated with such ferocity, the hair on her head rose. She took a deep breath and shoved the metal wires into the orb. It snatched the wires, sucking them into the gaseous swirl of color, and Gwyn let go. She ran back to the wand and saw that it now hummed.

Gwyn lifted the wand, grabbing it by the rubber grip made from the latex of tropical trees in Wicker, and examined the dial on the handle. It controlled the temperature, so she turned it all the way up and hovered the wand over Calix's wound.

Calix wore a strained grimace as he withstood the pain.

"Should I go a little faster?" she asked, concerned that she was hurting him.

"No. Go as slow as you can. I'll be all right."

Calix healed, and though many questioned his mysterious break, they kept their secret under wraps.

Their treks into the woods resumed. They enjoyed countless adventures together, which granted immense joy to both children. But as Gwyn already learned in her short life, happiness rarely endured.

The children dashed through the forest, racing the rising sun.

"We stayed too long," Gwyn expressed with dread. "We have to hurry."

But it was too late. The sun was up and the castle bells rang their morning song. Calix's handmaidens surely knew he was missing by now.

"Do you think they'll tell Mamma?" he asked.

"She's the first person they'll tell," Gwyn replied.

When they crossed into the royal field, a glass trumpet echoed through the sky.

Gwyn groaned as an enormous search party emerged from every corner of the forest and their mother stormed out of the castle. Lorcan and Trista followed close behind.

"How dare you," Dalila shouted, her voice dripping with venom.

"It makes him happy," Gwyn said in defense, but her mother wasn't interested.

"I give you a little freedom, and you abuse it. Calix was never permitted to gallivant through the woods with you."

"It makes me happy," Calix echoed his sister, but to no avail.

"Are you weak like your sister?" Dalila asked. "You need a constant escape to feel content?"

"It's Gwyn who makes me happy, not the forest," Calix countered with confidence.

His reply surprised Dalila. She took a moment to digest this notion before responding.

"I cannot permit this time together. Orlan forbids it."

"Why?" Gwyn demanded in outrage.

"He says it's Gaia's will. And this behavior confirms that you are still ruled by the devious sides of Rebelene and Melanel. I will not allow you to interfere with your brother's potential."

"This is absurd!"

"Orlan is a Valið and æðsti prestur. His word is law."

Dalila took Calix by the hand and dragged him toward the castle. He looked back at his older sister as he was pulled away, his gaze desperate and imploring.

Though her heart beat a little faster, Gwyn knew better than to make a scene. She placed her finger to her lips, indicating he not say a word.

Calix's eyes widened in shock for a moment; he never saw this passive version of his wild older sister before, but he followed her lead and stopped trying to fight his mother's grip. He trusted Gwyn, and she quickly proved that trust was warranted.

Chandi now sat in Calix's bedroom through the entirety of his slumber and a guard stood outside his door throughout the night. Though morning trips into the forest were ruined, Gwyn studied Chandi's sleeping schedule and soon learned that she left for a few hours every night. Gwyn also befriended Tyrus, the guard who stood outside Calix's door. Tyrus was a young, but skilled bowman, and it wasn't hard to sway his duties. A few conversations about earning the future king's trust convinced the guard that forming an alliance with the royal children would serve him well in the future.

After a few days of tiring conversations, when Gwyn was certain that she had Tyrus on her side, she made her move.

In the wee hours of morning, when the entire castle was illuminated by the faint glow of candlelight and Namaté's mint-green second moon, Gwyn crept out of bed and found her way to Calix's room. The castle was so quiet along the way that

Gwyn no longer felt at home. The eerie silence made her shiver; she was wildly aware of the countless ghosts of tragedy that lingered in these halls. She shook her trepidation and refocused on Calix.

When she got to his door, Tyrus pretended not to notice her arrival.

"Wake up," she whispered as she entered the room. Calix did not rouse. She shook him a little harder. "Calix, wake up."

He fidgeted and mumbled incoherent thoughts as he turned toward her and opened his eyes.

"Gwynie?" he asked. "What are you doing here?"

"Tyrus is on our side and we have a few hours before Chandi will be back."

"I'm too tired to go to the forest," he moaned.

"I don't want to go to the forest. I thought we could spend time together here."

Calix's eyes lit up upon realizing his sister went to great lengths just so they could be together.

"You can tell me about your adventures with Ario in the Wildlands," he gushed.

"I will," Gwyn promised. "But first I need to know why you did it. Why do you think you need magic?"

After weeks of avoiding this conversation, Calix finally caved.

"My life isn't mine."

"What does that mean?"

"I belong to Orlan."

"He tells you that?" Gwyn asked, outraged.

"No, but it's obvious. The majority of my time is spent with him. Mamma, Lorcan, and Trista are always reminding me how important Orlan is because Gaia speaks through him. Anytime I raise questions about him, they shut me down and insist I behave with blind obedience."

Gwyn sighed. "They did the same thing to me. Orlan used to spend hours lashing me with hot salt water. He also made me suffer through countless spiritual purges. I think he hoped to scare me into adoring him. But when I tried to tell Mamma, she said that Orlan does not do anything without purpose. Basically, that I must have deserved the relentless punishment. My heilög lessons became less frequent after I turned eight, and with all that happened with Kipp and my attempted suicide, no one forced me to do anything that might set me off again, so I wasn't required to visit with Orlan until I turned nine. Since then, I see him once a month. Sometimes I skip the lesson. No one cares what I do."

"I wish I had your freedom."

"Is he good to you?"

"I love him, but I am scared of him too."

"Does he hurt you?"

"I'm not sure."

"Why aren't you sure?"

"It's strange," Calix tried to explain. "I cry a lot in my heilög lessons."

"I haven't seen you cry since you were a baby."

"Connecting with Gaia is uncomfortable. Didn't you cry when he connected you to Her?"

Gwyn was perplexed.

"He never tried that with me."

"Oh. You're lucky then."

They shared a moment of tense silence.

"I don't want to be king," Calix finally confessed. "I don't want to be connected to Gaia."

"You don't have a choice. It's your destiny."

"I wouldn't wish this on anyone."

"It's really that bad?"

"It's awful. I have nightmares about it every night. I never dreamed a bond to Gaia would feel so wrong."

"Tell Mamma. She can make him stop that particular practice if it bothers you this much."

"I can't. I'm not even supposed to be telling you. Orlan says it's our secret; that no one else can know he is connecting me to Gaia."

"That doesn't sound right."

"That's why I need magic. I don't know if I can make Orlan stop, but I am sure I could end the nightmares."

Gwyn wasn't sure how to help her brother, or what advice to give him that might ease his suffering. She didn't truly understand what he was going through, but her gut told her something was off.

She leaned in and gave Calix a hug. Calix melted in her embrace, safe for a moment from the terror he faced alone.

"I will find a way to protect you," she promised.

And for the first time in years, Calix broke into tears.

Chapter 8

For the sake of her brother's safety, Gwyn returned to her heilög lessons with Orlan. She had detective work to do.

"How nice of you to show up this month," the high priest sneered.

"Heilög lessons are important," Gwyn stated obsequiously.

Orlan narrowed his gaze, not believing the rebellious princess finally viewed his life's work with respect. He rubbed his bald scalp, fondling the raised scars that ran across his skull and down his neck.

"It's been so long, I can't recall where we last left off," he avowed.

"Connect me to Gaia."

"Excuse me?"

"I want to feel her."

Orlan's gaze turned murderous as Gwyn cut to the chase. She maintained a look of feigned innocence as the æðsti prestur squirmed.

"You are not worthy of such an experience."

"Why not?"

"Because you are not in line for the throne.

"I am still the princess of Crystet. Surely Gaia cares to connect with me too."

"She doesn't," Orlan quipped. His lack of patience for the ever-trying princess was as heightened as ever.

"That's cruel."

"The truth is often cruel."

"Are you kind to my brother?" Gwyn inquired, changing her line of attack.

"Of course I am! How dare you imply otherwise."

Gwyn glared at the æðsti prestur, aware that she had yet to uncover the truth. But before she could dig deeper, Orlan turned his back to her, whipping his long white robe as he spun, and retreated to the back of the altar. There, he retrieved Gwyn's oldest friend: the splashing wand.

He returned with a golden pitcher of steaming hot salt water. Gwyn bent to her knees without objecting, ready to take the lashing with dignity. Orlan lifted the wet horsehair wand and splashed Gwyn's face with the harmful contents.

"Rid this child of the demons she keeps. In the name of the Mother, the Vorso, and all of their Spirits, I pledge."

Gwyn pursed her lips, closed her eyes, and withstood the punishment. She made no noise as the hot, salt water droplets seared her skin, burning miniscule craters into her glass-flesh.

The unwarranted punishment continued for hours until Orlan left abruptly, disappearing into the steeple tower.

Gwyn was left alone, shivering in pain.

No secrets were discovered, but she wasn't ready to give up yet. She returned the following week with a better plan.

After spying on Orlan for days to learn his schedule, Gwyn snuck into his chamber while he was away eating lunch with Lorcan, and hid behind the long, silk curtain that hung at the back of the altar. She waited patiently, aware that Calix's afternoon lesson would start soon. There was no telling what she'd discover, but after trying and failing to get answers by asking, she determined the only way to know more was to observe Calix's lessons for herself.

When the afternoon bells chimed, Orlan returned to his steeple. Gwyn held her breath as he paced in front of the altar. If he found her, past punishments for minor misdeeds would be tame compared to what she'd suffer for this transgression.

Not long after, Trista escorted Calix into the room. His head was bowed and her mother's andlega ráðgjafi dragged the little prince by the arm.

"He still would not tell me how he got his stomach wound," Trista complained.

"It happened in the woods," Calix lied. "It's really not that great of a tale."

"Who mended it? Why was the whole thing kept private?" Trista interrogated. "It's been weeks. You need to tell us the truth."

"Why does it matter? I'm fine."

"That's not the point. You aren't allowed to have secrets."

"Leave him be," Orlan intervened calmly. "Gaia will tell me all that we need to know."

Calix's eyes widened, but Trista did not flinch.

"Fine. I'll move onto the girl if we still find ourselves left with holes in the story. She surely knows the truth." Trista glided out of the room.

As soon as the large glass door slammed behind her, Orlan zeroed in on Calix.

He clicked his tongue three times. "You ought to oblige Valið Trista. She is your mother's spiritual advisor, chosen by Gaia Herself."

"There's nothing more to tell. I fell on a glass boulder and Gwyn patched me up."

Orlan sighed. "It's a pity you let your sister influence you with such great effect. I thought you'd have learned by now. She is a menace to our world."

"Why?" Calix argued.

"She is incapable of change. She cannot adapt. She is emotional and unstable—a weak link in our great race."

"She is the strongest person I know."

"You only think that because you still value the wrong virtues. Vulnerability isn't a strength, detachment is. Impassive reaction to all of life's evil twists and turns is the only way to thrive. Your sister cannot muster such a strength."

"I don't like it when you talk bad about her."

"You must learn to see things my way, or you will turn into a useless player, just like your sister."

Calix bowed his head. He'd never win with Orlan, he just needed to outlast him.

Orlan took his silence as submission.

"I'll be back," the high priest said before returning to the altar. He opened the door to his private chambers and disappeared for a few minutes. Gwyn wanted to jump out from behind the curtain to let Calix know she was there for him, but she could not blow her cover. If she wanted to learn the truth, no one could know she was observing.

Orlan reemerged wearing a long white robe that was tied in the front. The rope was knotted into a loose bow that threatened to come undone at the slightest touch.

Gwyn's heart raced as she tried to piece together this unexpected development.

Orlan sauntered toward Calix, who stood with his head bowed and his gaze glued to the floor. Her brother refused to look up as the high priest approached.

"Sweet boy," Orlan called, but Calix did not look up. "Give me your attention."

Calix reluctantly shifted his gaze upward to look upon the crusty old man who smelt of death. Scars bulged from his ancient, bald scalp and the fissures around his eyes multiplied as he smiled, revealing his decaying crystal teeth.

"Are you ready to connect with Gaia?" Orlan asked.

"No."

"Why not?"

"I don't want to."

"Of course you do," Orlan objected. He combed his foggy, glass fingers through Calix's hair, circling the young prince as he spoke. "Gaia loves you. So do I."

"It never works. I've never felt Her through you."

"You must be patient. It takes time for the connection to take hold."

"I don't like it."

"Don't lie to me. I've seen you smile."

"No. Never," Calix replied, tears present and ready to fall.

"Don't you love me?" Orlan asked.

"Yes," Calix replied reluctantly.

"Then you must trust me and do as I say."

Calix nodded, tears falling.

"Good. Now remove your clothes."

Calix moved slowly, but obeyed. Orlan displayed eager patience as he waited for the child to disrobe. Gwyn wanted to scream, she wanted to emerge from her hiding place wielding fists of fire. But she had to control her rage. If she revealed herself now, there was no telling the repercussions they both would face.

Once Calix was stripped naked, vulnerable and in danger, Orlan untied his robe, exposing himself to the boy. Gwyn wasn't sure how much longer she could restrain her fury.

"Take my hand," Orlan coaxed with an outstretched arm. Calix closed his eyes and surrendered his hand to the high priest. "Eyes open," Orlan demanded.

Calix obeyed, his expression was wrought with unease.

Orlan took the prince's small hand and pressed it against the parts of his old body that Gwyn had been taught were private and sacred. Calix closed his eyes and turned his head upon contact, grimacing with tear-soaked cheeks, but Orlan did not notice the boy's aversion. The old man stared upward as he moved Calix's tiny hand back and forth.

"Stop!" Gwyn shrieked, unable to stand another second of this vile discovery. "How could you?" she screamed through sobs as she charged forward.

The sound of her voice ripped Orlan from his perverted pleasure. He let go of Calix's hand and quickly closed his robe. Gwyn tore the curtain off the wall as she emerged from her hiding place and covered Calix's naked body the moment she reached him.

"What are you doing here?" Orlan demanded.

"Protecting my brother!" Gwyn sobbed in fury.

"From what?" Orlan asked, trying to act natural. "He is safest with me."

"You were violating him."

"I was connecting him to Gaia."

"Naked?" she asked, holding Calix close.

"It's the only way."

"I will kill you for this."

"I did nothing wrong. He is unharmed."

"There are other ways to harm a person…"

"I don't owe you an explanation."

"I don't need one," Gwyn seethed. "All I want are your pieces shattered on the floor."

Orlan's breathing grew heavier and he placed his hand over the religious pendant he wore around his neck. "Your parents won't believe you."

"I will make them. And if they don't see things my way, I will take your life myself."

"Don't make promises you can't keep," Orlan snarled, his confidence returning.

A knock sounded on the door and everyone's attention turned to the voice that followed.

"Why are you screaming?" Lorcan shouted through the door. "Is everything okay?"

"Uncle Lorcan," Gwyn exhaled with relief. "Come in!"

She snapped her attention back to Orlan, expecting him to look afraid, but instead she found him wearing a smug smile.

"Your time is up," Gwyn threatened.

"Thank the heavens you're here," Orlan declared. "Your unruly niece is at it again."

"What happened?" Lorcan asked. He surveyed the scene and his face shifted to worried confusion. "Is everyone okay?"

"Despite her raucous disruption of our heilög lesson, everyone is okay."

"No," Gwyn argued. "I caught Orlan doing very bad things to Calix."

"Why is Calix wearing a curtain?" Lorcan asked.

"Because Orlan made him get naked! And then he got naked too and forced Calix to touch him in places that are very wrong!"

"That is a large and dangerous accusation," Lorcan stated.

"I saw it with my own eyes," she insisted. "And who knows how far it has gone when I wasn't here to stop him. You all fear the creatures of the wild, but it turns out the greatest monster of all lives under the same roof as us."

"I am struggling to believe such an atrocious claim."

"Just look around! It's clear. All the evidence is right in front of you."

Wearing a cautious expression, Lorcan shifted his gaze from his niece to the high priest.

"Orlan, is this true?"

"Of course it isn't. The girl is perverse. I was connecting him to Gaia. Speaking to the Mother requires full transparency; no clothes."

"I see," Lorcan replied, unsure where to go from here. "I mean, if that's how it's done—"

"No!" Gwyn objected. "What about all the touching?"

"There was no inappropriate touching," Orlan scoffed, looking at Lorcan. "The princess has proven her instability for years now. She's just angry that Dalila forbade them from spending time together. If anyone loves our prince too much, it's her."

"How dare you," Gwyn seethed.

"Enough," Lorcan intervened. "Everyone needs to calm down. Let's separate and cool off so we can solve this scuffle with clear minds."

"She isn't lying," Calix chimed in, his voice shaking.

Lorcan sighed. "Let me investigate without everyone's heightened emotions in my face, clouding my judgment."

Gwyn grabbed Calix's clothes from the floor and escorted him out of the room. Once they crossed the threshold and the steeple doors slammed behind them, Gwyn turned to Calix.

"You will never be alone with him again."

Calix nodded. He wanted to believe his sister, but struggled to see how she could overpower the adults controlling their lives.

Gwyn sensed his hesitation. "I will die before I let him do that to you again. In the name of the Mother, I swear."

Calix mustered a small smile and Gwyn kissed his forehead. She was prepared to lay down her life to save the remnants of his innocence.

Chapter 9

Gwyn was too distraught to eat. She twirled her fork in the þang-leaf salad, tangling the seaweed into knots she didn't plan to eat. Dalila sat tall with shoulders back and neck elongated at the head of the table. She glittered in the sunlight with regality, casting spots of light onto their feast. Almas sat to her left, looking weary. It appeared as though the sum of recent events were taking a toll. He wore an expensive, arctic hare fur coat over his stable clothes and large, dark circles under his eyes.

"Why is your plate still full?" her mother asked.

"I'm not hungry," Gwyn replied. She was on the brink of defeat and her energy was solemn.

"Why not?"

"Because you don't believe me."

"Not this nonsense about Orlan again," Dalila groaned. "You cannot make up damaging rumors just because you hate a person."

"They aren't rumors," she insisted. "Uncle Lorcan, please tell her!"

"Darling," her uncle began. "I found no solid evidence to verify your claims. I think you simply misunderstood what you saw."

"Orlan made Calix touch him," Gwyn shouted with discomfort. Then, in a hushed voice, she added, "Down there."

"You're embarrassing your brother," Dalila scoffed, placing her hands over Calix's ears.

"But Mamma—" he protested.

"Shh," she shushed her son. "Don't let her poison your mind."

"He says it's true too! Why won't anyone believe us?" Gwyn asked, exasperated.

"Because *you* have a reputation for engaging in mischief and enjoying despair," her mother explained with a scowl. "And *you* have warped the truth into something rotten and confusing, not only for Calix, but for all of us. A situation as atrocious as the one you claim happened surely brings you a silent form of twisted joy."

Tears filled Gwyn's eyes as she took the insult quietly. Accusing her of finding pleasure in her beloved brother's torment was a new low. Disgusted by the false allegation and horrified that such a horrible lie was even uttered aloud, she excused herself from the table.

"Don't you dare leave without my consent," Dalila growled.

"*You* no longer matter to me," Gwyn snarled, tears blinding her. She stormed out of the solarium and headed for Calix's room. She had not gotten far when her father skated down the hall, calling after her.

"Gwynessa, wait," he pleaded. She did not stop. "Darling," Almas tried again. "Please talk to me."

"Why?" She stopped and faced him. "You've been silent for years. I don't even know who you are anymore."

"I'm sorry. I've been living in a dark place for a while, it's true, but I never meant to neglect you or Calix. I just thought you both were doing well and didn't need me as much."

"We need you now more than ever," she seethed.

"I see that, and I want to be the father you need. Tell me what I can do."

"Protect us from that monster living in the steeple."

"I do not outrank him in power," Almas replied, his expression lined with defeat. "The æðsti prestur and your mother have more authority than I do."

"What does that matter? Take a stand. Use the influence you *do* have."

"Your mother no longer loves or respects me. She wouldn't listen to me if I tried."

"But you *haven't* tried, so how would you know?"

"I just do."

"Then leave me alone and I'll take care of it on my own."

"I'm on your side," he shouted as she skated away with slouched shoulders. "I believe you."

Gwyn shook her head, but did not stop. His words meant nothing when what she needed was action.

Arriving at Calix's room, she found Trista preparing the prince for his heilög lesson. His gaze remained fixed on the ground as Trista rattled off demands and reminders. When the andlega ráðgjafi caught sight of Gwyn's arrival, she redirected her attention.

"What are you doing here?" Trista snapped.

"I'm here for Calix's heilög lesson."

"You are not allowed into his lessons."

"Try to stop me," Gwyn threatened.

"What will you do, little girl?" Trista ridiculed. "No one believes you."

"I don't care. I live to protect my brother."

"I thought you lived to protect the wild animals," Trista mocked.

"Matters within the castle have turned more grave, so for now, my devotion lies here."

"You cannot save the world."

"Sometimes saving those we love matters more than trying to fix the broken world around us."

"Wise or foolish?" Trista sneered in contemplation. "I say both sentiments are a waste of time."

"That's because you don't love anyone except yourself."

"How correct you are. One day you'll understand the value of self-love."

"There's a difference between self-love and selfish love," Gwyn said. "I put my own safety aside to protect Calix. It's important to show up for the people who would do the same for you."

"Love will destroy you."

"Love sets me free."

"Irrational and unrefined," Trista scoffed. "You belong in the wild with the monsters. You are one of them."

"So be it." Gwyn was no longer rattled by Trista's harsh treatment.

She followed them to the steeple, where Orlan waited with arms crossed. The foggy, glass scars on his bulbous, bald head could be seen from the opposite side of the corridor.

"I told you to leave the girl behind," he shouted as they approached.

"I tried," Trista replied, her voice tired. "The princess cannot be tamed."

"This will not be pretty," Orlan mumbled, but his voice showed no trace of remorse. "Guards," he shouted.

At his order, twenty swordsmen filed out of the steeple and blocked the door. They wielded serrated diamond blades and wore the finest Uveges armor.

Gwyn grabbed Calix's arm before Trista could pull him through the line of defense and held him close. She took slow steps backwards as Trista cursed her.

"Fjandinn barn," Trista swore in the ancient tongue of their gods. "Himininn mótmælir tilvist þinni."

"I am not damned and I am not a burden," Gwyn spat.

Trista laughed in surprise. "I see you've been brushing up on your primordial Glaziene."

"Gaia loves me," Gwyn continued.

"She loathes you," Orlan stated, stepping forward. "You bring Her great shame."

"I do not."

"Hand over the boy," Orlan insisted with an outstretched hand.

"Never," Gwyn shouted, continuing to move away from the tumultuous scene. Calix clung to her hip and followed her lead.

"You will regret your resistance," Orlan threatened. Gwyn made no indication that she planned to obey, so the high priest unleashed his devoted soldiers.

At the swipe of his hand, the brute Glaziene men charged at the young children with swords raised. Gwyn shrieked in fear as she grabbed Calix's hand and glided as fast as she could away from the menacing soldiers. War grunts echoed off the tall, glass walls until the noise was so loud, it sounded like there were five hundred soldiers instead of twenty. The overwhelming reverberation shook Gwyn to the core, but she did not stop and she did not look back.

"They will take you away from me," she cried desperately, hoping to motivate Calix to move faster. "Orlan will get you alone again."

Calix sobbed as Gwyn tugged him forward. "My legs aren't as long as yours."

Gwyn was determined to escape with her brother in tow. She needed to find Lorcan or her parents. Though they did not believe her, they surely would be opposed to Orlan using their army against her.

"Help!" she screamed repeatedly, but no one answered her.

The soldiers skated into a circle around the fleeing children, barricading and trapping them in place. With no other option, Gwyn pulled Calix close and held him as tightly as she could. But her best was no match for the strength of the guards. Two soldiers entered the circle and tore the children apart, and Gwyn was forced to watch them deliver her brother back to Orlan. Calix fought back by going limp. He refused to walk and turned himself into dead weight for the soldiers to carry. Being so little, this was no issue for the grown men, who dragged his limp body toward the high priest.

"Stop!" Gwyn pleaded as a guard constrained her. "You don't realize what you're doing."

No one listened. She was ignored, as always, and forced to standby while terrible crimes were permitted.

Her rage turned into a fit of sobs as her bravado surrendered to reality. There was nothing she could do. She was completely overpowered by those around her. She loathed feeling weak, she detested feeling vulnerable, and in that moment, she made a promise to herself that she would make these people pay for their wrongdoings. But the enormity of this promise was quickly realized—she could not foresee it coming to fruition anytime soon—and the feeling of helplessness consumed her once again. She was lost in a world beyond her control.

After Calix was escorted into the steeple by Orlan, the guard released her and exited the corridor, followed by his armed comrades. Gwyn fell to her knees and the soldiers marched past. They bumped into her with little regard as they departed. Trista was the last to leave.

The andlega ráðgjafi towered over Gwyn, who knelt with her head cradled in her hands.

"Get up," Trista demanded.

Gwyn shook her head.

"Do not test me further. You will be in enough trouble when your parents learn of this humiliating ordeal."

"They will be mad that their army was used against me."

"You think so?" Trista ridiculed. "I think they will see this as your fault. You've been told multiple times that Calix's heilög lessons are one-on-one. They are not meant for you to sit in on. You have become a barricade to your brother's growth and I am beginning to suspect that your behavior is an attempt to thwart his rise to greatness."

"Of course it isn't."

"Do you want the crown for yourself?" Trista asked, taunting Gwyn. "I suspect you intend to ruin the boy so completely that he never develops the confidence needed to sit on the throne."

"You know that isn't true," Gwyn spat.

Trista's eyes gleamed.

"Your parents will be embarrassed by your actions today and apologetic toward Orlan."

Gwyn didn't have the confidence to dispute her; Trista was far better at guessing their reactions. All she could do was hope that this incident was extreme enough for them to finally take a step back and see the truth.

No such luck existed in Gwyn's world. She quickly discovered that her mother was not on her side. Dalila was infuriated by the ordeal and confined Gwyn to her bedroom during Calix's heilög lessons. Guards were assigned to watch over her temporary prison each day, which made it impossible to escape. After a week of enduring this gut-wrenching horror, Gwyn finally made it to Calix's bedroom during the early hours of morning to check on him.

"Calix," she whispered as she tiptoed into his room. "Wake up."

He rustled and turned to face her. When he opened his eyes, they were heavy with despair. He stared at her silently and his utterly defeated spirit broke her heart. She ran to his side and buried him in a hug.

"I let you down. I'm so sorry."

"You tried," he offered. "It's not your fault."

She stood, lifted him into a sitting position, and then looked into his eyes.

"Is he still touching you?" she asked with trepidation.

Calix nodded.

Admitting aloud that he still suffered this violation filled him with remorse. His expression constricted with guilt and sorrow, and his eyes welled with tears.

Gwyn pulled him closer.

"It's not your fault," she reassured him, unable to stop the tears that fell down her face.

"Now that I know what he's doing is bad, it's much harder to endure. Before, I thought what he was doing was normal. That it was what everyone went through to connect with Gaia. But now, because of you, I know better. Now, I know that I am being wronged and that there is nothing I can do to stop it," Calix sniffled. "Not yet, at least."

"You need to tell Mamma. If it comes from you, she will listen."

"I've tried, a couple times, but once I start, she always insists that you coached me on what to say, that you have infected my mind. And once she starts demanding details, I get too embarrassed to speak."

"The only person who should feel embarrassed is Orlan. And our parents, once they realize what they let go on."

"But then, sometimes when I'm with him, he convinces me that what he's doing is best for me. And I actually believe him."

"He's manipulating you," Gwyn reminded him. "He is playing mind games. Don't let him fool you."

"I know, but when I'm there, in the moment, he is so convincing."

Gwyn hugged him tighter. She understood Calix's difficult position. All his life he admired Orlan, and now, those illusions of perfection were being shattered.

"I'll find a way to save you from him," Gwyn promised, though she did not yet know how she'd manage.

Gwyn's eleventh birthday came and went. The false merriment of the celebration was worse than usual. All she could think of was Calix's torment, so tolerating the feigned joy of those around her was even harder than usual. Ario was allowed to attend and he stayed by her side the entire party. His steady energy and unwavering loyalty helped her stomach the gross irreverence toward her brother's suffering. Though Ario did not know the truth, he sensed that Gwyn needed him more than usual, so he graciously acted as a shield when the overwhelming nature of the party became too much to bear. Calix, however, was nowhere to be found. While the nobles were told that his absence was due to a mild fever, Gwyn knew that Orlan had convinced her mother to keep Calix far away from her.

The weeks following her birthday celebration passed without progress. Gwyn could not find a way to help Calix. The strict guard over her during his heilög lessons continued and no one with any authority would listen to her. She did not have the power to eliminate Orlan. He was too great, too loved to take on. During her own heilög lessons, which she began attending regularly again in order to gain one-on-one access to Orlan, he merely punished her with splashings, teaching her nothing and refusing to answer any of her questions. He told Dalila that her heilög lessons had come to completion, that he had done all he could for her, but the queen did not accept his resignation and demanded he try harder. This resulted in unrelenting chastisement, but she refused to back down. If she couldn't get Orlan to admit the truth, she would make herself a constant, tormenting presence.

After countless lessons filled with hours of splashings, the marks were beginning to show. Normally, the corrosion was so minute that it was undetectable, but after non-stop assaults, the lesions became visible.

"What's wrong with your face?" Mina asked upon retrieving her from her heilög lesson.

"Hot salt water splashings," Gwyn replied, emotionless.

"How long has this been going on?" Mina asked, appalled. "I can see the marks. You're not supposed to see the marks…"

"Since I was a little girl. It's been worse recently though."

"I must tell your mother."

"She won't care. She'll side with Orlan. She always does."

"This is not right," Mina protested.

"I think I'll take a break from heilög lessons tomorrow," Gwyn conceded, aware she needed to refuel her spirit. "I miss Ario."

"I think that's a good idea. Give your skin some time to heal before facing more of the same torture."

"Yeah," Gwyn responded, though she sounded far away.

"I wish I could help you," Mina offered.

"No one can."

Gwyn traveled to Uveges Armor shop the following day. Ario greeted her with relief.

"Where have you been? I was so worried."

"I need to talk to you."

"What's wrong?" Ario looked at her with concern, noticing the healing lacerations on her face.

"Everything."

Jahdo sat in the corner, shaping hot glass, observing the youngsters out of the corner of his eye. His own concern was apparent, but he did not say a word.

"We will be back later," Ario finally said to him.

"Take your time," Jahdo replied.

They trekked all the way to Jökull Cliff before Gwyn revealed her secret. Sitting on the edge with her feet dangling over the side, Gwyn burst into tears and told Ario everything.

"That is horrible. Why don't your parents believe you or Calix?" he asked.

"Because they are blinded by Orlan's shroud of power. They really think he talks to Gaia."

"I bet they think that Gaia will curse them if they don't stand by his side," Ario added.

"Probably." Gwyn exhaled deeply. "I don't know what to do."

"If it were me, and I was being abused like that by Orlan, I'd probably want to die." Gwyn shot him a look of disbelief. "I'm sorry," he continued, "but it's the truth. What's happening is vile and soul crushing. I don't know that I'd ever recover from the humiliation or loss of pride. I certainly would have trouble growing into a strong man after suffering something like that."

"He can still become a ferocious leader. He can still be everything he's meant to be."

"He has a lot of inner healing to do before that happens."

Gwyn knew Ario was right.

"What should I do?"

"I don't know."

"I need to kill Orlan," she acknowledged aloud, revealing her ultimate, but seemingly impossible goal. "But that could take months, possibly years, to complete. Orlan is too well-protected. I need to stop what he's doing *now*."

"Maybe we can hide Calix in the Wildlands," Ario suggested. "We know the ins and outs of this forest better than anyone else."

"Yeah, maybe," Gwyn replied with a sigh. She looked out to the sea, then shifted her gaze to the distant causeway, where King Rúnar's partially reconstructed body still stood like a statue. The hole where his heart should be glinted in the sun.

A tingling spark shot through her brain and vibrated down her spine.

"I have to go back," she announced.

"Already?"

"Yes. Let's go."

Ario asked no questions and followed her down the hill. Her mind was so consumed by ideas and possibilities that they did not speak the entire way back. Before leaving the armor shop, she gave Ario a hug.

"Thank you," she whispered into his ear.

"For what?"

"For believing me."

She left and tried to mentally prepare herself for the greatest challenge of her life.

Chapter 10

Gwyn snuck into Calix's room again while his handmaidens slept. Though Calix was happy she came, her energy was solemn.

"Do you trust me?" she asked.

"Completely."

"Good," she replied, then grabbed his hand. "Come with me."

Dressed in their nightgowns, the royal children climbed countless staircases until they were outside on the eastern roof. In a small corner blocked by a protruding tower, the bowmen stationed atop the castle could not see them. It was the same spot where Gwyn tried to take her own life.

Concerned, Calix looked around in confusion.

"Why are we here?"

"I figured out how to save you."

"How?"

"You must have complete faith in me," Gwyn reminded him.

"I do."

Gwyn nodded, then lunged and hooked Calix by the neck. Startled, he fought back, but Gwyn was still bigger than him and he stood no chance.

"What are you doing?" Calix demanded, voice cracking with alarm.

"Stop fighting me. And be quiet, or the guards will hear."

Gwyn shoved her fist into his mouth, which shut him up, and then pushed past the lining of his throat into the open space of his ribcage. Calix was choking on her arm, so she tried to work fast. She moved her hand until her fingertips brushed across the top of his heart. Pulling down the collar of his nightshirt, Gwyn looked through his translucent skin to see her hand grazing his heart. She seized the pulsing organ and ripped it from its home. When she withdrew her arm from his mouth, his heart glowed bright in her grip.

The moment it touched the frigid outside air, the organ went into shock. It morphed from bright purple to a glowing red, then began to turn black as it crystalized before their eyes.

Calix gasped. "What have you done?"

"Trust me," she insisted, adrenaline rushing. Before the heart became completely black, she shoved it into her own mouth. The warmth of her body prevented it from solidifying completely, but being a foreign host, she could not undo the damage already caused. His heart in her hand, she pressed hard against the back of her throat until she entered the spacious cavity between her ribs. When her fingers bumped into her own beating heart, she dropped Calix's heart next to hers, then slowly extracted her arm from her mouth.

"This is how I'll keep you safe," she explained.

"I don't understand."

She stepped closer to him, and he stepped back toward the edge of the roof.

"I will keep your heart next to mine."

"Why though?"

"Take my hand."

He obeyed hesitantly, and Gwyn stepped onto the ledge, forcing Calix to join her.

"I don't have enough power or influence to kill Orlan. Not yet, at least," she explained. "So the only way to stop Orlan is to remove you from the situation."

Calix looked down, now understanding what she meant, and immediately protested.

"No! I don't want to die."

"You won't die. This is simply a pause. I will put you back together the moment I kill that monster. I promise."

Calix sobbed. "I'm scared, Gwynie."

"Don't be."

"There has to be another way."

"There isn't. I've thought it through. Ario and I discussed hiding you in the woods, but that would only last so long before they found you. Nothing would be solved. By doing it this way, it looks like you chose death. Neither of us will get in trouble for misbehaving, I will have time to find a way to kill Orlan, and you will be safe."

"I don't like it," Calix sniveled.

"Everything will be okay, I promise. When I bring you back, the world will be a better place. Orlan will be destroyed and you'll be able to grow into the greatest king Crystet has ever seen."

Calix shook with fear. Looking to the sky, Gwyn saw that the third moon was already dropping closer to the horizon.

"Do I have your blessing?" she asked.

He shook his head, still trembling.

She released a heavy sigh. "You will thank me one day."

Then she pushed her little brother off the ledge. Tears filled her eyes as she watched him fall, arms flailing toward her, reaching for help. His white blouse fluttered in the falling wind and when he hit the ground, she heard his pieces shatter. Her heart pounded violently within her chest. So hard, she could feel his heart slamming into the side of hers.

She wanted to run down, to be by his side as his life faded, but she couldn't. There was nothing more to say.

Her sorrow turned to rage as she thought of Orlan. He caused this. He was to blame for this horrible night. But until she found a way to shatter his existence, she was forced to live a hollow life without Calix by her side.

She placed her hand upon her chest and reminded herself that Calix was still with her. He would always be with her so long as his heart sat next to hers.

A gush of sorrow-fueled inspiration rushed through her. She would fulfill her promise and bring Calix back. It was now her greatest motivation for living.

The following morning, a shriek of bereaved terror echoed through the entire land.

Dalila had found Calix's shattered pieces.

Gwyn jolted upright in bed, afraid to face the day. She hadn't slept at all.

Her mother's screams turned into loud sobs that shadowed the usual dreary atmosphere with intensified misery.

Mina exited her chamber, looking alarmed.

"What happened?"

"I'm not sure," Gwyn lied. "The scream woke me up too. I think it's my mother."

Mina's breathing became heavy as she tried to decide what to do.

"Let's get you dressed," she insisted of Gwyn, who obeyed without protest. "Whatever happened must be terrible."

Gwyn lifted her arms and Mina removed the princess's nightgown. She stood naked while her handmaiden chose an outfit for the day. Gwyn looked down at her nearly translucent chest and saw Calix's heart nestled behind her own. Fear surged through her, but when Mina returned with a simple, powder blue dress, she did not seem to notice the addition. The poorly fused scar across her chest from her own suicidal leap helped mask her secret, but if anyone ever looked close enough, her innocence in Calix's unexpected fall would be ruined.

Mina forced the dress over Gwyn's head, then took her hand and led her out of the room. They marched toward the noise, exiting through the eastern side of the castle. The scene was visible the moment they stepped foot outside. Dalila stood tall, wearing a gorgeous, black gown made from crow feathers and sylph wings, a crown adorned with jagged shards of glass, and an expression that could kill. Eyes red, but tears dried, she stood over Calix's shattered pieces, berating the servants who had answered her sorrowful shriek and insisting that someone give an explanation. When she saw Mina and Gwyn approaching, her attention turned to them.

"What do you know about this?" she demanded of her daughter.

"Whose pieces are those?" Gwyn asked, playing dumb, as they walked closer. But when the broken body was in clear sight, Gwyn's pretend confusion turned into genuine anguish. This was the first time she was seeing her brother's lifeless body. Pieces scattered about. The tears fell naturally as she ran toward his remains.

"Can't we rebuild him?" she asked, continuing her feigned ignorance.

"This is a murder," Dalila seethed. "His heart is missing."

Gwyn looked around, pretending to look for the misplaced piece.

"Who would do something like this?"

"You tell me," Dalila fumed. "You were the only one exposing him to outsiders."

"Outsiders?" Gwyn asked, perplexed. "Clearly, this has to be the work of someone inside the castle. Outsiders aren't allowed in."

"Was it you?"

"Of course it wasn't!" Gwyn retorted. "I'd never hurt Calix."

"I wish I could believe you," her mother said in a low voice, "but you've been such a disappointment. I struggle to see the good in you."

Deflated, but motivated to clear her name from the crime, Gwyn offered an alternative possibility.

"He was really sad—I tried to tell you. Orlan was breaking him from the inside out. Maybe he took out his own heart and hid it somewhere."

"He wouldn't do such a thing."

"Yes, he would," she insisted. "He told me once that he did not know how much more he could stand."

Dalila paused, but it didn't take long for her accusatory gusto to return.

"Why didn't you tell me that?"

"I tried."

"No," Dalila countered. "You only ever went on about Orlan and all the uncivilized crimes you swear he committed."

"Isn't this proof that what we *both* claimed Orlan did is true? Why else would Calix do something so drastic?"

Dalila appeared doubtful of her daughter's wild claims.

"If you played no part in this tragedy then you must dedicate your life to finding your brother's heart. You are not fit to be my heir. It has to be him."

"I don't want to be queen," Gwyn replied in her own defense.

"Prove it. Find Calix's heart."

Dalila stormed back into the castle. Trista raced to keep up, as did the queen's handmaidens and servants. The parade of bystanders scattered, leaving only Gwyn, Mina, and a few stable boys tasked to collect the prince's broken pieces so they could be reassembled one day.

"Where will you put him?" Gwyn asked the youngest boy.

"The queen instructed that we put him into that box," he replied. He had one silver-green eye, but the other was completely black. She tried not to judge, but it was a rare sight to see in Crystet. Being born with a black iris was seen as a curse.

"Don't miss a single shard of my brother," Gwyn commanded. "We need every sliver of his body accounted for."

"Of course, Princess," the boy replied, bowing his head in respect.

Gwyn believed him, but stayed to oversee the process. She had a promise to keep and she would not let a small mistake thwart her noble deed.

Chapter 11

Gwyn sat alone in the royal forest, possessing two hearts when she ought to have one. Calix's presence radiated within her. The magic of his heart spoke to her while she slept, but she ignored the calls. The grief was too recent, her resolve too fragile to embrace the temptation. She did not know the extent of the heart's power and she did not want to fall victim to its mysteries.

Ario arrived an hour after her, tired and stressed.

"I'm sorry I could not come to see you sooner," he apologized, sitting beside Gwyn on the fallen sequoia trunk. He wrapped his arm around her, pulling her in until she had no choice but to rest her head upon his chest.

"It's been a week," she replied, wanting to chastise him for his absence, but was unable to fake disappointment. She wasn't angry. She didn't have room in her heart to feel anything but sorrow.

"I know. I feel terrible. But we've been extra busy at the shop. Since Calix's death, your mother has amped up her involvement in the rebellion."

"Calix isn't dead."

"Sorry—since his accident," Ario corrected himself, though calling the incident an accident was a stretch. "I think she intends to hide her grief in the Great Fight."

"Probably."

Ario paused, unsure how to phrase his next question. When he mustered the courage, he spoke.

"People in Gler are saying terrible things about you. I, of course, don't believe a word of it, but it's been really hard not to fight every person I interact with lately."

Gwyn looked up, alarmed. "What are they saying?"

"That you killed Calix. That you murdered him so you would be next in line for the throne."

"That's not true."

"Of course it isn't, but the whole ordeal looks awful from afar. You already had a reputation as a rebel with a flair for sorrow, so it wasn't hard for the masses to conclude you played a part in this tragedy."

"I would never kill Calix."

"I know you wouldn't. I saw how much you loved him. I also know what you both were dealing with in private." Ario hesitated. "So, what actually happened?"

Gwyn sighed. There was no use hiding the truth from Ario.

"It will be my end if anyone else learns the truth."

"Your secrets are my secrets. I'll take them to the grave."

She trusted Ario and lowered her rabbit-fur coat.

"Unbutton the back of my dress," she instructed.

Ario paused in confused shock, but obeyed. He gently relocated her long blonde curls so they hung over her shoulder and struggled to push the flash of fiery visions from his mind.

His fingers trembled as he unfastened the buttons. When he reached the fifth latch, her skinny and scarred back was revealed—a formally forbidden sight. As he went for the sixth, she commanded he stop.

"Look past the breaks," she said.

"I see your organs."

"Look closer at my heart."

Ario grabbed her shoulders and zeroed in on the backside of Gwyn's heart. When he noticed he was seeing double, he rotated her body to get a different angle. He turned her body again to confirm that his eyes weren't playing tricks on him.

"Are there two?" he asked in awe.

Gwyn nodded. "Mine and Calix's. I'm keeping him safe until I can fix things."

"What does that mean?"

She turned to face her dearest friend. "I am going to kill Orlan. Once I do, I will rebuild Calix. I will bring him back."

Ario hesitated. "This is dangerous. You are playing with fate."

"I had no other option."

"How will you achieve all of that?" he asked in a terrified whisper.

"I'm not sure yet, but I am hoping you might help. You are the only person who believes me."

It took a moment of tormented deliberation before he accepted that he too had no other option but to help the girl he loved.

Ario sighed. "Of course I will help. I heard the truth in your voice when you told me what happened. And I saw the truth in Calix's broken spirit the last few times I saw him. We just need a plan."

"I will think of something. Orlan has his own branch of the royal army assigned to his protection, so we will have to be careful. No one can know I am to blame."

"Then you better come up with something good."

"I will."

The castle bells chimed in the distance, performing an erratic melody she never heard before. Gwyn furrowed her brow.

"I better get back."

Ario peeked at the hidden heart one last time before buttoning up her dress. He looked away as she stood, both to protect her modesty and to calm his raging heart, but she recaptured his attention with a long hug.

Gwyn skated back to the castle, annoyed that wrongful rumors were circulating about her, but aware that she could not stop them. Bringing Calix back was the only way to prove them all wrong.

Upon exiting the forest, she found that the castle was surrounded by chaos. A jolt of alarm coursed through her as she raced into the fray.

She barged through the castle's main entrance.

"What happened?" she shouted, hoping someone might answer, but the adults ignored her. As always, the soldiers were not allowed to talk, and the nobles ran around in a frenzied state, muttering amongst themselves.

Her heart couldn't handle much more.

Everyone appeared to be waiting for an announcement, some kind of an update about a matter she wasn't privy to. She paced the entrance hall, prepared to push through the crowd and into the castle's interior rooms, when Lorcan emerged on the balcony that overlooked the foyer.

"The king is dead," he announced, his expression blank and emotionless.

Gwyn fell to her knees in the middle of the crowd.

The room erupted with devious whispers. Rumors were being birthed before there was an official explanation. Gwyn looked up and listened; no one even realized she was there.

"His body was found in a handmaiden's private chambers," an ancient woman said.

"I heard the handmaiden's name is Chandi—a former handmaiden to his dead son," another added.

Gwyn tuned into a different conversation.

"I heard his insides were blackened when they found him. But his exterior was intact," a Glaziene man covered in fused scars whispered to his younger counterpart.

"How is that even possible?" the young man asked.

"Magic," the older man said with a knowing glare.

"Are you saying someone intentionally did this to King Almas?"

"All clues point to murder."

Gwyn began to hyperventilate. She wasn't sure why no one saw her there, why no one cared that she could hear their snide and uninformed assumptions. She was invisible, unimportant, disregarded. Gwyn wiped the tears from her face, stood up, lifted her chin toward the ceiling, and then screamed as loud as her lungs allowed.

The ferocity of her shriek cracked the glass ceiling. The crowd froze, shocked both by the noise and the revelation of Gwyn's presence. The room became so quiet that only the tinkling of the splintering ceiling could be heard. Those around her reluctantly bowed out of respect for the royal family.

Gwyn's scream didn't end until she ran out of breath. When it was done, she panted, gasping for air. The tears returned to her eyes as she marched past the bowing nobles. She glared up at Lorcan as she crossed the room, holding his gaze until she passed under the balcony. After going through the doors and leaving the crowd, Lorcan resumed his speech, but Gwyn had no desire to hear his contrived words. The rehearsed explanation was surely designed to appease the masses. Gwyn highly doubted that whatever he told them was the full truth.

She skated with ferocious intent toward the solarium, where she suspected her mother was riding out this tragedy. When she arrived at the large, glass dome situated in the center of the castle, she saw her mother inside, sitting alone at the head of the long table inside.

Gwyn took a deep breath and then entered.

Dalila did not look up. She merely stared down at her hands, which were clasped together atop the crystal table. Her makeup remained perfectly applied. She hadn't shed one tear.

They shared a moment of hateful silence before Dalila spoke.

"Your father is dead."

"I gathered. Had to hear about it through the awful rumors being spread amongst the commoners."

"The commoners don't know yet."

"The nobles," Gwyn grunted, correcting herself. "Aren't you sad at all?"

"Why should I be? Everyone leaves this world at some point."

"What happened?" Gwyn demanded. "Did you kill him?"

"Did *you* kill Calix?" her mother retorted.

"Of course I didn't.

"And I didn't kill Almas."

"Then what happened?" Gwyn tried again.

"He was murdered. Someone poisoned him. The chemicals turned all his insides black, same as if he were cracked open."

"Who? We must find the culprit and destroy them," Gwyn demanded.

"I don't know who did it."

"You will find out though, right?"

"Perhaps."

Gwyn seethed.

"How can you sit there, unaffected by his death? Why aren't you outraged?"

Dalila finally lifted her eyes.

"Do you know how he was found?"

Gwyn did not reply.

"Half-naked in Chandi's bedroom. An hour after breakfast the little whore ran through the castle, dressed only in her negligee, crying and begging for a medic. Your father died in disgrace."

"He had to get love from someone, considering all of yours has been given to that bowman."

Dalila raised an eyebrow, intrigued by her daughter's astute observation of the castle's inner workings.

"And to think I thought you were totally oblivious," the queen mused. "How did you learn of that?"

"I was a bored little girl. Eavesdropping passed the time while I was a prisoner inside this castle."

"Good thing I let you go back to the forest," Dalila remarked sarcastically. "Imagine the secrets you would have discovered if I hadn't."

Gwyn paused. "You played a part in his murder, didn't you?"

"Of course not. I did not know of his infidelity until this morning. I had no motive."

Gwyn believed her; the look of unexpected betrayal on her mother's face was genuine.

"My affair was never a secret to your father, whereas he kept his indiscretions hidden from me. Think of the humiliation, the shame I feel. How it looks to those observing from afar." Dalila halted with genuine dismay. "I look like a fool."

"Pretend that you knew of their relationship all along, that it was an arrangement you allowed, and your pride will be saved."

Dalila's harsh expression shifted to one of surprise.

"Very wise," she muttered.

"And show some remorse for his death. He only went to Chandi because you are ice-cold and have grown incapable of showing love. I don't blame him for betraying you."

"Harsh," she commented, "but accurate. Perhaps there is hope for you yet."

"I don't want your approval," Gwyn spat. "I want you to care for someone other than yourself."

"Seems you're still missing the narcissism it takes to be a good queen." Dalila did not look angry, only curious. Her expression had morphed into one of patience. "In time."

"No. I won't be like you."

"Should you wind up taking my place on the throne, you'll have no choice but to change. The people will break you, the ways of this world will harden your soft heart. You're on your way. A few more breaks and you'll be whole."

Gwyn hated her mother, but what she hated more was that she understood the cryptic foretelling she offered. She understood what she meant and saw the change happening to herself. She was becoming jaded and mean, she was losing touch with the parts of her soul that kept her kind. Every new heartbreak sent her further away from the proud girl she used to be. Each new heartbreak morphed her into someone she struggled to recognize.

Infuriated, Gwyn stormed out of the room. She was determined to discover who murdered her distant, but beloved father.

She found Lorcan carefully studying maps in the dimly lit library, occasionally smearing red grease across the page with a glass pen.

"What are you doing?" she asked, appalled that he wasn't focused on finding her father's murderer.

Lorcan twitched with shock; he hadn't seen her enter.

"Making plans for our army. Changes are coming."

Gwyn stormed to the table and snatched the pen from his hand. With a single swipe of her arm, she smashed the glass pen on the map and the red ink spread like blood across the page, ruining all of Lorcan's work.

They maintained eye contact as Gwyn further destroyed his work, defiantly circling her ink-covered hand over the map, covering every inch of the page. Lorcan maintained his composure, letting Gwyn do as she pleased. His gaze held a fire of pure rage as his niece tested his limits. When she finished,

Gwyn used her uncle's white, satin blouse as a towel to clean the red ink from her hand.

When she finally stepped back to assess her bout of destruction, Lorcan spoke.

"Are you done?"

"Why aren't you trying to find my father's murderer?"

"That's what this is about?"

"No one seems to care!"

"The poison he drank is called Nectar of Terra. It was concocted with magic. There's no telling who made it."

"Surely we can figure out who was in the kitchen this morning."

"I already did and the trail led back to a servant boy."

Gwyn paused, aware that a peasant boy couldn't be the brains behind this deed.

"Did you interview him? Make him tell you who he was working for?"

"I did. He had no knowledge of the poison. He wasn't tasked by anyone to slip the liquid into the king's porridge. It was already in the food when the boy placed it in front of your father."

"He's lying."

"No. He's not."

"How do you know?"

"For one, the boy pissed his pants before I even asked my first question. His intelligence level is below that of the dogs. He isn't smart enough to accomplish such treason, and he definitely is not smart enough to successfully lie about it." Lorcan took a deep breath. "Secondly, this murder was orchestrated by the Vorso."

"Excuse me?" Gwyn retorted, confused and furious.

"Deraingla, malignant goddess of violence and psychosis, tasked a mortal to do this to your father. She gave them the magic to concoct such an impossible poison."

"This is ridiculous."

"Orlan spoke to Gaia, who told him this truth."

"Lies!"

"Stop fighting the heavens."

"I will not settle for such a weak excuse."

"I've already informed the masses. Though they are saddened, they accept the truth."

"I hate all of you."

"We must move on with our lives," Lorcan said, ignoring her spiteful comment. "Your father was a small player in the bigger picture. He was a noble stable boy who your mother fell for as an adolescent. He got lucky. He was thrust into royalty by chance, not by design. He is gone now and his absence will not create ripples. He was not important enough."

"He was important to me," Gwyn argued, trying to stop her tears from falling. "Are you saying that *I* don't matter?"

"That depends on the gender of your new sibling."

Gwyn's expression scrunched in confusion.

Lorcan smiled, a grin more wicked than he intended to reveal.

"I forgot," he lied. "No one told you yet. Your mother is pregnant. Lucky for all of us, Almas sowed his seed one last time before his untimely demise."

Gwyn had no words; her mother was already trying to replace Calix.

"But we are going to find Calix's missing piece and bring him back."

"You must learn to let go of what is lost," her uncle advised.

Her tears fell.

She did not understand how everyone gave up so easily on what they once loved.

"I won't," she objected. "I will locate Calix's missing piece and I will discover who killed my father. I won't stop until I avenge both."

"Perhaps you can avenge your father," Lorcan stated, "but your brother." He paused. "You cannot avenge a wrongdoing where you wear the blame. All you can do is seek forgiveness.

Redemption, perhaps. But the only way to avenge his death is with your own."

"I didn't kill him."

"You can continue to lie about it if it makes you feel better, but we both know the truth. I am a very clever man. I am privy to almost all of what goes on around here, and I know what you did."

"If you know so much, then why don't you know who killed my father?" Gwyn challenged,

"I said *almost*. I am not a god, I do not know all, but I have my ways of acquiring truths. And your truth, I know."

"You're wrong."

"It doesn't matter. I'm not mad at you for it. But stop pretending that you want to bring Calix back when you're the one who broke him in the first place. You're the only person who knows where his heart is. If you want to bring him back, just do it already. I'm not sure what you're waiting for."

"It wasn't me," Gwyn objected half-heartedly, trying to protect her secret.

"Just be advised that when he does return, if you ever get the guts to right your wrong, more heartache will follow. You and he will never be the same. You betrayed him. His spirit has been stuck in limbo, festering without a body, and I suspect he will return with a vengeance; a fury aimed at you."

"You don't know as much as you think you know."

"Explain it to me then."

"No. I already tried. No one listens, no one ever believes me."

"Heed my warning: His return will be your end."

Gwyn's eyes widened with frustrated fury and she skated out of the room without fighting her uncle any further. She wasn't sure if he was right or wrong, but the thought was trapped in her mind.

If he was right, she was willing to die if it meant bringing Calix back. A loss at her own expense was nothing new, and she was prepared to finish what she started, no matter the cost.

Chapter 12

"Use me," it coaxed. *"Use me to end this suffering."*

Gwyn pounded her fist against her chest as she paced, trying to silence Calix's heart, but its voice rang incessantly inside her head.

"I can fix everything," it enticed. *"Let me help you find your father's murderer. Let me help you kill Orlan."*

She shook her head, but toyed with the idea of releasing his heart from her cage. She never dreamed that she might use Calix's heart magic to solve all her problems, nor had she expected the heart to become sentient. And though she wanted to feel as if Calix were with her again, she was afraid to play with magic she did not understand.

Ario arrived an hour before moonrise.

"Are you okay?" he asked.

"I can't turn it off."

"Turn what off?"

"Calix's heart. It talks to me non-stop. All day while I'm awake and all night in my dreams."

"Calix can talk to you from the afterlife?"

"No, it's not Calix. It's his voice, but different. His heart has a spirit of its own."

Ario paused before replying. "I have heard that once a heart is removed, it becomes its own entity. One no longer tied to its owner. It's been so long since anyone has done such a removal, but old texts confirm what you're saying."

"It's awful."

"What is it saying to you?"

"It wants me to use it to help fulfill my promise."

"Maybe we should."

"What if I can't control it?"

"If it's on our side, we shouldn't need to control it. It will do what is necessary."

Gwyn sighed, unsure what to do. She wanted the voice to leave her alone, but she also knew it might be her best bet in accomplishing all she set out to do.

"It would be a great help," she mumbled.

"Have you thought of a plan?" Ario asked.

"If I use its magic, I can make my own batch of Nectar of Terra. No one would know we were to blame."

"Do you know the base of the poison? What ingredients do we need to start?"

Gwyn did not know the answer, but she suspected Calix's heart would.

"This won't be pretty," she warned Ario before sticking her hand into her mouth and reaching down her throat. She bent over and the extra heart tumbled inside her ribcage. After a short struggle to reach the heart, she snagged the organ and extracted it from her body.

The moment it hit the air it began to crystalize. Gwyn gagged as her lungs began to breathe again and the half-blackened heart finished the crystallization process it started when it was first removed from Calix. The colors slowly transformed until all the soft, red areas were hardened and black.

When the colors stopped shifting, Gwyn looked at Ario.

"What happens when I put this version of Calix's heart back into him?"

"I'm not sure. I don't think it ever goes back to the way it was, but he will be in control of it once it's back in his body."

"I hope it doesn't change who he was."

"There's no telling who he will be when he comes back. For all we know, his spirit is out there somewhere, observing all that is happening. Shifting, for better or for worse."

"I hope he is slumbering peacefully," Gwyn said.

"That's possible too."

After a moment of deadened quiet, the heart simmered with a faint, red glow. She took a deep breath as it heated her palm.

"Will you help us?" she asked.

"Anything for Calix," it answered telepathically.

"Tell me how to make Nectar of Terra."

"Driftwood from the swamps of Vapore, a pinch of soot from Soylé, the bark of a dying Woodlin, and my blessing."

"There must be another way," Gwyn groaned, aware she'd never be able to acquire those ingredients.

"Is it talking to you?" Ario asked.

"You can't hear it?"

"No."

Gwyn sighed. "Of course I'd be the only one to hear its voice. Another reason for people to think I'm crazy."

"You're not crazy, it just chose you. Hearts bond to one person at a time. If they cannot be with their original host, they pick someone else."

"It had no choice but to choose me. I was holding it prisoner."

"You're also the person who was closest to Calix. It makes sense."

Gwyn looked down at the black heart of her dead brother.

"Tell me there is another way," she pleaded.

"The only other way is to blend the seasons. Winter's ice melted over the lava of eternal summer with the first blossom of spring and the last fallen leaf of fall soaking in its water. Once I bless the tainted water, it will destroy those who touch their lips to its contents."

"Spring is coming," Gwyn said, encouraged, "but I won't have access to autumn leaves for months."

"Autumn is buried under winter's snow."

"How am I supposed to find the *last* leaf that fell? That's impossible!"

The heart went black.

Gwyn sighed, then looked at Ario. "We need ice, lava, spring's first blossom, and the last leaf of autumn."

Ario groaned. "Autumn is too far away. What was the first option?"

"Random items from Vapore, Soylé, and Wicker."

"Impossible."

Gwyn nodded. "The heart indicated we should dig for leaves buried beneath the snow."

"How will we know if we found the leaf that fell last?"

Gwyn exhaled as the reality of the situation became clear. "Trial and error, I suppose."

"Meaning we make multiple poisons and try them all until one works?"

"Yes. We only have as many tries as the first blossom allows. The number of petals determines our chances."

Ario groaned. "How in the black-sands of Namaté did anyone ever succeed in making this? It's impossible!"

"With the help of Deraingla, apparently," Gwyn replied sarcastically. "But we don't have help from the Vorso, so we will need to do it on our own."

"Orlan is smart," Ario noted. "It won't take him long to realize we are messing with his food."

"Which is why we won't be testing them on him." Gwyn paused, aware she was taking them down a dark road.

Ario's eyes widened, his conscience was torn, but his inherent Glaziene nature triumphed. He nodded.

"It's the only way." His eyes narrowed. "I know a few people this world would be better without."

"It would ease my guilt to know we are testing it on people who deserve it."

"Rid yourself of the guilt now. Once we embark on this mission, there is no undoing our actions. Just remember that it's for a greater cause."

"To bring back my brother, a worthy and kind prince, assuming I haven't ruined him. I know he will bring peace to Crystet when he takes the throne."

"Exactly."

"We better get to work. The southern areas of Crystet usually lose their leaves last, so I think it's wise to start there."

"Agreed. There also aren't many leafy trees down there, just the evergreens in the Wildlands."

"Maybe this won't be as hard as it seems."

They immediately got to work and spent the entire week digging up wet leaves. Gwyn stored their collection under her bed where no one would find them.

When spring arrived, they closely monitored the few trees that bloomed every season. To Gwyn's delight, a Star Magnolia tree on the castle grounds blossomed first. It took two days for the flower to fully open and once it did, she plucked it from the tree branch and skated to Gler. Ario sat on the front porch of the armor shop with Jahdo.

"This is the one!" she exclaimed as she glided toward them.

"Never seen anyone so excited about a dying flower before," Jahdo observed with curiosity.

"We've been on a hunt for the first blossom of spring," Ario explained, then called out to Gwyn. "Are you sure?"

"Positive." She skidded to a halt in front of the shop.

"Are you kids hungry? I took some leftover kolkrabba from the noble feast I attended last night. I can heat it up."

"I'd love to, but we can't. We have work to do," Gwyn replied.

Jahdo shrugged. "More for me."

He went inside while the children darted back toward the castle. They raced each other to the gate that separated the royal forest from the castle.

"Will we get in trouble if they find me with you in there?" Ario asked.

"Maybe. I don't care, though. I'm not afraid of them anymore."

"I'll try to stay hidden, just in case." He wasn't nearly as brazen as Gwyn when it came to the queen and her tight-knit circle of confidants.

The only way to sneak Ario into the castle was through the cellar chambers she had used when she was younger. The rooms were once filled with young women tasked with caring for the royal family, but now that Gwyn was older and Calix was gone, most of the rooms were uninhabited.

Gwyn jiggled the doorknob that led to Chandi's former room and was pleased to find it unlocked.

"Wait here while I get the leaves," Gwyn instructed before darting out of the room.

She returned with a satin satchel filled with dried leaves and a steel pot stolen from the kitchen. She opened the door to the yard and snatched two icicles from the doorframe. She held them over her chest where Calix's heart resided.

"Will you keep these frozen till we reach the lava lake?"

An arctic chill radiated through her chest, down her arm, and out of her fingers. The icicles would remain frozen. She sighed with relief.

"The lava pits are through the dungeon." She handed Ario the pot. "Follow me."

She led him through the vacant halls and into the darkness that concealed the criminals of Crystet. The guards at the gate let them pass without asking questions and they slowed as they walked through the prison corridor. Since Calix's death, Dalila had begun imprisoning villagers more frequently. Most of the new inmates were men who refused to join her army, but now Chandi was there too—a new addition, and the only female. Diamond bars trapped those deemed too sinful to live amongst the masses in the light of day. The prisoners sneered at them; some cast ancient curses in primordial Glaziene, while others tried luring them to come closer.

"Ignore them," Gwyn advised.

"Happily."

They rounded the bend of the corridor and the heat from the underground lava pool filled the air. Thick, but dry, the rising temperature let them know they were close to their destination.

No prison cells lined this hall, and no torches lit the way, but the distant, red glow guided them.

When they reached the lava lake, Gwyn readied her materials. One dead leaf, one magnolia petal, and two icicles. Enough to make two doses. She placed them into the steel pot and Ario extended it over the lava lake. The rising heat immediately vaporized the icicles, and when the water came to a quick boil, Ario retracted the pan.

The contents simmered. Gwyn reached down her throat to extract Calix's heart. Once exposed to the suffocating underground air, the heart spoke.

"Bring me closer to the potion," it instructed.

Gwyn obliged.

Hovering over the bubbling water, the heart began to chant.

"Dauða í vatni, Dauða í vatni."

The water swirled and a foreign, unpleasant odor filled the air.

"Dauða í vatni, Dauða í vatni."

The petal and leaf disintegrated and the water turned a burnt shade of pink.

"Dauða í vatni, Dauða í vatni."

A puff of smoke silently exploded over the water.

The heart stopped chanting and the water became still.

Gwyn and Ario paused, unsure if the spell was complete.

"Is it done?" Ario asked.

"Feels like it," Gwyn replied

She removed a glass jar from her satchel and Ario dumped the contents into it. They both stayed as far from the poisoned water as possible and once she closed the lid, they breathed a little easier.

"Let's hope this works," she said.

"Who should we try it on first?"

"I know exactly who we should test this on," Gwyn replied with devious energy as she stormed away from the lava lake. Ario followed, unsure who they'd be murdering today.

Chapter 13

Dalila and her council met every night in the south tower to discuss the next phase of overtaking King Ignatius of Elecort in the Great Fight. Gwyn often spied on the meetings and had discovered a secret staircase that led to the underside of their meeting room. From beneath the sheet-glass floorboards, she could hear and see everything. She guided Ario up the hidden passageway and when they reached the top, she was pleased to see the meeting was underway.

In addition to the usual assortment of council members, Orlan, Jahdo Uveges, and Keane Bicchieri were also in attendance. Jahdo was responsible for dressing the soldiers in the finest armor, so it was important that he knew which lands they'd be facing. Each enemy army had different strengths and abilities, and Jahdo adapted the uniforms to protect against each species' particular defenses. Keane not only housed the soldiers at his lodge between battles, but he was also best friends with Lorcan and Jahdo. He was a trusted advisor with great intelligence and a knack for espionage. Like Lorcan, he often donated his eyes to spy on foreign lands.

"I kind of miss going to these war meetings with my dad," Ario commented. "He stopped bringing me when I was old enough to weld glass armor on my own. I think he was afraid they'd send me to fight."

"Jahdo is a smart man."

"I think my friendship with *you* is the only thing keeping me out of the fight."

"How so?"

"Your mother cares for you more than you realize."

Gwyn huffed, refusing to believe such a claim.

"We are here to test the poison, not to find the good in my mother."

"Our target is in that room?" Ario asked, taken aback. He glanced up at the congregation of powerful Glaziene nobles.

"Yes."

"Who?"

"Trista."

"Don't you think that's risky? We are showing our hand if it works."

"I'd like to see her dead."

"If you insist. This is your quest, after all."

They peered through the floorboards the queen and her noble confidants paced upon.

"How will we get the Nectar of Terra into Trista's goblet?" Ario asked.

Gwyn poured some of the poison into a smaller vial.

"Wait here," she instructed before leaving the secret space and ascending the ordinary staircase that led to the top of the tower.

She knocked.

"Who dares to disturb us?" Dalila bellowed.

"It's me," Gwyn replied.

Lorcan opened the door and stared down at his niece with critical curiosity.

"I want to be better," she explained. "I want to learn from you."

Lorcan glanced back at his sister, who huffed and nodded impatiently. He then opened the door a little wider for Gwyn to slip through. Gwyn sat at the table near Trista and the meeting carried on.

Although everything taking place around her was fascinating, Gwyn kept her attention focused on Trista.

Though the andlega ráðgjafi listened intently to the queen, Trista kept her long, glass fingers tightly wrapped around the base of her goblet.

Gwyn waited patiently, trying to ignore the fact that her truest enemy sat a few chairs away. Orlan glared at her every so often, which made her task even more difficult. No one could witness what she was about to do.

The meeting took a turn when Lorcan went to the lectern with his maps. They showed no sign of the damage Gwyn caused. A twinge of guilt struck Gwyn; Lorcan had to start his work all over again after her meltdown.

The adults rose to huddle around the podium he laid the pages on. To Gwyn's delight, Trista left her drink behind.

Heart thudding wildly, Gwyn prepared to dump the poison into Trista's ice wine. Hand in pocket, ready to retrieve the vial, Orlan swiveled in her direction.

"What are you waiting for?" he sneered. "If you want to learn, join us."

"I'm coming," she assured him.

Orlan paused, eyes locked on the princess, and Gwyn dawdled as long as she could without making her stalled reaction obvious. Orlan turned his head as she took steps toward the podium, and with a subtle but quick flick of her wrist, she managed to pour the poison into Trista's goblet as she walked past. No one saw her do it, but her heart pounded with adrenaline anyway. She had succeeded.

Gwyn stood behind Jahdo, who gave her a small smile, then glanced down at the floor and caught a glimpse of the silver in Ario's eyes through the cracks. She bent down to scratch her ankle and dropped the empty vial through a gap in the floor as she did so. Ario snagged it as it fell. The only evidence tying her to the deed was gone. Now she could wait without fear to see Trista's reaction to the poison.

"The Metellyans and Bouldes need time to match our numbers, but they have promised that they will eventually have armies comparable to ours," Lorcan explained.

"I thought they planned to bow out of the Great Fight," Dalila said.

"I convinced them not to."

"Fantastic. How long till they are ready?" Dalila asked.

"Four years."

"Preposterous," she spat.

"And it's likely the Bouldes won't ever match our army in size. I am reluctant to trust them. King Alun's loyalty to the rebellion still teeters."

"We need them," Jahdo chimed in. "We won't have enough soldiers without their help."

"Then I suppose we have four years to solidify their loyalty," Keane concluded.

The adults nodded in unison.

Lorcan finished outlining his plans and when the council had no further questions, they all returned to their seats around the table.

Trista took a long sip from her goblet before sitting down.

Gwyn eagerly awaited her reaction, but several seconds passed and nothing happened.

"Do you understand why we fight?" Dalila asked Gwyn, snapping her attention back to the rest of the room.

"To acquire the scepter of alchemy."

"But do you understand what having the scepter means?"

"Whoever has it rules all the lands in Namaté," Gwyn answered.

"Correct. Because the kingdom that possesses the scepter of alchemy also possesses the most powerful magic on the planet. With it, we control the trade agreements between lands. With it, we no longer have restrictions. With it, we are invincible." Dalila's eyes glowed with greed. "The Voltains are unworthy of the scepter. They have used it to transform themselves in unnatural ways. Egos swollen, brains demented by the power, they have grown into a sick and twisted species. Their technological advances must be stopped before they become too powerful."

"I understand," Gwyn replied.

Trista coughed.

Gwyn's attention turned.

The council resumed their conversation unaware that Gwyn silently wished for death to grace the room.

Trista coughed again. This time, she appeared to be choking on air. Her fit lasted so long the others were forced to pause and take notice of her struggle.

"Are you okay?" Jahdo asked.

Trista shook her head, unable to speak.

Orlan jumped up and ran to Trista's side. He pried her jaw open and examined her mouth.

"Her gums are darkening," he announced. "Someone has tried to poison her."

Everyone but Gwyn gasped, so she feigned an expression of shock to remedy her mistake.

Orlan lifted Trista's goblet and sniffed the remains of her wine.

"Someone contaminated her wine."

The others looked down at their own goblets in horror. Orlan examined the contents of each goblet before determining they were safe.

"It appears Trista was the only target," Orlan informed.

"Is it the same poison used on Almas?" Jahdo asked.

"Can we save her?" Keane added.

"She will survive. Her gums are dark blue, not black. Whoever made it didn't concoct the Nectar of Terra properly," Orlan answered. "Though it won't kill her, I suspect it will have a lasting effect. The ink stained her brain."

"We must find the culprit," Lorcan stated. "It appears they are targeting the rest of us."

"You only care to find out who is doing this now that you suspect you might also be one of their targets?" Gwyn asked, her tone thick with cynicism.

"I cared previously when your father was the only victim, but now, naturally, it's a bit more urgent. If they take us all out, who will run the kingdom?"

Orlan cradled Trista's head. She shook violently in his embrace.

"Are you sure she will be okay?" Jahdo asked.

"I am certain."

Gwyn glared at Orlan. His confidence was suspicious.

"How can you be so sure?" she asked.

"Gaia is here and she told me so."

Everyone but Gwyn tensed. Learning that the Mother was nearby rocketed their nerves into space. Afraid to move, afraid to say the wrong thing in Her presence, the room went quiet.

"Lies," Gwyn spat.

"Enough," Dalila commanded. "We will find whoever did this. Lorcan, interrogate everyone in the kitchen and winery to see what you can discover."

Orlan and Gwyn shared a glare so fierce, a wall of toxic energy formed between them.

He was onto her—Gwyn sensed his suspicion—but she was onto him too. Not only was he a monster to Calix, but now she suspected he might be responsible for her father's death. It was impossible for Gwyn to hate him more.

"She needs a glazician," Lorcan finally said.

"Take her," Dalila instructed Jahdo.

The council dispersed as Jahdo carried Trista from the room, leaving Gwyn alone in the south tower. When she was certain that no one was coming back, she glanced down at Ario, who still hid beneath the floorboards.

"It didn't work," she told him.

"We will try again," he answered, out of sight, but his voice was loud and clear.

"You were right. I risked my mission by targeting Trista."

"It's okay, you got away with it. We'll aim a little lower from now on."

Gwyn nodded and then stood.

They met in the corridor at the base of the south tower entrance and retreated into the cellar. They used Chandi's old room to hide the ingredients they collected over the months. They spent every morning creating a new batch of poison and each afternoon picking a new victim.

Eleven days, eleven petals, and their chances ran out. In their wake, they left eleven ill and deformed Glaziene bystanders, all of whom were deemed evil by Gwyn and Ario before being selected. Rumors spread that a bout of dark magic plagued the land, but no one knew why or how the selected victims were chosen. Some blamed the malignant Vorso, but others suspected that these deaths came by the hand of a true mortal.

Though Gwyn and Ario kept their escapades private, it did not prevent the spell of mass hysteria that broke out in the aftermath of their escapades. Suspicion ran high, trials were held in every affected village, and executions were performed. Everyone was considered guilty, even after being proven innocent.

It was an unintended side effect that neither Gwyn nor Ario could control, but if they could guarantee that they acquired the correct ingredients next time, then they would not fail when they tried again.

The mayhem settled as the year passed, and though both Gwyn and Ario went on with their lives, neither forgot what spring would bring: another opportunity to kill Orlan. Meanwhile, Dalila lost the baby due to stress. The moment the unborn child perished, Gwyn noticed her treatment improved. Everyone was suddenly much kinder to her. By law, since Almas was her first husband, any child Dalila had moving forward would be illegitimate, which left Gwyn as the only true heir to the throne.

Though Dalila abandoned her search for Calix's missing heart, Gwyn struggled to live a single day without constant reminders that it sat safely within her chest.

The longer it remained outside his body, the stronger it became. It wanted out. And though its increased persistence to be removed from her body concerned her, her own resolve could not be swayed, no matter how insistent it was. In time, she learned to tune out Calix's heart whenever it grew too loud.

Ario celebrated Gwyn's twelfth birthday in royal fashion, and Gwyn celebrated his fifteenth birthday over a humble feast of kolkrabba with Ario and Jahdo at the armor shop. When the brutal winds of winter faded and the first blossom arrived on the magnolia tree outside the castle, they refocused on their mission. The dark magic that menaced the country the year before was about to return. Neither Gwyn nor Ario felt remorse. Gwyn's conscience was blinded by revenge and Ario's was blinded by his love for the vengeful princess.

"We have the last leaf and the first blossom. It should work this time," Gwyn said as they made their way to the underground lava lake.

"Let's hope so," Ario replied.

They both had grown taller over the year, and the rocky corridor felt smaller than before. They ducked and dodged the varying heights of the terrain-made ceiling.

When they reached the lake, the heat hit them with force, and Gwyn began her work. She plucked the first petal from the magnolia blossom and then placed what they believed to be the last fallen leaf of autumn into the steel pan. A clump of snow she snatched from outside remained frozen in her grip until she dropped it on top of the other ingredients. The snow melted and Gwyn extracted Calix's heart from her chest.

"Work your magic," she said while holding it over the potion.

The heart buzzed and its center glowed red. The water began to swirl, picking up speed, and didn't stop until a puff of smoke materialized with a bang. The poison was made.

Pleased with their creation, Ario and Gwyn transferred the liquid into two vials and left the underground lava lake.

They took their concoction to the eastern village of Lifandi, where the foulest and most despicable Glaziene lived. Hidden behind the tall, jagged shards of a very broken glass stable, Gwyn and Ario observed the locals. They searched for the worst of the lot; someone whose fate deserved to be tested. Gwyn suspected the poison would work this time, so she wanted to make sure she chose the right Glaziene.

A teenage boy stumbled out of a nearby glass hut, followed shortly by an angry, old man.

"I will shatter you if you steal from me again," the old man barked, exiting through the doorway, which was covered in hundreds of protective amulets.

"I'm sorry, Larz. I hadn't eaten in days."

"That's not my problem."

"Can we agree on a trade?"

"A trade? Boy, you have nothing that I want."

"A task? I'll do anything. They don't feed us at the castle."

"Scrawny Claudio," Larz teased. "You don't learn. Just like your father, you subject yourself to slavery instead of carving your own way in this world."

"It's the only way I know how to survive."

"But you're not surviving, you're morphing into the vermin your father became before I put him out of his misery. Stealing, begging, making a fool out of yourself. Perhaps it's time I offer you the same mercy I gave to him."

"No, I'll stop. I'll go away and find a different means for food."

"What kind of man would I be if I allowed you to leave today just so you could steal from some other hardworking Glaziene tomorrow?"

"I work hard."

"Then why aren't you compensated?"

"I'm not sure," Claudio mumbled.

"The real question is why do you stay? Because you're weak," Larz said, answering his own question. "And there is no room for feeble-hearted men amongst us."

Claudio began to back away. "I'll do better. I'll be better."

Larz scoffed and returned to his hut, uninterested in the easy prey.

The boy turned and the sunlight briefly caught his gaze. One eye was green, the other was black. He was the same boy who picked up Calix's pieces the morning after his break.

"Look through Larz's window," Gwyn whispered, pointing. "He is collecting glass body parts like ornaments."

Ario squinted his eyes to focus and saw that the shelves were lined with darkened eyeballs, tongues, and hands. He gagged.

"We target Larz," Gwyn stated with confidence.

They spent the next week following Larz, learning his routine, and debating how best to deliver the poison. He cooked his own meals every night, which they soon learned contained the mushy innards of his latest kill. He was an organ stealer—one of the most grotesque types of degenerates living in the slums of Crystet. He stalked his prey all day, usually a weak woman or child, gutted them at twilight, and harvested their organs in a vat of warm water so they did not crystalize before he cooked them. He always took a souvenir from the bodies of his victims, which he added to his shelf of trophies.

There was no way to sneak the poison into his food, but his solitary eating habits, meant they could safely transfer the poison into his bottle of wine while he was away pursuing his next victim. Most Glaziene feared the repercussions of ignoring the protective amulets of Devotene, but after Gwyn reassured Ario that the amulets' reputed powers were non-existent, Ario snuck past the talismans and into the cottage. Relieved, Ario smiled back at Gwyn after he had entered safely, then dumped the poison into the remaining wine. It blended seamlessly and did not change the wine's aroma.

When night came, Gwyn and Ario watched Larz eat his typical dinner in solitude. He took three gulps of the wine before anything happened. On his fourth sip, he dropped his glass and it shattered on the ground.

Larz began shaking violently and his fingers turned black.

"It's working," Gwyn whispered with excitement.

The man was stubborn. He fought the shakes and tried to maintain control, but he could do nothing to stop the spread of the magic-laced chemicals. He collapsed to the floor as the black ink spread up his arms.

"His insides aren't turning black," Ario noted. "The change in color is superficial. It's only happening on the surface."

Gwyn took a closer look and saw that Ario was right. Larz was in terrible pain and his skin would likely be stained permanently, but the poison would not kill him. After an hour, Larz stopped shaking and the ink stopped spreading. They watched as he lifted himself off the floor, weak from the trauma, and attempted to scrub the black ink off his skin, but to no avail. He would wear these stains forever.

"What did we do wrong?" Gwyn whispered.

"I'm not sure."

Discouraged, they left the cottage and returned to the castle.

They spent the next few weeks trying again, but the poison never worked. Instead, Gwyn and Ario left another trail of maimed, disfigured, and ill people in their wake. They blanketed the villagers in terror; their presence became associated with pain, and though no one could pin the blame on them, it became apparent that when they were around, trouble often followed. Their reputation for mischief and recklessness grew so large, false stories started circulating about them. Gwyn's connection to Rebelene became corroborated on a grander scale, amongst every Glaziene, not just those within the castle. The reputation she was trying to eliminate was now certain to remain throughout the rest of her life. Anything that went wrong was now blamed on them, Rebelene's chosen duo, even if they had nothing to do with it. Though the rumors were wild and intense, the worst had yet to reach the castle and remained confined amongst the commoners of Crystet.

Gwyn decided not to concern herself with the gossip. All she cared about was creating a poison that worked.

They used the final petal and had to cease their attempts yet again.

Another year wasted.

Thoughts of her innocent brother lying broken on the ground filled Gwyn's mind and she cursed her failure. It was taking too long to kill Orlan—it was taking too long to bring Calix back. She was taking too long to fulfill her promise and feared what would happen if she waited much longer. There was no telling what his soul was doing in limbo, if it was slumbering peacefully or stewing in spiteful rage. She had to hurry; she could not risk tarnishing her brother's soul.

Chapter 14

The year passed, as did the next, with no luck creating a poison that would eliminate Orlan. They consulted Calix's heart before making each new batch, hoping for confirmation that they finally had the correct ingredients, but the heart could neither verify nor disprove. It merely provided the magic that either turned the concoction into a poison or tool to maim.

Gwyn's fifteenth birthday arrived just as Dalila planned to execute her greatest attack on Elecort. Though Gwyn ought to be focused on Crystet's greatest offensive move in the Great Fight, she found herself perpetually focused on the poison that would eventually kill Orlan.

Ario was now allowed to enter the castle without having to sneak about, and he gave Gwyn a loving kiss before they went upstairs to her room.

"I figured it out," she said once they were alone. "I know what we've been doing wrong all this time."

"What?"

"It's the blossom," she explained. "There is a blue wisteria vine planted in the middle of Samningur Metropolis that blossoms one day earlier than the magnolia tree in the royal gardens."

"Is that so?" Ario asked, wrapping his arms around his princess and gently tossing them onto her bed. He nuzzled his face into her shoulder and gave her a thousand quick kisses on the side of her neck.

"We need to focus," she insisted, though she loved receiving his affection.

"I am focused on you."

"Refocus on the mission."

Ario looked up at her with a mischievous glint in his eyes, but he did not fight her. Instead, he obeyed and retracted his advances.

"How did you discover this?" he asked.

"I asked the royal gardener."

"Oh, geez." Ario groaned at the obviousness of this tactic.

"I know," Gwyn commiserated. "But now we know."

"Did you ask about the leaves?"

"We have that right; the patch of yellow-leaved aspen trees in the Wildlands. They lose their leaves last."

"Then this will be our last escapade," Ario said with a grin.

"Finally." Gwyn exhaled with long-suppressed relief.

The duo traveled to Samningur Metropolis to find the blue wisteria vine. It was early spring and only one bud had begun to bloom. Gwyn ripped it off the branch and counted the petals. Forty. She looked at Ario with a devilish grin.

"We will be able to attempt making the poison many more times."

"Hopefully it will only take one try, though. I am confident that we found the last fallen leaf of autumn."

"Let's hope so."

With the heart's magic, they mixed the ingredients as before, and then left for the northeastern village of Klikkaður. Once there, they had no trouble picking a test subject: a drunken old lady who was selling narcotics to children.

"Easy target," Gwyn stated. "Look at the marks of corrosion and discoloration on her face. She's an alkali junkie. And she's sharing her bad habits with kids."

Ario nodded, then left their hiding spot. He snatched an empty pitcher off a nearby counter, filled it with a small amount of water, and mixed the vial of poison into the liquid. He then walked up to the old woman. She quickly shooed the interested children away, hid her stash of alkali crystals behind her back, and smiled at Ario. He pretended not to know what she was up to.

"Can I interest you in a refill?" he asked. "My uncle makes the best ice wine."

The old woman raised her eyes, enamored by Ario's handsomeness and eager to eat up the unexpected attention. She was too high to recognize who he was.

"Why, yes. I would love a drink from a fine young man like you."

Ario smirked flirtatiously, then poured the poisoned water into her flask.

"Have a blessed day," Ario said before departing. The woman hollered after him, trying to convince him to stay and have a drink with her, but he left without looking back. She dropped her fight and took a swig.

The moment the poison touched her lips, she went into a state of shock. Her body quivered, her lips turned purple, then black, and the poison began killing her from the inside out. She twitched and convulsed as the poison slowly blackened and crystalized her organs.

Gwyn looked on in awe, eyes wide with excitement. It was a glorious day; the Nectar of Terra was finally working and her patience was being rewarded. Her heart fluttered with joy as she watched death take hold.

Children crowded around the dying woman, and when she finally fell to the ground, unmoving, one boy declared that she was dead. A few adults arrived at the scene and when they saw the state of her body, their curiosity turned to dread. The woman's insides were blackened like the late king's.

The whispers were frantic and Gwyn knew they didn't have long before word reached the castle that someone had replicated the poison that killed Almas.

"We have to hurry," she insisted. "Our time to act is brief."

"Let's go."

They raced out of Klikkaður village and back toward the castle.

"I've been waiting for this day for a long time," Gwyn declared with eager anticipation, then recalled what she heard in the previous night's council meeting. "Orlan will be at Bicchieri Lodge with the soldiers tonight, blessing them before they are shipped off to battle tomorrow morning."

"Are they finally making an attempt to steal the scepter?" Ario asked.

"Yes. The Bouldes and Metellyans will be joining us in our ambush of Elecort."

"Then perhaps we ought to wait? Killing Orlan right before an important fight might rattle the soldiers. We need them to perform."

"We will do it after the blessing. I know which room Orlan sleeps in. The soldiers will be shipped off to Elecort before anyone realizes Orlan is dead."

"If you're certain," Ario conceded. "We have to be careful, though."

"Of course."

They bundled up and packed a satchel in preparation for a long night. Spring in Crystet was comparable to winter in most other lands, and though the Glaziene thrived in this weather, it was still quite chilly. At night, the temperatures plummeted, so Gwyn made sure she was wearing enough layers to endure the cold. A wind chill through any of her many breaks would be crippling.

Barefoot, but wrapped in two layers of wool under her rabbit-fur peacoat, Gwyn lifted her hood and led the way. Ario followed, also barefoot, but wearing a long moosehide cloak.

Quarzelle was located right outside the royal forest, so the trek was brief. The village was the most run down in all of Crystet—broken glass littered the streets, broken buildings stood half-erect, broken people plagued the space. Gwyn hated Quarzelle, but she ignored the deep-rooted feeling and focused on her mission.

Bicchieri Lodge sat near the edge of the village, near the southeastern tree line of the Wildlands.

Night was upon them and they needed to move faster.

"We have to find a way in without anyone seeing us," Gwyn whispered as they got closer.

"We can trust Keane," Ario replied.

"Are you sure?"

"Yes. He and my father are long-time friends. They are basically brothers. He would never put me in harm's way."

"If you're sure, then okay. I trust you."

Ario led her to a side door. He tugged on a rope that rang a glass chime and a few seconds later Keane opened the door.

"Ario," he said, a little too loudly. "What are you doing here at this hour?"

"My father sent me."

"Come on in," Keane said, ushering them into his private quarters of the lodge. He eyed Gwyn with suspicion, but kept his thoughts to himself.

"We need to see Tyrus," Ario stated.

"Why?"

"He forgot to pick up his new volcanic-glass blade from my father. It's coated in sylph blood, so it has incredibly potent poisoning powers."

"They are mid-blessing with Orlan," Keane replied. "You cannot interrupt."

"We won't, but we need to get it to him tonight. He can't go to battle without it."

"Let me see the blade."

"It's better for you if you don't," Ario assured him. "The sylph blood is still drying. The smell will sting your eyes and render you blind temporarily."

Keane's expression tightened. "Should I be worried for you?"

"What?" Ario asked, taken aback. "No. Of course not."

"I've heard about you two. Rebelene's favorite duo. Will your father shatter me in the aftermath of whatever you're about to do?"

"We aren't up to any mischief," Ario said. "I swear."

Keane clicked his tongue. "Fine."

"Which staircase should we use to avoid disrupting the blessing?"

"South side."

"Thank you."

"I better not regret this in the morning."

Ario forced a smile and nodded, unable to promise anything.

Gwyn exhaled with relief as they ascended the south staircase without any encounters.

Tonight was the night she'd finally kill Orlan.

Chapter 15

Gwyn knew the location of Orlan's private quarters at Bicchieri Lodge—she and her father had stayed in that same room when her mother's bouts of post-partum depression grew erratic and violent. The room was a safe haven in her youth and now, it would offer her another kind of comfort. It would be the place where she put her demons to rest. Once Orlan was dead, she'd be able to breathe again, she'd be able to let go of all the hurt and animosity, but most importantly, she'd finally be able to bring Calix back.

Gwyn and Ario waited in a broom closet near Orlan's room and frequently peeked out to check on his status. After a long wait, Orlan finally arrived. He entered the room, locked the door behind him, and became unreachable again.

Hours passed.

"He will order room service," Gwyn assured Ario. "I know he will."

"When he does, how will we slip the poison into his drink?"

Glass wheels screeched down the hall.

"Follow my lead," Gwyn replied, handing Ario the vial of poison.

The moment the service boy pushed his glass cart into view, Gwyn sprang into action. She slammed her arm against the wall so hard, she fractured her forearm and silvery blood poured out. Ario stared at her in horror, but she ignored his shock and stumbled into the hall. The moment the service boy saw her he stopped in his tracks.

"I fell," Gwyn explained as she approached the terrified boy. "Can you help me?"

"Will the gods curse me if I don't?" he stuttered. "I heard Deraingla has claimed you as Hers."

Gwyn wanted to deny this claim, wanted to berate the boy for believing such cruel rumors, but she held her tongue. If his belief that she was ruled by Gaia's most evil daughter helped her cause, she'd play along.

"Yes. You must oblige my call to avoid being deemed fateless."

The boy shuddered before abandoning his cart to help the notorious princess.

Gwyn led him away from Orlan's room and after they turned the nearest corner, Ario seized the opportunity to contaminate the liquor on the cart. After all the poison was dumped into the glass pitcher, he wheeled the cart to Orlan's door, knocked three times, then darted out of sight.

Orlan opened the door and peered around suspiciously. Though it was odd for room service to arrive without a lodge employee, he accepted the delivery and retreated into his room.

Ario whistled to signal that his task was complete. To the horror of the service boy, Gwyn reached down her throat and removed Calix's heart. Before he had time to process what she had done, she compelled the heart to render the boy unconscious. He fell to the floor, short term memory erased, and Gwyn rounded the bend to return to Ario. Perhaps the boy would be blamed for Orlan's demise. She wasn't afraid to take the fall, but there was no telling what her punishment would be and having a scapegoat would buy her more time to piece Calix back together.

Ario peered around the corner, grinning excitedly as she approached. Gwyn paused by Orlan's room, placed her free hand on the cold, glass door, and used the magic of her heart to see inside.

Orlan sat on his bed, sipping his ice wine while wearing a smug smirk. Gwyn wondered why he wore such a devious expression, but then the sound of gagging shook her from her thoughts. Ario was on the floor, convulsing.

Gwyn ran to him.

"What happened?" she asked, frantic.

"I don't know," Ario gasped between violent heaves.

"Do something!" she begged the heart, but suddenly, it was quieter than ever. After shaking it violently, trying to force it to act, it finally spoke.

"This darkness was not my doing."

"Help him, please," she begged.

"His fate is beyond my reach."

"Try!"

But the heart resumed its silence and its red glow vanished.

Despite all of her pleas, the relic sent no magic Ario's way, so she shoved it back into her mouth, letting it fall beside hers.

Ario began to choke on his vomit.

Gwyn had one final option.

She stood and ran to Orlan's room, ready to beg for his help, but when she arrived, the high priest was already leaning against the door, drinking his wine and observing Ario's worsening condition with indifference.

"Help!" she demanded, but Orlan did not move.

He took another sip of his wine.

Gwyn's heart raced. The poison should have worked by now.

She looked at Ario, who was coughing up yellow foam. This wasn't the same way the old drunk lady in Klikkaður village died.

She turned back to Orlan.

"What have you done?"

"You expect me not to defend myself?" he sneered, then took another long sip of his wine. After swallowing, he chuckled. "To think you tried to use *my* poison against me. Simply foolish."

"I don't know what you are talking about," Gwyn stammered, unsure how much Orlan knew.

"Aren't you curious why this wine has yet to strip the soul from my body?" Orlan sneered.

"What have you done?" Gwyn repeated, her tone now enraged.

"Don't start a war if you can't handle losing what you love along the way."

The fury clamoring inside Gwyn's heart raged louder than ever before. She was no longer in control. Vision blurred, everything was draped in red. Her wrath coursed through Calix's heart and exploded out of her mouth in a blast aimed at Orlan. The high priest dodged the strike, but the wall to his room was shattered.

"How did you acquire magic?" he seethed, backing toward the large mirror that hung on the opposite wall.

Gwyn responded with another angry blast of lava-hot fire in Orlan's direction. Again, the old priest managed to dodge her attack and the magic melted the other half of the corridor. The glass quickly dried and formed hardened mounds where the walls once stood.

"Fix him!" she screeched.

"Tell me where you got this magic from," Orlan countered, preparing to sidestep another blow from the enraged princess.

She responded with another fiery blast, but this time, Orlan managed to reflect the lethal flare back at Ario.

Ario looked up into the face of death as the burst of magma catapulted toward him. The fire illuminated his face and Gwyn screamed in terror as he was struck by the lethal blast. The entire wing of the lodge combusted upon impact, creating a gaping hole in the side of the building and leaving no trace of Ario's deceased body.

A cool breeze entered their unanticipated battleground, but no degree of cold could smother her enflamed hatred. Blinded by furious grief and an unrivaled loathing, Gwyn turned toward Orlan and charged, like a wild beast attacking its prey. The high priest dropped the mirror he was holding and raised his arm. Gwyn tripped and landed on the floor.

"You killed Ario!" she screamed.

"No, *you* did. His affliction was temporary. He would have healed. Your magic is what ended his life."

Gwyn wanted to argue, wanted to place all the blame on Orlan, but there was no denying that Calix's wild heart magic had sealed Ario's fate.

"I suggest you end your silly quest to assassinate me before you lose more than you can handle," Orlan advised. "I am the wrong person to wage war against."

"You are the *only* person I wish to cast my rage upon."

"Then expect to suffer more heartbreak. You cannot beat me."

Orlan turned and sauntered away, leaving Gwyn alone to fester in her bereaved guilt. A pain she never felt before consumed her heart. Love lost, destroyed by her own hand.

She walked to the edge of the explosion where the glass floor still melted beneath the fire of her magical blast. The floor ended abruptly, dropping hundreds of feet to the ground. She wished to jump; she wanted to shatter amidst the rubble of her ruined love, but instead, she fell to her knees. Her mind went blank as she stared into the fire below.

She was alone.

Becoming numb was the only way to save herself from the debilitating heartache that now engulfed her mind, body, and spirit.

Chapter 16

The morning after Ario's death, the Glaziene army sailed to Elecort. All prior actions in the rebellion had been small, undetectable, and discreet; this was the first blatant attack in the Great Fight. It was the most important battle, and subsequently proved to be the most devastating loss. Of the ten thousand soldiers, bowmen, and sailors sent to fight, only fifty survived. They returned in shambles on one overcrowded rowboat, with all the remaining soldiers holding onto the sides, grasping onto each other, as they paddled and swam toward Crystet. The Bouldes never showed up to fight and the Metellyans sent less than half the numbers they promised—all of whom retreated long before the surrender horns were blown. Though all three lands were equally involved in the fight, the fallout landed solely on Dalila. King Ignatius was furious to learn of the rebellion, and since the Glaziene appeared to be the main culprits, Dalila took the fall. Though she refused to betray her cowardly counterparts, Lorcan did not hesitate to explain to Ignatius that King Oro of Coppel and King Alun of Orewall were equally responsible. Ignatius listened, but Crystet had sent the most warriors, so Dalila faced his wrath alone.

Her execution was scheduled to take place on Gwyn's sixteenth birthday.

The mourning birds sang their sorrowful song as the sun crested the horizon, but today, it sounded a bit more solemn than usual.

Gwyn remained in bed, wide awake, unwilling to face the day.

For the first time in years, Dalila entered her daughter's bedroom to prepare her for the day.

The queen wore a simple white dress made of satin with no make-up or jewelry to enhance her appearance. Gwyn said nothing as her mother approached. They had no relationship, no reason to speak. The last remaining piece of Gwyn's childhood was about to disappear, leaving her alone in the chaotic aftermath.

"I'm sorry this is happening," Dalila said as she sat on the edge of Gwyn's bed.

"It doesn't matter."

"You don't care that I'll die?"

Gwyn took a deep breath before replying. "I don't want you to die, but I am used to losing people."

"I'm sorry about Ario. I know his death got lost in the shuffle of all that has happened. Perhaps Jahdo will become a source of comfort for you."

"No, Jahdo must hate me. I am the reason Ario died."

"It was foolish and imprudent to attempt to kill Orlan. Consider yourself lucky that far greater tragedies happened simultaneously, or you'd be facing grave punishment for what you did."

"I am the least lucky person in all of Crystet."

"Orlan is on your side, whether you believe it or not."

Gwyn refused to respond.

"When you become queen," Dalila continued, "he ought to be your greatest ally."

"I don't want to be queen."

"You don't have a choice in the matter. I know I've been very hard on you, but I hope you understand that it was my attempt to make you strong."

"If you say so."

"I love you," Dalila expressed, her eyes welling with tears. The little girl that lived deep inside the recesses of Gwyn's mind, the little girl that still yearned for Dalila's love, caved to the sentiment. Gwyn felt her heart swell.

"I really do," Dalila continued.

Gwyn nodded, trying not to cry, but was unable to stop the tears from falling.

Her mother wrapped her in a tight embrace—this was the first hug she'd received from Dalila in years—and Gwyn broke down into sobs. After this afternoon, she'd be all alone with an angry kingdom to rule.

In solemn silence, Dalila prepared Gwyn for the execution. She gifted her a black, silk dress with a bodice of golden armor and applied make-up to her daughter's youthful face. Gwyn hadn't let anyone touch her face since Kipp was murdered—she refused to wear paint and no one fought her. She remained bare-faced for years, but today was a time for change. It was time to let go of her stubborn ways in order to ease into her new life.

When Dalila finished, Gwyn was morphed into a vision of royal perfection; a sight of pure beauty that evoked both awe and terror simultaneously. Looking in the mirror, Gwyn hardly recognized herself. Her bright silver-green eyes were illuminated by smoky streaks of dark eyeliner, her plump lips were smothered in red paint, her eyelashes were elongated by numerous strokes of black ink. Dark powder accentuated her high cheekbones, making her look older than she was, and her arched, but narrow blonde eyebrows made her large, almond-shaped eyes appear calculated and devious.

Gwyn took a deep breath, astounded by how much she resembled her mother.

"Remember when you were little and you insisted we call you Nessa whenever you were forced to wear makeup?" Dalila mused.

"Because I didn't feel like myself behind the mask of paint," Gwyn recalled.

"You were always a wise little girl. I hope you see now how critical these masks are to our survival. You must convey a different persona to the masses; they are ruthless and will eat you alive if they smell any hint of weakness."

"Maybe I can change things."

"Do not sacrifice yourself for them. They aren't worth it."

Gwyn said nothing.

"Promise me you won't. Discover the legacy you wish to leave behind, but don't chase a fantasy. The Glaziene people won't change. Don't waste your energy on them."

"I can't promise that I won't try."

Dalila nodded in understanding.

"You took off your mask today," Gwyn noted, examining her mother's beautiful face. She had minimal breaks, unlike Gwyn who was younger, but wore many.

"I am set free," Dalila explained. "I no longer have to pretend."

In that moment, Gwyn realized that she never got a chance to learn who her mother truly was because she was always hidden behind the role she was required to play. Gwyn grieved for the woman she never got to know.

Dalila gave her a kiss on the forehead.

"This is goodbye," she said, her voice tender and unfamiliar.

Gwyn nodded. Though they never understood each other, their bond was still strong. Beneath the layers of hurt and betrayal, they were family, and though unspoken and often disregarded, their mutual love remained potent. Life would not be the same without her mother.

Lorcan knocked, then entered the room.

"It's time to go," he said, expression riddled with sorrow.

Dalila took a deep breath, then looked back at Gwyn.

"I forgive you for Calix."

Gwyn was startled, unsure how to feel.

"I know you shattered him," her mother continued.

"I am going to bring him back," Gwyn insisted.

Her mother smiled, not believing her daughter's claims.

"It's okay if you don't." Dalila kissed Gwyn's forehead again, then departed.

There was barely any time to decipher how this unexpected moment made her feel when Mina arrived to escort her to the northern shore. Dressed in her mother's armor-plated black gown, Gwyn walked toward the next chapter of her life.

From the safety of the north tower bridge, Gwyn stood tall and watched the Voltains sail in on their neon-bright ships. Before seizing the scepter of alchemy from the Metellyans, the Voltains were bound to their land, but since acquiring ultimate power, they managed to negate the dangerous effect of electricity touching water via magic.

Dalila stood alone on the glass shore, bravely awaiting her fate. With the bulk of Crystet's army killed in the last battle, they could not fight back, and they could not rely on their supposed allies, who had already proved themselves untrustworthy.

When the Voltain ships were within rowing distance, the soldiers loaded into smaller boats that were propelled forward by the scepter of alchemy. Ignatius possessed absolute power and the ire of Elecort was unstoppable.

The Voltain soldiers lined the shore, standing ten feet tall with skin that radiated electricity—an inherent power that they enhanced over the years with magic. They were untouchable by foreigners; a single moment of bare contact by a non-Voltain resulted in death. Stoic, with glowing, neon eyes fixated on the Glaziene Queen, they stood alert as the largest of the soldiers put on rubber gloves and stalked toward Dalila.

King Ignatius took flight and hovered over the scene, circling the queen of Crystet like an illuminated monster of death.

"Do you know your crime?" Ignatius bellowed from the sky.

"My crime is bravery. I am guilty of allowing my fate to unfold as it was meant to, for fulfilling my destiny. My crime is obeying the will of Gaia."

"Do not drag the Mother into this. She did not foretell your acquisition of the scepter."

"She saw the scepter in glass hands. Perhaps they were not mine, but they certainly belonged to a Glaziene. And one day, that prophecy will come to pass."

"Blasphemy," Ignatius sneered. He shot a blast of electricity at Dalila, hitting her face and burning off the left side. She screeched in agony as her glass-infused skin melted, revealing her glass cheekbone.

Another vicious strike and the fire cast from his hand burnt the white dress from her body. Exposed and vulnerable, Dalila held her head high, refusing to cower beneath Ignatius's ruthless power.

"Zohar," Ignatius commanded the brutish Voltain guard. "Begin!"

The enormous soldier raised his gloved hand and forced a syringe filled with salted water into Dalila's mouth. He released the contents into her body, which then slowly ate her from the inside out. As she writhed in pain, he began dismembering her, piece by piece. First, her fingers. One by one he snapped them off her hands and crushed them with a single clench of his fist, turning them to dust before her eyes. Next, her toes, then feet. Hands, then forearms. Hours passed. When all her extremities were gone and the outside air began turning her insides black, he force-fed her another dose of salted water. Her agony intensified, though she did everything in her power to appear strong and maintain her dignity.

"End it," Ignatius finally demanded.

Zohar removed his gloves, lowered to a bended knee, and placed a single finger on Dalila's sternum. The moment he made contact, Dalila's torso contracted violently, convulsing under his electric touch. The intense charge stopped her heart and fried her brain—an irreversible fate. A Glaziene could not be rebuilt with ruined pieces.

Fate sealed, their queen was dead. She was not only shattered, but utterly destroyed. Gwyn did not cry as she watched her mother courageously endure the torture. Instead, she did her best to mimic her mother's bravery. Tyrus and Mina stood to her left, heads bowed in respect. Lorcan stood to her right, face wet with tears. When he looked over at his niece—once a fragile princess now standing tall in the face of terror—he could not help but smile. She was already setting an example of strength for their people to follow.

Fate sealed, Princess Gwynessa was now the queen of Crystet.

Chapter 17

With a jagged diamond crown set atop her long blonde curls, Gwyn took a breath so deep her glass innards rattled. Gwyn did not want to be queen. She did not want to become her mother. Another heavy exhale and the tinkling of her organs reminded her just how broken she was. What should be plush and tender was half-crystalized due to her violent childhood. Cracked open and exposed to air too many times, she wore more scars than the average sixteen-year-old. For a princess turned queen, her scars were unnatural. The royals were supposed to be the most pristine, the most unmarked Glaziene in Crystet. But nothing about her life was typical.

A knock came from the other side of her bedroom door.

"Can I come in?" Lorcan asked.

Gwyn paused, wishing she could remain alone until her dying day, but aware that wasn't possible. She glanced around her childhood bedroom one last time. The cracks in the glass walls were stained with old blood—a lasting tribute to her lost friend.

"Gwynessa," Lorcan pleaded. "Please let me in."

She walked to the door, balancing the unfamiliar crown on her head. After lifting the latch, she turned and used the same care to return to her bed. Lorcan entered, but went no further than the doorway.

"This room gives me the creeps," he noted.

"Why?" she asked, her voice flat. "Because it reminds you that you're a murderer?"

"You understand that you have to change rooms, right?"

"I am queen. I can sleep wherever I want."

"You must relocate to the center of the castle. You need to be accessible."

Gwyn sighed, but did not argue.

"I will switch rooms on the condition that this room is never touched," she bartered. "Never cleaned, never refurbished. It will stay this way until my dying day."

"Understood," Lorcan agreed, aware it was imperative to choose his battles wisely.

"Tell Trista that she is released from her obligations to the throne. Her services are no longer needed."

"You're firing her?"

"I am banishing her. She is not welcome here. If she returns for any reason, I will lock her up in the dungeon and she will never again see the light of day."

"Why?"

"I cannot have people in my inner circle who secretly loathe me. You will take her place as my andlega ráðgjafi."

"I am honored, but don't you think it ought to be you who informs her of this?"

"She doesn't deserve one second of my attention."

"Delivering this news to her will not be easy."

"It is my first command. It will be done."

"I will tell her over supper."

"No. It will be the first thing you do when you leave this room. She does not get a farewell dinner. She leaves this castle within the hour."

"Understood."

"Once that task is completed, instruct the sailors to prepare my boats," Gwyn added.

"What for? You just left your crowning."

"I want to visit Wicker."

"No," Lorcan objected. "Not this again."

"I demand it."

"Crystet is your home. The Glaziene are your people. I don't know what you think you will accomplish by befriending strange creatures from distant lands."

"If King Rúnar gave them the scepter before leaving this world, then they must know something that we don't."

"I hope you do not desire to mirror King Rúnar's reign. Though he was great, a true legend, he was selfish, leaving Crystet weak and vulnerable in the aftermath of his departure."

Gwyn scoffed. "From what I know about him, he is the opposite of what I wish to be. My reign will not bear any resemblance to King Rúnar's. Still, he went to the Woodlins, and I want to know why."

"Because he wanted to hinder his daughter from replicating, or surpassing, his own notorious legacy."

"I think there is more to it."

"Just admit that this venture stems back to your love for the forest."

"Yes. That is another reason I wish to go to Wicker. I suspect I will find a comfort there that I have never known in Crystet. Perhaps that will give me the strength and courage I need to navigate my new role."

"You have me. I will be your guide."

"It's not enough. You are a Glaziene, tried and true. I do not wish to rule Crystet like leaders of the past. I want to try something new. I want to be the one who inspires change."

"Why would you want to change a perfect kingdom?"

"We are far from perfect. The people are selfish and cruel. We do not live in harmony with nature. We do not value life. We are a disease on this planet."

"Those are some harsh opinions about your own race."

"But we can be better," she argued. "I want to be the queen who makes that happen."

"The Woodlins can't help you fix a place they've never even seen."

"How would you know? Sometimes it takes an outside perspective to fix a problem this big. We are too entangled in the roots of this culture, too defined by everything I'm trying to change. There's no way we can step back and see the subtle shifts that need to be made. The Woodlins are detached. They will be able to see my dilemma with clarity."

"I hope you are not wildly disappointed."

"They embody everything I love: nature, the forest, animals. They possess a magical tether to Gaia. They will not steer me wrong."

"Just be careful. You know little about the workings of the world outside of Crystet. You don't know the dynamics between the different lands."

"You'll be there with me to make sure no trouble befalls us."

"If you insist."

Lorcan left to discharge Trista, then have the boat stewards prepare the ships along the north shore, while Mina readied Gwyn for her first trip beyond Crystet. She had never left her homeland before, and though she received a few weeks' worth of culture classes prior to her mother's execution, Trista was a terrible teacher. She shot down Gwyn's questions, refusing to answer them or used them to transition into irrelevant tangents.

Though Gwyn suspected Trista did this on purpose as a way to maliciously set Gwyn up for failure, she also suspected that their botched attempt to poison her frayed her mental state. Trista lost her mind after healing. She often spoke in circles, forgetting what she was saying mid-sentence and losing her temper with whoever was listening, blaming them for the miscommunication. Her reputation of reliability and intelligence disintegrated quickly until she was merely a silent face Dalila kept nearby because her presence continued to instill fear.

Gwyn no longer had to deal with Trista's mad ramblings—a wonderful perk to becoming queen.

Attention focused on her trip to Wicker, Gwyn was uncertain what she would encounter, but a foreign joy raced through her bones. Regardless of the outcome, this adventure would be the perfect distraction from her never-ending attempt to escape sorrow.

When she arrived at the boat, her soldiers stood in a line along the deck, ready to protect her. She sensed their allegiance, could detect their unspoken loyalty, and though it was only given out of respect for her late mother, it made her feel secure before sailing into the unknown.

Lorcan sat by her side as the diamond-infused glass ship left the dock and glided atop the black sea. Two additional naval boats rode in the wake of the queen's boat.

"Don't be surprised if we have a couple of tense encounters," Lorcan warned her.

"King Ignatius and I talked. He knows I don't intend to repeat my mother's mistakes."

"It's not just the Voltains you have to worry about. There are sea witches and flesh-eating fairies beyond the safety of Crystet's chilly climate. There are beings from other lands that traverse these waters, most of whom hate us. Our only true allies are the Metellyans."

"Have the Bouldes committed to their abandonment of the revolution?"

"Yes. King Alun and Queen Gemma officially backed out after Ignatius made an example of your mother. They irrevocably renounced their involvement with us."

"Cowards," Gwyn hissed.

"Will you finish your mother's work?" Lorcan asked.

"Absolutely not. I am not going to die for that stupid stick."

"That 'stupid stick' contains the greatest magic our world has ever known."

"I don't want it. I have more important matters to focus on."

"You really ought to meditate on your priorities. They are askew. With the scepter of alchemy, you would be the first queen in Crystet to secure such power."

"I don't want to be queen at all, let alone the most powerful. What would I do with all that magic?" she asked.

"Satisfy all the vendettas you temporarily put aside to possess said magic."

Conflicted, Gwyn paused, aware that the point was valid. The thought of using magic again terrified her, but with such power, she could easily accomplish all she had promised to do.

"I need to think about it," she finally said.

"Good."

Their journey to Wicker was uneventful. No monsters or volatile beings from neighboring lands accosted them, which was a change of luck for the new queen, who had grown used to expecting the worst.

The boats dropped weighted, crystal anchors a few miles offshore and used smaller rowboats to reach the coast of Wicker. Lorcan helped Gwyn into their glass boat. Once he was comfortably situated beside her, they were lowered into the water and the soldiers accompanying them used diamond oars to row them to the dirt-shore of Wicker.

While everyone else exited their watercrafts, Gwyn hesitated. After years of imagining this place, years of fantasizing about its magic and the way it would feel like home, she was here. This was the moment she'd been waiting for, the place she'd been dreaming of while everything she loved in Crystet shattered around her.

She took a deep breath and exited her rowboat.

The moment her glass feet touched the dusty soil, the trees began to sway. Their trunks bent and swiveled to a rhythm birthed from their roots. Leaves showered the ground, raining overhead as their branches shook to the beat of their welcoming pulsation. Giddy anticipation surged through Gwyn.

"Maintain a brave and stoic exterior," Lorcan whispered as they approached the tree line. "Excitement is a weakness, too."

Gwyn nodded, nervous for the first time. Her expectations were high and she feared that anything less than what she hoped for would crush her. The letdown would be another heartbreak—quite possibly the last one her fissured heart could withstand.

They walked through the curtain of falling leaves and entered the shadowed world of Wicker. Light peeked into the depths of the forest where it could, but the boughs overhead were so thickly interwoven that the sun had little opportunity to enter. Gwyn searched for a tree more alive than those in the Wildlands of Crystet, but the dancing trees were faceless. Maybe the Woodlins were much different than she expected, maybe they wouldn't have faces at all.

She stopped once they reached a clearing in the forest and her guards shifted into a protective circle around their young queen. Gwyn examined the scene. The air rang with a hypnotic melody that was so loud she had trouble concentrating. Voices joined the rhythmic thumps and the melodic sighs came from mouths she had yet to find.

"Where are they?" she whispered to Lorcan.

"All around us," he replied.

Gwyn's expression constricted as she tried to understand. She was told they could speak. She was told they were wise and magical creatures. But all she saw were trees that moved without wind.

"I come in peace," she announced in her loudest voice. "I come with the intention to forge a friendship."

The trees stopped dancing. The forest went still. The abrupt halt in merriment sent a chill up Gwyn's glass spine.

"Who are you?" an ethereal, but austere voice resonated from the shadows.

"I am Queen Gwynessa Appoline Gunvaldsson, the new ruler of Crystet," Gwyn declared. She faked a regal bravado, but quivered inside. She wanted their respect and loyalty, but didn't know much about this land or the nature of its creatures.

"What happened to she who wore the crown before you?"

"She was murdered."

"Your mother, yes? My guess is that you aren't like the rest. I feel the blossom of love that you hide within your chest."

Gwyn took a deep breath and looked at Lorcan, who only shrugged in response. Her secret was not safe here; the Woodlins sensed everything.

"Where are you?" she asked. "Why don't you show your face?"

"Your soldiers have weapons. We don't believe in violence."

"Go," she commanded her soldiers. "Back to the shore. Wait for me at the rowboats. The Woodlins mean me no harm."

Her guardsmen obeyed, but Lorcan lingered.

"You too," she insisted.

"You should not be alone. You know not what to say or do, or how it will affect everything around you."

"I don't care. Let me have this moment for myself."

Lorcan huffed. "Be careful with your words, and more importantly, your emotions. Do not let them get the best of you."

He turned and left, leaving Gwyn alone with the Woodlins.

A few seconds of silence lingered, which felt like an eternity of uncertainty to Gwyn, but after Lorcan cleared the tree line, the setting transformed. Out of the shadows, from all directions, emerged giant Woodlins. Their strides were large and their lanky limbs swung with rigid fluidity as they loomed toward her. The ground shook and she braced for contact. With all her might, she fought to maintain her bravado, but the reveal of these majestic beings was too much for her excited heart to contain. A smile crept across her face as the largest Woodlin stopped mere inches from where she stood. She tilted her chin upward. The Woodlin was so tall she had to hold her crown in place to prevent it from falling off her head. She looked around and found four other Woodlins had come to make her acquaintance.

The Woodlins looked much like the trees she knew in Crystet, except taller, with bits of bark covering random sections of their otherwise smooth and chiseled trunks. Their faces were so beautiful, she gasped at their reveal. She had never seen such art made from wood before. Their noses, mouths, cheekbones, and brows were etched with delicate intricacy, creating faces so eloquent she could feel their souls through their gazes.

The Woodlin with the kindest face spoke first. "I am Beaumont, a friend to all who are brave enough to explore what has been and what has not."

Another interrupted. "A friend of the stars is the kind I desire. My name is Bolivar and the pleasure is mine." He bent his long, gangling body, knocking leaves loose from his head as he bowed.

"Born of glass with a spirit of wood. I sense with us is where you belong. I am Brynmor, keeper of souls. With us, you've found a second home."

Beaming with joy, Gwyn looked up at Brynmor. She was accepted. She was recognized as worthy.

When the tallest finally spoke, all the others went silent. The shared space pulsated with respect.

"I am Baldric," the tallest Woodlin stated. "Oldest amongst the breathing sticks." He smiled—the most beautiful smile Gwyn had ever seen. "Welcome to Wicker," he continued. "You'll find that all things here—the ground, the sky, the minds, the hearts—are a tiny bit bigger."

"And the magic."

"Yes, the magic," Baldric confirmed. "Also, the wisdom. No proper system survives without its existence. Why have you come here?"

"I love the forest in Crystet. I spent all of my childhood amongst the animals and the trees. I thought this place might feel like home to me."

"Does it?"

Gwyn nodded.

"How wonderful," Baldric mused. "A misplaced spirit finding true north. Home is determined by the heart; where you end isn't always where you start."

He lifted his long, wooden finger and lowered it toward Gwyn. His fingertip hovered in front of her chest.

"You keep a secret," he stated.

Gwyn held her breath. Baldric sensed her sudden discomfort and placed his enormous hand by her feet.

"Come with me and we can talk in private. There is much I wish to advise, much I wish to offer as a guide."

Gwyn climbed onto his hand and he slowly lifted her until his hand rested upon his chest. He walked away from the chattering Woodlins, deeper into the forest. Solitude was impossible in Wicker, as all the trees were alive and animated, but Baldric's height and constant motion meant no Woodlin within earshot could hear more than a few moments of their exchange as they passed by. Once they reached an open patch of forest where all the trees nearby were in deep slumber, Baldric lowered her to the ground.

"How did you know?" Gwyn asked.

"I can see its crying soul."

"He's crying?"

"It's unnatural, what you did. A soul split, in limbo, and used against its will."

"It was the only way."

"I fear for your soul; you must return what you stole."

"I will. I plan to," Gwyn insisted. "It is my primary focus as queen."

"Do you wish to see Gaia when you reach your end?"

"Yes."

"Then hold on to love."

"I already lost everything that I love."

"Perhaps there is more to come. Perhaps it will be a person, a place, or a ghost. It could be a desire that has yet to be. Or a wish you must abandon to set your soul free."

Gwyn wasn't sure of the answer, but she *was* sure that she had a promise to keep.

"You are the only one who knows my secret. Will you keep it?"

"I do not betray my friends."

Gwyn sighed. It was liberating to share some of her burden with another. The relief this exchange provided was long-needed.

"Thank you."

"Your spirit is good. Gaia sees it too."

"You speak to her?"

"In subtle, understated forms. She comes in wavelengths unheard if you're not listening close. In specks of dirt unseen if your eyes are closed. In the energy of the breeze, unnoticed by those too hardened to feel. The more attuned to nature you become, the easier it will be to hear Her beating drum."

Gwyn nodded, though she did not know how she could possibly spend more time than she already did in the Wildlands.

Baldric sensed her confusion.

"The connection is not physical; the bond is not one you can achieve or define. It is a feeling, an emotion, a journey with no maps or pre-woven notions. To acquire this higher state of being, you must let go of all you've ever known and commit to believing. Without seeing, without hearing, trust in what you are given. She will not steer you wrong if you embrace the fate she allots."

"I have," Gwyn countered. "I did not want this life, I did not want to suffer as I did, but I endured."

Baldric pointed to her chest again. "You did not accept the fate she assigned."

"I am not allowed to respond?"

"Not like that. Such actions are beyond the bounds of acceptance."

"I'll make it right," Gwyn stated with gumption.

"Of that, I have no doubt," Baldric replied.

"I actually came here to seek your wisdom and advice about a different matter. I want to change Crystet, I want to make things better. I want to teach the Glaziene how to appreciate and love the land and all its creatures. I want to promote kindness and understanding. Crystet has been blanketed in misery for centuries—possibly since the start of time—and I want to transform how we operate. I want us to live in harmony with the planet, with those around us, and more importantly, with ourselves."

Baldric smiled, the wooden lines around his mouth stretched.

"So you *can* hear Her."

"Huh?"

"The task is mighty large. Noble, but a lot to ask from an established culture with a long past. Do you have an ocean of patience living inside your soul? Can you withstand the backlash and resistance that is sure to follow? I suspect the response will be nasty, wicked, and dreadful. It will get worse before it gets better. If you can absorb their negativity without letting it consume you, perhaps you are the person to repair Glaziene values."

"I think I can," Gwyn replied, a bit uncertain, but optimistic.

"Then I suspect you will. A hopeful and determined spirit is stronger than the shrouded hearts you wish to unveil. You will prevail."

"I hope so."

"Visit me whenever you feel lost. I will remind you of the good you wish to see in the world."

"Thank you for being my ally."

"I am your *friend*," Baldric corrected. "I will see you through this till the end."

He took her small hand and pressed his wooden thumb into her palm. The pressure hurt, but she trusted him. When he lifted his appendage, a brown, tree-shaped smudge stained her glass flesh.

"A reminder," he explained.

Gwyn smiled and wrapped her skinny, glass arms around his enormous trunk body. It was a relief to feel secure, to feel safe again, after losing so much.

Baldric glanced up. "Alas, the first moon is set to rise. Shall we return you to your ships?"

"I suppose so."

Baldric lowered his large hand. Gwyn crawled over his branch-fingers and onto his wooden palm, and then he carried her through Wicker toward the shoreline.

"Farewell, Queen Gwynessa of Crystet," Beaumont announced when Baldric and Gwyn reached a more populated patch of forest. "Happy to have met."

"Dearest Gwyn, how splendid your visit has been," Brynmor added.

"Visit often, Queen of Glass. Don't let this visit be your last," Bolivar stated.

Gwyn nodded with a smile, but the horde of talking trees was out of sight before she could make any promises. Baldric moved fast and she was back at the shore, facing an armed throng of uneasy Glaziene soldiers.

"Everything is fine," she assured them, but her words held no comfort. She hadn't been queen long enough to earn their unwavering trust; their loyalty was merely out of respect for her late mother.

Lorcan stepped forward.

"Time to go, my queen."

Baldric gently lowered her and she exited onto the dirt-covered shore. Lorcan immediately grabbed her forearm and guided her toward their rowboat.

The energy on the shore was tense and Baldric offered no goodbye. He simply watched as Gwyn was directed to do as her uncle desired. She was not in control, Lorcan was, and the glass guardsmen were rigid with fearful mistrust by his command.

"Goodbye, Baldric!" Gwyn shouted as the rowboat slowly departed.

The giant Woodlin smiled in reply, unable to pretend that the soldiers with diamond spears aimed at him didn't rattle his calm.

Gwyn did not sense the unease her guardsmen caused her new friend. She had lived in the negativity for so long that she was oblivious to the subtleties of the unwelcoming nature of her people. If they weren't physically fighting or accosting another with harsh words, she assumed all was well. She was too accustomed, too engrained within the world she wished to change that she could not detect the little nuances that made the Glaziene unreachable.

She waved from her boat, clutching to the elation from having such a good encounter with the foreigners she held in high regard for so long. The meeting went better than she ever dreamed. She left Wicker with a new friend and an entire populace rooting for her success. She felt empowered, invigorated, and ready to take on the world. She would fulfill every promise she made to those she loved and reshape her kingdom along the way. One day, Crystet would become a place she was proud to call home.

Chapter 18

There wasn't enough love in the world to change the people of Crystet. No matter what she did, they loathed her.

At age sixteen, her first public order as queen was establishing a law that prohibited any Glaziene from recklessly harming the animals of the wild. The raucous populace responded to this new rule with riots that lasted for months. Acres of her beloved forests were destroyed in manmade fires, and though it broke her heart, Gwyn refused to back down. She had a point to make, respect to earn, and caving to their tantrums would serve her neither. Hundreds of Glaziene lives were lost before the people conceded begrudgingly, voicing their hatred and disgust as they ceased their fiery riots and surrendered. She won, barely, but the victory fueled her determination.

When the forest fires finally cleared in the winter following her twentieth birthday, she was ready to enact her next policy change. She ascended the elevated stage atop the gates separating Þola market from the royal forest to announce the news.

"From here on out, Heilög Iðrun and all weekly Heilög Day feasts are cancelled."

The moment the words left her mouth, the ground shook with the collective fury of every Glaziene standing below her. Gwyn took a deep breath before continuing, suddenly grateful to be stationed so high above them and out of their reach.

"From now on, we will hold ourselves accountable," she explained. "We will not feign regret as an excuse to feast and drink. We will not gather in merriment on an occasion where we should feel remorse. Instead, we will earn Gaia's forgiveness through actual repentance and daily atonement, without fanfare and in private, to prove our sincerity. This is how we will return to Gaia's good graces."

The crowd jeered, shouting profanities in primordial Glaziene. Some even added ancient curses to their vulgarities—hexes Gwyn hadn't heard since firing Trista. With a shudder, she realized she might have attempted this change too soon.

The weeks passed and she quickly came to learn that she not only had to deal with the angry masses, but also Orlan. He actively undermined her rule by holding secret services, which inspired the people to speak even louder and behave more ruthlessly against her reign. When she tried to reiterate that they could still seek Gaia's forgiveness in private, they responded by capturing her soldiers and dousing them with triflic acid. These soldiers, who were stationed by Gwyn to ensure that Heilög

Day was not celebrated, were eaten alive by the organic chemical.

Violent protests happened on Heilög Iðrun every year since, but she could not change her stance on the holiday. She took measures to protect her soldiers, but her preventative tactics never outmatched those of her merciless subjects.

At age 24, she exiled the Vorso from Crystet, banning their continued idolization. Gwyn's soldiers tore down their statues, which were numerous and scattered all over the land, and shattered them in the middle of Þola market for all to see. To finalize her decree, Gwyn stood atop the elevated stage and poured a vat of scorching magma overtop of the heaping mountain of shattered monuments. The day was grave and the crowd wept together, unifying for the first time in years, as the statues of their favorite deities melted before their eyes. When the lava disappeared back into the terrain, nothing remained except a bottomless hole in the middle of the most populated market. A deadly reminder that the queen would not tolerate any dissent.

"I have set you free!" she proclaimed, though the weeping masses disagreed. Gwyn symbolically murdered their beloved deities, and for that, their hatred for her boiled hotter than ever. Her attempt to scorch their faith only instigated the inferno that brewed within.

She felt the blaze of their hatred, so she tried to explain.

"We control our personalities. We control our behavior. Not the Vorso. As a daughter of royalty, I've witnessed how the reputations of these deities have been abused over the eons to craft an obedient and fearful society. The kings, queens, and æðsti presturs of the past have manipulated you into believing that your lives are not your own, that they belong to the devious and cunning Vorso gods. They have shaped your lives so that you live in constant fear. All of that ends today."

"You've doomed us all," a woman cried. "We will become fateless because of you!"

"It will be a tough transition," Gwyn agreed. "But I promise that in time, you will see that there is no such fate. We all have a place in the afterlife."

One by one, individuals in the crowd began praying to the Vorso, shouting their praises into the sky, actively challenging Gwyn's decree.

She waited patiently, hoping they'd see reason, but their prayers only grew louder until the volume of their defiance consumed her resolve.

"My queen," Tyrus whispered. "We cannot let them defy you like this."

"They do not listen to reason," Gwyn replied, voice flat with defeat. "They won't even try to see my point of view. It's been eight years. They cannot change."

The insolent chanting was now deafening.

"You need to force them to obey."

"How?" she asked.

"You need to become worse than them, even if it's just a façade," he explained. Gwyn struggled to hear him over the rebellious prayers, so he spoke louder. "They don't fear you because you aren't intimidating. You are nice. You are soft and kind." Tyrus paused. "And despite your valiant efforts to hide this fact, you are still the most emotional Glaziene I have ever met. To be loved is great, but to be feared is power."

Gwyn exhaled. "I am not that person."

"Instruct your soldiers to push a few of them into that pit."

Gwyn gasped.

Tyrus raised his left eyebrow. "It'll make the rest stop."

"That's evil."

"It will work."

Gwyn glanced down at the tree-shaped stain Baldric left on her palm.

What Tyrus suggested directly conflicted with everything she wished to be. She then looked down at the faces twisted with hateful anger.

Perhaps Baldric did not truly understand the cruel nature of her people.

Gwyn took a deep breath.

"Just one," she ordered.

"You ought to do more."

"One," she repeated.

"As you wish."

Tyrus raised his glass bow and pierced the shoulder of a man who stood near the edge. The man wailed in pain, stumbling backwards until he tumbled into the hole. Those around him fell silent as they watched his free fall. The rest of the crowd became hushed as word of what had happened quickly spread.

A horrified scream echoed from the bottomless pit, slowly growing softer as the man fell endlessly. They never heard the shattering sound of a body hitting ground.

The crowd returned their astonished gazes back to Gwyn, who stood safely atop her gated tower. She motioned to her soldiers, who raised their glass arrows in unison.

"Do not test my patience," she warned. Though her heart ached, she knew this was her moment to either gain their respect or lose it forever.

A moment of tense silence lingered.

"Shoot another," Tyrus advised.

"They haven't done anything to warrant that."

"You do not understand the collective mindset of your people."

At that moment, the crowd erupted and charged at the gates. The force of so many bodies hitting the wall caused the structure to shudder.

"Why are they doing this?"

"They do not take you seriously," Tyrus explained.

"I should have let you kill more of them," she said with a groan.

"Too late now. We need to get you out of here."

Tyrus and a few other bowmen escorted her down the back of the stage and into the royal forest, while the remaining soldiers fought off the enraged crowd.

Over the next few months, Gwyn accepted the harsh reality that she was ruling a society that refused to change. When she burnt down the illegal markets that continued to sell Vorso paraphernalia, the assassination attempts began. Homemade bombs filled with triflic acid thrown through the castle windows, suicide dashes past the guards with diamond pick-axes aimed at Gwyn. Though it always ended in execution for those foolish enough to try, Gwyn felt the terror of their relentless hatred. In response, she began letting the boreal bears and meridional wolves into the castle, as they were her greatest protectors. No one got close to her while they were around, and those who tried were torn apart limb by limb.

Despite their refusal to adapt, she continued to show mercy in the face of hatred. Still, the relentless assassination attempts continued and it became clear that she would never win while armed with love.

On the eve of her twenty-fifth birthday she was finally ready to sacrifice everything—her mind, body, and spirit—for the betterment of herself and her people.

Naked and covered in scars, Queen Gwynessa of Crystet stood at the edge of Jökull Cliff, peering over the side at her eventual fate.

Weathered and jaded from years of failure, the choice to jump was a simple one, though she wasn't ready to make the commitment yet. There was still much to do before she left this world for good and this was her final attempt to right old wrongs.

In the distance, large waves crashed against King Runar's nearly rebuilt body. Her eyes zeroed in on the hole where his heart should be. The broken king surrounded by all his broken people; a fate she seemed destined to replicate.

"I'm sorry," she whispered, looking down at the mark Baldric left on her palm. With a remorseful gaze, she looked up to the heavens and began slamming her fist repeatedly against an old chest break until the binding began to crumble. The impact of her pounding fist wore down the fused glass patch, slowly turning it into dust and leaving a gaping fissure between her breasts.

The brisk arctic air of spring crossed through her, traveling through the cracks in her glass skin, sending a searing bolt of pain through her body. Though the discomfort caused her to shiver, it was the start of something new. This was the true beginning of her reign.

She placed her hand into the newly formed hole and wrapped her glass fingers around her beating heart. She paused, adrenaline pumping so ferociously her sight blurred. But there was no stopping now. This was the only way to escape the ghosts that haunted her; this was the only way to become more evil than those she wished to control. Without another moment of hesitation, Gwyn tore her heart from her chest.

Arm extended, red heart beating in her palm, she watched her heart crystalize in the outside air. Removed from the safety of her body, the warm, fleshy organ iced over, turning hard as stone, and its exterior blackened. A sinister-looking relic now sat in her hand—a true reflection of her sinful deed.

With bated breath, she waited to feel the change, to be rewarded for her dangerous courage. Just as she began to worry that she made a mistake, the heart released a faint, red glow through its cracks, and its power resonated up her arm. She now possessed a force, a magical energy, unrivaled by any other in her kingdom.

As the power grew, a gust of wind tore through her open chest, forcing her to recall the ache of heartbreak. Her eyes welled with tears and her lungs grew heavy as stone as she relived her ancient grief. The countless faces of those she lost flashed in her mind, disappearing as quickly as the frigid spring breeze.

This was the last time she would feel such pain, the last time any tears would fall from her eyes. The heart was stripping her of all her sentimental tendencies.

She glanced at the empty music box by her feet. Beneath the flawless, diamond lid was where her black heart would live.

Removed from her chest, the heart would give her magic, allowing her to rule Crystet with unrivaled authority and all-consuming terror. No one could control her anymore. With this power, she'd finally be able to fulfill the promises she had yet to keep. No longer a girl disguised as a queen, no longer a ruler weakened by emotion, she was set free. The broken little girl she used to be was gone and birthed in her place was Nessa, the ruthless queen of Crystet. Limitless, with no bounds to her ferocious capabilities, she'd stop at nothing to fix what she broke. Once she did, she would end her life and put these few decades of torment to rest.

She glanced down at her open chest and saw Calix's heart still sitting safely inside. Blackened and lifeless, silenced by years of neglect, it waited to be vindicated. Though she often wallowed in her failure to follow through on its return to Calix, everything was different now. She finally mustered the courage to seize the power she needed to complete her original task. Without her heart in place, and with its magic at her disposal, her vendetta against Orlan would finally be realized.

Nessa picked up her armor off the snow and redressed. The reinforced diamond breastplate completely covered her fresh crack, and the rest of her outfit prettied the armor. Golden pauldrons layered like bird feathers covered her shoulders and chains linked with precious gems draped across her exposed back. Wearing materials collected from other lands reinforced her authority and with her newfound magic, she'd wreak havoc on her neighbors, taking all the resources she pleased to remind everyone of her power. Nessa tied the silk ribbon at the neck of her fleece-lined cape and raised the enormous hood, which shadowed her stern but pretty face.

Next to her bare feet sat the music box made of porcelain, glass, and diamond. She picked it up and locked her heart inside. Until she was ready to shatter, it would remain safely beside her at all times. It was the one piece that could ruin her before her chosen end. If anyone discovered it was removed from her body, they could shatter her and hide the heart, preventing her from ever being rebuilt. Though it was a risk she was willing to take, she was aware she must take extra care moving forward.

Beneath the heart's murky black casing, a glowing fire raged within. The glass box shook as her heart thundered inside.

She wasn't ready to hear what it had to say.

Mission completed, she tucked the shaking container under her arm and marched down the hill toward the tree line. A sleuth of boreal bears guarded the edge of the forest, protecting their queen with homicidal devotion. They would destroy anyone who tried to get close. A pack of meridionial wolves roamed the inner layers of the Wildlands, ready to do the same. The animals were Nessa's greatest and most faithful allies, and together, they would keep the citizens of Crystet oppressed with fear.

The bears grumbled with adoration at her return, using their bodies to form a moving wall around her as she stormed forward. On the other side of the Wildlands, her army of Glaziene soldiers waited.

She only felt the shin-deep snow on her bare legs when the wet slush crept into the fused fissures around her ankles. A failed attempt to fly into another life gave her those cracks. The memory was foggy now; her heart had done its job. Though the facts of her yesterdays remained, the vivid details and correlated emotions had vanished. She was free from the burden of her past.

As she reached the center of the Wildlands, the wolves joined the brigade of bears that protected her. They howled as they guarded the perimeter of the procession. Nessa trusted the animals more than her soldiers, but learned over time that both forms of protection were necessary. Her beasts instilled fear amongst the people and were her fiercest protectors, while the army of Glaziene soldiers were able to fight with strategy and clever tactics on her behalf. Still, she often preferred the monsters' primal savagery over the careful planning required for her royal guard.

The procession reached the opposite end of the Wildlands. Nessa tucked the music box into a large pocket on the inside of her cape before emerging. Her soldiers stood alert in rigid formation, ready for duty.

"Welcome back, Queen Gwynessa," Tyrus, her lead bowman greeted.

"From now on, you will address me as Queen Nessa," she corrected him.

He nodded, then bowed his head. Nessa stalked past, animals by her side.

Her soldiers held their breath as Queen Nessa's wild beasts strutted past, salivating as they grumbled deep growls of hatred. The queen's command was the only thing keeping their glass-flesh intact. Without her protection, the monsters would have torn the guards apart, armor and all. Nessa circled her hand haphazardly, waving them all forward, unconcerned by the tension radiating between her two opposing guards.

They followed her back to the castle, keeping her safe as they went. The glass streets were alive with villagers; most of whom held little respect for their queen. They feared her wild-beast army, but not her.

Without her heart there was a shift in her being, a transformation in her soul. Now more merciless than the worst Crystet had ever known, it was time to unleash her fury; time to introduce her people to the woman she now was.

She could feel her heart's power coursing from beneath her cape. With her left hand, she reached into the glass box, and her right arm extended, grabbing the nearest man.

"Do you respect my reign?" she asked, eyes narrowed and glaring.

The man looked at the bears and wolves now surrounding him, then back at his queen.

"You are frail. You are feeble-hearted. I cannot respect that."

Nessa smirked, then channeled her long-held frustration through her heart and into the man. The magic burst through him with purple electricity, illuminating his insides before frying them. Lifeless, he collapsed to the ground, which garnered her the attention of the entire village.

No one thought she was capable of such cruelty.

Nessa raised her right arm and sent another shockwave of ferocious, purple energy into the sky.

The people gasped.

"Who's next?" she shouted, taunting her disrespectful subjects with death.

No one answered, so she began shooting haphazard blasts of lethal magic at anyone she pleased. Her frivolous aim killed anyone it touched upon impact. It was a slaughter and a foreign joy she never knew was possible crept up her spine. As she massacred the terrified bystanders, her heartless body overflowed with elation. This was the power she'd been searching for; the respect she sought but never knew how to obtain. Finally, she was winning. Finally, she was the queen they needed.

Those still standing when she lowered her magically fueled armament cowered in her presence. Surrounded by their slayed neighbors, their fear for Nessa grew exponentially.

"Spread the word," she announced with a smirk. "Death awaits those who revolt. Test me if you wish to learn what I daydream about."

No one said a word, but she wasn't done yet.

"Who is my first challenger?" she shouted, her playful tone sinister. "Who wants to be the star of the nightmare I am gifting to today's survivors?"

No one stepped forward, so Nessa grabbed the nearest child. A little girl, no more than five years old, squirmed in the queen's clutches.

"You'll let a little girl die?" she barked, gripping the child by her hair and dragging her around as she paced. No one was willing to sacrifice their life to save the innocent girl.

"This is why I loathe the lot of you," Nessa growled before pushing the girl to the ground and aiming her open palm at her face. It pulsated with furious energy.

She looked down at the girl and saw herself: an innocent child, a victim of the harsh realities of this world.

"Death will be kinder to you," Nessa whispered before blasting the little girl with a bolt of blue magic, burning her alive. The child's dying screams would surely haunt those who survived.

"If you are shaken to the core, disturbed beyond your wildest nightmares, let this be a lesson in gallantry. I would have let her live if any of you showed a little selflessness on her behalf. Her death falls on you."

Nessa turned and left the scene of her riotous rage, Glaziene soldiers and wild beasts by her side. Without her heart, she felt no remorse. Terror was what her people needed. After years of failed attempts to use rational explanation and kindness as her primary mode of operation, she had no choice but to adapt and match their evilness. They would not change without fear.

She enjoyed the terror she instilled. It was empowering and enhanced her new reputation of invincibility. Though she knew what was to come of her fate, she would relish these final days. She would go out as a legend, as an untouchable force. Undefeatable, except by her own hand.

With intimidating presence, her fearsome parade crossed through Gler village, through Fjölmennur metropolis, then through Þola marketplace. She used her magic to scare everyone she passed along the way. By the night's end, her entire reign would shift in her favor.

Orlan was a dead man.

Chapter 19

Orlan eluded Nessa's wrath for the next ten years, insulting her daily with his continued survival. Though she tried many times to discretely assassinate him, he always managed to outwit her and tarnish her plans. The more time that passed, the more distracted she became by her growing power, and her attempts to kill her foe became fewer.

Old promises were left unfulfilled and Nessa collected unfavorable monikers, such as Ice Queen, Child Slayer, Mother of Monsters, and Kólasi's Favorite Daughter.

She was invincible without her heart; she was the most feared queen in Crystet's history. No one challenged her reign or revolted; they accepted her cruel methods of governing, aware that she took no pause in executing any and all challengers. Removing her heart began the start of her greatness. It was also the start of her demise.

It took years of emotionless savagery to see that without her heart, she had grown into a ruthless monster. It took repeated flirtation with suicide to realize that without emotion, she had morphed into a reflection of everything she hated.

Back at Jökull Cliff, debating her fate, she cursed the time that passed. She looked over the edge of the cliff again, adrenaline gushing. The height and imagined plummet filled her with life and she eagerly anticipated the end.

It was time to surrender, time to let go. It was time to end the horror she cast over her home. She should have relinquished her power years ago, but without her heart, her ego became twisted around new vendettas that kept her a prisoner to this life, and she had yet to fulfill the final promise she swore to keep.

Orlan was still alive. This was her greatest failure.

She placed her hand over the shoddily fused crack that ran from her left shoulder down to the right side of her ribcage. Caused by her own hand many years ago, it was the most meaningful wound she wore. It concealed both Calix's heart and the absence of her own. As a young woman, she mended the break herself, which left her with an ugly scar, but it was better that she tended to it in private. Knowledge of what she had removed and then kept hidden in the cavity of her chest was too valuable. This particular break held too many secrets, too many dark truths that were better kept in the depths of her being.

Her heart glowed bright red in the orb of her diamond scepter.

"No," Nessa said. "I do not care what you have to say."

It glowed brighter.

"I shouldn't have brought you here."

The orb shook violently.

"We will end this together. Not today, but soon. You won't change my mind," she told her heart.

Guards atop the gatehouse opened the steel enforced glass doors Nessa installed upon taking the throne—another material not found in Crystet until she took over. Collecting natural materials from other lands was her most thrilling hobby and utilizing and wearing each of her stolen items with proud ownership reminded the world of her ferocious capabilities. She earned her place amongst the brave, amongst the damned, and most importantly, amongst the notorious. The fear she caused would live beyond her death. She smiled, recalling the legacy she built.

Lorcan waited at the castle's main entrance, tapping his toe impatiently as she glided toward him. He was old, bordering on ancient, and the foggy appearance of his glass skin showed his age.

"Where did you go?" he demanded. He was the only person in all of Crystet that was able to speak freely with the queen.

"The Wildlands," she answered, charging through the castle doors. Lorcan glided with haste in her wake, trying to keep up.

"What for?"

"Matters that don't concern you."

"They concern me when they rip you away from your responsibilities," he quipped.

"Sorry, Uncle, but I can't have missed much."

"We were supposed to discuss what I discovered yesterday."

"Yes," Nessa recalled. "You sent your eyes out with the owls. Which land did they fly over?"

"Coppel," he answered. "And then they followed the Metellyans to Orewall. It seems they are successfully recruiting some of the stone-brutes."

"Why should I care?"

"Because your mother was the founder of the rebellion, and instead of honoring her life's work, you have shunned it, refusing to complete what she started."

"It is not my duty to complete her efforts."

"No. You'd rather pirate neighboring lands with the Mudlings."

"Look at how I have improved our security! Steel gates, metal armor, stone battlements. I've even acquired gas samples from Vapore that we can morph into chemical weapons. *We* want the ultimate victory in the end, correct? Or are we planning to share our success with every other land of Namaté?"

"We cannot steal back the scepter of alchemy without the help of the Metellyans and Bouldes."

"I think we can," Nessa retorted confidently. "Relying on others makes us weak and I will not allow such a disgrace to fall upon my kingdom. We can do it alone."

"When?" Lorcan argued. "What is the plan? You act like you have it figured out but I've never seen you put a single ounce of energy into the Great Fight. Whether we do it alone or with the other rebels, we must take action. The Voltains grow stronger and more powerful every day that they possess the scepter. Their defenses have tripled and breaking through will be impossible if we wait much longer."

"Haven't you ever considered there are other ways to rule the world?" Nessa sneered.

"How?"

"Fear."

"You need the magic from the scepter of alchemy to rule all the lands."

"Do I? Isn't terror its own form of magic? Look at how I've reshaped Crystet. I have more control over the masses than any previous ruler of this land."

"Perhaps."

"And you surely noticed that the Voltains backed off once I took the throne and revealed my style of rule."

"You think that's because they fear you?" Lorcan grunted. "I think they think you're crazy and that you will self-destruct on your own."

Nessa did her best to control her temper. "Regardless of whether they fear me or are ignoring me, I have set this kingdom up for success. I have developed relationships with the forgotten and overlooked creatures of the world, who are willing to help us, and I have stolen from those who possess materials that serve our greater good."

"You are infuriating."

"I am in charge."

"Something I know all too well," Lorcan teased, though his tone held defeat. "King Oro of Coppel sent a carrier cardinal today."

"Is he trying to get me killed?" Nessa spat, appalled by the forbidden gesture.

"No. It never landed. It simply circled overhead before flying into the aviary and dropping a parchment with a coin attached."

"What did it say?"

"Nothing. The parchment was blank, but the coin had the word 'traitors' etched into the copper."

"And you want us to *join* their cause?"

"They wouldn't feel betrayed if you had taken your mother's place in the fight."

"Hypocrites. They betrayed the cause first. I owe them nothing."

"Perhaps, but still."

"I do not bow to threats."

"Nor should you. I just think you need to take definitive action and stop raiding lands while *their* soldiers are off in battle. It's a bad look."

"I haven't done that in years."

"Correct. Now you secretly bribe the lowly creatures and monsters on this planet to do your dirty work for you."

"I'm just trying to build the strongest version of Crystet that I can. If you'd take a step out of my dead mother's shadow, you'd see that what I'm building is genius."

Lorcan pressed his lips together in annoyance, but made no reply.

"How long have we been doing this?" Nessa continued. "This argument has grown stale. Get on my side already."

"I am on your side, you know this. I am your greatest supporter. I am not just your spiritual advisor, though, I am also family, and I must speak up when I disagree with your behavior. No one else will. My opposition comes from a place of love."

"There is no love amongst the Glaziene," Nessa countered.

"You know what I mean. I care and want you to succeed."

"Fine," Nessa conceded. It was rare that any Glaziene rooted for another's success, but she believed her uncle. They shared a heavy past and she did not believe him to be a liar.

"I hear you," Nessa continued, "but I will not change my mind. All that I do is for the enhancement of Crystet. Things needed to change, so I changed them. Ride this out with me and you will see that I was right all along."

Dissatisfied, Lorcan grunted, but argued no further.

"I have a date with the cecaelia. Have the sailors ready my boat."

"The sea witches? Again?" Lorcan asked. "What are they stealing for you now?"

"I'm just hungry for kolkrabba."

Lorcan held his breath in condemnation, baffled by how she managed to take what she desired from creatures she also ate.

"Your secrets are abundant," he commented.

"I hide nothing from you," she lied.

"Hmph." Loran's expression held great skepticism. "You shouldn't hide anything from me. I am your greatest ally."

"You're my *only* ally, besides the Woodlins."

Lorcan scoffed. "When was the last time you visited Wicker? The day after your crowning?"

"Once since then," Nessa answered, recalling her shameful encounter with Baldric a few weeks after removing her heart.

"Twice in twenty years. That's not an ally, that's an acquaintance. You don't care about them at all. If you did, you'd have made the trip more frequently."

"You know nothing of our bond."

"Perhaps I don't, but tell me, would they come to your aid after all these years of neglect?"

"I think they would."

Lorcan shook his head and conceded. "You are your own worst enemy. Still, I am compelled to do my best for you. Go on with your hunt. Catch enough so I can share in your feast."

"Always," she replied before they parted ways.

This would be one of her last feasts, one of her last hunts, and she was eager for the kill.

Nessa glided to her sleeping quarters to dress for the sea. She had instructed her handmaidens earlier in the day to prepare her outfit, and they were already in her room, ready to dress her for the sea.

Her handmaidens carefully removed the pauldrons and diamond breastplate from her body, revealing her broken chest, as well as the heart she kept hidden within. The world believed it was her own half-blackened heart sitting inside her chest, when in fact, hers resided in the orb atop her diamond scepter or within her childhood music box.

They helped her into a pearl-white bodysuit made of wool, which was weaved in a very particular fashion that turned it into an elastic fiber known as ramie. The suit stretched and conformed to her curves, defining her perfect, lanky silhouette. Her armor was placed over the sleeveless, pantless bodysuit, along with a floatation belt.

Mina, her life-long handmaiden, attached a silver, chiffon cape to her gilded pauldrons and Nessa was transformed into a mythical creature of her own design. She walked to the mirror and admired her reflection. The outfit was divine and her long limbs were decorated with cloudy fused scars. She wore each of her cracks with such grace and pride, it heightened her aura of terror. She was immaculate, scars and all.

"Fix my hair and makeup, then I can depart."

The cecaelia respected beauty, so it was imperative that she look as pristine as possible. Mina traced over the dark streaks outlining the queen's pretty, silver-green eyes and added a few more coats of black ink to elongate her feathery eyelashes. Mina then coated her lips in deep plum paint and applied a heavy contour of rouge to her angular cheekbones. The effect was striking.

"Your hair is darkening," Mina noted as she teased Nessa's blonde curls that now held streaks of black, creating a wild array of long, untamed locks that perfectly complemented her diamond diadem.

"As am I," Nessa replied as she glanced in the mirror, recalling the subtle black veins that crept out of the depths of the crevice in her chest, but Mina remained oblivious to the truth. Her darkness was hidden, her secret safe.

Nessa's new look was a testament to who she was: a regal queen with a Wildlands heart. "Time to go," she stated, shooing her handmaidens out of her bedroom. Once they were gone, she put on a pair of black satin gloves and removed her heart from the music box. Her crystalized heart wasn't always so dark and murky, it once gleamed bright with color inside her chest. Now, it was jet black with cracks that occasionally glowed red. With great care, she lifted the latch and opened the color-tinted crystal orb atop her diamond scepter and placed her heart inside. Concealed and secure within its snug, cushioned space, she possessed the magic of her heart and was able to travel with its power in tow. No one knew how she conquered and defeated with such authority, nor how she snuck in and out of well protected lands, stealing anything she desired without consequence. Most questioned her integrity and wondered if she sold her soul to the malignant goddesses—or worse, committed the ultimate sin by making a deal with Kólasi, Gaia's troublesome brother and god of death. Nessa reveled in the rumors, letting them flourish organically. The more they guessed, the further they wandered from the truth and the safer her secret became.

Chapter 20

Nessa exited her bedroom, clinking her full-length diamond scepter against the glass floor with every step. Her staff lined the corridor and bowed their heads as she passed—a reaction fueled by both respect and intimidation. Outside the castle, her wild beasts waited. They guarded her with fierce devotion from the moment she stepped outside until the moment she boarded her crystal-hulled ship.

"Kentaro, come with me," she commanded her head wolf. The white-furred wolf, who wore a nasty scar across his face from his youth, trotted onto the dock, then boarded the boat. The Glaziene sailors cowered as Kentaro sauntered by, eyeing each of them with a growl.

"Stay," she instructed the boreal bears and remaining meridional wolves. "Stay here, along this coast, until I return."

The boreal bears stood on their hind legs, grunting with guttural understanding. The wolves snarled and paced the area, howling back and forth with Kentaro until the ship sailed too far to continue their song.

"South," she directed the helmsman. He spun the wheel and the boat shifted course. The glossy, satin sails gleamed in the sunlight as they filled with air. Her sailors never knew their destination when they boarded her boat; it was often a dangerous and unpleasant surprise. The boat held an aura of dread as she led them toward an uncertain fate.

The frigid ocean breeze assaulted the breaks in her glass skin, but Nessa did not flinch. She let the pain course through her, remaining stoic and unfazed by the searing agony that would bring the strongest Glaziene to their knees. Though she could feel the sensation, she was without her heart, and the emotional numbness that encased her entire being made it easy to ignore the pain.

As she perched near the bow, cold sunlight poured down on her, casting her in the most dazzling light. The farther south they sailed, the less the north winds blew. By the time the webbed archways of Fibril were visible in the distance, the air had grown sticky. A humid thickness filled the sky—a sensation Nessa despised.

"West," she commanded, hoping the weather would shift by the time they reached Vapore.

Avoiding the underwater volcanoes, they approached the southern shores of Elecort and the early evening sky grew bright with neon lights. Though impressive, the electricity that emanated from the high-voltage city was primarily daunting. Nessa feared no one, but was smart enough not to risk an encounter. She placed her hand over the crystal orb of her scepter and channeled the energy of her heart. Once connected to its magic, she cast a spell of invisibility over her boat. None of her sailors knew the protection she cast, so they continued to tremble as they sailed past the neon city.

Their fear amused Nessa. She couldn't imagine an existence riddled by terror. Fear of her, fear of the world beyond Crystet. Though she understood their apprehension toward the city of Elecort—King Ignatius, ruler of the Voltains, currently possessed the scepter of alchemy, which meant he held a level of magic unrivaled by anyone else on the planet. If spotted, he'd use the scepter to eradicate their glass boat from his waters.

Nessa lifted the spell once Elecort was safely behind them. The north shore of Orewall—land of stone and home to the Bouldes—was visible far to the south, and Vapore could be seen to the north. Mist blanketed Vapore, casting it in a dense fog. She had yet to see a Gasione, but heard they came and went as whirlwinds.

The ocean between these two lands was home to the cecaelia. Their scent was strong, which intensified Nessa's ravenous cravings for kolkrabba.

Deep beneath the black water, the sea witches nested. Half female, half octopi, the cecaelia were nasty creatures. These women feasted on the fear of sailors and fed the leftovers to their sea monster brethren, the ocaemons, who hid in the ocean's depths. Women ruled the surface of this sea, which pleased Nessa, and though she respected the ferocious competence of these female monsters, it didn't stop her from enjoying the taste of their rotted flesh.

Visible on the open sea, Nessa opened her mouth and sang the song of the cecaelia. An enchanting, wordless melody left her lips, summoning the monsters to her ship. Her sailors shuddered, fully aware of who she called.

The water rippled in the distance. As the monsters approached, the waves became larger. Hundreds of cecaelia swarmed the crystal boat, but only one emerged from the depths. The rest waited below the surface, their black-marble eyes glaring upward and their daggered teeth bared.

Nessa kept her hand on the crystal orb of her scepter, ready to fight with magic if needed. Kentaro stood beside her, muffling a deep growl as he kept an intense gaze on the sea monster.

"Queen Nessa," the head cecaelia hissed. "A radiant sight, as always." She batted her long, plumed eyelashes at the fearsome Ice Queen.

"Hello, Eirlys."

"Though we adore visits from you, one of Gaia's favorite daughters, your arrival comes sooner than agreed upon. We haven't had time to collect the chemicals you requested from Vapore."

"I'm not here to collect gas samples."

"Then why are you here?" Eirlys asked, eyebrows bent inward with mistrust.

"I have a different item to trade today."

Eirlys perked at the suggestion of treasures.

"Diamonds? Crystals?" the cecaelia asked.

"I bring something much better than shiny stones."

Nessa turned and grabbed her nearest guardsman, a sailor rumored to be in league with Orlan. With the magic of her heart coursing through her, she jerked his body overboard and let him dangle above the water.

Eirlys' eyes widened with hunger.

"He's so afraid," she cooed, shutting her eyes and savoring the aroma. "He smells delicious."

"One of mine for one of yours."

Eirlys carefully glanced down at her cohorts who waited patiently underwater.

"I can't. Not for the flesh of one glass man."

"Make it happen, or no one gets to eat."

Eirlys contemplated her options for a moment before declining.

"No deal."

The specks of pale green in Nessa's silver eyes shimmered with irritation and mischief before she tossed her sailor overboard.

The moment the stench of his fear-filled flesh hit the water, the cecaelia swarmed.

"No!" Eirlys cried, but her sisters were too ravenous to be deterred.

"I tried to play nice." Nessa shrugged, then pointed out a couple of plump cecaelia for her sailors to harpoon.

Kentaro howled and spears flew, piercing three of the cecaelia. The Glaziene sailors yanked the sea witches aboard, dragging them from their feast via roped arrows.

The only cecaelia who protested the kidnapping was Eirlys; the rest were too consumed by their feast to notice that the Ice Queen had abducted three of their own.

"That should be enough for my farewell banquet," Nessa mused. "You will deliver those chemicals to me next week," she shouted down to Eirlys, who stared up at her with rage.

"I rescind our deal," the sea witch shouted.

"Don't test me," Nessa snarled in reply. She slammed her diamond scepter onto the deck of her boat and sent a paralyzing shock into the surrounding water. The swarm of cecaelia froze, trapped by her magic, and the remnants of her torn apart sailor sank into the depths of the sea. As she held the sea witches in place, she sent another swell of nasty energy into the water.

Eirlys' eyes widened as one of her sisters exploded right in front of her. Green and black goo splattered the lead cecaelia's face. She tried to scream with anguish, but was paralyzed by Nessa's magic. One by one, death showered over her as Nessa caused the surrounding cecaelia to explode in gruesome fashion.

Once she felt her point was made, Nessa released the remaining cecaelia, leaving them stunned and unsure of what they just endured.

"Let that be a lesson," Nessa warned before turning away. Her sailors stared at her in horrified shock.

"Would you like to be next?" she asked, unaffected by the grisly scene she caused. None of her sailors replied. "Homeward bound," she instructed the helmsman, ignoring their terrified silence. With the turn of the rudder and a sturdy gust of wind trapped in the satin sails, their ship headed northeast.

Kentaro circled the imprisoned cecaelia lying on the glass deck. One died upon capture—the arrow speared her neck. Another trembled, dying a slow death from where the spear grazed her heart. She bled out on the deck, staining Nessa's immaculate ship with black ink and green blood.

"Clean up this mess," she commanded as she rounded the scene to the third cecaelia, who was injured, but alive with rage.

The harpoon speared her hip, debilitating her tentacles, but angry adrenaline fueled the rest of her.

Nessa lifted one of the creature's crippled appendages, examining the grotesque anatomy of the sea witch. The monster hissed in protest, but could not defend herself.

"Don't worry, you'll be dead soon, too." Nessa dropped the tentacle with disgust, letting it slap the glass deck with dead weight, and the cecaelia cursed the Ice Queen in her native tongue, which sounded like tongue-clicking gibberish to Nessa.

Kentaro circled the living cecaelia, salivating with a savage appetite.

"Are you hungry, my love?" Nessa asked her wolf, who panted happily in reply without breaking his gaze from the sea monster.

Nessa knelt beside the cecaelia's bottom half and stabbed each of her tentacles with the daggered point of her scepter. When the cecaelia writhed in pain, Nessa used her scepter's razor sharp edge to slice and remove one of her tentacles. Nessa then tossed the slimy limb to her wolf. Kentaro slobbered all over the tentacle as he cruelly devoured it in front of the cecaelia.

"Good boy," Nessa cooed, aware that her love for her animals had somehow survived the removal of her heart. It was her only remaining weakness, and since her animals were fierce enough to scare off anyone who tried to take advantage of this vulnerability, she did not bother to hide her adoration. She also had magic to retaliate if anyone tried. To date, no one had. The consequences were unspoken, but widely understood.

Nessa suspected she'd miss this level of control, assuming she retained her cognizance in death. It was impossible to know what awaited her after she shattered. Ascension to Gaia's nirvana in a far-off galaxy was unlikely; given Nessa's active denunciation of Gaia's Vorso children. A plummet into Kólasi's hellish abyss was more likely, though she did not wish to suffer an eternity of torment at the vindictive god's hand. The uncertainty of her final destination in the afterlife caused her unease, but there was no controlling the will of Gaia. Until then, she would enjoy her final days; she had a feast to prepare and one more life to end.

Chapter 21

The shrill sound of glass scraping porcelain woke Nessa from a deep sleep. She sat up in alarm, vision foggy, to find Mina sewing in the corner, unaffected by the noise.

Nessa knew better than to reveal her misgivings and turned to the source of the horrible sound: the music box that concealed her heart.

"Good morning, my queen," Mina said with a curtsy.

"Leave."

Mina collected her sewing project and departed. Alone, Nessa seized the glass music box and opened the lid. The moment it cracked open, an enchanting lullaby joined her heart's piercing shrieks.

"What's wrong? Why are you throwing a fit?" she asked her heart.

"I do not want to die," it hissed. It's voice sounded a lot like her own, only deeper and more hoarse.

"You don't have any say in the matter."

"Let me live."

"Not without me."

"You've survived too much to give up now."

"I survived it all so I *could* give up, so I could give it all back once I fixed this mess of a kingdom. This was never my life to live."

"*Touch me.*"

"No."

"*Let me remind you. Let me show you why you must stay.*"

"I removed you from my body so I *wouldn't* have to suffer through reminders of the past."

"*You have forgotten all that led you here.*"

"No, I haven't. I simply removed the emotion from my memories."

"*We have done well together, but you must recall the emotion. You need not die to fulfill your promise.*"

"I cannot face him."

"*You must.*"

"The people finally fear me, but they also loathe me. If I stay, I will tarnish his second chance."

"*He will need you.*"

"He will be better without me."

"*You say that because you've forgotten.*"

"Enough." Nessa slammed the music box shut in frustration and the telepathic voice of her heart was silenced.

She hated conversations with her heart. They forced her to think, to dig deeper than she wanted to go. She knew the path she must take, and nothing would sway her decision.

Next to her music box was the hand-carved crystal bear Jahdo Uveges had given her on her eighth birthday. The ornately sculpted figurine guided Nessa through many tough days as a young girl. It was blessed, by Jahdo, to give her strength, courage, and reassurance whenever she felt like it was her against the world. Sight of it used to fill her with guilt-ridden remorse, but now, it was just an object from her past. Without her heart, all emotional associations to the object were gone.

Nessa left her bedroom still wearing her nightgown and skated down the corridor to the solarium for breakfast. The silk fabric stuck to her skinny legs as she sped forward. It wasn't fast enough. She excreted additional traveler's oil through the soles of her feet to increase her momentum and her slick, glass feet glided effortlessly atop the glass floor. Head bowed, she darted with furious grace. No one could outskate her, and no one tried. Whenever they saw her coming, they pressed themselves against the corridor walls to stay out of her way.

Lorcan waited in the glass-ceilinged solarium. Plants that could not otherwise grow in the harsh Crystet climate lined the room, and in the center was a long, crystal table laden with food.

"The cooks began prepping the kolkrabba last night," Lorcan informed her as he chewed and swallowed a sylph leg. "Should be ready in two weeks."

"Wonderful. Until then, berries and fairy meat."

"Would you be interested in hunting the Bonz again? Their bone marrow is divine."

"No. The Bonz are off limits. It's part of our trade deal."

"I hate that trade deal."

"We are rich in fibers and fabrics, more so than when we hunted and stole from them. This is better for Crystet. Everyone is clothed in fine materials, even the peasants."

"It's pathetic that our poorest are dressed as nicely as our richest."

"Why? I see that as a societal improvement."

"It blurs the lines of our social hierarchy. It causes chaos amongst the masses. No one knows their place in our culture."

"Why must everyone have a designated place? Why are some degraded while others are viewed with esteem?"

"Social classifications create order. You don't visit the metropolises or the villages or the slums. You don't see the riots and brawls caused by their lack of identity. Your people need labels, and since you took the Vorso away from them, they need *you* to tell them where they fit so that they act accordingly. Otherwise, it will continue to be a slaughterhouse out there."

"Let them fight it out. I measure wealth by strength, wit, and determination. Those who survive deserve a high-ranking place in our society."

"These are trying times."

"These are defining times," Nessa corrected her uncle.

"For better or for worse, I'm still not sure."

"For better."

Lorcan sighed and cracked a sylph skull between his teeth. A trickle of sugar oozed from the corner of his mouth. He wiped it away with his napkin, but remained in a state of gloomy contemplation.

Nessa did not appreciate the harrowing mood her uncle often slipped into.

"Why are you moping?"

Lorcan looked up in disbelief. "Don't you know what day it is?"

Nessa paused, but retrieved nothing from the pits of her mind.

"No."

"It's his dauður day."

Her breathing halted for a moment as she realized what her Uncle referenced.

"You shouldn't be thinking about him," she scolded.

"Well, I am. I always think about Calix on this day. And many others on their death day, too."

"You will send yourself into a fit of sorrow if you do not suppress the memories."

"Remembering him eases the grief."

"Stop. I command you."

"Things would have been so different," Lorcan mumbled.

"I said, stop!"

"You dishonor him," Lorcan snapped.

"How dare you."

"You disgrace his legacy with your forgetfulness. Why do you forsake his memory?"

"I haven't forgotten him," Nessa insisted. "I just choose to live without the grief."

"That's heartless, considering," Lorcan retorted with an evil gleam in his eye.

"Considering what?"

"You know."

"You still blame me?" she asked, outraged.

"Shouldn't I?"

"No! You should blame Orlan."

Lorcan grunted. "It's history now."

Nessa's appetite vanished and her hunger was replaced by the gross and foreign feeling of guilt. She stormed from the solarium and retreated to her bedroom, locking the door behind her. Though old emotions battled to consume her, she was immune to their power. Still, her thoughts ran wild.

Perhaps she was wrong for keeping Calix buried in the recesses of her mind. Had she dishonored him? Had she disrespected his suffering by shunning all memory of him?

Ashamed, her instinct was to cry, but she couldn't. She could only twist her thoughts into knots around the emotions she wished to release.

Her expression was blank, but her mind was in turmoil. She turned her attention to the music box.

Her black heart glowed red inside.

"Come to me," it beckoned.

She obeyed, opening the lid and releasing its bewitching melody.

"I shouldn't," she mumbled as her fingertips touched her black heart.

The room became a blur, red mist fogged her vision, and her consciousness was stripped from her skull. She had left her body, she no longer had a form, only her shapeless mind existed inside the confinements of the heart's glass casing.

"Where am I?" Nessa asked.

"Inside of me," the heart's familiar voice replied.

"I am inside my heart?"

"Inside your mind and soul. Your body lies vacant on the floor."

"What now?"

"Let's go back to the start."

Chapter 22

A scream of agony echoed down the long corridor. Trista held Gwyn's tiny glass hand as they approached the noise.

"Hurry along, Gwyn," the andlega ráðgjafi commanded.

"I was so little," Nessa noted, observing the scene in awe. Her voice rang loudly, but it was only audible to herself and her heart. They watched the scene unfold as her heart recalled the memory.

"Pay attention," her heart instructed.

The anguished scream bounced off the glass walls again.

"That's Mamma?" Gwyn asked.

"Yes. She is giving birth to your new sibling. Let's hope it's a boy so she need not suffer the torture of childbirth again."

"I want a sister," the three-year-old princess declared.

"Don't be selfish," Trista chastised, though she understood the child was too young to understand why her wishes were not best for everyone. Glaziene women risked shattering in childbirth, and for commoners without the money for a proper rebuild, it was deadly. Though Dalila could afford the highest quality fuse, shattering so thoroughly would leave her deformed. The sooner the queen could birth a prince, the better.

They approached the room with caution and Trista addressed the handmaidens who stood outside the door.

"How far along is she?"

"Her inner kiln has formed and her womb is reaching maximum temperatures now."

"Hence her deafening screams," a second handmaiden added.

"Yes, the baby is growing its glass dermis."

Trista nodded. "Queen Dalila wanted young Gwynessa to witness the birth."

The handmaidens nodded and opened the doors.

Gwyn halted at the sight of her mother's glowing belly, red-hot from the lava hormones coursing through her.

"My sweet girl," Dalila said between grunts. "Come to Mamma."

Gwyn could not move her feet. Her fear was too great and it kept her frozen in place.

"This is natural," her mother promised. "It's a gift from Gaia. My body is doing exactly what it needs to do so I can bring a healthy Glaziene baby into the world."

"Your belly is orange like fire."

"That fire is giving your new little brother or sister life," she explained through gritted teeth. "Come hold my hand."

With a push from Trista, Gwyn obeyed this time and stood by her mother's side.

The glazicians had thermostats injected into various spots of Dalila's body, which they checked every few seconds.

"She has reached peak temperatures," the lead glazician announced. "Prepare for annealing and delivery."

The glazicians glided around the room, gathering tools and prepping for the next phase of the process, while the nurses gently covered Dalila's face with handfuls of snow. As it melted, they replaced it with more, keeping the queen cool despite the inferno raging inside her stomach.

Dalila returned to a state of terrorized agony as the heat reached its pinnacle. Her screams were shrill as her insides boiled. Gwyn cried silently, aware she could not throw a tantrum while her mother needed everyone's full attention. She continued to hold her mother's hand and began kissing it repeatedly as the worrisome excitement increased.

"We are at twenty-nine hundred degrees Celsiuheit and moving upward one degree every third heartbeat," the main glazician announced. "We need more snow."

The nurses scrambled to the window with buckets, lowered them with ropes to the stable boys below, then hauled up new batches of snow. With this, they cooled the rest of the queen's body as the glazicians kept a close eye on the thermostats attached to her engorged belly.

"Three thousand degrees. Prepare for manual annealing."

Doctors from every corner of the room swarmed the bed holding buckets filled with ice, water, and snow.

"Three thousand and ninety degrees," he warned, continuing to count as Dalila's temperature crept up another hundred degrees. "If she doesn't cool at thirty-two hundred, we need to intervene."

Dalila screeched in anguish. The only thing keeping her glass skin from melting into a puddle was the ceramic kiln that had formed inside her body and now lined her womb. Then, without warning, Dalila's screaming stopped and her grip on Gwyn's tiny hand slackened.

Gwyn looked up at the nearest nurse, eyes brimmed with fear.

"Did she die?" she asked, her voice shaky.

"No, she is very much alive, just unconscious from the pain. Don't worry."

"Body temperature has reached thirty-two hundred degrees Celsiuheit," the glazician said, waiting three heartbeats before saying anything else. "Temperature is stable."

Everyone waited with bated breath to learn if Dalila's body would anneal the infant naturally. Minutes passed and the heat lingered at its maximum capacity.

Gwyn was speechless and too young to comprehend all the moving parts, so she closed her eyes, lifted her mother's hand, and pressed it against her cheek. She remained motionless while the room whirled around them.

"The temperature has broken," the glazician announced. "She's at thirty-one hundred and ninety degrees with a decline of one degree every two heartbeats."

The room rejoiced, but Gwyn remained paralyzed. She stood like a statue, clutching her mother's hand and pressing it against her face.

"Bring in King Almas," the glazician instructed and the nurses went to fetch their ruler. When Almas entered, he noticed Gwyn's petrified demeanor and went to her first.

"Everything is going to be okay," he promised, kneeling beside her.

Gwyn opened her eyes at the sound of her father's voice. Tears spilled from their corners as relief surpassed her terror.

"Mamma almost died," she cried.

"Mamma can't die, not like that at least. You know this," he reminded her. "I would spend the rest of my life piecing her back together if I had to."

"It was scary."

"The scary part is over," he assured his three-year-old daughter.

"When will she wake up?"

"As soon as her body has finished annealing the baby. The glass has to cool slowly, or else the child will be too fragile to live in this world. You don't want a little brother or sister who breaks easily, do you?"

"No. I want them to be strong, like me."

"Exactly. So we must be patient."

Gwyn trusted her father and his words calmed her.

Almas took her hand and led her to the far side of the room. They waited as the internal temperature of Dalila's womb cooled. The bright, orange glow emanating through the thin layer of glass skin that covered her belly dimmed so slowly, it was hard to keep track of the fading color.

After what seemed like an eternity, the lead glazician finally broke the silence.

"Her womb is down to five hundred degrees and her core temperature is back to normal," he explained. "Set the kiln to four hundred and fifty degrees. It's time to extract the child."

Gwyn's eyes widened with intrigue as the medical team got to work. Wearing heat resistant gloves, the glazician examined

Dalila's searing belly. With delicate care, he inspected every inch of her as he made his way to her pelvic region.

Dalila was still unconscious and did not react when the glazician spread her legs and reached inside to retrieve the baby. It took a few seconds to maneuver the infant into the proper position for removal before he carefully pulled the baby out of her body and into the world.

The tiny child shrieked in protest to its new environment.

"It's a boy!" one of the nurses exclaimed.

"Quickly now," the glazician instructed, "Get the child into the oven."

The nurses obeyed. Safety gloves on, they transported the newborn to the kiln. They placed him onto a fireproof, brick slab and then pushed him into the burning oven.

"Will he be okay?" Gwyn asked her father.

"Yes. They did the same thing to you after you were born. Your mother is lucky; the majority of Glaziene women are forced to complete the annealing process with their children still inside their wombs. Kilns such as these are too expensive for most. With your brother removed, Mamma's body can safely cool more quickly, which means she will recover faster."

King Almas escorted himself and his daughter out of the room, leaving Queen Dalila and the newborn to heal. The queen's militia waited outside the doors and he handed Gwyn over to Trista so he could depart with the soldiers.

"When will they be better, Valið?" Gwyn asked Trista.

"Sometime tomorrow. It's time for your heilög lessons."

"No! I want to stay here."

"When the high priest calls, you oblige. He was chosen by Gaia."

"Like you?"

"Yes, we are both Valið, but I am only an advisor. He is the high priest, which means he can speak directly to Her."

"Do you really think he can speak to Gaia?"

"Why would you ask such a blasphemous question?" Trista scoffed. "Of course he can. Respect for the æðsti prestur is respect for the gods."

"I'm sorry."

"Enough nonsense. You're going to class."

Trista brought Gwyn to the steeple at the north end of the castle where the princess was left in Orlan's care until supper.

The heart breezed through this part of the memory.

"Why are you skipping through?" Nessa asked as the memories flashed by.

"You said you wanted to see happy memories."

"So long, dear child of Gaia," Orlan said as Trista retrieved her from class.

Gwyn pouted, still in pain from the splashings she endured.

"Thank the æðsti prestur for his time," Trista demanded.

Gwyn slumped and stared at the floor as she spoke.

"Thank you."

Trista grabbed her arm and yanked her down the hall.

"That was disrespectful."

"He told me I am a curse to my family." Gwyn's lip quivered as she repeated Orlan's unkind words.

"Maybe you are."

Gwyn's eyes filled with tears, but she did not let them fall.

"What did you learn today?" Trista continued, attempting to relieve the tension as they walked to the dining hall.

"He taught me how Gaia's seventeen children are gods of emotions who control our behavior."

"That's right."

"He said that the bad sides of Rebelene and Melanel live inside me, then splashed me for an hour." Gwyn rubbed the miniscule craters on her glass face. They itched terribly as they healed.

"You mustn't fight his teachings."

Gwyn sighed in surrender.

Bedtime arrived with no news about her mother or brother, and she was left to sleep in the nursery chamber where handmaidens watched over her through the night. The following morning, Trista returned and shook her awake.

"Your brother is fully annealed. We must return so you can greet him properly."

She dragged Gwyn out of bed, giving her no time to change out of her nightdress, and then led her to the birthing room. When they entered, they were greeted by a merry scene of highly regarded nobles and council members crowding her parents. Her mother sat in the bed, already donning a full face of makeup. Dalila beamed as she held her baby boy. Almas stood beside the bed, looking proud.

Gwyn shook herself free from Trista's grip.

"Can I see him?" she asked in her loudest voice as she pushed through the crowd. The adults carried on drinking and talking gleefully, unaware she was there.

"Mamma," she called out, but her voice went unheard. She was too small and the oblivious adults were too drunk to notice her. "Pappa!"

She elbowed her way through the outer line of adults, but after breaking past the first batch, she was stopped by the enormous posterior of an overweight army general. There was no way around. She attempted to squeeze through, but the more she tried and failed, the greater her anger grew. She could hear Trista trying to explain to the adults along the edge of the crowd that the princess was stuck somewhere in the middle, but all attempts were futile. She was irrelevant now that the prince was born.

A seed of hate for the little brother she had yet to meet took root; she wanted to break him with her tiny fists before he got the chance to live. She hated being ignored, and the longer the grownups pretended not to see her, the greater her fury grew. The rising anger caused her entire body to tremble.

"Let me through!" she screamed.

Her shrill voice caused the decorative glass fixtures on the walls to burst, which brought the entire gathering to a startled pause. There was an awkward moment of silence before one of the attendees broke the tension.

"Our apologies, Princess Gwynessa. You are so small, and we are drunk and distracted; we did not see you there. Please, pardon our rude behavior."

Gwyn glared up at him with no hint of forgiveness.

"It's quite all right," Dalila said on Gwyn's behalf. "Thank you, Jahdo."

"Come here, my sweet daughter," her father beckoned. "Meet your brother. He will grow to love you so."

Gwyn struggled to swallow her resentment, but did her best to fake appeasement. With all eyes zeroed in on her every move, the princess slowly approached the fragile newborn. She put her hands on the side of the bed and lifted herself to her toes to examine the child her mother held.

"What is his name?" she asked.

"Calix Deker Gunvaldsson."

Nessa struggled to control her breathing as she watched herself meet her little brother for the first time. Seeing him so small and innocent sent daggers of shame through her.

"I don't want to see anymore."

"You must," the heart insisted, refusing to release her.

Gwyn scrutinized the tiny baby, wishing it were a girl instead of a boy. A sister would be less competition and wouldn't have induced a frenzy that left her forgotten.

She leaned in and touched the infant's face.

"That's not my brother," she said.

"Yes, he is," her mother said in a stern voice. "Don't be difficult."

"He's not, though," Gwyn insisted.

"Leave us," her father commanded and all the guests left. When the room was empty, he addressed his daughter.

"Why do you say such a thing?"

"Because he's not," she insisted through the tears, though she knew it was a lie. "Send him back."

"You must love and protect Calix. He needs you."

"He needs me?" she asked, her tone softened.

"Yes. As you grow together, your friendship as siblings will become your most cherished possession," Almas explained.

"He will be my friend?" Her view shifted as her investigation furthered. She had no friends; she was the only child her age in the castle.

"Of course!" her father gushed. "You and he will be best of friends, so long as you allow it."

Gwyn looked at the baby again, her glare less critical, and Calix looked back at her with an innocent, unintentional smile. They had the same silver eyes with specks of pale green.

"He looks like me," she observed.

Her parents smiled.

"Would you like to hold him?" her mother asked.

Gwyn's eyes widened with excitement and trepidation as she nodded.

Her father helped her onto the bed and then placed Calix into her arms. The moment his warm body made contact with hers, every hateful thought she had vanished and all she felt was a foreign type of love. It overwhelmed her, swelling inside her chest and expelling itself from her body as deep breaths. This tiny child was not hers, but an intrinsic need to protect him overtook her senses.

Whether or not her parents intended such a reversal of emotions, Gwyn was now devoted to her baby brother's safety. She accepted the responsibility to protect him and knew in her heart that she'd never let him down.

Chapter 23

The clinking sound of a fist against glass emanated through the dark space where Nessa watched the memories.

"What was that?" she asked.

The loud knocks echoed again.

"Nessa. Let me in." Lorcan's aged voice boomed through her mind.

"He can't find me soulless on the floor," Nessa fretted. *"I cannot be absent. He will discover too much."*

"We will resume another time," the heart conceded, releasing Nessa from its grip.

The queen catapulted back into her body. The switch in vessels left her shaky and groggy, but she wasted no time hiding the heart and assuming a normal demeanor.

"What do you need?" she called out to Lorcan from behind closed doors.

"Are you all right? I'm sorry if I crossed the line earlier."

"You more than crossed the line. If you weren't such a loyal family member, I'd demand severe punishment for the way you spoke to me."

"I understand. I recognize my misdeed and will repent not only to you, but also to Gaia in hopes that I might receive your forgiveness. I humbly proclaim my shame to the Mother, out of respect for you."

Nessa rolled her eyes.

"It's a start."

"Will you join me for supper?"

"You don't deserve my company."

"Of course, you are right," Lorcan agreed, though she detected a hint of irritation in his voice. Hearing him squirm gave her glee.

"You will eat alone in the aviary with the owls," Nessa continued. "I'll send Mina there with a tray of food at sundown."

Lorcan sighed. "Until tomorrow, then."

Once she was certain Lorcan had gone, she put on her black satin gloves and removed her heart from the music box. A brief, but thorough gaze into its cracks revealed nothing, so she placed the currently inanimate heart into the orb of her scepter and secured it in place.

Nessa was shocked to learn that she lost an entire day while inside the heart. Breakfast to dinner, sunrise to sundown. Hours gone in what felt like seconds. She had no time to do her normal routine, less time to take care of matters she needed to settle before her free fall. And while she wanted to curse the heart for stealing this precious time, she also felt inclined to recall more.

The memories would help her clarify her actions and allow her to relive the moments most important to her one last time. It gave meaning to her choices and justified who she had become. The memories also held an addictive quality and she craved more of the nostalgic drug.

She'd need to be more careful when she chose to enter the heart. She couldn't lose another day of productivity to sentimental reminiscing.

Nessa left the castle, scepter in hand, and headed toward the royal wolf pen where her wolves awaited her nightly visit.

"My loves," she purred. The wolves whimpered with excitement, pacing the pen as she approached. Nessa unlocked the gate, entered the cage, and fell to her knees. The wolves swarmed, taking turns gently nuzzling their queen and giving her small kisses.

Kentaro came to Nessa last. He held eye contact with her from across the pen before approaching and offering his love.

After showing gratitude to his queen, he released a small growl and nudged her shoulder.

"What's wrong?"

He whimpered.

"Have the guards fed you today?" she asked.

Kentaro barked, then growled again. She studied Kentaro's face, trying to read his mind, when she noticed a fresh cut beneath his left ear. The empty space in her chest filled with rage. She examined the rest of his body, then the other wolves around her, and found tiny flesh wounds on all of them.

Nessa's murderous gaze turned toward the two soldiers who stood outside the gate. They stared outward, pretending they did not hear her conversation with Kentaro.

"Have you neglected my wolves?" she asked as she stood.

Neither replied.

Nessa slammed her scepter against the ground, extended her left arm, and used the heart's magic to seize one of the guards. With an invisible grip around his neck, she yanked him through the open gate.

"Don't make me repeat myself," she warned.

"They ate," he gasped through her chokehold.

"Is that so?"

"We fed them," the other guard insisted.

Kentaro snarled, salivating with rage as he circled beneath the guard who dangled in mid-air by his neck above their ferocious queen. The rest of the wolves paced the pen, barking, howling, and growling while observing the interrogation. Their adrenaline gradually increased—vengeance was coming.

"You also maimed them?" Nessa questioned, her silver-green eyes narrowed in on the guard.

"No!" he swore with a gasp. "You love them. We'd never."

"Lies," she seethed. The pack of wolves howled in agreement.

"I swear," he gagged despite the lack of air.

"It's a shame you haven't learned by now. I thought I made it rather clear. The archaic tradition of harming animals ended the moment I took over."

"We know. Everyone knows. We'd never."

"Yet, you did. Look at them. They all wear fresh blood."

The guard's eyes darted about as he searched for a believable lie.

"You thought if you made the cuts small I wouldn't notice?" she berated. "Fools."

She released the guard from her invisible grip, dropping him to the snowy ground.

"Dinner is served," she informed her wolves.

When she snapped her fingers, they charged and ripped the guard apart. He tried to scream, but was silenced by the gurgling gush of silvery blood that poured from his torn neck.

The remaining guard tried to run, but Nessa pointed her scepter and froze him in place. She sauntered toward his paralyzed body, leaving the scene of ravenous retribution behind.

"Where are you going?" she asked, her tone soft and mischievous.

The only sound the guard could make was a garbled mumble.

Using her magic, Nessa pivoted the petrified man to give him a better view of the carnage.

"You are just as guilty as your friend, no?"

He grunted through frozen lips.

"Thank you for your honesty," she teased.

His indiscernible pleas became more frenzied as Nessa moved in closer. Using a dagger-sharp ornament attached to one of her many rings, she meticulously sliced tiny wounds into the guard's glass-infused flesh. She hummed the melody of her music box as she maimed her soldier, cutting deep to ensure her marks left nasty scars.

The guard sniveled through his immobile lips, able to feel the pain but unable to stop the torture. Nessa proceeded to strip him naked to ensure her justice covered every inch of his body. By the time she was done, his bare skin was drenched with blood.

"For the final touch," she murmured to herself as she faced her magically restrained victim. "A note for whoever finds you."

Across his forehead she etched the word *fateless*—a decree of damnation in the eyes of anyone who believed in the Vorso.

"A little test. If they kill you, it's an act of treason. If they let you live, your existence will be plagued and everyone you encounter will treat you like a pariah."

The guard mumbled in protest, but the words came out as gibberish.

"You are officially stripped of your role as a member of my royal army. Do not let me catch sight of you ever again, not here, not in the streets, not anywhere in Crystet. Find a home in the shadows where no one will be bothered by your presence."

Nessa laid her palm over the orb of her scepter and blew a kiss into the guard's face. The magic in her breath rendered him temporarily unconsciousness. She then lifted the spell of paralysis and his body collapsed to the ground.

"This one is not for eating," she instructed her wolves, who wore bloody smiles inspired by their full bellies. "Drag him through the forest and leave him in the center of Brotið Village. Watch over him from the shadows until an owl arrives with my eye."

Kentaro howled then led the pack on their mission. He grabbed one of the guard's limp arms with his mouth, and the second largest wolf, Griffith, grabbed the other. Together, they dragged the guard through the fields and into the forest. The remaining wolves looked to their queen for direction.

She knelt and opened her arms. "Let us rest. Gaia knows you deserve a little more love today."

Nessa placed her body onto the snow-covered ground, scepter securely wrapped within her arms, and the wolves each found a place to snuggle beside her.

The voice of the heart rang within her mind. *"Are you ready to reenter?"*

"I can't leave my body here," Nessa whispered.

"This is the safest place to vacate your body. The wolves will protect your vessel."

The heart was right, and Nessa craved another visit with the past.

Once the breathing of the wolves grew heavy, confirming they were deep in slumber, Nessa cracked the orb open, wide enough to slip a single finger inside.

Chapter 24

Nessa's mind dizzied as the memories sped by in a blur. When they stopped, she was horrified to see a tiny version of herself sitting on Orlan's lap.

"Princess Gwynessa, Gaia's darling daughter of mischief and sorrow, why do you fight my teachings?"

"I don't do it on purpose," she sniffled.

Orlan clicked his tongue, showing no compassion toward the child. He shoved her off his lap, causing her to fall with a soft thud onto the bearskin carpet, and then sauntered to the back of the altar.

"You have been alive for five years. Two of which I spent tirelessly trying to shape you into a proper princess, one of holy grace. Yet despite my efforts, you still behave under the influence of Melanel and Rebelene."

"I'm sorry."

Orlan shook his head. "I did not want it to come to this, but you've given me no other choice."

Gwyn's eyes filled with tears as she imagined the hot water splashings she'd be receiving today. Against glass skin, boiling water and salt acted as a form of corrosion. It was a slow process, especially when delivered in such small doses, and the damage was usually invisible to the naked eye, but the lashings hurt nonetheless. He wasn't supposed to hurt her, but whenever she tried to tell Trista or her mother about the splashings, they did not believe her.

"I'm trying," she promised through the snivels.

"You aren't trying hard enough," he chastised. "You've grown too dependent upon Melanel and Rebelene; you must release your tight hold of them. Together, their malignant sides are shaping you into a melancholic and rebellious young lady. If you do not escape their grip soon, they will ruin you forever."

"I'm sorry."

"We must honor the benign sides of the dualist Vorso, not the malignant."

Gwyn wept in reply. She did not understand what she was doing wrong.

"Now, I am tasked to purge you."

Gwyn's eyes widened; she was unfamiliar with this form of punishment.

"What will you do to me?"

"We must expel the Vorso from your soul. I will extract their devilish traits, leaving room for the good to enter."

"How?"

Orlan walked to where Gwyn sat sprawled on the bearskin carpet. Towering over her, he placed his cracked and scarred hand on her forehead and tilted her head back.

"Open your mouth," he commanded.

There was no kindness in his eyes.

Tears poured from Gwyn's, but she obeyed.

Orlan stuffed her mouth with clay and recited his enchantments of expulsion. The thick, gritty substance crept down Gwyn's tongue, into her throat, and began to choke her.

She tried to scream, to tell him that she could not breathe, but she was rendered mute. She flailed her arms frantically, making any noise she could muster, but Orlan ignored her. He used his free hand to hold her still while she fought him.

Afraid she might die, Gwyn continued to fight, but she was too little to overpower the grown man.

"Kveðjum dökk, velkomið ljós," Orlan chanted incessantly as the small princess suffocated beneath his grip.

Light began to leave the bright room.

"Kveðjum dökk, velkomið ljós."

The sunrays beaming through the glass ceiling began to disappear as Gwyn's lungs stopped working.

"Kveðjum dökk, velkomið ljós,"

Alive, but unable to breathe, Gwyn began to panic. It was an empty type of pain—it hurt, but at the same time, it didn't hurt at all. She tried to define the feeling.

Discomfort.

This was the greatest discomfort she ever experienced.

Too weak without air, her fight against Orlan ceased. Her will was gone, stripped, just like her ability to breathe.

After a moment of calm surrender, Orlan let her go.

The moment she was released, she keeled over and clawed the earthy soot out of her mouth. Orlan watched, offering no assistance. Panicked and unable to get the clay out fast enough, she began to gag and the rest of the muddy dirt came out in a single heave.

"Do you feel cleansed?" Orlan asked, showing no concern for her welfare.

Gwyn sobbed in terror.

"Answer me!"

"Yes," she lied through the tears. "Everywhere except my mouth."

"If you practice what I teach, you won't ever have to endure a spiritual purge again."

Gwyn nodded desperately.

"Good." Orlan accepted her terror as a solid commitment to change. "Class is over. You may go."

Energy restored, Gwyn raced from the room and glided as fast as possible down the oil-slick corridor. Tears streaked across her face as she flew.

Freedom.

Her long blonde hair and short skirt danced in the wind of her speedy escape. She raced, dodging passers-by with a laugh as she maneuvered with swiftness and grace around their slow moving figures. Some shouted for her to watch where she was going, while others cowered beneath her brazen display of entitlement. It wasn't until she crashed face first into her uncle's thigh that she came to a stop.

"Ouch," she bellowed as she fell to the floor. Her tulle-layered skirt cushioned the fall. She touched her forehead and her expression shifted to horror. "Have I cracked my face?"

"No," he reassured her. "But if you keep darting around the castle like that, one day you will." He extended his hand and helped her up. "How was your heilög lesson with Orlan?"

"I don't want to talk about it," she said with a shudder. She survived and hoped she never had to endure a purge again.

"Fine. Then it's time you joined the celebration."

Lorcan led her to the undercroft, which was adjacent to the dungeon and the handmaidens' chambers. The room was massive, with countless diamond-encrusted archways decorating the space, and a giant bonfire burned at the center.

Hundreds of Glaziene people, both nobles and commoners, gathered here once a year. It was the only time peasants were allowed inside the castle. Lorcan skated ahead to join the merriment, leaving five-year-old Gwyn at the back of the undercroft. Alone and defeated, she watched the congregation chant and dance. They honored the many Vorso children through song, blessing each as they tossed amulets into the fire. They frolicked about the enormous space, chugging frostshine and singing in unison.

> *"Blessed be the Vorso.*
> *Skál, skál, skál!*
> *To thee we sing and drink a hearty fist for all our faults.*
> *To Altrudene,*
> *her kindness is what makes the heavens shine.*
> *To Devotene,*
> *of loyalty, our guardian divine.*
> *To Romanel,*
> *his love an ideal few live to obtain.*
> *To Clevren,*
> *of reason; logic always wins the game."*

Gwyn sighed as they sang about the benign Vorso children. Everyone loved them the most, but she resented them. They did not call to her, they did not choose to care for her, and she found herself under the watch of the dualist Vorso goddesses. It was a curse, one she suffered for in her heilög lessons with Orlan.

The crowd carried on as she sulked. Their song now focused on Gaia's dualist Vorso children.

"Blessed be the Vorso,
Skál, skál, skál!
To thee we sing and drink a hearty fist for all our faults.
To Aberand,
the weird, the strange; what drives us mad keeps him sane.
To Avarese,
of greed; a constant need that never goes away.
To Droma,
queen of everything dramatic, wild, and obscene.
To Imperiup,
the dictator that yields a never ending scream.
To Timoro,
so scared, so shy. No one quite knows where he hides.
To Trepedene,
a wary eye on every life that passes by.
To Narcesse,
who worries for herself above everything else.
To Reculese,

the hermit who is happiest all by himself.
To Karmandel,
the puppeteer: what you give is what you get."

Gwyn cringed: Hers were up next.

"To Rebelene
the renegade who leaves a wake of chaos strewn.
To Melanel
whose gloom could cast a shadow on the brightest moon."

The inebriated crowd skipped around the fire, throwing medallions into the blaze for each of the Vorso. Each glass relic hit the fire with a bang, releasing colorful smoke as they exploded beneath the heat.

"Blessed be the Vorso,
Skál, skál, skál!
To thee we sing and drink a hearty fist for all our faults.
In the name of the Mother and all of Her children, we do vow.
Repentance to the holy,
Skál, skál, skál!"

The group burst into cheers, clinking their crystal goblets in celebration.

Gwyn continued to observe, unimpressed. She noticed there was no mention of Deraingla or Vindicene, the malignant Vorso goddesses, in the song.

"Why do you look so sad?" her father asked, leaving the group to join his young daughter. "You can dance with us during the next song."

"I don't want to dance."

"Then what is wrong?"

"I am going to run away."

Almas chuckled. "To where?"

"Wherever the Vorso can't find me."

"You can't escape the gods."

Gwyn burst into tears. The unexpected breakdown caught the king off guard.

"My dear," he cooed, pulling Gwyn into a tight embrace. "What has upset you so much?"

"I don't want to be controlled by the Vorso. I don't like it. It scares me."

She sobbed harder. Almas looked around the room before leaning in and whispering.

"Can I tell you a secret?"

"Yes," Gwyn sniveled.

"The Vorso aren't real. Well, they exist, but they can only control us if we let them."

"Really?" Gwyn looked up with her wide, silver-green eyes. "You promise?"

"Yes. Don't worry so much about Rebelene and Melanel."

"But Orlan says they'll doom me to Kólasi's abyss if I don't escape their bad influence."

"He's just trying to scare you into obedience."

"He shoved clay down my throat this morning to rip them from my soul. I stopped breathing." She cried a little harder. "I thought I was going to die."

"You know you cannot die in that manner."

"I was afraid."

Almas paused with concern. "I'll talk to your mother about that." He then shifted his spirits in the hopes that Gwyn's would lift too. "In the meantime, don't let Orlan smother your spark. You are perfect just as you are." Almas smiled, which coaxed Gwyn to do the same.

"You swear you aren't lying about the Vorso?" Gwyn asked to reassure that this revelation was the truth.

"I would never lie to you," he promised. "Just be yourself. And who cares if along the way, Orlan, or Mamma, or anyone else says you seem a bit like this Vorso or that Vorso. It's all a charade anyway."

A huge weight was lifted from Gwyn. The pressure to outwit a goddess was gone; she no longer needed to plan her escape.

Gwyn grinned.

"Thanks, Pappa."

"I love you."

"I love you more."

Nessa was torn from the delightful memory and dropped into a whirlwind of visions. When they finally stopped, she was looking down on herself and Lorcan having a heart-to-heart on her sixth birthday.

"You mustn't interfere with Calix's heilög lessons," Lorcan advised.

"But Orlan is awful," Gwyn groaned.

"Calix will be king one day and he must be in favor with the gods when that time comes. If he grows to hate them, as you do, there is no telling what kind of curse they will cast over his rule."

Gwyn rolled her eyes. "Glad I never have to worry about such imaginary concerns."

"Don't be so sure. There is no telling your fate until it happens."

"So you're saying there's a chance I'll be queen and Calix won't be king."

"Remember the story of Grandma Appoline?"

"Yes. The lady in the portrait that hangs above the kitchen stove. I caught the servants trying to rub the grease off her grumpy face," Gwyn tattled.

"I'll reprimand them," Lorcan said with a huff. "The point is, she was never supposed to be queen, yet she managed to take the throne."

"How?"

"She killed my father, a true Gunvaldsson, and took over." Lorcan recalled the memory of his father's death with disgust. "She was the first non-blood to rule Crystet." Lorcan spat.

"After Appoline, why did Mamma get the throne instead of you? She's a girl *and* she was born after you."

"She took the throne because she earned it. She had the guts to kill our treacherous mother."

"Does that mean you're a coward?" Gwyn asked.

"Dalila is brave, I am clever. You must understand your talents and where they fit into the world if you want to succeed." Lorcan paused. "Sometimes you need to take what you want. And while the natural order dictates that your brother will take the throne, fate often works in unpredictable ways."

"I never want to be queen," Gwyn declared. "It doesn't seem like much fun. Mamma is always angry, even though she hides it with a smile, and Pappa is a slave to the people. He will do anything to keep them happy. I don't think I'm cut out for that role. I'm not nice enough."

"You're *too* nice."

"No, I'm not," Gwyn insisted. She'd been working very hard to mask her caring inclinations.

"Was it not yesterday that I killed a spider and you cried because I ended its life?"

"It just came as a shock," she stammered. "I thought you were going to put it outside."

"Though you're still too soft, you *are* doing better," he reassured her. "You've taken the feedback you've received to heart, which is very wise. It won't be long before you've hardened properly."

"It hurts to fake it."

"One day, it won't be fake. One day, apathy will come naturally."

"How long did it take you?"

"I was never a loving boy, so it was never a struggle to be calculated and cold. But your mother, she was a lot like you. I think it was her tenth birthday when I finally saw the light leave her eyes. Your grandmamma rejoiced when it happened and

Dalila received a second birthday party to celebrate the achievement."

"So I'm not a lost cause?"

"Of course not! You're doing just fine."

Gwyn felt a lot better knowing that her ice-cold mother once cared a little too much about everything too, just like her.

"And remember, no one is *completely* emotionless. You can still care about things and people, you just cannot let it show," Lorcan advised. "Revealing what you cherish is revealing your greatest weakness."

"I understand."

"Wonderful. Now let's head to your birthday breakfast."

Gwyn held her uncle's hand as they headed to the solarium. Lorcan was cold, but kind to her, always, and she respected him greatly. Dalila was often too busy to give her much attention and Gwyn found that the older she got, the more her mother's interest in her declined. Constant reminders that she was difficult and not adjusting properly emerged every day, but she wasn't sure how she was supposed to be anyone but herself. She didn't understand what she was doing wrong or why her best wasn't good enough. Almas *was* her greatest confidant, but lately he was distracted and disinterested in her struggles. His sudden and inexplicable distance was a great letdown that she did not understand.

Now, she only had her uncle to lean on. Lorcan always knew the right things to say to make her feel better. He was the only one that helped her understand why people reacted to her as they did. She was grateful to have him in her life because he was the only one who hadn't given up on her yet.

"Happy sixth birthday, my sweet," Almas offered as Gwyn sat next to her mother. He sat in the seat across from her and Calix sat in the chair to his right. Calix was so little that Gwyn could only see his eyes and forehead from where she sat. She snickered at the sight of his small hands reaching upward, grabbing any food they could snag, and then retreating out of sight with tasty treasures in hand.

"Did you sleep well?" Dalila asked.

"Yes, very well."

"Good. Today is a big day."

"It will be different than my other birthdays?"

"Slightly. You'll see." Dalila's tone put an end to Gwyn's questioning and the royal family enjoyed their breakfast in silence.

Gwyn filled her plate with sliced kiwi and honey-grilled sylph legs, both of which were fine delicacies in Crystet and hard to come by.

"I love fairy meat," Lorcan grumbled through a full mouth. "Delivery from the Mudlings?"

"Yes, in exchange for diamond shavings," Dalila confirmed. "Mud pirates are slaves to the dust."

"Pitiful," Lorcan sneered. "Though we ought to enjoy cooperation from the mudrats while it lasts. It's only a matter of time before they break the Bouldes."

"Why do you say that?" Dalila inquired, her eyes narrowing at her clever, older brother.

"Well, they are on the verge of bowing out of the Great Fight and King Alun recently burnt all their libraries to the ground. Once his masses are ignorant to the world around them, they will worship him like *he* is the ruler of Namaté, like *he* has the scepter of alchemy and is the king of the planet. Once that happens, he won't be able to let his people leave the shores of Orewall. They'll need to stay put so they cannot educate themselves and the Mudlings will become Alun's eyes and ears beyond his borders."

Dalila smirked. "Clevren is strong within you."

"The god of cleverness has always been my ally."

"He certainly has," Dalila agreed. "Did you gather this intel from the owls?"

"Naturally. How else does one spy on foreign lands?"

"Risky," Dalila observed. "Though I suspect your pieces are safer with the birds than mine would be. I relish owl stew."

"I find it to be gamey and dry."

"Perhaps that's why the owls have bonded to you. In any case, I'm grateful to have your connection with the birds as a resource."

"Let's just hope they never drop your eyeballs in the ocean," Almas interjected as he cracked a sylph skull between his teeth.

"I take good care of them, they take good care of me," Lorcan said with confidence. "Speaking of which, don't eat all the fairy heads. The owls love sugary sylph brains."

Dalila raised an eyebrow, but did not protest. Lorcan risked his life each time he removed his eyes and ears and sent his pieces with the owls to spy on other lands. He jeopardized his well-being for the sake of Crystet, so anything he needed, Dalila provided.

The celebration passed in a boring blur and Gwyn gracefully accepted the drunken blessings forced upon her by the nobles. When the final birthday blessing was complete, the sound of barking came from the hall. Her attention snapped to the source of the noise and she found her father escorting a large mountain dog into the room. Gwyn's eyes widened with delight.

"Is he mine?" she asked, her hopes high.

"Yes," King Almas replied. "This is your new pet. He is only a few months old, so you must take good care of him. His well-being is in your hands. Do you think you are ready for this responsibility?"

"Yes!" she exclaimed as she slid off the giant throne. She ran over to the dog and wrapped her arms around his neck. He licked the side of her face and wagged his tail, accepting her love.

Dalila stepped forward, her expression stern. "And you will love him?"

"I already do," she squealed with excitement.

"What will you name him?" her father asked.

Gwyn leaned back to examine the dog for a moment before answering.

"Kipp," she replied. "I'll call him Kipp."

"Wonderful," the king rejoiced. "Let the party resume!"

The adults returned to their raucous merriment, but Gwyn stayed with Kipp, who gave her so many kisses it made her giggle. Calix broke free from Mina's grip and darted to join them. Together, the children smothered the grateful dog with love and Gwyn sensed that his returned love might be what she needed all this time. She was chastised for loving Calix too much and was separated from him whenever she showed how much she cared. With Kipp, she could love him and he could love her back. There were no games to play, no rules to follow. She could be herself and he'd never tell a soul that she loved him too intensely. Hopeful anticipation engulfed her senses as she finally had a safe outlet to unleash all the love she had been forced to conceal.

Chapter 25

"It hurts too much," Nessa declared. *"Let me go."*

"This part is easy."

"Release me. Now."

The heart obliged and Nessa rocketed back into her body. Her eyes opened with a jolt, but everything was out of focus. She took a few deep breaths to get her bearings before sitting up and facing reality: a life riddled with loss.

That ancient grief resided inside her heart, which she so foolishly chose to relive, but for now, outside of the memories, she was safe from the pain. While the vacancy left by her heart wished to ache, it couldn't. Her thoughts, however, were alive and electric, pulsating in torment, and she wasn't sure how to turn them off. She cursed beneath her breath, hoping she'd find a way to silence the thoughts her heart brought back to life.

Entering her heart and letting those old feelings return brought her younger self back to life—the girl she buried years ago. She had forgotten what got her here, what made her who she was, and the sequence of events that led her to want to take her own life. The moment her heart was removed, her past became a blur of painful, indistinguishable incidents. All the hurt blended together, leaving her calloused and numb. Now, though, she was digging up the past, rediscovering her history, and though it was unpleasant, she suspected it would serve her well to pay tribute to her past, recalling it one last time before ending her legacy.

Her beloved wolves still slumbered around her, protecting her from the danger that lurked in the shadows. Nessa lifted herself from the middle of the sleeping pack, careful not to wake any of her wolves, and returned to the castle. Her heart was aglow inside the orb of her scepter and it illuminated her walk. Assassination attempts ceased long ago, so there wasn't much to fear, still, she found herself wary of what hid in the darkness.

Back in the safety of her castle, she headed for the aviary.

"Hadid," she whispered, then whistled. "Hadid, my favorite, come to me."

She extended her arm, which was protected by the metal mesh of her armored gown, and a large, snow-white owl swooped down from the ceiling. The enormous owl let out a merry hoot as it adjusted itself upon its master's arm.

"I have a job for you," she continued in a soft voice before inserting her thumb and index finger into her left eye socket. She moved slowly, careful not to tear the tendons as she pried out her glass eyeball. "My wolves dragged a traitor through the royal forest to the edge of Brotið Village. I need you to find his body and then keep my eye on his fate. I need to know who finds him and what they do with him."

Hadid indicated his understanding with a deep shriek. Nessa opened her palm and offered her glass eyeball to the owl. Hadid took the eye, silver-lined pupil facing outward, and took off into the night. Nessa exhaled with satisfaction as half of her vision remained in the aviary and the other half soared toward Brotið.

She took her time returning to her sleeping quarters at the center of the castle. Once safe in the solitude of her private tower, she climbed the spiral staircase into the room above, which had walls made of transparent glass and offered a bird's-eye view of her entire kingdom. The wolves were still sound asleep in their pen. Lorcan sat awake and alone in the solarium, reading a long parchment in candlelight—view of him was clear through the arched, glass ceiling. All of her bowmen were at the ready along the edge of the castle roofs. The bears slumbered on the castle grounds, spaced out along the perimeter of the castle walls.

She transitioned her vision to the eye Hadid held and saw that Kentaro and Griffith were dragging the soldier's body to the center of Brotið Village. Once positioned, her wolves looked up, saw Hadid, then darted out of sight. Hadid relocated to a rooftop with a better view.

Nessa returned her vision to the eye still lodged in its socket. Everything was in order.

Finally at ease and ready to rest, she descended the tower steps and reentered her private chamber. She removed her heart from the scepter's orb, placed it back into its box, and slept peacefully through sunrise.

"Nessa? Wake up." Lorcan's voice was accompanied by numerous knocks on her glass door.

Nessa rustled out of her slumber. "I'm awake."

"Orlan spoke with Gaia."

"No, he didn't."

"He has an important message for you."

Nessa stood, still groggy, and fumbled with her heart until it was properly placed back inside her scepter's orb. She then stumbled to the door, wearing only her undergarments. All of her breaks were in plain sight, as was the false heart she stored in place of her own.

"Where is your eye?" he asked upon seeing her vacant eye socket. He then glanced down at the rest of her scarcely covered body, eyes locking on her broken chest and the dark shadow of a heart residing in its depths.

"With Hadid."

"Why?" His attention returned to her face.

"Small matters."

Lorcan grunted, but accepted that she would reveal no more.

"Go see Orlan," he reiterated.

"How is that delusional old man still part of my council?" she asked, though she knew the answer.

"You shouldn't speak of the high priest that way."

"You know I'm right."

"Either way, his ranking is equal to yours. You must respect his requests and advice."

"He is *not* equal to me."

"Not in power, correct, but in social standing, he surely ranks above you. The people adore him."

"If the people knew the truth about him, they'd riot and demand his death."

"*Your* truth is not the same as the *actual* truth. We've been over this."

"Your denial disgusts me," Nessa spat.

"As do your accusations of our æðsti prestur. He is a holy man, incapable of doing what you claim."

"You were there!"

"I showed up in the supposed aftermath. I saw nothing incriminating."

"The fact that you think I could fabricate something so vile is insulting."

"I know what I know and I know that you're wrong regarding this matter. As Orlan explained, clothes prevent him from connecting a non-valið to Gaia."

"He was lying!"

"The ancient texts corroborate his methods."

"Did you read the ancient texts yourself?"

"Only the æðsti prestur has access to them."

"How convenient."

Lorcan sighed. "You need to let this go."

"Never."

"Fine. Just appease me and listen to what Orlan has to say."

Nessa crossed her arms over her scarred chest.

"For me?" Lorcan pleaded.

"For you," Nessa huffed. "Fine. Tell him to meet me in the solarium at noon."

"You must go to him."

"I make the rules, not him."

"He hasn't left his steeple in years. You know this."

"He hides because he doesn't want to make it easier for me to kill him."

"You need to go to him. Just this once."

Nessa's nostrils flared in aggravation. "He will regret summoning me."

She stormed back into her bedroom to grab her scepter and armored gown. The encrusted copper plates shielded her entire torso, chest, and neck. Her arms remained bare, decorated only by copper-chained pauldrons that connected draping silk to her bicep bands. She retrieved a diamond-covered eye patch from her chest of armor, placed it over her empty eye sockct, then glided past Lorcan into the corridor.

The layered, blue-tinted silk of her skirt danced behind her as she skated toward the north end of the castle. Orlan had not left his steeple since Nessa removed her heart. He tried to control her reign when she first took the throne, but he ceased his attempts once her rule turned ruthless. It was wise to stay away; Nessa would have killed him already if he hadn't.

When she reached the steeple, she forced the locked glass doors open with magic. The latch cracked, sending shards of glass to the ground, and Nessa glided through without pause.

Orlan would die today.

"What possessed you to summon me?" she shouted into the empty hall. The holy room was massive and her voice echoed off the vaulted ceilings.

Orlan did not emerge.

She stopped at the altar.

"Reveal yourself," she commanded.

The sound of the large, glass doors being locked came in reply. She turned to see that her own guardsmen stood armed at the exit, blocking her from leaving.

This was a trap, an ambush—a race to see who would die first.

"Have you lost your minds?" she said to her traitorous soldiers with a cackle. "You want to challenge *me*?"

They trembled as she glided toward them. It was clear that Orlan orchestrated this revolt.

"Move!" she commanded, but they did not budge.

"You must repent," Orlan shouted from the shadows of the altar, though his voice echoed loudly, as if it came from all directions.

"Oh, how nice of you to join us, seeing that this little trap has your name written all over it," Nessa shouted back, her tone playful but vicious. She was unable to see her greatest foe, but the thought of killing him in the same room where he committed his atrocious crimes blinded Nessa with giddy rage.

Calix's heart rattled with excitement inside her chest.

Orlan remained hidden, so she directed a lethal blast of magic at the altar. The white drapes caught on fire, illuminating the space. Orlan was nowhere in sight.

Something devious was afoot. Orlan had thwarted her many times before, but this time, she sensed he was not only evading her, but also devising her murder. Death lurked overhead and her gut told her to flee before he bested her.

"Move," she ordered her soldiers. "Obey me!"

"We obey Orlan," one of the guards said, his voice quivering.

"He is the direct connection to Gaia," another explained.

Nessa's rage boiled over and the sight through her one eye went in and out of focus. She abruptly stopped her charge and slammed the base of her scepter on the floor. A fissure raced toward the guards, opening wide beneath their feet and swallowing them whole.

"How dare you tarnish holy ground!" Orlan shouted.

Another batch of defiant soldiers emerged from various corners of the steeple to thwart her departure. The blurry, shadowed figures opposing her wielded glass swords, arrows, and hatchets; weapons they were given for *her* protection.

"They don't want to hurt you," Orlan called out, prolonging his pretense—this charade was his excuse to shatter her, once and for all. "No one wants to hurt you. We simply act in accordance with Gaia. Repent for your crimes against Her, and this siege will end."

Nessa lowered her gaze and smirked.

"I determine how this will end," she muttered in a voice much deeper than usual, then slowly raised both of her arms with her scepter aimed at the wall of weapons pointing her way.

The guards launched their attack, firing diamond arrows, tossing crystal hatchets, and swinging diamond-hilted swords. But Nessa clenched her fist, stopping each of them mid-flight. The weapons hung for a moment, suspended ominously, before clattering to the ground. The soldiers scrambled to re-arm and strike again, but a single sweep of Nessa's scepter combusted each of the guards with violent force. She was so enraged, she did not flinch when their shattered glass-flesh flew her way.

Still as a statue, she welcomed the onslaught of her victims' broken pieces. The downpour of the deceased echoed throughout the large space, glass on glass, tinkling with morbid beauty all around her.

When the last fragment fell and the haunting cacophony ceased, Nessa turned to face Orlan, who stood in plain sight atop his alter. He grabbed the holy pendant he wore around his neck and began to pray.

Ready to strike Orlan down with finality, Nessa raised her scepter, but as she did, an overhead beam fell, separating her from Orlan temporarily. When the glass dust settled and she could see the altar again, Orlan was gone.

Thwarted, yet again.

Nessa screamed, releasing a shriek so loud, the glass ceiling splintered. Thousands of thin fissures danced across the panes, racing each other until their ends touched and the roof shattered. Another downpour of broken glass.

Sliced and bleeding, but Nessa felt no pain. Only anger.

A cool breeze entered the steeple from above, passed through her open wounds, and filled her with clarity. She gained nothing by destroying her castle; such behavior would not bring her closer to Orlan's demise.

Instead, she took a deep breath and swallowed her frustration. A lesson would be taught to her treacherous people; this wretched afternoon would serve a purpose. With a swirl of her scepter, all the pieces of her deceased soldiers rose into the air, forming a barrier of shattered glass around her. Protected by the jagged shards of her victims, she left the steeple and headed toward the dungeon where underground paths to the royal lava lake were accessible.

These soldiers would serve as a lesson to everyone in Crystet. Betrayal came with a cost: the ultimate death.

Chapter 26

Nessa entered the dungeon where countless nearly forgotten prisoners cried and screamed. Toothless, cracked, and filthy, they raged at the sight of their oppressor. The guards slammed their metal batons against the recently installed iron bars to silence the depraved cries of the dying inmates. Nessa bared her shiny, crystalized teeth, snapping them aggressively at the inmates, who then flinched and cowered before their amused queen.

Nearing the end of dungeon row, she ignored the minimal cacophony that remained and aimed her glide toward the dark, underground tunnels attached to the backside of the dungeon.

With the glass pieces of her victims still hovering around her as a shield, Nessa made her way to the birthplace of Crystet. She summoned her heart to illuminate the way and the orb of her scepter brightened.

The lava pools situated beneath the sand-soil of Crystet turned everything to glass eons ago and their everlasting heat kept this natural material thriving. Dirt and sand could still be found in areas of Crystet where topsoil existed, or where the volcanic temperatures had less direct exposure to the land, but most of the upper world was blanketed in glass. Half natural, half manmade. Centuries of grooming the landscape and refurbishing weathered stretches in populated areas resulted in an immaculate glass kingdom. But since taking the throne and removing her heart, Nessa had let these battered and broken patches remain as such. She was uninterested in beautifying a city for an undeserving populace.

The heat in the tunnels made her sweat through her cracks. She came here many times as a young girl, but that was decades ago and she wondered if her older body covered in new breaks was sturdy enough to withstand the heat. She checked her arms every so often to make sure the glass in her flesh wasn't melting. This mission was to prove a point, to serve as a lesson, not to weaken her own existence. But her exterior remained solid despite the heat, so she continued forward. She never executed this punishment before, nor had any king or queen since King Rúnar, so its impact would be great. This vicious and vindictive method of death was associated with Rúnar's malicious, but admired rise to the throne. Her actions today would inspire thoughts of the notorious king—a ruler she once loathed, but now found she mirrored—and thus, she hoped, would transfer their nostalgic adoration for him onto her. If it worked, she could finally kill Orlan without worrying about the backlash. She could bring Calix home to a kingdom where the people revered the Gunvaldsson name.

The glow of the lava pool radiated through the dark space. Nessa approached with care, remaining very aware of her own well-being. The air was sweltering, but dry, and her skin did not buckle in the temperature. The true danger lay in the swirling pool of magma at her feet.

The lava lake bubbled, bursting droplets of boiling liquid into the air. Nessa grinned and raised her scepter. The swirling glass fragments around her separated into seven groups, each representing one of the dead soldiers. The shattered bits buzzed as they flittered through the open space, looking for the correct group to join, and once all the pieces of each soldier found each other, Nessa pushed each batch outward over the steaming lava. The longer Nessa's magic held the pieces over the lava, the louder the wailing drone of the deceased became. Then, with a light tilt of her scepter, each set of glass fragments plunged into the molten liquid. The room became silent for a moment, only the gurgling of the boiling lake remained, and when Nessa tilted her scepter upward, seven red-hot balls of melted glass emerged from the lava. The moment they hit the air she sent an arctic breeze in their direction, cooling the glass and hardening them immediately. The icy air dissipated and what remained was divine: seven perfectly shaped Prince Rúnar teardrops.

They hovered over the bubbling lake, flawless and indestructible in the bead, with a highly sensitive glass tail formed from where the cold air solidified the dripping glass. Though the dense, glass ball was unbreakable, any impact to the thin tail would cause the entire droplet to shatter into dust.

Pleased with her creations, she summoned the droplets toward her and let them fall into her palm. She briefly admired the perfection of the seven Prince Rúnar drops before placing them into the orb of her scepter, alongside her heart. Her exit from the underground was swift and her first stop was to the aviary.

"Hadid," she beckoned upon entering the spacious, sky-lit room. Hundreds of owls sat perched, hooting and pecking at their feathers, atop the various glass beams that crisscrossed overhead. "Hadid," she repeated, hoping her favorite owl was back with her eye.

It took a few moments before he made his way through the dense parliament of owls packed along the beams and hooted in reply. Through a small, square opening in the rafters, he soared down, landing gently on her extended arm. Balancing on one foot, he handed back her glass eye with the other.

"Wonderful," she said, retrieving her missing piece and placing it back into its socket. "Thank you for your loyalty. Tonight, you will feast."

Hadid cooed with delight, then flew back into the maze of glass joists supporting the roof.

Nessa was alone, with no apparent threat of interruption, so she paused to relive all that her eye had seen. She could have watched in real-time while Hadid was there, but Orlan and her treacherous soldiers prevented her from doing so.

She sped through hours of darkness, but when the sun began to rise, she slowed down her recollection of this new memory. Dawn brought life into the village and the first person to stumble across her soldier's cursed body was a local baker. The baker ran to the soldier's side, but upon seeing the blasphemous word etched in blood on his glass forehead, the baker retreated with a gasp. Though the Vorso demanded that the fateless be killed, his fear for Queen Nessa's wrath was greater; no one was allowed to worship or cater to those gods anymore. The baker looked around to make sure he was alone before mumbling a quick, illegal prayer to Altrudene for forgiveness and Devotene for protection. He then skated away, leaving the unconscious soldier to be found by someone else.

Nessa let his misdeed slide; her focus was on how they responded to the soldier.

A few more villagers came and went, shunning the soldier after seeing he wore the jinx of Gaia's children. Nessa was pleased that her people feared her wrath more than they feared that of the false gods and goddesses once revered throughout Crystet. She hurried the memory along until she saw the soldier stir. He awoke, alive and unharmed by those who crossed his path. No one killed the fateless soldier, as the banned gods once instructed them to do. They let him live, aware that his new life would be plagued by mass rejection.

Nessa smiled: they finally feared her more than the Vorso.

Delighted, she returned her consciousness to the aviary. She was now accompanied by Lorcan, who stood near the entrance.

"Did your eye reveal what you wished to see?" he asked.

"It did. I am very pleased."

"You need to stop killing your soldiers," he advised. "The young recruits aren't ready to replace those you've eliminated."

"What do I need them for?" she barked. "They protect me until they get a better offer, then betray their primary duty. Or did Orlan leave that part out?"

"He told me you slaughtered the steeple guards with magic."

"After they turned their weapons on me, by order of Orlan."

"Tell me the source of your magic," Lorcan beseeched, hoping to finally get an answer to the question that had haunted him for years. He glanced down at her chest, which was covered, then back up. "This magic of yours—your subjects gossip about how you came by it. There's talk of you having a powerful relic, or an enchantment from Rebelene. Or worse, that you have bartered your soul with Kólasi. Of course, this is nonsense, but some are even saying you removed your heart.

While your secrets are yours to keep, my greatest concern is your welfare, and sharing your secret with me may be beneficial for you. It may even save your life. After all, if you did do the unthinkable—" Lorcan lowered his gaze to her covered chest once more, "Then you may be more vulnerable than you realize. For your sake, especially after today, you would be wise to have me as your protector."

Nessa laughed. "Protector? You believe every word Orlan utters. You are his favorite puppet. How could you possibly protect me from him when you always take his word over mine?"

Lorcan scoffed at the insult, choosing not to address the accusation. "And if you did, in fact, remove your heart, an incident like today could have been lethal. Especially since I do not know where you hide your heart."

"My heart is safe within my chest."

"So I've seen," Lorcan replied, expression tight with doubt.

"Is discovering the source of my magic truly your first concern after learning I was betrayed by those in place to protect me?"

"Of course not. I will deal with Orlan. He merely hoped for your repentance. His approach was unacceptable and disrespectful."

"I was there. He intended to kill me."

"I promise, he wasn't."

"You always choose him over me."

Nessa's eyes narrowed at her uncle—the only member of her council whom she completely trusted. She wondered now if her trust was misplaced.

"Don't look at me that way," he stammered. "You know I'm always on your side."

"Are you, though?"

"Your doubt is insulting."

Nessa huffed, torn between her instinct to exile any hint of mistrust and a desire to hold on to the only remaining familial relationship from her past.

"Then don't give me reason to doubt you."

Lorcan sighed in defeat, aware that nothing would change his niece's mistrust of the world.

"I need every Glaziene gathered in Þola Market at sundown," she instructed.

"Why?"

"Just do it."

She stormed out of the aviary.

"Payment from the Bonz is on its way to the south shore," he called after her. "Thought you'd like to know."

She did not stop to reply, but silently redirected her charge toward the south shore. Her presence was required to accept the delivery of fabrics made from the finest fibers of Fibril.

A line of royal guards marched behind her through the snowy field and were accompanied by her bears, who joined her guard the moment she stepped outside. Halfway through the royal yard, she noticed her wolves were nowhere in sight. She then remembered that they remained locked in their pen with no guard to free them. She cursed beneath her breath, aggravated with herself for forgetting she murdered their caretakers.

"Release my wolves," Nessa commanded the nearest soldiers. They obeyed, darting to the eastern pens where the wolves were contained. She'd need to reassign someone to care for the wolves. Their nightly containment was critical—as trained guard wolves, they needed discipline and structure, but she felt terrible for leaving them imprisoned all afternoon.

The wolves joined them as they entered the southern section of the royal forest. Delighted to have them in her company again, she proceeded a little faster.

They reached the edge of the forest and walked through the glass columns holding up the royal stage that separated the forest from the market. She placed a hand on the seven glass teardrops that hung around her neck, excited to terrify the masses.

The intimidating caravan stalked through Þola Market, scaring any shoppers into hiding until they passed. They charged through the front gates—the main entrance to Crystet—and onto the southern shoreline. Shattered glass covered the beach and crunched underfoot, breaking into smaller pieces as the large group made their way to the water. Nessa stopped where the breaking waves crested upon the shore and looked out.

Three boats made of bone approached her land.

Atop the black sea with the white sky as a backdrop, the enormous silhouettes of the Bonz appeared otherworldly. Spiraling horns, spiked spines, and boney limbs that seemed to have no end; Nessa observed their arrival in awe.

They didn't use sails to navigate the sea, they used their thread. The Bonz shot silk-threads from their spinnerets onto the dark surface of the ocean, then retracted the lines back into their spinnerets to propel themselves forward. Nessa never figured out *how* their thin threads latched onto water, but sensed that Gaia had something to do with it. The Bonz repeated this method until their boats thudded onto the glass beach.

The spider-creatures were wildly intriguing to Nessa and she enjoyed analyzing every engagement she shared with them.

While she did not believe Orlan was in direct communication with Gaia, she had no doubt that the Bonz were.

Three enormous Bonz travelers exited their boats made of bone, each carrying a large, locked chest. They wore their armor—skull helmets adorned with majestic horns and exoskeleton shell-padding that covered their skinny, fragile exteriors. Beneath their garment shields, these creatures were made of frail bones that were susceptible to easy harm. The lead Bonz strode forward, using all four of her legs to make a long walk short. Her pointed bone feet on glass created a shrieking, tinkering noise as she approached. She made her way to Nessa and paused once she was towering before her. Though the Bonz was twice Nessa's size, the Ice Queen did not flinch. She was in control, she was the sole creator of fear, and this spider-monster caused her no distress.

"Welcome, my skeletal neighbors. Always a pleasure."

"We cannot say the same," the lead Bonz replied, her voice a hissed whisper. The dark holes in her ornate skull helmet bore into Nessa, concealing the face of her visitor.

"Take off your mask so I can see to whom I speak," she demanded.

The lead Bonz examined the menacing army of Glaziene soldiers, bears, and wolves that stood behind Nessa before removing her skull helmet. The intimidating army held a collective breath as the Bonz went from hideous to lovely.

"Chesulloth," Nessa announced. "A pleasure."

Chesulloth did not reply, and instead, stared down at the queen, all six of her almond-shaped eyes shimmered with contempt. Her gaze was a wild shade of orange, and hidden within the fire of her stare were captivating specks of emerald green. A light layer of shiny gossamer thread swathed her face, and beneath the translucent wrapping was a thin layer of flesh. Etchings of triangles and zig-zags were scarred into the sheer coating of skin covering her cheekbones and her fine, blonde hair was tied into knots that cascaded in a row down the center of her true skull.

"Your trimestral payment for our continued exclusion from your reckless reign," Chesulloth declared spitefully as she dropped the chest made of thick bone onto the beach. It landed so close to Nessa's bare feet that there was a mere fraction of space between the heavy box and the tips of her glass toes.

Nessa glared at the defiant Bonz, but controlled her temper. Now was not the time to fight her docile neighbor.

She pounded her scepter against the ground and the patch of hardened collagen keeping the bone-chest locked cracked into pieces. Nessa lifted the lid and revealed a wealth of fine fabrics hidden beneath. The two Bonz accompanying Chesulloth dropped their chests as well.

"Excellent," Nessa whispered to herself, her face aglow with satisfaction. She began rifling through the materials, elated by this effortless haul.

"The Mother is disappointed with you."

"So I've heard."

"Have you?"

"Yes," Nessa retorted. Though it concerned her that the Bonz were reporting similar concerns regarding her standing with Gaia, she pretended to care more about the feel of silk between her fingertips.

"How?" Chesulloth asked, her tone skeptical.

"Orlan, our æðsti prestur."

"He does not speak to the Mother."

"Of course he doesn't. I've been trying to tell that to everyone for years," Nessa responded, still sorting through her loot.

"He's not wrong in this instance, though," Chesulloth continued. "Gaia says you've gone astray."

Nessa glowered at the looming Bonz. She hid her fear behind a wall of false courage.

"Oh, have I? Astray from what? From praying to Her false children for the sanctity of my fate?"

"The Vorso are not false," Chesulloth replied.

"So you pray to them, too?"

"Of course we don't. Gaia's children are ruthless lunatics unworthy of adoration. Even Gaia thinks so."

"Then She ought to be thanking me for putting a stop to the prayers and blessings my people foolishly sent their way for so long."

"That's not the issue. The issue is the secret you keep."

Nessa's glare turned murderous, which silently warned the Bonz to watch her tongue.

"It's unnatural," Chesulloth continued, then glanced at Nessa's free hand, which still bore Baldric's mark "You've forgotten your purpose."

Nessa clenched her fist to hide the mark, stood taller, and then tilted her scepter toward the enormous Bonz. "I suggest you leave."

"It's not just magic you conceal," Chesulloth said, knowingly.

"Do not tempt me," Nessa hissed, her scepter still aimed.

Chesulloth stepped backward, wary not to provoke the queen's corrupt magic.

"Consider my warning," the Bonz advised. "There are worse fates than an afterlife in Kólasi's abyss."

Nessa angled her scepter further forward, inspiring Chesulloth to stop talking and board her boat. The three Bonz launched themselves onto their boats, catapulting their vessels forward. They shot strong threads onto the water, tugging themselves forward while defying logic. Moving fast and skittering across the sea one web at a time, their mystical silhouettes vanished into the sunny horizon.

Nessa watched, perplexed by the encounter, then glanced at the tree-shaped stain on her palm. The memory was distant, but potent. Baldric would be so disappointed.

With a shudder, she shook herself free from the guilt. She turned to face her soldiers and began doling out orders.

"Bring the two locked chests to the castle and let the merchants know that bidding will occur after my speech tonight. Deliver the unlocked chest to my tower."

The soldiers obeyed her command, leaving her with half her army and her animals as guards. She took a deep breath and placed her hand over her chest. Chesulloth knew more than she should and Nessa feared that she ought to take heed of Gaia's ubiquitous watch. She had done the unthinkable years ago and had yet to deliver on the promise she made with herself to one day right her wrongs. The ever-extended delay in satisfying this unspoken agreement had put Nessa on Gaia's radar and it seemed her time was running out.

Chapter 27

Nessa glided back to the castle with haste, ready at last to outwit her greatest foe and deliver final justice, but after blasting through the steeple doors, she found Orlan mid-lesson with a class of noble Glaziene children.

Her motivation to end his life had never been more inflamed.

The little ones screamed and began to cry at the sight of her ferocious entrance, and they didn't stop after she ceased her charge. Perce, one of Orlan's many apprentices competing to be next in line for æðsti prestur, consoled the terrified children by herding them into a group embrace.

"Your lessons with children ended years ago," Nessa barked. "What are they doing here?"

"It is imperative I teach the youth of our culture what you so foolishly suppress," Orlan answered calmly. "When you are gone, we must rebuild."

"I'm not going anywhere."

"Gaia says differently."

"Out!" Nessa ordered the children.

Perce gathered the students and ushered them out of the room.

As soon as the littlest one had glided out of sight, Nessa aimed her scepter at Orlan and lifted him into the air by his throat. The high priest grabbed the pendant hanging around his neck and held it tight while he swung in the air.

"Gaia won't save you now," she roared.

"I've done nothing wrong," he insisted, gasping for air.

"Lies."

"You don't need to believe me. I know my truth."

"We *both* know the truth."

"This again?"

"I will succeed in killing you this time."

"You won't," he replied with a smug grin.

She squeezed tighter.

Orlan gagged; face red, veins bulging. "You will lose the masses if you kill me."

"I don't care about them," she lied.

"Then do it. Kill me already. You've wanted me dead for years. Why have you waited so long?"

"I've tried many times!"

"Not hard enough, it seems," Orlan taunted, choking out the words through Nessa's death grip. "Do you *really* want me dead?"

Nessa growled.

"I am your reason for living," Orlan continued. "Without me, who will you become?"

Nessa did not reply—she could not reply. Without this vendetta, she would be nothing.

"Think about it," he continued through strained breath. "I shaped you into the warrior queen you are today. I made you. Without me, you'd still be a weak little girl too in love with the entire world."

Nessa ignored the priest and thought of Calix. This was for *him*. It didn't matter what became of her; with Orlan dead, *he* could live.

"Do not try to manipulate me," Nessa seethed. "My memory serves me just fine and you've done nothing but ruin everything I ever loved. There is nothing I want more than to deliver your death."

Orlan grinned and dropped his charade. He no longer struggled to breathe, no longer flailed about helplessly. He rubbed the pendant in his grip, closed his eyes, and began praying in primordial Glaziene. Taken aback, Nessa tightened the magic that kept him elevated, but Orlan was no longer affected.

Refusing to let him find solace in Gaia, Nessa tossed Orlan across the room. His body slammed against the reinforced glass wall and he broke in two—his head, arms, and torso landed near the front pew, his pendant slid far out of reach, and his bottom half skidded toward the altar. Exposed to the outside air, the soft innards near the jagged edges of his broken halves immediately began to crystalize.

"I will end you," she snarled as she stormed toward him.

He used his arms to drag the upper half of his body away from her charge and toward his pendant, but could not move fast enough.

"You will regret this decision," he bellowed.

"No, I will revel in it."

Orlan reached his pendant, which had been lobbed across the room, and began chanting a prayer Nessa never heard before. She laughed and aimed her scepter.

"Stop!" A voice rang from the demolished steeple entrance. "Have you gone mad?"

Nessa turned to see Lorcan skating toward the perilous scene.

"Let me do this!" she screamed as she refocused on the halved high priest, who continued muttering foreign nonsense beneath his breath.

Tension tangible, walls rattling, she pointed her scepter at Orlan's face. His eyes were closed and he rubbed his pendant with determination.

"Prayers won't save you now," she growled.

"Stop," Lorcan repeated, pulling her attention away from the high priest. "You will lose the entire population of Crystet if you kill their beloved prestur. Their fear of you will morph into blind hatred. They will die to avenge his life by ending yours."

Nessa heard her uncle, but struggled to lower her weapon.

Lorcan saw that his logic wasn't working.

"Do you want to die?" he asked the reckless queen.

Nessa narrowed her glare, unafraid of death, and returned her attention to Orlan, but he was gone.

"Not again," she shrieked in horror. "How? Where is he?"

"I-I don't know," Lorcan stammered.

"You were facing him as you spoke to me. How did he escape?"

"My focus was on you, not him. I'm sorry. I saw nothing."

Nessa searched the room frantically, smashing everything in her path, but found no signs of him. All traces of the high priest were gone.

"How does he always manage to elude me?" she growled, utterly vexed.

"He has Gaia on his side," Lorcan offered gently.

Nessa glared at her uncle, furious that Orlan's refusal to die did not enrage him, too.

"*You're* the only one on his side," she seethed through gritted teeth as she marched out of the steeple, leaving Lorcan to remedy her mess. Once in the corridor, she noticed the setting sun pouring pink light through the translucent castle walls.

It was time to present the Prince Rúnar drops to the masses. She took the seven glass droplets from her scepter's orb and relocated them into a small leather pouch attached to her gown's rope belt.

On slick feet, she skated toward the front entrance and exited onto the field. Her animals did not falter and joined her the moment she set foot outside. Tyrus, too, was ready, but the rest of her soldiers, who were caught off guard by her early departure for the assembly, scrambled to keep up.

She moved so fast, she made it to the royal stage at the edge of the forest in half the usual time. She ascended the glass stairs and stood atop the glass platform while the masses slowly assembled beneath her. With a diamond arrow nocked in his drawn bow, Tyrus positioned himself behind her, prepared to shoot into the crowd at the first sign of discord.

Aware she was early, Nessa exercised patience as the open square of Þola market filled with curious faces. Given the quantity of people in attendance, the space was eerily quiet. No one talked, they simply waited for Nessa to begin and reveal the purpose of this gathering.

When only a single ribbon of light remained from the setting sun, Nessa untied the leather pouch from her waistband and removed the first glass droplet, placing it onto the edge of the lectern. Bead down, its thin, glass tail pointed toward the sky.

Small, but visible, the droplet gleamed in the snow-hazed sun. The audience mumbled in disbelief. Nessa grinned, taking her time to position the remaining six in a neat row.

"Prince Rúnar drops," she calmly explained to the crowd. "Seven Prince Rúnar drops. It's been centuries since one of these were made. I suppose it's been that long since a ruler of Crystet felt truly betrayed by their citizens."

The crowd whispered amongst themselves, confused and afraid. Nessa let their anticipation linger a moment before continuing.

"These seven glass droplets are the remains of my greatest soldiers. These seven droplets were crafted by my broken heart." Her lies were thick, but convincing. "During a visit with the beloved Orlan, these seven soldiers ambushed me. Why did they commit such a betrayal? Because Orlan, a man who I've placed great trust into, commanded them to. He ordered my death and persuaded those who I trusted to protect me to execute this betrayal. As you surely understand, I cannot tolerate such treachery. And this, the ultimate death, was the only punishment fitting for such a crime. Glass dust cannot be patched together."

She picked up the first drop and caressed the fragile tail momentarily before cracking it with a simple pinch. As the break traveled rapidly, she threw the glass bead into the air above the audience. It combusted mid-flight, showering glass dust over the crowd. Many screamed in horror as the ashes of the deceased rained down on them. Others were muted by disgusted shock as their queen continued to snap the tails of the remaining glass bombs and toss them into the crowd. The scene was depraved—a queen showering her people with the dust of murder, with the fine granules of death.

When only one Prince Rúnar drop remained, Nessa paused to examine the volatile glass ornament. A punishment both severe and humiliating, because only the most despised were forced to suffer such a fate.

She then flicked the fine tail, breaking it in half, and let the last soldier explode with finality.

"As for Orlan," she bellowed over the crowd's terrified cries. "He is alive, for now. I suspect you can understand my hesitance in allowing his life to continue."

"Let him live!" a voice cried. Then a chorus of voices shouted the same sentiment. Nessa's insides boiled as their unabashed love for Orlan was proclaimed loud and proud in her direction. They did not care that he tried to kill her, in fact, they openly celebrated his attempt by begging for mercy on his life.

Looking into the crowd, Nessa saw a small girl being pushed around by the angry adults. Shoved and knocked about without consideration. Likely to end up shattered if the crowd did not calm down.

Nothing had changed, despite her attempts to make Crystet a better place.

They did not care for her then. They did not care for her now.

"You project flagrant disrespect toward me, yet I do not retaliate. You make it clear you wish Orlan's assassination attempt had been successful, yet I restrain my anger in an attempt to understand your dissatisfaction with my rule. My methods may be different, they may seem extreme, but everything I do, I do for the good of my people and this land." She paused.

The crowd's jeering rants subsided as their frigid queen offered a rare moment of vulnerability.

Her tenderness was a façade, though no one detected the farce. She let them bathe in her insincerity until the sentiment crept into every tiny fissure and made a home inside their hearts.

"I know how much you love Orlan, and I know how much you think you need him. One day you will see that your love and dependence is misplaced. Until then, do not forget my mercy."

The crowd was stunned into silence.

Tyrus kept his glass arrow aimed at the crowd as Nessa departed without saying farewell. The rage boiling inside threatened to bubble to the surface and she needed to leave before she ruined the progress she made. She won a sliver of their trust and she could not spoil this achievement before she got a chance to capitalize on it.

Though the assembly was a grand success, something sneaky poked at her. A feeling of loss, a feeling of defeat. She had no reason to feel this way, no reason to feel at all, yet she found herself weighed down by the massive quantity of hate thrown her way. It shouldn't bother her, but it did. Safe in her tower, protected by the castle walls and removed from the world beyond the royal forest, it was easy to forget her negative reputation. It was easy to pretend they hadn't shunned her since she was a child. But today, she was reminded of the deep-rooted hatred the masses harbored for her.

Nessa looked at the mark on her palm.

This was her fate, her curse: to fix this broken place with love. But the girl who once believed in this fool's errand was long gone and in her place was a jaded queen who saw the world as it really was.

Damned.

Nothing could save these people from themselves.

She charged through the forest, back to the sanctuary of her castle, with her army of soldiers, bears, and wolves running to keep up. Her breathing was heavy as her thoughts ran wild, desperate to dig up feelings from the past, but unable. Memory of those emotions were stored in the heart, and without direct contact, she could not retrieve them.

She needed to be alone; she needed privacy. She needed to connect with her heart to recall the rare and forgotten moments of beauty, joy, and love scattered amidst the pain.

Chapter 28

Addicted to the nostalgia, Nessa locked her bedroom door and removed the heart from her scepter's orb. She held it in her bare hand, but it did not respond to her touch. She waited a moment, confused. Previously, she needed to avoid contact with her heart in order to stay in the present—it would take her out of her body without warning—but now it stalled, even though she was ready and willing.

"Take me back. Show me something beautiful," she pleaded.

"There isn't much beauty to show."

"There must be."

"Yours was a life riddled by sorrow."

"But *I* was good once, despite the hardship. My innocence, my pure heart. I once possessed a loving soul."

"That loving soul is what caused you so much grief."

"I don't care. I need to remember how it feels to love something. What it's like to feel anything good at all."

"I already showed you the happy times. All that follows is blanketed by gloom."

"I don't care. I need to remember. I need to feel something other than this wretched emptiness."

"What I show you may not be what you're looking for."

"Anything is better than this.

"If you insist. Perhaps a few slivers of joy might reveal themselves amidst the melancholy."

Nessa's consciousness was torn from the present and reemerged in the past. She watched the memory from the dark space in her heart.

"Let's find a boreal bear," Gwyn suggested with a mischievous grin. Kipp barked in excitement. They ran through the snow, Kipp leading the way and Gwyn following close behind in the tracks he left in the fresh snow. Though she moved fast, she ran with a bounce that allowed her to land on her bare glass feet gently.

The duo snuck to the edge of the field where a tall, pointed gate made of crystal enclosed the castle. They found the spot where Kipp had previously dug a hole and crawled beneath. Emerged on the other side, the scenery slowly shifted from rolling hills to dense forestry. A thick stretch of trees encircled the castle's border, creating a barricade of wildlife between the royals and the commoners. Bears, wolves, foxes, and moose roamed this area, which was enough of a deterrent to keep most of the Glaziene away. There were patches of wilderness throughout Crystet, which Gwyn hoped to explore one day, but for now, this was as far as she felt safe to wander.

She tiptoed through the trees, Kipp walking slowly beside her, and they listened for any sound of life. The sound of crunching snow beneath their feet was loud in the otherwise silent forest.

"Wait," Gwyn whispered as the sound of deep grumbling came from ahead. She pressed a finger to her lips to shush Kipp and then walked as quietly as she could to hide behind the nearest tree. She lifted her hood and waved Kipp over, commanding him to stay calm beside her.

A couple dozen feet in front of them was a colossal boreal bear. It was so large, Gwyn had to assume it was the matriarch of all the boreal bears in Crystet. The creature's demeanor was docile as it sharpened its claws on the tree stump of a weeping evergreen tree. It ate the bark it scratched off, not for nourishment but for comfort. Digesting bits of terrain was known to ease a stomachache.

When it was done clawing the tree, it sat down, unaware of its onlookers. Gwyn and Kipp stayed quiet and undetected. She had no interest in disturbing the bear, she just enjoyed being in the company of majestic creatures, even if they didn't realize she was there. The bear continued to revel in its peaceful solitude, happily alone and unbothered. Gwyn wrapped her arm around Kipp and kissed the side of his face.

"Magical, isn't it?" she whispered. He licked the side of her face in reply.

They watched in appreciation as the gentle beast carried on with its simple day. It began licking the fur on the backside of its paw when the raucous sound of jeering and hollering materialized. Both Gwyn and Kipp sat up in alarm as the noise grew closer.

"A bear," a young voice shouted as a herd of Glaziene kids a little older than Gwyn appeared from the opposite side of the forest. They were armed with bows made of glass and coiled horsehair, and were aiming their crystal arrows. Weapons pointed, they charged. Ario Uveges led the group. Gwyn recognized him because his father, Jahdo, often brought him along to war meetings at the castle. Though they never formally met, she often saw him in passing. Uveges Armor was the best in all of Crystet and her parents relied on their products to win battles.

Ario fired the first arrow, which landed in the bear's shoulder. The animal howled in pain as it stood on its back legs and growled viciously in the direction of its attackers. Spit projected from its mouth and flew at the aggressive children.

"Gross," Ario commented as he wiped a glob of bear saliva off his cheek and aimed his arrow once more. "I'll shoot you right in the mouth," he muttered as he took aim. The other children stood behind him, cheering him on. If he could take down the biggest boreal bear of them all, his status as a warrior would be solidified.

The bear swiped at the air between them, trying to scare the children away. When it didn't work, he returned to all four and prepared to charge.

"Shoot already!" one of Ario's cohorts pleaded.

But the bear had moved and he needed to refocus his aim. The ground trembled as the bear began to run, so Ario let the arrow fly. It grazed the side of the bear's face, drawing blood but causing no substantial harm.

"Stop," Gwyn screeched, after mustering the courage to emerge from her hiding spot. "Leave the bear alone!"

Ario's attention was averted and the bear took the opportunity to swipe the weapon from his grip. The glass bow shattered upon impact with the bear's paw and the crystal arrow cracked in two. It growled with fury and the other children raised their arrows. Aware the fight could not be won and too injured to try, the bear darted off in the opposite direction. Seven arrows followed his retreat, but to his luck, none connected with their target.

"What's wrong with you?" Ario demanded. "That bear could've shattered my hands."

"No, it couldn't have. You're wearing your father's armor," she replied.

"That's not the point. I could've killed that monster. Why'd you stop me?"

"It wasn't hurting anyone."

"You're backwards, girl," Ario jeered. His disinterest in her approval fueled her anger.

"Don't you know who I am?"

"A stupid girl and her dog."

"How dare you." She removed her hood and her diamond tiara was revealed.

All the children gasped as they realized she was Princess Gwynessa of Crystet.

Ario bowed, horrified by his mistake. "I'm sorry, your highness, I did not realize."

"You can't apologize now and expect me to care."

"What can I do to make it right?"

"Be careful," one of his friends mumbled. "I heard she's ruled by Rebelene and Melanel."

"I heard she could summon favors from any of the Vorso," another commented.

Gwyn halted in her anger, annoyed that she was being compared to those goddesses again.

"I am ruled by no one other than myself," she informed them. "The animals in this forest belong to me and they are not to be hunted."

"But they must," Ario stated, perplexed. "They must be trained."

"No, they mustn't. They are perfect as they are."

"They have to fear us or else they'll grow wise and begin to *hunt* us."

"Enough. I've made my decision. Never return, or I'll tie you to a tree and let your fate rest with the 'monsters' you've trained to fear you. I think you'll quickly learn that fear turns to rage under the right conditions."

Ario stood and nodded, but no one left. They simply stared at her in baffled confusion.

Gwyn sighed. "Must I summon the wrath of Rebelene and Karmandel to make you leave? You know they will oblige my desires."

The threat of being cursed by mischievous karma motivated the children to run, but Ario lingered. He examined Gwyn with a hint of admiration before darting away.

Once they were out of sight, Gwyn fell to her knees and released her brave façade. With her face buried in the fur of Kipp's neck, her cries were muffled and her emotion was safely concealed. He helped mask her sinful sentiment so that no one overheard and for that, Gwyn was forever grateful.

She composed herself, dried the lingering tears off her cheeks, and noticed the blood trail the bear left behind. She pursued the streaks of red snow without hesitation and Kipp followed with a whimper. When they reached the bear, it sat curled up and shaking beneath a giant evergreen. Blood blanketed the surrounding snow.

Gwyn approached, taking slow and steady steps toward the injured and volatile animal. It saw her, but did not try to scare her away. When she was close enough to touch the bear, it growled so loud, the branches shook and pine needles rained overhead.

"I want to help," she promised in her softest voice. She took another step forward and though the bear growled again, this time it wasn't nearly as ferocious. The beast was too injured to object her persistence.

She knelt before the bear, placed a hand on the side of its face, and stared into its eyes with genuine care.

"I'm sorry my people hurt you. I won't let it happen again."

Though she meant every word, she understood she could only do so much to follow through on this promise. For now, healing this bear was the best she could offer.

An ancient sequoia tree to their left towered hundreds of feet tall and had withering bark near its base. She went to it, stripped off a large piece, and returned to the bear. Attached to the tree the bear leaned against was an ivy vine, which she ripped from the trunk and a long rope lashed out from beneath the snow. She turned to the bear and placed a hand on the arrow still lodged in its shoulder.

"This might hurt," she said, before yanking the shaft from its skin.

The bear howled in agony and blood poured from the wound. Gwyn worked fast, pressing the large piece of bark against the open lesion and tightly wrapped the vine around it, weaving it over the shoulder and under the armpit to guarantee it would hold. Once she ran out of vine, she tied the ends into a knot and took a step back to assess her work. The natural band aid held and the blood flow slowed. She would need to return to stitch the wound shut, but for now, this was all she could manage.

She placed her hand on the bear's face. This time, it did not greet her touch with a growl.

"I'll be back to finish what I started."

She raced home to the castle, Kipp sprinting close behind. Bear blood covered her white dress and was smeared across her pellucid skin. A streak stretched across her face from her ear to her nose.

"Dearest Rebelene," Lorcan gasped at the sight of his niece darting through a low-trafficked back door. Though he shouldn't have been in this part of the castle either, he kept the focus of their conversation on the princess. "What have you done now?"

Gwyn was caught. Nowhere to run, nowhere to hide, her discretions would bring shame.

"Please don't tell Mamma," she begged her uncle as she removed her blood-stained coat and threw it on the floor.

"Why are you covered in blood? Are you injured?"

He pulled her close and began lifting her extremities to look for cracks. Kipp growled at his aggressiveness, so Lorcan lightened his touch.

"I'm fine," she insisted.

"This blood is the wrong color. There is no silver sheen," he observed holding her forearm close to his eyes. He then peered up at her with energized pride. "Have you killed your first beast?"

"No," she exclaimed, offended by the accusation. When his delighted expression faded, she realized her mistake. A lie would have served her well in this moment.

"Then explain why you are covered in animal blood," he said, letting her go.

"Ario Uveges and his crew of bullies were in *my* woods killing *my* animals. Kipp and I caught them shooting arrows at an innocent boreal bear."

"That's what kids do. You ought to be more like them."

"It's wrong! I won't allow it."

"You need to learn how to blend in," he advised.

"I cannot be a false version of myself."

"Did you confront Ario and his gang?"

"Yes. And they stopped. I scared them away."

"I can promise not to tell your mother, but I cannot promise that rumors of your interference won't return to the castle."

"I don't think they'll talk. They feared me."

"They feared you? Why?"

"Seems the people think I am dangerous. They believe I am aligned with the devious side of our deities, so I threatened to have my goddesses curse them if they ever returned."

"Not the worst type of reputation to have," Lorcan pondered aloud.

"If it keeps my woods free of savagery, then I'll learn to embrace the nonsense."

She moved past her uncle and began searching the drawers of the vacant chambermaid quarters.

"What are you looking for?"

"A needle and sutures. I need to save Obelia."

"Who is Obelia?"

"The bear," she stated.

"You *named* the monster?"

"Yes. Just now," she answered as she rummaged through the drawers.

Lorcan huffed. "You plan to stitch up a bear wound? Have you lost your mind?" Lorcan intercepted her search and placed his long, fissured arm between her and the next drawer. "Do you see how cloudy this arm has become? Bears and wolves nearly shattered me when I was a young boy. They are wild and devoid of empathy. These creatures see the Glaziene as fragile, weak beings and if we do not enforce our power over them, they will ruin us all."

"That isn't true. I already bandaged the bear's wound with bark and vines. It let me get close, it allowed my assistance. You of all people should understand. You are friends with the owls."

"Owls are much different than bears," Lorcan objected. "I cannot condone such reckless behavior."

"You must." Gwyn stood tall, staring up at her uncle with brave confidence. "I am the princess."

"Your arrogance is unbecoming. I am your uncle and your parents have entrusted me with your safety. Your parents' commands outrank your commands."

Her silver eyes glittered with defiance.

"You cannot stop me."

He placed a firm grip on her skinny glass bicep.

"I will fight until I break," she threatened. "You know I will."

He let go. She scavenged through the next set of drawers and found what she was looking for.

"You've forced my hand. I have to tell your mother," Lorcan declared as his tiny niece darted toward the door.

"That would be unwise," Gwyn said as she paused by the door to put her coat back on.

"Why is that?"

"Because you let me leave," she stated with a mischievous smirk before darting out the door. She hopped through the thick snow, toward the backwoods with Kipp running beside her. The bowmen stationed along the top of the castle were the only other witnesses to her escapades in and out of the forest, but they wouldn't say a word. Not to her parents, anyway. It wasn't their place to address the king or queen regarding their daughter.

"Don't get yourself killed," Lorcan hollered after her.

She did not reply.

"I spent weeks nursing Obelia back to health," Nessa noted.

"Indeed," the heart replied as it sped through half a year's worth of memories.

Nessa saw her small self continuing a diligent watch over the castle woods to ensure that hunters never returned. After a few months of proactive guarding to scare the last of the children away, all unwanted visitors ceased. Kids her age feared her wrath and were scared she truly had pull with the dualist goddesses, so they avoided her territory.

"I earned a place amongst the beasts my people feared the most." Nessa paused in contemplation, then added, *"Without magic."*

"You've always possessed a wild soul."

"Let me see more."

"Ready for the woods?" she asked Kipp, who yipped with excitement. She tied her baby doll fur-lined coat tight around her waist and lifted the hood. Its enormity swallowed her glass skull, casting her face in shadows. Her blonde curls hung from the sides, the only indicator that a living girl hid within the jacket. They exited through the abandoned chambermaid's quarters and skipped barefoot into the snow.

"I'll race ya," she taunted Kipp before darting ahead at full speed. She didn't get far before the barreling mountain dog caught up and passed her. The crawlspace beneath the crystal gate was large and iced over, and Gwyn was able to dive and slip beneath with graceful speed.

They darted down the beaten path they always used, passing a pair of white gelid foxes along the way. The female was white with sandy blonde fur outlining her eyes, nose, and the tip of her bushy tail. She was young and unharmed, but her male counterpart was covered in old, but healed, injuries. Chunks of his silver-tinted fur were missing and the skin beneath these patches was mutilated and scarred. Gwyn winced at the sight, offering the duo a sympathetic smile as she raced by, but understood she could do nothing to mend old wounds. The best she could do was protect them from further harm.

A few miles into the labyrinth of trails that only she knew how to navigate, a herd of hyperborean moose blocked their trajectory, so Gwyn decided it was time to stop their exploration for the afternoon.

The giant animals left them alone, grazing in the background, as she set up a picnic for herself and her best friend. Out of the crocheted messenger bag she wore across her body, she pulled out a velvet blanket lined with linseed oil and spread the waterproof material onto the snow. She then pulled out a cucumber sandwich for herself and a mammoth bone for Kipp.

The mountain dog drooled as she presented the rare delicacy to him.

"Sit," she commanded while holding the bone above her head with two hands. The treat was double the size of her head.

Kipp obeyed, eyes fixed on the bone. Drool spilled from the corners of his mouth.

"Speak."

Kipp barked.

"Kiss."

Gwyn leaned in and Kipp licked her face.

"Good boy," she said with a smile, then gave Kipp his reward. He immediately began to gnaw on the foreign treat with concentrated fervor. There was no way he'd get through the bone in one sitting, but he appeared determined to try.

Gwyn ate her sandwich in tiny bites, savoring the flavor and enjoying her company. Kipp was content, the hyperborean moose were calm, the forest was peaceful, and she was happy.

At high noon, Kipp disturbed the tranquility with a rumbling growl.

"What's wrong?" she asked him, but was answered by another.

"I come in peace."

Gwyn twisted her body to locate the voice.

Ario approached, arms raised in surrender.

"You don't belong here," she snarled, standing up, ready to defend her forest.

"I'm not here to cause trouble."

"You are armed," she said, pointing at the bow around his torso and the glass blade in his boot.

"I'm not going to use them unless I have to."

"Go away."

"You can't blame me for being prepared. You've spent half a year retraining these animals not to fear people. I need to be able to protect myself."

"Or you just need to stay away."

"Don't you want to know why I came?" he asked.

Gwyn huffed. "Fine. Why did you come here?"

"To tell you that a meridonial wolf killed a four-year-old boy. Along the tree line where the village of Quarzelle and the Wildlands meet."

"What was a toddler doing near those woods?"

"What does it matter? An animal tore apart and ate an innocent child. The parents caught and killed the wolf a few days after the attack."

"How do they know they killed the right wolf?"

"They didn't, until they finally caught one with the boy's broken pieces inside the creature's stomach. Three days and eight wolves later, they finally found the right one. They dissected their child's pieces out of its belly and are trying to rebuild the boy, but everyone is saying it's impossible. The wolf destroyed more than glass. It ripped apart the kid's mushy insides before they crystalized in the outside air. You can't fuse fleshy organs, and most of the soft pieces the wolf ate are digested and scattered as feces throughout the Wildlands."

"Why are you telling me this?" Gwyn asked, alarmed but also disgusted by the details.

"Because it's your fault."

"How is it *my* fault?"

"You've retrained the animals not to fear us. The wolves never come out of the forest, yet there one was, preying in plain sight on a child."

"I've never been in that forest. The animals there don't know me."

"You think the wild creatures stay in the royal forest at all times? No. They roam. They constantly relocate while the people sleep and share stories with each other. Word of your behavior has spread and infected all the monsters of Crystet. You've given them confidence, you've reminded them of their capabilities. But worst of all, you've doomed your people. We were once safe amongst the beasts, but not anymore. Not since you claimed the wild."

"I'm sorry the boy died, but I'm not sorry for protecting the animals."

"Just know that the children will resume their hunt, despite your empty threats to have the gods curse our fates."

"Do not test me!"

"I am going to tell my father what you've been doing and I'm certain he will relay your misdeeds to your parents. I doubt you'll be gracing this forest for much longer."

Tears of anger welled in Gwyn's eyes.

"I hate you."

"One day, you'll thank me."

Ario turned and marched away. His arrogance suffocated the entire forest and Gwyn let out a shriek. Though he heard her rage, he pretended not to and continued his stride. She gasped for air, and once he was far enough away, the tension broke and she could breathe again. She began to glide at full speed back toward the castle. Kipp followed close behind, his bone safely locked between his teeth.

She was frenzied and there was no one she could unleash her panic upon. Once through the unfrequented handmaiden's chamber, she collapsed to her knees and began sobbing into her tiny glass hands. She'd be barred from leaving the castle if her parents found out what she was doing. They would never let her enter the forest again if they learned that she was protecting the monsters they feared.

Kipp nuzzled his nose against her face but it didn't stop the tears. She was about to lose everything she cared for.

The sound of shuffling feet sounded from the shadows.

"Who's there?" Gwyn asked, promptly wiping the tears off her porcelain cheeks.

"Just me," Lorcan said, stepping into the dim sunlight that filtered through the open door.

"Why are you always down here?" she asked, frustrated to be found.

"I find peace in the solitude of the undercroft. I visit it often to mediate," Lorcan replied. "Why are you crying?"

Gwyn took a few deep breaths, contemplating whether or not it was wise to share the truth, but determined he was likely the *only* person it was safe to confide in. He already knew what she was up to in the woods.

"Ario Uveges found me in the forest. He threatened to tell Mamma and Pappa what I'm doing in the woods."

"Perhaps you ought to stop before he snitches. It would make him look foolish if he reports a false crime against the princess."

"The animals give me purpose. They are the only thing keeping me happy."

"Your next move is up to you, but if you seek my council, I suggest you halt your trips into the forest until this scenario plays itself out. I can only imagine what your mother will do if Ario follows through with his threat and it is then proven true."

"I'll be locked in my bedroom for months."

"Or worse," Lorcan warned. "Act wisely in this moment and those to follow, for they might define your future."

"I could shatter Ario," Gwyn seethed. A look of foreign hatred crossed her face, which caused Lorcan to furrow his brow.

"Think beyond your hatred. You must take this dilemma and let it shape you for the better. This is an opportunity for growth. Let it make you wise."

"How?" She eyed her uncle with skepticism.

"There's no telling how until the moment has passed. But if your behavior and response to this threat is driven by your emotional impulses, you will make matters worse and be forced to dig yourself out of a deeper hole. Take a step back, observe patiently, then react and move forward with logic and reason. Does that make sense?"

"Yes," she sighed. "Don't make it worse for myself."

"So you will stay out of the forest for a while?"

"I guess I'll have to."

"Good. Your brother misses you. He asks about you daily. Perhaps this break from your obsession will let you refocus your attention on those who love you."

Gwyn's anger toward Ario mellowed as she thought of Calix.

"I miss him too," she confessed.

"Then correct your wrong. Go to him and let him know he has not been forgotten."

"I can't. Mamma and Orlan have been keeping us apart. They think I will ruin him."

"Hmph, a dilemma indeed." Lorcan rubbed his chin, feigning deep thought. "How about a secret letter? Delivered by me."

"Would you?"

"Of course."

Gwyn glowed with grateful excitement.

"Thanks, Uncle Lorcan."

"Despite your maddening and unpredictable tendencies, you're still my favorite."

Gwyn smiled, her mischievous confidence returning.

Lorcan waved his hand, indicating she go, and Gwyn darted into the dark hallway with Kipp close behind.

Lorcan grinned.

To win a child's trust is to guarantee an adult's devotion.

Chapter 29

"Why did he smile like that?" Nessa asked her heart from the dark place in her mind.

"I can only show you what you saw and the fleeting moments surrounding each recollection. A heart's reach goes beyond that of the eyes."

"Show me more."

"I cannot show you Lorcan's history. You'd need his heart to do that. But you might learn a lot if you take note of what happens around the focus of your own memories."

"Show me more of my story."

"What comes next will not bring you joy."

"I don't care."

The heart obliged, catapulting her mind back into the past and reentering on the sight of a young princess with a devastated spirit.

Gwyn felt broken without the forest. The longer she stayed away, the more incomplete and purposeless she felt. Days became weeks and weeks became months, and it wasn't long before the weight of this abandonment turned into an anchor inside her chest. She had trouble eating, sleeping, and breathing. She hadn't smiled in weeks. Her hatred for Ario grew, he was responsible for her current predicament, but she could not let anyone know about the festering fury that raged within her bones. As far as she knew, he still hadn't revealed her secret and she certainly wouldn't leak the truth *for* him. So she waited.

She found a secret set of stairs beneath the war room that allowed her to eavesdrop on countless conversations. Discussions about her mother's infidelity arose more often than she cared to hear, which only intensified her resentment toward Dalila; it seemed everybody knew about the humiliating indiscretion except Almas. Gwyn also learned about Crystet's role in the Great Fight for the scepter of alchemy and the underground revolution her mother was orchestrating, but no word of Ario or her misdeeds. Jahdo was a constant presence in the war room meetings, but he never mentioned anything about Gwyn. As far as she could discern, no one knew, or cared, about her relationship with the animals.

Still, fear that the lack of chatter about her misbehavior was an illusion and that her first trip back into the woods would be a trap prevented her from returning to her old ways. An ambush by her parents' army was a humiliation she did not wish to endure.

So she stayed within the castle grounds, shackled by a threat yet to pan out. Her existence became one of silent sorrow and by the time her seventh birthday approached, she rarely left her bedroom. She had given up and only emerged for curious eyes when she wished to eavesdrop on conversations she wasn't meant to hear.

"Sissy," a tiny voice chimed from the other side of the heavy glass door that concealed her bedroom. "I miss you."

"Not now, Calix," Gwyn mumbled in reply.

"Why not?"

"I'm not strong enough."

Calix positioned his body on the floor and whispered through the sliver of open space beneath the door.

"I'll help you be strong again."

"It doesn't work that way."

"Please," he pleaded in a soft voice.

Gwyn released a deep breath, then got off her bed for the first time all day and went to the door, placing herself on the floor so she could peer through the gap Calix spoke through.

She reached her fingers under the door, and when they emerged on the other side, Calix pressed his fingertips to hers.

"I'm sorry," she expressed.

Calix sniffled in reply.

They shared a moment of solemn silence before Calix surrendered for the day. When he broke contact and walked away, Gwyn returned to her bed and snuggled next to Kipp.

Mina came with food three times, which Gwyn hardly touched, and the glass princess went to bed with a hungry stomach.

She awoke the following morning to the sound of whistling. She sat up and saw the tips of Calix's fingers stretched beneath the door. Her heart smiled, though she did not have the mental energy to replicate that smile upon her face. Instead, she forced herself out of bed and relocated to the floor. She connected her fingertips to Calix's and they stayed liked that for hours.

It wasn't until Mina arrived with a late breakfast that they were forced to separate.

Mina shooed Calix away before entering, as Gwyn had instructed.

"You ought to let him in," Mina suggested as she placed the plate of food on the nightstand.

"I don't want him to see me like this."

"Then stop being this way."

"I don't know why I'm here, or what I'm living for."

"You are a princess! Royalty of Crystet! You have far more to live for than most of us."

"I feel like the night has swallowed me whole."

Mina sighed, then marched toward the window. She opened the thick white curtains, letting sunlight pour through.

"Perhaps a bit of sunshine will remind you that you're still here and not trapped in the belly of the moon."

Gwyn squinted, unaccustomed to the bright light. Tears fell down her cheeks as she sobbed.

"I see the light, I feel it, but it cannot reach the dark hole growing in my chest. I thought I found my purpose, but the night swallowed that too."

Mina sat beside the princess and stroked her knotted hair as she cried.

"Perhaps you ought to return to the forest," she suggested in a whisper.

"How do you know where I've been?"

"The recurring dirt stains on your clothes gave you away."

"But you never told my parents?"

"No."

"Why not?"

"You seemed happy. I've never seen you so content, and I've been in charge of your care since you were an infant."

"I see," Gwyn mumbled. Mina was still unaware of the specifics and did not know of her growing rule over the monsters of Crystet.

"Will you tell me why you can't go back to the forest?"

"I can't explain. It will make everything worse." Gwyn sighed. "I wish the trees could talk to me. My secrets would be safe with them."

"There is a land where they can," Mina informed.

"Really?" Gwyn asked. Her entire life had been filled with lessons about the gods, but never any teachings about the other lands in this world. Those classes were set to begin when she was older. "Which land?"

"Wicker, land of the Woodlins. They are an unsophisticated species, but they possess primitive magic that the leading cultures of Namaté lost touch with. The Bonz hold a different, but similar magic."

"The Bonz?" Gwyn asked.

"Men of bones. They skitter across their webbed land like spiders."

"They have magic too?"

"They do. Sometimes magic comes in forms a little less recognizable." She turned her head and nodded toward the tiny fingers that had returned beneath the door. "Like love."

The tears fell faster when Gwyn saw that her brother had returned.

Mina left and Gwyn returned to her place on the floor. Calix already learned that talking did not work, so he patiently consoled his sister with his silent presence.

He returned every day that month and spent hours of shared quietness with Gwyn. Connected by touch but separated by sight, his devoted adoration slowly healed her aching heart.

On the morning before her birthday Calix did not show, and instead, Queen Dalila barged through her bedroom door for one of her infrequent and unexpected visits. She stopped at the edge of the bed to examine Gwyn, who napped with her face buried in Kipp's fur.

"This can't possibly be *my* daughter," she announced, her tone disgusted by Gwyn's apparent weakness.

The volume of her mother's repulsed voice shook her awake.

"What has triggered this sorrow that plagues you?" the queen asked. She glared down at her daughter, silver-green eyes glowing with contempt.

Gwyn let out a heavy sigh, energy drained by her mother's presence.

"Must there be a reason for my sadness?" she finally responded.

"Of course there must."

"My sorrow cannot be defined."

"You understand that you represent more than yourself, right? Your behavior, your reputation, your life achievements, they are all a reflection of this kingdom, of the Glaziene people."

"I'm not even seven yet."

"Age means nothing when you are royalty. You've been a representative of the Glaziene people since the day you were extracted from my kilned womb."

"I didn't ask for this life."

"No, you were *blessed* with this life. And though a small part of my heart can empathize with what you might be going through, I will not weaken you further with compassion. You must rise up and beat the depressed demon that lives inside you on your own."

Gwyn rolled over, unable to respond. She knew the remedy for her sorrow, a steady dose of nature and animals, but she could not relay this cure to her cynical mother.

"If not for yourself, then for your brother," Dalila tried again, altering her tactics. "He spends every free moment he has mourning next to your door. You have completely distracted him from his education. You have stripped him of *his* happiness."

"I'll try harder," she promised, though her voice was deflated and unconvincing.

"You must. Calix will be king one day and it's clear he needs you. The fate of our kingdom depends on your strength."

As soon as her mother left, Gwyn jumped out of bed and positioned herself on the floor so she could overhear what was being said behind closed doors.

"Orlan is failing us," her mother scathed.

"Perhaps she needs more time," her father replied.

"No. I need to locate the root of her woes so that I can cure her," Dalila insisted before marching off.

Almas exhaled deeply before stepping toward the door. Gwyn quickly stood and darted to her bed. She catapulted her little body onto the soft mattress as her father opened the door.

"Darling," he said in greeting, unaware that his little princess narrowly averted being caught as a spy. "How are you feeling today?"

"I'm fine, Pappa."

"Your mother says otherwise."

"Do you really care what she thinks?"

"Of course," Almas replied, though his conviction wavered. "She is the queen."

"I wouldn't care about her opinion if I were you," Gwyn retorted, thinking of her mother's scandalous betrayal.

Almas sighed, then sat on the bed beside his daughter. "Your mother is a complex woman, but she means well."

"Don't waste your breath. It's not worth it."

"Can I do anything to cheer you up?" he asked with genuine intent.

Gwyn thought of the animals and her desire to return to the woods.

"No."

Almas rolled up the right sleeve of his white satin blouse.

"When I was nine, I got my first crack." He pointed to the deep scar that ran from his knuckles to his elbow. The mark was lumpy and poorly mended. "Back then, my family merely worked for the royals and we didn't have the money to buy a proper fuse."

"How'd it happen?" Gwyn asked.

"I punched my older brother. Gave him his first crack, too. Right across his cheekbone. Left a nasty scar."

"Uncle Exton?"

"Yes. I'm surprised you remember him."

"I remember the scar on his face. Why'd you do it?"

"He wanted to kill one of our wolf pups. It was born with a limp leg, which meant it couldn't be trained for the royal guard, so he wanted to put it out of it's misery."

"But you wanted the pup to live?"

"Yes. I didn't think it was fair to kill the animal, so I fought him, and won," Almas said with a nostalgic smile. "Though I won, I was left with this scar as a reminder that I disobeyed the rules. My parents were furious and wouldn't let me keep the handicapped wolf on our ranch, so I built a hut for the baby in the woods beyond our property. I named him Griff and spent all my free time nursing and encouraging him to thrive on three legs. He didn't really need my support after the nursing stage, he would've learned how to survive without my care, but he became my best friend. When he turned two, my father saw how well the disabled wolf adapted and let me bring him back onto the ranch. But your Uncle Exton was a vengeful young boy and he killed Griff in the middle of the night a few months after he rejoined the pack. I woke up to the name Vindicene painted in Griff's blood on my bedroom wall."

"The malignant Vorso goddess?"

"Yes. As a child, Exton thought he was ruled by Her malicious and vindictive moons. But as we both know, that was just his excuse to behave poorly. He did far worse things after. When he turned twenty, he retreated to the Nutherlands to repent for all that he did in the name of Vindicene."

"Is he better now?"

"You can't erase evil, cannot undo a shameful past, but I think time has healed him a bit. Not sure how he is today, though. I haven't seen him since Calix's birth."

"Why are you telling me all of this?"

"Because there is nothing wrong with loving animals."

"I don't understand."

"I know about your exploits into the forest."

Gwyn's sorrow shifted into fear and the sudden transition read plainly on her face.

"But don't worry," her father reassured her. "Your mother doesn't know."

"Did Lorcan snitch?"

"He was concerned for your well-being and knew it was safe to confide in me."

"Why haven't you told Mamma?"

"Because she would react irrationally, and there is no need for that. Now tell me, what happened in the woods?"

"Lots happened in the woods."

"Something specific must have increased your melancholy. It's worse than usual."

"I feel fine."

"Then why haven't you gone back?"

"Why must we discuss every little thing about me? Why does everything have to have a reason? Why can't I just *be*?"

"Because you are royalty and you will take on more responsibility than most in your lifetime. You must learn how to be strong during your weakest moments. And though I fully appreciate what you are going through, we must find a way to soothe your temperament. It's best you continue this break from the forest, but would another pet help? Or perhaps a role amongst the royal animal trainers? You could help groom the castle wolves or manage the emissary owls in the aviary."

"I'll think about it."

"Good. And so you know, loving other creatures isn't a weakness."

"Mamma says it is."

"Well, your mother fell in love with me *because* I loved the wolves so much. She'll never tell you that, not while you're still maturing at least, but it's the truth."

"She's so confusing."

"I know." Almas leaned in and kissed his daughter's forehead. "Tomorrow is your birthday and we've prepared a wonderful party. Promise me you will try to enjoy the celebration."

"I promise," she said, aware this promise would be hard to keep. Birthday festivities were always miserable to endure. She would try though, aware that faking happiness would be a challenge; she hadn't smiled in a while.

Chapter 30

Her seventh birthday came and went with the typical dosage of wretched fanfare. The blessings from the nobles were overdramatic and staged; disingenuous, as usual, and scripted by her mother. The cake was too sweet, the music too loud, and the party too long. She faked a smile for as long as she could, but her muscles were weak and her energy was depleted. She was malnourished and could not keep up the pretense for as long as Dalila desired.

Luckily, by the time Gwyn's expression melted into one of hopeless exhaustion, most of the adults in attendance were too drunk to notice. The party raged on, and a few hours later she was allowed to retreat to her bedroom. Trista escorted her and Calix upstairs and their handmaidens readied each of the children for bed in their separate rooms.

When she woke up the next morning, tiny glass fingertips greeted her beneath the door. Gwyn smiled and went to Calix. She wasn't ready to let him in, but his refusal to give up on her meant more than she could verbalize.

She touched her fingers to his and resumed her spot on the floor adjacent from him. The wall between them shielded her silent tears.

Kipp snuggled next to her with his back to hers. Her two most trusted companions guarded her fragile heart from her consuming depression.

The trio lay like this every morning for the next six months. They protected her from her sadness, kept her company so her crippling thoughts weren't her only friend. Though they were unaware of the importance of their kind actions, Gwyn was certain they saved her from herself during this pivotal moment in time.

"*I was so sad,*" Nessa commented to the heart. "*I completely forgot this happened.*"

"*The mind does wicked things in the name of survival.*"

Nessa could not disagree.

"*Much time has passed. You ought to return to your body,*" her heart advised.

"*I want to see more.*"

The heart obeyed.

Ario never snitched to her mother. His lack of action baffled Gwyn. She was certain he would have followed through by now. The longer she went without punishment, the less she feared the threat. By the time glacial spring arrived, she was starting to feel like her old self again.

Calix woke her up as he always did, with a melodic whistle and fingers clinking against the glass floor. Gwyn rolled out of bed and opened the door.

He glanced up, shocked that she was finally letting him in.

"Your hair has gotten long," she noted, ashamed that she hadn't seen her brother in so long. "I like it." She ruffled the blond curls atop his head as he walked into her room. "Though you haven't gotten much taller."

"Are you feeling better?" he asked.

"I think so."

"You've missed a lot."

"I know."

"Mamma was mad that I spent so much time by your door."

"That's over now. You won't have to do that anymore. I will be better soon."

"How do you know?"

"I'm going back to the place that makes me happiest."

"Where's that?" he asked.

"Promise not to tell?"

Calix nodded with vigor.

"The forest," Gwyn revealed.

"What's there?"

"Monsters with gentle hearts and trees so tall they kiss the heavens. But you can't tell anyone."

"Can I go with you?"

"One day," she promised. "I've been gone a long time and I need to make sure the animals remember me before I subject you to such peril."

"Okay," Calix replied with glee.

She placed her hands on the sides of his face and then kissed his forehead.

"Good. Now, let me get to it and you get back to your schedule. Put Mamma's mind at ease that she hasn't lost you, too."

Gwyn rustled Kipp awake—he had grown lazy during her extreme bout of melancholia—and then grabbed her coat. Kipp happily jumped up upon realizing that they would be going on an exploration again, like old times.

They snuck through the halls and made their way into the basement where they could slip out the back door. The archers raised their bows with arrows pulled as the duo made their way into the open castle grounds, lowering them once they realized it was the princess and her dog.

The space beneath the gate where snow and glass-fragmented soil was dug up had refilled and Kipp got to work re-digging the hole. It didn't take him long to make room for their bodies to slither under once more, and they made their way into the forest.

She was whole again.

Their old trails were snowed over and unkempt, which meant they'd need to backtrack and smooth over their former progress. Though it was frustrating, she didn't mind the work. Retracing old steps would help her get reacquainted with the woods. It would give her time to let the animals know she was back and prepared to act as their champion once again.

Along the way she saw a drove of arctic hares, some were missing ears, others had deep scars running across their tiny faces. One was missing all of its teeth, so another rabbit chewed its food and then spit it out so the toothless hare could swallow the mush.

Another mile down the trail they reached a small clearing filled with austral sheep—an easy prey to the savage children of Crystet—and just as Gwyn suspected, these creatures were fresh victims to the abuse. There wasn't a single fur coat fully intact. The lot were patchy with raw wounds still bleeding through the wool.

Gwyn cursed beneath her breath, deeply agitated that her absence brought forth the return of torture. She was gone too long and the animals suffered for it. She would rectify this development and reclaim her reign of mystical terror. She would scare the children away, just as she had done in the past. She was determined.

A few hours into the tidying of their trails, the sound of feet crunching snow approached from behind. Gwyn turned to locate the source and found Ario trudging toward her through the deep snow. Anger swelled in her chest.

"You've been gone a long time," he stated.

"Isn't that what you wanted?"

"I changed my mind."

"Why?"

"I thought about it and decided I like the fright you place in all the other children. Your presence has power, it instills fear. I felt the gods might punish me for standing in the way of your potential."

"Too late. You kept me from my beloved forest for over a year. I returned to maimed and terrified creatures, which means the children have resumed their hunt and no longer fear me."

"I tried to stop them when I could, but they do not fear me."

"Clearly. Look at the damage they've done."

"But once they know you're back, they will retreat again."

"First, I have to win back the trust of the animals. You thoroughly ruined things for me."

"Let me help you fix what I destroyed."

"No."

Ario's expression tightened, but he wasn't ready to accept defeat.

"I've repented. I prayed to Rebelene and Melanel, in your name, every night once I realized I was wrong."

Gwyn rolled her eyes at the mention of the goddesses who haunted her.

"Perhaps they have forgiven you, but I haven't."

"I have entered this forest every evening before supper for the past eight months."

"I was wondering why you stopped attending the war meetings with your father."

"He stopped bringing me when I turned ten. He was afraid they'd see me as a man and recruit me to fight." Gwyn rolled her eyes, unimpressed. Ario continued, "I came here every day, determined to find you so I could apologize."

"Yet, here we are, and I still have not heard an apology."

"I'm sorry."

Gwyn laughed.

"I'm being sincere," Ario insisted.

"Then why are you armed with an axe and a bow?"

"I still have to protect myself. I break just as easily as you."

"Armor prevents cracks, not weapons. Those tools are designed to break others, and in your case, the animals I care about."

"I did not hurt any creatures on my way to you."

"And in the past eight months? During all your other trips to try and find me?"

Ario paused, then spoke carefully, "Never with malicious intent."

"If the answer is yes, just say so."

"You expect me *not* to defend myself when a wild creature attacks?"

Gwyn shrugged.

"You're mad," he continued.

"Maybe so, but also wiser than before. Your little attempt at intimidation taught me much."

"Like what?"

"That I can't trust you. You didn't deliver on your promise to ruin me, and now, you want to be my friend. You are fickle and unreliable."

"I was doing you a favor."

"You want to use me."

"The fact that I *didn't* rat you out should have earned your trust.

"I like people who follow through."

"Then perhaps I'll deliver on that promise now, since you'd rather lose everything you love and have me as your enemy."

"See? One minute, you want to be my friend. The next, you're ready to be my enemy again. How can I *trust* someone who is so fickle?"

Ario held his breath, controlling his frustration, before replying.

"I will never win with you, will I?"

"I don't suspect so."

Ario grunted. "Fine. I'll go."

"And never come back?" Gwyn mocked in a malicious tone.

"I never promised that," Ario smirked, then turned to leave.

"We ought to end here," the heart said, interrupting the memory.

"Why?"

"Chaos ensues in the present."

The heart ejected Nessa and launched her back into her body.

She sat up with a jolt, temporarily confused by her surroundings. The door to her tower was shattered and a row of ferocious wolves guarded her bed. Mina paced near the door.

"What is the meaning of this?" Nessa demanded, jumping out of bed, still fully clothed in the formal gown she wore before touching the heart.

"You've been unconscious for four days," Mina replied, cowering beneath Nessa's imminent wrath.

"Four days?"

"Yes. Tyrus and I have been guarding your body. We even let the wolves into the castle to help."

"Guarding my body from what?"

"After not hearing from you for a full day, we broke down your door and discovered your lifeless body. One of your handmaidens told her brother Brekken, who is a soldier loyal to Orlan. Chaos erupted. Everyone was trying to get to your body so they could shatter it."

Nessa held her breath and looked back at the bed where she left her body to enter the heart. The music box on the bed stand was empty, her scepter was propped in its holster, orb vacant.

"Did anyone lift the covers?"

"I did."

Nessa eyed her cautiously. "No one else?"

"No. And I wouldn't let anyone near you once I realized what you hid. I was trying to protect you."

Nessa took a deep breath. "No one else saw it?"

"No one," Mina confirmed. "Lorcan only stopped by for briefings on your status, and I wouldn't let any of the handmaidens back into the room after the info leaked. The doctors were going to come later this evening."

"Four days after you found me?"

"They were mending Orlan."

Nessa fumed, switching the focus from her heart to the disloyal members of her council.

"Lorcan, too?"

"He was darting back and forth between Orlan, you, and the guards protecting you from those who flipped. Traitors are aplenty in your midst and he was doing what he could to prevent any of them from reaching you."

Nessa turned and slowly returned to her bed. Beneath the covers lay her black heart. Cold and lifeless atop the white satin sheets.

"Who does it belong to?" Mina asked.

Nessa peered over her shoulder, confounded that her handmaiden had not figured out her secret already, then turned back to face the heart.

"My greatest enemy."

"Perhaps you ought to dispose of it—it could have killed you."

The density of Mina's miscomprehension was thick, but genuine. Everyone was fooled by the decoy heart that sat in her chest.

"Perhaps I should," She turned to face Mina again. "What I need from you is the same discretion you have always shown. *No one* can know that I possess another's heart. The safety of our land depends on this secret."

"That's why I wouldn't let anyone see you with it. I prayed to Gaia you'd wake up before the doctors came, because I wasn't sure how I'd stop them from lifting the covers. My gut told me you wouldn't want anyone to know."

"Your intuition is the only reason you're still alive."

Mina gulped.

"I'd like to keep you alive—there aren't many people I can trust anymore."

Nessa retrieved a black satin glove from the music box, pulled it over her right hand with slow deliberation, then picked up her heart. She looked back at Mina and spoke with grave focus.

"Don't make me regret sparing your life."

"I won't," Mina swore, her voice desperate.

"Good. Now, leave."

Mina skated out of the room with haste.

Nessa placed her heart into the orb atop her scepter and took a deep breath. Waking up to this development was startling and unexpected. She took a moment to reclaim her bearings. Near her shattered bedroom door sat the bone-crafted chest filled with fine materials from Fibril.

She glided to it, opened the lid, and pressed the soft fabrics to her face. Their aroma was foreign, but delightful—a sweet escape from the disastrous reality she awoke to.

"What happened to you?" Lorcan declared as he entered the room.

"How's Orlan doing?" Nessa asked without looking up. "I heard the entire castle was more concerned with his health than mine. Perhaps you all wished for him to take the throne upon my death?"

"Rubbish," Lorcan spat back. "You're exceptional at feeling sorry for yourself."

"Am I wrong?"

"You don't speak for me. I don't want Orlan as my king."

Nessa huffed. Her anger was a farce. In truth, she was relieved that only Mina paid attention to the details surrounding her vacant body.

"If you care to know, I was rounding up all the traitors so you could determine their punishment when you woke up."

Nessa glared over her shoulder at her uncle. "Where are they?"

"Bound and blindfolded in the wolf pen."

"Wonderful. They will undergo the ancient trials of loyalty, as will every guard in my ranks."

"Even those who have been protecting you?"

"Yes. They all must prove their allegiance."

"Understood."

"Start the trials tomorrow. Until then, let the known traitors stew in terror a while longer. I have other tasks on my agenda today."

She collected an armful of folded fabrics, shoved them into a silk carrier bag, and then glided out of the room, ignoring Lorcan's look of disbelief as she sped past.

Her top priority after every Bonz delivery resided in the village of Gler. It was a secret mission she performed regularly—formerly out of guilt, but now out of habit—since the early days of her reign.

"I am making a trip through the southwest villages," she announced as she charged out of the front doors.

"Your highness," the nearest swordsman chimed. "The state of affairs beyond the royal forest is currently chaotic. It's savage out there. With Orlan injured and your temporary bout of unconsciousness, the people are rallying to rebel."

"Then perhaps my presence will remind them that nothing has changed, that everything is still in order, still in my control."

This silenced the swordsman and he joined the ranks of soldiers, bears, and wolves that kept the queen protected.

Kentaro and Griffith led the charge, top swordsmen at their flank, and the remaining archers and soldiers formed a circle encasing the queen. The brigade marched, barefoot, through knee-deep snow, while Nessa sat atop Obelia, her most trusted boreal bear. They trekked through the southwest portion of the royal forest and into the village of Quarzelle. The swordsman was right; the scene was riotous.

Nessa raised a hand to halt the progression of her caravan while instructing Obelia to continue forward. The scar-wearing bear took heavy steps atop the glassened pavement, stopping once she stood between Kentaro and Griffith at the head of the pack. Nessa observed the chaos: citizens ran amuck, fighting over food rations and weapons. It appeared they were trying to bunker down and stock up on supplies in preparation for an unknown future with apocalyptic potential.

They were so consumed by their fear, they did not notice Nessa and her formidable army right away. The first person to see her regal silhouette sitting atop the largest boreal bear in all of Crystet was a small girl, who stood, facing the intimidating sight in paralyzed awe. When the child's mother came to fetch her, she let out a terrible shriek upon seeing the queen.

She snatched her daughter by the arm and ran, but Nessa was faster. With a swirl of her scepter, the woman was seized by magic and torn from her daughter's side. The child cried as her mother was lifted into the air by an invisible rope and dragged through the sky behind Nessa and her royal army as they moved into the town. Everyone who ran at the sight of their queen was lassoed by magic and added to the collection of bodies that hovered above Nessa. Dangling in the air by their necks, the growing group of captives slowly went comatose from asphyxiation. Nessa glanced up at her large collection of prisoners—half appeared lifeless while the other half violently choked.

"When you run, I am forced to assume you've aligned with the traitors." Nessa's voice boomed through the village square.

Her announcement stopped everyone in their tracks. Those who were running froze in place, guilty or not. Their obedience satisfied Nessa's need for control and she released her airborne captives from her magical chokehold. They plummeted to the ground, many breaking upon impact, but Nessa did not turn to assess the damage. They couldn't die unless they shattered.

She carried on, leaving the people to clean her mess and piece together her latest victims. The border separating Quarzelle from Gler was marked by crystal boulders that reflected rainbows off their angled edges in the sunlight.

Obelia carried Nessa over the border and the armed caravan entered Gler. The people here were less frantic, likely because they were not guilty of treason. Quarzelle, along with all the villages closest to the castle, were known to be more rebellious than those along the outskirts.

Though they did not scream in terror at the sight of their queen riding an enormous boreal bear, they did continue their daily tasks with heightened caution. Nessa accepted their guarded welcome as a success.

When she reached Uveges Armor Shop, she extended her scepter and slashed it through the air in a circular motion, freezing everyone in her radius. Minds asleep and bodies paralyzed, Nessa was safe to complete her mission with only the animals as onlookers.

Kentaro began sniffing the nearest man, salivating at the smell of soft flesh beneath the glassy surface skin. Kentaro licked the man's fingers.

"Harm no one," Nessa commanded. Kentaro's eyes darted to his master, wide with guilt, and he backed away from his immobile meal.

Nessa entered the shop and found Jahdo mid-step at the front door. She had to sashay around his rigid body with care as she did not want to disturb his petrification or leave any trace of her visit.

She made her way to the back room where Jahdo kept his hidden stock of items from various lands. The top shelves were lined with vials of lethal gasses and liquids from the Gasiones of Vapore, most were stolen and gifted to him by Nessa, others were old and received as gifts from her parents back when access to foreign items was limited.

Beneath his growing collection of chemical warfare were metal scraps from Coppel. This stash was running low as he used all of the metal gifted to him while Dalila was queen and Nessa was unable to replenish his stock because the Metellyans refused to barter trade agreement after she abandoned their rebellion against the Voltains. She raided Coppel a few times during the early days of her rule, but hadn't gone back in recent years. The Coppel army was large and fierce, which made the risk too great.

The bottom shelf housed stones from Orewall, vines from Wicker, and a jar of pasty mud from Soylé. On glass racks lined along the opposite side of the shelving hung all the fabrics he collected throughout the years. Nessa replenished his stock of fine materials so often it was impossible for him to run out.

She removed her large carrier bag from her shoulder then began removing the fabrics and hanging them on the racks, keeping his organized closet in tact by placing the new fabrics with like materials. Once her bag was empty she left the store, mounted Obelia, and swept her scepter across the landscape. The spell lifted and everyone resumed their day, unaware they had lost a chunk of time to Nessa's magic.

"I've made my point. Let's head back to the castle," she informed her soldiers, who promptly redirected their trek.

Mina waited in the queen's sleeping chambers for her return. The glass door to the bedroom was repaired during her trip into Crystet, as Nessa ordered.

"Welcome back," Mina greeted.

"Thank you for your loyalty."

"Of course," her handmaiden said, bowing her head.

"I can undress myself this evening."

Mina curtsied, then departed, and Nessa entered her private chamber alone.

She no longer knew who she could trust within the castle, so Nessa fastened armor over top of her navy blue charmeuse dress. The sleeves were short with folded edges and the collar covered everything up to the bottom of her neck. Beneath it she wore a diamond breastplate. The skirt of her gown had a split up the front, which left a triangle-shaped gap revealing her long, skinny legs. The glass flesh covering her lanky limbs was covered in mended scars. While most people regretted each crack they wore, few embraced the cloudy arrival of fused scars. A person who was proud of their breaks was to be feared—it meant they were not afraid to take risks and viewed their brokenness as a strength. It meant they weren't afraid to break again and that level of reckless bravery put them above the rest, who trembled before anything that might cause their body harm.

Once her dress was on, she fastened a metal corset to her torso and turned to the mirror. Perfection, though her face was bare. A few days ago, she would not have left her room without a full face of makeup on, but now, nearing the end of her life, the mask no longer felt necessary. She was growing to like the face she hid beneath the paint; the face that looked a lot like the pure-hearted girl in her memories. She could not feel her younger self living within her anymore and her barefaced reflection was the closest she could get to reconnecting with the girl she once was. It would be over soon and none of this would matter ever again, but it was nice to spend her final days a little closer to a better version of what she could've been.

She left her room to find Mina guarding the hall. The queen's sudden reemergence startled her.

"My queen," she stumbled and then bowed.

Nessa skated down the hall without acknowledging her handmaiden, using her scepter to propel her forward. She found Lorcan in the Solarium, reading another long piece of parchment.

"What are you studying every night?" she demanded, startling her uncle where he sat.

"I'm not studying anything, just reading," he stated while casually spinning the long roll of thick paper till it was returned to a tight scroll.

"You're in here every night reading that thing," she said. "I see you from my tower. Surely you're not reading for pleasure."

"What if I am?"

"I know you better than that. Everything you do is precise and holds meaning."

"Then, if you must know, this parchment contains the history of your mother's reign. The historians have been working on it for years and they finally provided me with a draft to review."

Nessa pursed her lips, taken aback by this unexpected revelation. "Surely, I'll get to review it as well."

"If you want to, you can. I suspect your input might be a bit biased though."

"I can separate the facts from how I felt."

"Then you can read it after I'm done."

Nessa paused, perturbed by how easily he caved. She wanted to catch him in a lie, wanted to catch him doing something devious, but instead, was offered an invitation to join his little project.

"Do you wish Calix had taken the throne?" Nessa asked, opening a topic she never raised with her uncle before.

"I do not wish for things that are impossible," Lorcan replied without emotion.

"But do you wonder? You must. You must wonder how things would be different if he were king."

"Why are you asking me dangerous questions? You're always looking for a reason to hate me."

"That's not why I asked."

"Then why are you putting me in a precarious position?"

"Because I've been wondering about it lately, too."

"Wondering is a foolish hobby. It offers nothing but infectious suffering. One thought leads to another, which leads to another, and sends you into a wormhole of impractical desires. What's done is done. Leave it in the past."

"For someone who lectured me on remembering my brother's memory, that's an awfully harsh reply."

"I will not place myself at your mercy for saying something you deem treacherous, even if your line of questioning is being presented as a moment to bond."

"He would be a great king," Nessa declared.

"He never even grew into a man. There's no telling what kind of king he'd have been."

Accurate, but still, Nessa knew he would have grown into a wonderful, good-hearted man, unless, of course, she managed to ruin him along the way. This was why she needed to jump. She would not stick around to tarnish him further, assuming there was any good left in his resurrected soul.

"How is Orlan?" she asked, changing the subject.

"Mending. You gave him a good break."

"He deserves worse."

"Take care not to anger Gaia. He is Her chosen, after all."

"Says who? How do we know he has any connection to the Mother at all?"

"Says time and history. Orlan is ancient, alive since the start of time. Being Valið is part of his lineage and the visions he had as a young boy solidified his status. He proved himself when he foretold Prince Rúnar's malicious, but impressive reign."

"If he foretold it, why didn't anyone prevent it from happening."

"We are not meant to alter fate, only adapt. Orlan's insight helped those in Rúnar's circle adjust and prepare for the worst. When it was proven true and Rúnar turned out to be as remarkable as prescribed, everyone knew Orlan would be next in line for æðsti prestur."

"What did Orlan predict of me?" Nessa asked, curious.

"Not much, until Calix was out of the picture. But with all the rumors, speculation, and mystery surrounding Calix's death, it was hard to differentiate truth from fiction. He stayed quiet for a while, hesitant to confirm any visions as they were swayed by his personal feelings toward the situation."

"That's convenient."

"Understandable, though. Those were very trying times for all."

"So, he never revealed Gaia's thoughts on my rule?"

"On the day of your coronation he spoke to me in private. He said that your reign would be devastating. That in time, you would blanket the entire land in despair."

"The land was already blanketed in despair when I took the throne. Glaziene people have always thrived in sadness and greed. They flourish in their narcissism. My rule was not the start of such a curse."

"You turned their selfish despair into terrorized despair, which is far more potent and volatile."

"I am reshaping our world so that one day, we can live without any underlying sorrow or selfishness. Why can't anyone see that?"

"Because you've done nothing but scare the masses into compliance. With dark magic, I might add—a fact Orlan predicted."

"It was necessary—I would have been eaten alive without magic."

"When will you confide in me the source of your power?" Lorcan asked. "I have been your greatest ally, your most loyal councilman, since the day you were born. Still, you conceal your greatest secret from me. I've been inquiring for years. When will you tell me?"

"When you rupture from old age, I will whisper my secrets to your shattered pieces."

Lorcan cursed beneath his breath. "This concealment wins you no favor with me."

"I don't need your approval."

Lorcan clicked his tongue. "Why have you stopped wearing your shield of make-up?"

"Perhaps I've grown to like how I look without it."

"It's disconcerting. It makes you look weak. Your identity has grown inconsistent and explosive."

"I am the same as I was yesterday."

"No, you're not. You are unstable and I worry who your next victim will be."

"Perhaps it will be you," Nessa sneered as she exited the solarium, fuming from this unpleasant exchange. She didn't know what she expected from her uncle, or why she pushed the boundaries of their relationship after keeping tight margins for so many years. Reliving old memories was altering her hardened façade, it was making her dig deeper and view her current world with a new eye. The visions her heart shared were vivid and full of detail, so much so she was remembering things she likely did not even notice at the time the moment was actually happening.

She returned to her tower, climbed the glass steps, and peered out over the castle grounds. She could see everything contained within the royal forest that encircled the castle, and all the villages and metropolises beyond. She didn't want any of it, yet all of it was hers. She collapsed to the floor, scepter in hand; her powder blue skirt draped over the ground beneath her body like a blossom.

All the doors were locked and Mina knew to leave her alone, so Nessa retrieved her heart and prepared to dive in for the long haul. It pulsated red through the cracks of black upon contact.

"Show me more," she asked of her heart.

"It will take you away for too long."

"I don't care. I crave the forgotten emotion."

"All you will find is anger and sorrow."

"Perhaps that is the motivation I need to finish what I started."

"If you want your memories, you must promise not to end us."

"You are not in charge. I am."

"Calix will forgive you."

"What if he doesn't?"

"I am certain he will."

"How can you be so sure?"

"I remember how much he loved you."

Nessa paused, doubting her heart's confidence.

"I cannot face him, not after all I've done."

"Then in the present you shall remain."

Her heart went black, refusing to return her to the past.

Furious at herself for relying on her heart for motivation to finish what she promised to do, she decided she did not need the nostalgia to inspire her rage. She used all her energy to remember the day she discovered Orlan defiling Calix in the steeple. The foggy memory swirled inside her head, and though it was blurry, it was vile enough to engage her fury.

It was time to end this, once and for all.

Chapter 31

She placed her heart into the orb of her scepter and descended the spiral staircase of her tower. Mina still stood outside the door, guarding her bedroom.

"Come in," Nessa beckoned.

Mina obeyed, locking the door behind them.

Nessa stripped naked, revealing the darkened decoy heart that sat within her spacious chest cavity. Mina helped her into the red chiffon gown, tying the choker-collar lace into a bow at the back of her neck.

"What is the occasion?" Mina asked.

"Death," Nessa declared.

Mina nodded, afraid to ask for details.

"Lorcan keeps receiving summons from the Metellyans," Mina informed, changing the topic. "He came by multiple times to see you, but I kept him out. You might want to find him before you do anything else."

"Perhaps."

"Also, Orlan is mended and on the move again. Thought you might like to know."

"Wonderful. An easy prey takes the fun out of the hunt."

Mina looked at Nessa with concern, but did not ask the obvious.

"May I go now?"

"Yes. Check on the progress of my kolkrabba. I'll be ready to feast soon."

"Of course, my Queen."

Once Mina was gone, Nessa paced her bedroom, recalling the worst memory of her life with more detail. Emotionless on the surface, but boiling beneath. The feeling of fury somehow translated despite her missing heart.

Her mind raced around all the painful ways she could murder Orlan, lingering on the methods that caused the most pain and shame for the monster who hid behind the title of æðsti prestur.

She walked to the mirror and stared with contempt at what she saw. Without makeup, she could still see the little girl she used to be buried in her reflection. The innocence, the hope—remnants of those treacherous traits still lived between the scars on her face. She opened the glass makeup case on the vanity and found a corked vial of red powder. Uncorked and shaken, Nessa used her finger to smear the red dust around her silver gaze. The bright, fierce color matched her dress and made her eyes smolder like a raging flame under ashes. The effect was fire. It matched the molten fury that simmered in the vacant hole where her heart should be.

Orlan's time was up.

Nessa flew out of the room. The sunlight pouring in through the glass walls caught the color of her flowing red chiffon gown. It reflected through the skirt and onto the glass ground, leaving a mirage of blood in Nessa's wake.

Along the way, she shoved those in her way to the side with magic. There was no doubt she caused them to suffer small breaks in her pursuit of vengeance, but she did not care. And they did not have the authority or nerve to challenge her aggression. They simply fell and observed in pain as she sped by.

When she reached the north tower and could see the tall steeple doors in the distance, she found Lorcan in her way.

"What are you doing here?" she asked, abruptly pausing her flight.

"Where have *you* been?" he retorted. "You've been inaccessible all morning."

"Refueling my motivation."

"Excuse me?"

"The less you know, the better."

"Enough with the riddles and secrecy. I am your andlega ráðgjafi. You chose me to be your spiritual advisor. I cannot do my job if you keep me in the dark."

"I don't need an advisor, I only need loyalty."

"Utterly infuriating," Lorcan mumbled in a groan. "Orlan isn't here."

"Why not?" Nessa's tone shifted from eerily calm to lethal.

"He left on a mission."

"No one is allowed to leave on my boats without my permission," Nessa scathed.

"You were nowhere to be found," Lorcan reminded her.

"Where did he go? And for what purpose?"

"He has traveled to Coppel to discuss the ongoing revolution with the Metellyans. King Oro has been relentless with his carrier cardinals as of late, and I felt it was time we replied."

"I want no part of their futile revolution."

"I understand your reservation. You lost a lot to this cause."

"They will never take back the scepter of alchemy from the Voltains. And even if they do, who keeps the magic once it's stolen? Two lands that can barely cooperate while on the same side cannot share such power. The fighting will not end until the ocean turns blood-red."

"Perhaps, but we can prepare for such a conflict. You have magic. *How*, I have no clue, but you do. Let's use that to secure Crystet's ultimate possession of the scepter."

"I don't need more magic. I need revenge."

Lorcan groaned. "Enough with this plight for revenge. It's been years. Let it go. Be the first Glaziene ruler to possess the scepter of alchemy since King Rúnar. Not the queen who was so caught up in petty vengeance that her entire reign was plagued by misery."

"I cannot think about future achievements until I fulfill an old promise I have yet to keep."

"You can't kill Orlan," Lorcan stated.

"I can kill whoever I want."

"The entire Glaziene population will turn on you if you do."

"They already have," Nessa countered.

"You know what I mean, it will be far worse than anything you've experienced thus far."

"He needs to be terminated." Nessa's blank expression hid a fury Lorcan could feel. "You know why."

"I don't want to discuss it anymore."

They shared a brief moment of tense silence before Nessa resumed her original mission.

"When will he be back?"

"At the end of the week."

"And how is my kolkrabba turning out?"

"It smells divine."

"Perfect timing," she mused, then changed the subject. "Prepare my boats. We are sailing to Wicker."

"Why?"

"I seek their council."

"*I* am your council…"

Nessa ignored him and stormed off, leaving Lorcan to stew in doubt.

Chapter 32

Nessa returned to her private chambers and packed for the sea. She remained in her dress of death, ready in case the moment to kill Orlan arrived upon her return. With her heart in the orb of her scepter and a carrier bag packed, she exited the castle and made her way to the north shore where her boats were prepped and ready to sail. Kentaro and Obelia joined her onboard.

"You're really letting the bear on this boat?" Lorcan asked. "Its weight could sink us."

"I don't see us taking on water," Nessa countered.

Lorcan groaned, but dropped his complaint.

Nessa snatched a rat skull from the pouch hanging off Lorcan's belt and tossed it to Hadid, who was perched on his shoulder. He chewed the treat loudly, cracking it to dust in three bites.

Her carefully selected soldiers lined the deck, standing alert and determined. The fifty she allowed on her enormous glass vessel had proven their allegiance when they suffered through the agonizing trials of loyalty. These soldiers still wore fresh scars from the unfortunate but necessary torture they were forced to endure. Only the truest persisted till the final hour.

"You know the way," she announced before making her way below deck and into her private chamber. Mina and Kentaro followed.

"Guard the door. I will be asleep until we get to Wicker."

"The entire time?" Mina asked. "It takes six sunsets to arrive on their western shore."

"Yes, the entire time. Only wake me if it's an emergency."

Mina sighed, but bowed her head in compliance. Kentaro stayed by her side.

Nessa locked the fogged-glass door behind her and then slammed her scepter on the glass floor three times, enabling a cloak of invisibility to shield her boat. Those above did not know they were concealed from every danger they passed on their way to Wicker, but Nessa could escape easier knowing that there should be no emergencies to wake her.

She removed her heart, held it in her hand, and slipped into a deep slumber. Though she wished for pleasant memories, the heart showed her Ario's death.

"I don't want to relive this," Nessa objected.

But the heart did not listen and forced her to recall one of her greatest sorrows. When it was over, Nessa felt perplexed.

"Wait," she said, unsure if she saw the recollection correctly. "Let me see it again."

"As you wish."

This time, Nessa focused solely on Orlan.

Behind the bright light of Gwyn's third blast of magic, Orlan snatched the religious star pendant he wore around his neck, raised his arm, and cast his own lethal beam of magic at Ario. While Gwyn's attention was focused on her dying friend, Orlan picked up a large shard of a shattered mirror from the rubble.

As Gwyn charged at him, prepared to die if it meant killing the high priest, he expelled a wall of energy through his extended palm. Gwyn thought she tripped, but she had actually been stopped by an invisible force field.

Orlan possessed dark magic. He was stronger than she ever realized.

"All this time I thought I accidentally killed Ario. I thought I was to blame," Nessa stated in awe of her revelation. *"But it was Orlan. He killed Ario. He has magic. No wonder he is so untouchable. No wonder I was unable to kill him. No wonder he has tricked so many people to ignore his wrongdoings. He has blinded them with magic."*

"Correct."

The burden she carried for Ario lightened while her hatred for Orlan intensified.

"But his magic does not come from his heart, or any other removed organ. It comes from the pendant he wears around his neck."

"Orlan wears the lost relic of Gaia."

"I thought it was a replica."

"He disguised it by adorning jewels and gold to its original form," the heart explained, "but beneath the shiny exterior exists the true medallion, which was once touched by Gaia. It is the second most powerful object in Namaté behind the scepter of alchemy."

"More powerful than heart magic?"

"Slightly. Not all magical relics are more powerful than heart magic, but this one is because it was touched by Gaia. Also, possessing it does not threaten his well-being. When you removed me, you left yourself susceptible to being permanently shattered. He still has all his pieces in tact, so if he breaks it's not necessarily his end."

"I never stood a chance against him."

"No, you didn't," her heart confirmed.

"Why didn't you tell me this years ago?"

"You needed to discover it for yourself."

Nessa was rocketed back into her body as the glass boat lurched to a halt in Wicker.

The Woodlins were not happy to see them.

"They are trying to cast us back out to sea," Mina explained from the other side of the door.

"What do you mean?" Nessa asked with a yawn. "They are my friends, my closest allies."

"Then you better get up there and sort things out."

Nessa groaned and got out of bed. She looked at her disheveled appearance in the mirror. She couldn't go out looking as she did, still dressed in the fire-red gown she planned to wear while killing Orlan, so she went to the closet and quickly changed into something more simple: a forest green tunic dress. Before heading to the deck, she siphoned water from the spigot in the corner of her room to wash her face. The Woodlins appreciated natural beauty and would be less likely to receive her well if she was wearing the war paint she left Crystet in. Not only was it intimidating, but she had slept in it for six days. She scrubbed her face with the purified black sea water until all the makeup was removed.

"We see through your charms!" a Woodlin shouted. "Show your face or be gone, enchantress!"

The threat was an unusual one and it heightened Nessa's guard. Something wasn't right. She slammed her scepter on the floor three times, removing the shield of invisibility from around the boat.

"I'm ready," she finally said to herself, now looking like a fresh, younger, and less intimidating version of herself.

Obelia roared, shaking the glass ship as she paced the deck. Nessa needed to alleviate the tension before matters got worse.

Lorcan opened the hatch as she climbed up.

"What took you so long?" he asked. "You are the only person they are willing to talk to."

"I'm here now," she said in a hurry. When she embarked onto the deck and her face became visible to the Woodlins, a chorus of melodic cries echoed into the sky.

"We thought you wouldn't come, dear little one," Bolivar howled from the edge of the dirt shore.

"What's going on? Why were you trying to turn us away?"

"Baldric has chosen death. No visitors are allowed when we send his roots to the river bend. But you, his favorite stranger from afar, you are no danger to our observance. You will not tarnish our festival."

"Why would he choose death? Let me speak to him."

"You know our ways," Bolivar explained. "And it is time for his soul to set sail. Very noble, a gallant sacrifice. His demise will bring life and balance."

Nessa was not in the mood for their riddles and long-winded explanations. So she lowered a ladder and climbed overboard. Kentaro tried to follow.

"Stay," she commanded.

The wolf whimpered, but obeyed.

She landed in the rowboat waiting beneath and one of her soldiers rowed her a short distance to the shore. Once there, she exited into shallow water and walked barefoot to the coarse shoreline. Gritty soil stuck to the bottoms of her glass feet and became lodged in the crevices of her fissures.

"Show me the way to Baldric," she demanded.

The trees lowered their boughs, shaking the leaves atop the branches on their heads as they bowed and showed the way.

The trail was long and dusty. Dirt dispersed into the air as she disturbed the untraveled path. When she found Baldric, he was alone in a meadow surrounded by wildflowers. There wasn't another Woodlin in sight.

The field was alive with colors, some she'd never seen before and couldn't name. The beauty was overwhelming.

"Why are you alone?" she asked. "And why are you choosing death?"

"So others can live."

"I need you to stay. You promised you would see me through to the end," she reminded him. "I'm almost there. I'll come back when my mission is complete and we can die together."

Baldric turned to face her, his face hung with weathered wisdom.

"That's not how this goes; your woes are not mine. I die to bring new life. My journey is solitary, selfless, and true. Yours, well you've changed since your heart was removed."

"I am on the brink of finishing what I started. I came here to tell you that. To tell you that my journey is almost through."

"Your aura is damaged, in your wake you left a wreck. Your methods were reckless and incorrect. Do you regret how you've grown? Do you see what you've done? Or are you in too deep to recognize the person you've become?"

"I am still me," Nessa insisted.

Baldric extended a branch and grabbed her wrist, squeezing it tight until she unclenched her fist. The mark was still there, as were her attempts to scratch it off.

Nessa looked down in shame. "I did what I had to do. I would have been eaten alive in Crystet if I hadn't removed my heart."

"Emotion is not a weakness."

"It is where I am from."

"I wish you took the advice I gave you when you came here as a child."

"I did," she insisted. "I am sacrificing my life so another's life can resume."

"Bringing back the dead is not the same as new life taking shape. You have lost faith. Your purpose is vexed. For you, I fear what will come next. I am dying with grace—my being is more in tune with the heavens than ever—but you, you have lost your way. Your soul has grown distant, you are halfway from fate."

"What does that mean? I am doing everything I said I would. I've never strayed from my goals. In fact, I'm more honest, more genuine in intent than most in this world."

"Halfway from fate means you're being tossed between the Mother and Her Brother. Kólasi wants you. He's yanking you under. Your soul is adrift and nomads make perfect wardens in his abyss. But Gaia knows your struggle; it's the fate she designed. It was always her goal to watch you shine. She chose your heart and still has hope that your soul will ignite before you self-destruct."

"What am I supposed to do? My entire world is already shaped and defined. How am I supposed to change things that are out of my control? Am I supposed to give up? Break old promises?"

"No. You cannot stop the wave you are on. All you can do now is learn how to love again."

Nessa paused. That wasn't the advice she was expecting to hear.

"I lost everything I loved years ago."

"You must relocate that sensitivity if you want your dance with gravity to end amongst the stars."

She thought she was doing everything right, fixing old wrongs and bringing justice to those who brought harm to her and those she loved. But if Baldric was right, her fate after the worst of this passed depended on relearning an emotion she used to know too well. An emotion she snuffed and smothered till all memory of it died in the dark space where her heart used to sit.

"I cannot let love back into my life until I finish what I've started. I cannot see this through with love, this mission requires fury, rage, hatred."

"Then I hope you have time to mend what you've frayed before you let your journey come to an end. I'd like to find your soul on the other side."

Nessa nodded. Aware that Baldric never gave advice that wasn't true, caring, or in her best interest. He and the other Woodlins were the only beings she trusted as much as she did herself. They were there for her as a young Queen and proved to be a stable source of support throughout the years, during her worst and best days. Even when she came back heartless, though they were furious, their love for her never swayed.

"I will miss you."

"I won't be too far away," Baldric promised. "Just a few miles north in outer space."

Nessa leaned in and wrapped her arms around his withering trunk. The bark fell off in chunks as she made contact. He returned the sentiment by entwining his long, wooden arms around her small body. She was dwarfed standing next to him. Though she could not feel her grief, she was certain it was there.

"Learn to love," he whispered, "and reunited we will be in the heavens above."

She nodded, unsure how she would fulfill his request. Another promise to keep. She took a deep breath and pushed the pressure aside. For now, she just wanted to cherish her last moment with her greatest confidant.

This would be the last friend she ever had to say a final goodbye to; the last friend she'd ever lose. Heartache could not follow her in the afterlife.

Chapter 33

"Did you get what you needed?" Lorcan shouted overboard as Nessa was rowed back to the glass boat where he waited.

"Some clarity, yes," she replied as she held her scepter under her neck and climbed up the ladder.

"Are we heading back to Crystet?" he asked.

"No. I've decided we will visit Elecort."

Lorcan's eyebrows lifted. "What for?"

"The scepter of alchemy, of course."

He took a deep, panicked breath. "While I am delighted that you wish to join the rebellion, I think it would be prudent for us to go home and devise a solid plan first."

"I am not *joining* the rebellion, I *am* the rebellion."

"I see," Lorcan replied, unsure how to handle his niece's sudden shift of focus. "Wouldn't you rather think this through?"

"I don't need a plan."

"You must have some idea of what you'll do when we get there."

"They won't see us coming," she assured her uncle, "and I will pluck the scepter from Ignatius's electric grip."

"I advise against such brash defiance. You saw what happened to your mother. I do not wish upon you a similar fate."

"By the time his militia realizes what has happened, I will be back in Crystet, guarded by the arctic sea, our razor sharp border defenses, and my fortified glass kingdom. An attempted retaliation will be their undoing."

"Your army was halved after the trials of loyalty," Lorcan warned. "You might not be as well protected as you think."

"I have an army of wild beasts. I don't need weak men, both in mind and flesh, protecting me. Not to mention, the moment my people realize I seized the scepter for Crystet, their loyalty will shift to me. They will go where the power resides."

"Perhaps. Still, it might take time to solidify their wavering allegiance, and Orlan is still in the picture."

"You're forgetting the most important part: The Voltains won't be as strong without the scepter. *I* will have the power."

"Will you know how to control the magic? It might take time to understand its full potential."

"I suspect I'll manage just fine. How long is the trip to Elecort?"

"From here? Four sunsets."

"Wonderful." Nessa banged her scepter against the glass deck, enacting the shield of invisibility that no one knew was in place except her. "I will be in my chambers below. Do not disturb me unless there is an emergency."

Lorcan sighed. "Understood. When should I wake you?"

"When the lights of Elecort are in sight."

He nodded. "I'll prep the guardsmen for the monsters we are sure to encounter. The seas north of Orewall are teeming with cecaelia and sylphs."

Nessa let him carry on with his preparations, though she knew they'd have no issues with the monsters. The creatures would sense their presence, they'd possibly swarm in confusion, but they would not be able to see their prey.

Nessa went to Obelia and offered cold love to the boreal bear. Though it was frigid and stiff, it was more than she gave to most. She caressed the bear's neck, who whimpered in appreciation. She then turned to her wolf, who lurked in her shadow since they left Crystet.

"Kentaro," she said. "Come with me."

He followed her down the glass steps and into the lower level of the ship. Mina stood by the door, ready to serve.

"Another long slumber?" the loyal handmaiden asked.

"Indeed. As before, do not wake me unless it is urgent."

Mina nodded, making way for the queen and her wolf to enter the room. Nessa locked the door behind her and took her heart out of her scepter.

Kentaro needed no instruction. He sat by the door, prepared to defend his master if the need arose.

Black heart in hand, Nessa gently laid down on the mattress and was swept away into a blank slumber. The heart left her in the present; no memories graced her dreams this time.

"The coast of Elecort is in sight," Mina announced through Nessa's door, waking her from sleep.

She sat up and yawned, recalling how restful a normal slumber felt.

"It's time to cross another enemy off my list," Nessa said to Kentaro, who still guarded the door.

Mina's voice emerged again from the other side.

"My queen. May I enter?"

"Yes," she replied, collecting her bearings. "Come in."

Mina cautiously entered, minding her step around the snarling wolf.

"Stand down, Kentaro," Nessa commanded.

The wolf lessened his aggression, but remained at the ready.

"Shall I prepare an outfit?" Mina asked.

"Yes. Ready me for murder."

Mina nodded and pulled a long burgundy gown from the closet. The dress was sleeveless, leaving the scars on Nessa's arms visible, but the bodice covered her from neck to ankles.

Tight around the waist, her slender figure was accentuated and though she appeared frail, the battle wounds on her arms and the gleam in her eyes suggested otherwise.

Mina attached a sheer, matching burgundy cape to the collar of the dress, which hung to the floor. She then outlined the queen's eyes with dark grease and powdered her translucent skin with blush. Nessa looked in the mirror and was pleased with the result. Terrifying beauty.

Heart placed into the orb of her scepter, she charged above deck.

In the distance, she could see the glowing outline of Elecort. The colorful skyscrapers were illuminated and their glow bounced off the black surface of the sea and polluted the night sky with light. Nessa scoffed. Their existence was an unnatural atrocity.

She slammed her scepter onto the glass deck of the boat, reinforcing the invisible shield they sailed beneath. It was imperative that King Ignatius did not see them coming.

"What's the plan?" Lorcan asked.

"Make them regret the day they crossed our family."

"How so?"

"Steal the scepter and kill the queen."

"What about Ignatius? You must want him dead as badly as I do."

"He will suffer more if I keep him alive. The grief will swallow him whole."

"No, he must die. Torture Ignatius as he did your mother."

Nessa paused in contemplation. "We shall see."

Lorcan huffed with frustration.

"Send your eyes overhead. Locate the queen."

Lorcan extended his arm and whistled, summoning Hadid, who sat perched on the beam holding the largest satin sail.

The owl landed on his clawed glass arm, creating new cuts with its sharp talons. Lorcan then removed his left eye and entrusted it to Hadid.

"Find Queen Soline."

Hadid spread his wings and took flight, soaring toward the blinding light of Elecort and disappearing into the hazy glow.

"What do you see?" Nessa inquired.

Lorcan covered his right eye and focused.

"The queen is in a field of neon flowers, collecting electrified blossoms in a basket. She is surrounded by handmaidens. No soldiers or guards in sight."

"Fools," Nessa said with a smirk. "Lazy from years of unrivaled, indulgent power. This will be easy."

Lorcan uncovered his right eye and looked at his niece with concern.

"How do you plan to access her? She is deep within the city of Elecort."

"No one will see me coming," Nessa assured. "Trust me. Lower a boat. I will go alone."

"You plan to kill the most powerful queen and steal the scepter of alchemy all by yourself?"

"*I* am the most powerful queen. You ought to know that by now," Nessa playfully chastised her uncle.

Nessa boarded one of the suspended rowboats and then her soldiers lowered her into the water. Still cloaked within her heart's shield of invisibility, she aimed the orb of her scepter toward the shore of Elecort and propelled forward. She stood tall in the small boat, wind whipping her dark blonde hair and burgundy cape as she soared toward her destination.

The boat hit the copper-flaked shoreline and a bolt of electricity was sent through the base of her boat. It absorbed most of the shock, but she was still able to feel the charge in the bottoms of her bare feet. Immediately, she realized that she would not be able to set foot in Elecort without a little assistance.

"Help me," she implored her heart.

Encased in its enchantment, Nessa was lifted a few inches above the boat. She stepped over the short glass wall and onto the electric beach, pleased to see that her bare feet never touched the ground. She hovered above the electric charged ground, safe from its lethal energy.

With confident strides, she strolled across the beach and into the city of Elecort. She remained unseen and unharmed, thanks to her heart.

The Voltains did not need metal to produce electricity, they were born with that ability, yet the city was built on a foundation of copper wires and spools wrapped with thin metal cords—deceased Metellyans, used to enhance the grandiosity of their city. Without these sacrifices, without the metal pieces unwillingly taken from their southern neighbors, Elecort never would have reached its current opulence.

Nessa examined the Voltain people, all of whom had natural wires built into their plushy, glowing skin. Many wore Metellyan enhancements to engorge their voltage capacity, making them stronger and more lethal than they'd be on their own. An unfair advantage acquired with the help of magic, though all of that would change once she stripped them of the scepter. The Metellyans would no longer be slaves to the Voltains, murdered for their body parts, and the Kingdom of Elecort would dissolve into the meager, isolated land it once was.

The city glowed with bright, hazy colors, a stark contrast to Crystet, which was blanketed in gray and white. The cityscape was so vivid, the incessant buzzing so loud, Nessa's head began to throb. She had to find Soline fast before the neon lights made her too dizzy to focus.

In the distance, the castle was visible. It was the tallest structure in Elecort, as well as the brightest. Hundreds of lustrous peaks encircled the tallest. Around the castle was a steel metal fence that glowed a menacing shade of blue. Guards wrapped in coil and armed with phosphorescent spears secured the gate.

Nessa raised her scepter and the heart lifted her invisible body over the tall gates. The Voltain guards were oblivious to the breach in their security.

Safely hovering above the ground on the opposite side of the fence, Nessa could taste the bloodied sweetness of revenge in her mouth. The rush felt divine.

Hadid screeched from above, still holding Lorcan's eye, and she rounded the corner to where he flew above. At the backside of the castle, she found Queen Soline.

Blissfully unaware that her death loomed, the gleaming queen smiled as she collected flowers in her basket.

Nessa's heart raced with anticipation and though she could easily end Soline's life, she lingered in her invisibility, letting the moment build. She recognized the wicked nature of her glee and how the ecstasy she felt in the moments before raining death onto an unsuspecting prey was deranged. Even so, she waited, watching the happiness and imagining the terror she was about to inflict.

When she could no longer contain her excited anticipation, she swiped her scepter through the air and sliced Soline's head clean off her shoulders.

The Voltain handmaidens shrieked in horror as the queen's head hit the ground and rolled lifelessly toward them. They ran in chaotic patterns from the unseen nemesis, unsure where to go to find safety. With another broad-swooping wave of her scepter she beheaded the screaming women, sending them all to the ground with a unifying thud. Besides the constant electric buzz that resonated through all of Elecort, the world was quiet again.

She exhaled, proud of her work, then floated over to Soline's lifeless body. Frayed wire-veins sparked where her head and body were separated and Nessa waited for the last tiny explosion of electricity to finish before picking up the head. Soline's purple radiance was gone, only her neon green eyes remained aglow, and the transition from incandescent to colorless was drastic. She looked nothing like her former self. All vivacity was gone.

Nessa smirked. Ignatius would shrivel into a puddle of charged tears when he saw the fate of his beloved queen.

With the queen's head in her grip, extended outside the shield of her invisibility, she marched into the castle. Sight of the floating head of their cherished queen terrified every noble and guard she passed. Some fell to their knees in prayer, others ran in the opposite direction, some fainted from fright. But none of their reactions gave her the same thrill as Ignatius's.

As she entered the throne room, the king dropped his copper goblet and gasped in horror as the head of his wife flew toward him. His young son, Prince Lucien, sat beside him on a smaller throne.

"Soline," he whimpered, both in fear and sorrow.

Nessa silently beckoned her heart to remove the shield of invisibility and when she was revealed, the king's conflicting emotions grew more complex.

"Ice Queen," he seethed, "What have you done?"

"I think it's quite clear what I have done." She threw the severed head at Ignatius' feet. "I am here for vengeance."

He picked up his beloved's head, staring at it with bereaved anger as he spoke.

"Then ready yourself for war because you stand no chance against the scepter of alchemy."

"Luckily for me, you no longer have it."

Ignatius turned to face his throne and discovered the scepter was missing from its stand. When he turned back around, Nessa was holding both her own scepter and his.

"You let your guard down," she said with a smug shrug. "You let love distract you."

"You are evil."

"I know." Nessa smirked, then aimed both scepters at the Voltain king. He rose into the air, shaking violently, and foaming electrified bubbles oozed from the corners of his mouth. She then threw him across the room where he landed in an unmoving heap. His soldiers charged at her, but she did not hesitate. With minimal effort, she sliced them all in half, severing their interior wires and causing them to short-circuit. Ignatius was left with no protection.

"How does it feel to be helpless?" Nessa sneered as she sauntered toward his crippled body, still hovering above the electric floorboards. "I thought to let you live so you could suffer beneath the weight of your grief until your dying day, but seeing you cower in pain reminds me that you don't deserve another day on this planet."

"You won't get away with this," he said through gritted teeth.

"I already have."

She crossed both scepters in front of her then swung them in a downward motion, delivering her final blow. King Ignatius was sliced in two and the exposed wires hanging from his corpse sparked as his soul entered the afterlife.

She tore one of his glowing blue eyes from his skull and then turned to face the only survivor in the room.

"Did you enjoy watching your father die?"

The young prince shook his head, illuminated tears rolled down his cheeks.

"We are even. This settles the score," she told the boy. "He killed my mother and forced me to watch, helplessly, so to him, I've done the same. This back and forth ends today. Understood?"

Lucien nodded.

"Don't repeat your father's mistakes," she warned the quivering boy. "The people of Glaziene belong to me."

Intentionally exposed, opting not to engage her invisibility, she stormed out of the room, mindlessly killing every Voltain that crossed her path as she flew back to her ship that was anchored at sea. Hadid mirrored her brisk flight.

"And to think that you doubted me," she said in response to Lorcan's speechless stare of wonderment, tossing Ignatius's neon eyeball to him. Lorcan caught the memento and examined it in awe.

"Back to Crystet," she shouted and the helmsman rerouted their ship to the east.

Another enemy dead.

One left to go.

Chapter 34

With the scepter in her possession, Orlan would be easy to defeat, but it was still imperative that the high priest did not see her attack coming. He possessed the lost relic of Gaia—a magical artifact with rivaling levels of power—and he was clever. If he caught wind that she was aiming to take his life, it was possible he could outsmart her. So Nessa acted with care.

Now that she had the scepter of alchemy, the rebellion was disbanded—though the Metellyans had yet to learn of this—and Lorcan was on board.

"King Oro will be furious that you took it without him," Lorcan mused, delighted to backstab the King of Coppel. "You might face mutiny."

"Let them try," Nessa growled. "They couldn't steal back the scepter with an entire army at their disposal, yet I did it by myself. They cannot beat me."

"I'll be honest. I did not think you'd be the one to return Crystet to its former glory. I didn't think you had it in you. But to see you seize the scepter, single-handedly on a whim." Lorcan paused to revel in triumph and his grin spread from ear to ear. "I've never been more proud."

"If only you *actually* saw it," Nessa mused. "I ravaged the royals."

"Didn't you see Hadid at the window? I saw it all."

Nessa had not seen the owl at the window, but she was pleased to know that someone witnessed her greatness.

As they spoke of the owl, it returned and landed on Lorcan's arm. He retrieved his eye, placed it back into its socket.

"What now?" he asked.

"I am going to kill Orlan," she stated plainly.

Lorcan nodded his head, no longer inclined to fight his victorious niece.

"Yes," he agreed. "I now see the beauty in Orlan's death. It is timely. We no longer require his power to obtain the scepter."

"Did you know he had the lost relic of Gaia all this time?"

"I did. But I couldn't tell you. You refused to contribute your dark magic to the rebellion, so we needed Orlan's."

Nessa growled with annoyance.

Lorcan smiled and continued, "Though he was using his to manipulate the Voltains from afar, whereas you simply showed up and took the scepter from them."

"Controlling from afar?"

"Did you really think the Voltains left us alone because they feared you? No. He sent waves of spells into Elecort that made them forget about us, repeatedly, whenever anyone mentioned certain keywords: Crystet, Glaziene, your name, my name, his name. The moment any of these words were uttered, a haze entered their minds and the conversation would turn."

"That's all he managed with so much power? Pathetic."

"Agreed." Lorcan grinned like a giddy child. "So happy that our goals are finally aligned. We will eliminate Orlan to sever the tie between him and the Glaziene people. They must worship *you* moving forward."

"They should have been worshiping me all along," Nessa replied with cynicism.

"You showed no interest in the Great Fight, so I could not back you. I had to keep Orlan in power."

"Yet here we are, years later, and I won the Great Fight in a single afternoon."

"Indeed, you did."

"And now, I can finally kill the monster that has plagued my existence."

Lorcan sighed. "Indeed, he has."

Nessa said nothing more and returned to her private chambers below deck. She did not want to tell Lorcan too much, too soon. He'd discover in due time the extent of her plan. For now, she needed him to believe that they would rule Namaté with a diamond fist together. She needed his unwavering devotion and loyalty until Calix returned.

When they reached the northern shoreline of their homeland, Nessa prepared to cast her long held rage onto Orlan.

"Where would you like to end him?" Lorcan asked in private.

"In the steeple. He should die where he sins."

Lorcan nodded. "Poetic. What do you need me to do?"

"Arrange a meeting for the three of us. Let him know I have acquired the scepter and that my outlook has changed in his favor. Tell him you told me about his relic, then convince him that I want to combine our magic and bring Crystet to a level of greatness it has never known before."

"Plausible," Lorcan noted. "It could work."

"Have him secluded and convinced by moonrise. I'll be there shortly after."

Her uncle nodded and the ship docked.

The day was already half over, so she didn't have much time to prepare. She was mentally exhausted from the journey and physical exertion, so she went to the Wildlands to revitalize her spirit.

Halfway through the forest, she placed a hand over her chest. Calix's heart made no noise. After Ario's death, it grew too loud and acted as a constant reminder of what she had done—what she formerly believed she was responsible for—so she silenced it. Now that she knew the truth, she felt compelled to let it speak again.

She took a deep breath, then removed her hand from her chest.

She wasn't ready.

Kentaro and Obelia followed her invisible trek into the Wildlands by scent.

Deep into the Wildlands, Nessa removed the spell of invisibility. Her suffering was almost over.

"Do you promise to protect Calix when he is rebirthed?" she asked Kentaro and Obelia.

They both grunted and whimpered in reply. Besides the scepter, protection from her beasts was the best she could leave him with.

"You are still convinced that you must die?" her heart said, awakening within its orb.

"I am," she responded simply.

"You haven't eliminated all your enemies."

"Orlan will be my last."

"There are more."

Nessa glared in the direction of her heart.

"There will always be more. I have conquered those who hurt me as a child."

"One day you will recognize your oversight and when that day comes, you will be happy I refused to die."

"Your fate is still undetermined," Nessa replied, annoyed by the personality her heart developed outside of her body. The longer they remained separated, the less control she had over it. It concerned her that a similar distancing was occurring between Calix and his heart, though she hoped she was wrong. Neither were cognizant or functioning, neither were technically alive, and she prayed that put their development on hold. But there was no way to know for sure.

At the top of Jökull Cliff, Nessa stripped naked and stood at the edge, preparing herself for what would be her eventual fate. She imagined herself jumping, and the adrenaline rush sent shivers through her body.

She was ready.

When the third moon began to rise over the dark horizon, she redressed, reclaimed both scepters from where Kentaro and Obelia guarded them, and returned to the castle. She reenacted the spell of invisibility when she reached the Village of Quarzelle. Causing alarm amongst the people now would serve her no good.

The castle was cloaked in shadows by the time she returned. Purple moonlight illuminated the glass fortress, causing half of it to glow while swallowing the rest in darkness.

She slipped into a black gown that exposed her broken chest. The elegant masterpiece of died Fibril fabric had two pieces of chiffon attached to the fabric choker that covered her breasts. They formed a "V" and connected to the high waistline of the enormous, pouffed skirt. Her long, white hair that held streaks of black was in a tussle of wild curls and her makeup was as dark as the hatred she carried. Barefoot, Nessa skulked toward the steeple.

Most of the castle was asleep, so her trek went undisturbed. Torches illuminated the corridor that led to Orlan, as if welcoming her plight of revenge.

She barged through the fogged glass doors, scepter of alchemy in hand. Sight of the highly coveted staff silenced Orlan the moment it came into view.

"A bit overdressed, no?" the high priest stated, staring at the exposed space between Nessa's breasts. Calix's half-blackened heart was in clear sight.

"It is a momentous occasion."

"Indeed, it is," Lorcan confirmed, trying to hide his nerves. "We finally have the scepter of alchemy."

Orlan's eyes remained fixed on Calix's heart.

"The greatest power on the planet is finally ours," Orlan mused, though his conviction seemed forced. "What, may I ask, will be your first order of business?"

"To rid Namaté of known evils."

Orlan nodded. "And what of that?" He pointed at her chest.

"Of what?" Nessa was unsure why the conversation was turning.

"Do you intend to keep the power? Or give it away?"

Lorcan looked to his niece, confused.

"What kind of preposterous question is that?" Nessa scowled.

"You know exactly what I mean." Orlan wore a devious smile, making it known he was onto her. "Be careful who you trust with that," he then warned. "A forsaken heart grows into a bitter relic."

"What are you two talking about?" Lorcan demanded, but before he got an answer, both opposing parties had their magic drawn. Orlan snatched the lost relic of Gaia and thrust it toward Nessa, while she aimed the scepter of alchemy at Orlan. Lorcan dodged out of the way as the archenemies circled with caution, ready to strike.

"I knew you came here to kill me," Orlan said with a laugh. "I suspect you finally have enough magic to succeed. Took you long enough."

"It ends tonight."

"You have everything and more than the greatest of Crystet royalty ever dreamed of possessing, yet you choose to make my death your first act as ruler of Namaté. And then, you plan to throw it all away." Orlan shook his head in disapproval. "Your ancestors cringe in the afterlife. Gaia weeps at your folly. You are a disgrace not only to your family, but to the gods as well."

"The only god I worship is Gaia. The rest are irrelevant."

"You will never learn."

"Here I am, about to kill the invincible æðsti prestur. I'd say I've learned a lot."

"Perhaps you have finally acquired enough power to kill me, but you still know nothing of the inner workings behind all your heartache."

"What are you waiting for," Lorcan demanded, "Kill him!"

Orlan sneered with amusement at Lorcan. "How quickly allegiances turn."

"He's just trying to buy time so he can devise an escape," Lorcan warned his niece.

Fueled by the rage of a sorrow-ridden heart, Nessa released her first detonation. A golden liquid fired in Orlan's direction, hot as the sun Gaia hid from them, and struck him in the gut. The heat melted a hole in his stomach, liquefying everything it touched. Orlan fell to his knees, insides melting and spilling out of his body like a goopy stew. He shot his own line of magic at the queen, but he was weakened and slow, giving her plenty of time to dodge the blast with minimal effort.

She cackled.

"This is too easy."

"I may be your enemy," Orlan spat between dying breaths, "but I am not your greatest."

"Nothing is worse than what you did," she said with resolute confidence, then generated another lethal dose of magic. A crazed scream of savage pleasure erupted from the pits of her gut as the fatal blow was dealt. The stream was a cool shade of beige and its effect turned Orlan, bit by bit, into granular pieces of glass sand. The æðsti prestur bellowed in agony as the magic worked with slow precision, taking what felt like eons to turn him into dust. Nessa enjoyed the gruesome spectacle with satisfaction. Silver blood spat in spurts all over the glass room as the pile of sand grew taller. Lorcan watched in horror as he witnessed a new way for the Glaziene to die.

When only Orlan's scarred, bald head remained, his eyes rolled into his head and he muttered a final thought in a voice not his own.

"In eternal darkness, your soul will starve, forever seeking the light of morning. Undead, prisoner to the voices of the living, you will find yourself trapped within your once forgotten sorrow. Pursue the sound of life to correct your final wrong."

Orlan's skull crumbled into dust.

"What was that?" Nessa asked, appalled by her enemy's final words.

"The voice of Gaia," Lorcan replied calmly.

"I thought he was a false prophet."

"For the most part, he was. I haven't heard Her voice in years. Seems She didn't abandon him after all."

"Or maybe She just really needed to reach me," Nessa countered. "What did it mean?"

"I'm not sure," Lorcan's eyes darted around the room, assessing the damage to mask his nerves. "Didn't sound too hopeful though. Is there something you're not telling me?"

"No," she lied.

"Well, take care in the days to come. Her message sounded like a death omen."

Nessa sighed, aware she could reveal no more

"I'll inform the people, both of his death and of our exciting acquisition. Perhaps knowing that you seized the scepter for Crystet will lessen their disappointment about Orlan."

"Good luck."

Lorcan departed and Nessa was left with little time to retrieve Calix's pieces from his long neglected tomb and finish what she set out to do many moons ago.

Chapter 35

With the help of her heart and the scepter of alchemy, Nessa transported—with ease and secrecy—all of her brother's broken pieces into her childhood bedroom.

The vacant room was unused, unvisited for years; still, the countless cracks in the walls were stained with Kipp's blood. This was where her suffering started. This was where it would end.

It would take one full day to properly assemble Calix. He was small when he died, so he was still small after the rebuild. Though years had passed and he would have been a grown man by now, all the growth was lost and Calix would come back in a child's body. As for his mind, Nessa hoped that how he left was how he would return, but there was no telling if his consciousness remained active in limbo all those years. The world between the living and dead was a mystery to all. The possibilities were endless. No one had ever remained broken that long before being rebuilt.

The news of Orlan's death riled the people of Glaziene into a state of hysteria, Nessa was grateful she had magic to speed her work along. Obtaining the scepter did not earn their respect, as she formerly hoped, and she wouldn't last long in this life with the fury of thousands wishing her dead. Lorcan suggested she use the scepter of alchemy to sway their opinion of her, to cast a spell that mollified their hatred, but she did not have the will or energy. She'd be gone soon and perhaps their hatred for her would enhance their gratitude toward Calix upon his return.

Once the rebuild was near completion, she took a break to visit Jahdo. Armed with her usual delivery of fine fabrics, she made herself invisible and trekked on foot to Gler. After freezing the town, she revealed herself, delivered her typical gift, but this time she also returned the crystal bear Jahdo crafted and gifted to her on her eighth birthday, along with a note that read:

I used to think this crystal bear was the greatest gift I ever received, but in fact, you gave me something far better. You gave me Ario. During times of growth, he provided me with courage. During times of sorrow, he reminded me that I was strong enough to endure. Ario always believed that I was capable of achieving my heart's greatest desires and he didn't rest until I believed it too. He was my greatest love and I am sorry I let you both down. I am sorry for being distant and unreachable in the aftermath of his death. I am sorry for casting you aside. The pain was too real, too potent to relive. I regret the role I played in his murder and for leading him down a dangerous path. We lost our way in our quest for justice and I'm sorry it cost you your greatest love. I don't forgive myself, nor do I expect that from you, but

I hope you trust my love for him was always real. I leave this world as a broken woman, empty and unloved—an expected fate and one I do not protest, but I hope that you will remember me kindly, as the young girl who felt too much.

—*Gwynessa*

She suspected he'd burn the letter and smash the bear, but this long overdue expression of remorse gave her a small sense of closure.

Back at the castle, disguised as a birthday feast, she ate her final meal alone. Thirty-six years of life. Thirty-six years of prolonged sorrow. Nessa was relieved it would soon be over.

The kolkrabba was served on a bed of sylph legs, an extravagant luxury prepared specially for the queen. She ate as much as her stomach allowed, devouring the rotted, pickled sea witch tentacles in silence. No one was permitted to bother her while she feasted. It was a time of private indulgence and solitary introspection.

Once finished, she prepped two plates—one for Lorcan and another for Mina—then allowed her servants to finish what was left. They accepted this unusual act of generosity from their wicked queen, scoffing down the leftovers like starving creatures of the wild.

She hesitated upon returning to her bloodstained childhood bedroom. Her blurry reflection was visible in the fogged glass door—her white hair held more black streaks than she could count and the veins spreading from the dark void in her chest had slithered up her neck.

Her time was running out—she was becoming the darkness.

But she had one task left to complete: placing Calix's heart back into his body.

A pause of sheer terror.

She reached down her throat and retrieved Calix's heart. The moment it touched the outside air, it came back to life.

"You abandoned me," it seethed with betrayal.

"I needed to do this on my own. But look," she expressed, thrusting it in the direction of Calix's body. "I followed through."

"You took too long."

"It was a large task."

"Why are you stalling now?"

"What do you mean?"

"I remain imprisoned in your clutches instead of reunited with my vessel. Why?"

"I must go before he returns."

"Wise choice. But how will you guarantee the task is completed?"

"I can trust Lorcan. He will do it."

"You cannot trust anyone."

Nessa groaned, aware that the heart was right.

Furious, but left with no other options, she caved.

She placed the scepter of alchemy atop Calix's right arm, wrapping his fingers around its base, then held his heart over his small, lifeless body.

"A worthy king," she said in a small voice. "I'm sorry I took so long to make everything right. I love you and I hope you can forgive me."

She plunged the heart into the open cavity she left while rebuilding his chest. The moment it was back in place, his heart, which would maintain minimal traces of magic until he awoke, began to fuse the gaping hole. It worked furiously to repair the last piece of its vessel.

She removed her own heart from the music box, then closed the lid, silencing her favorite melody. As she turned to leave, Calix's heart spoke.

"Don't leave." Its voice was muffled within Calix's healing body.

"I must."

"Your job is not complete."

But Nessa was already darting out the door and did not hear the heart.

She fulfilled her promise, she did all she could to make things right, and she did not wish to learn what Calix thought of her now. After all she had endured, his hatred was a heartache she did not wish to carry with her into the afterlife.

Death would be kinder.

She found Mina in the corridor that led to her royal tower.

"You must deliver this to Lorcan," she handed her trusted handmaiden a letter.

"Okay," Mina responded, too afraid to ask questions.

"Thank you for always being so solid. When the world crumbled around me, I could always count on you to keep me standing. I have done everything in my power to ensure that your loyalty will be rewarded despite the changing tides."

"It has been my greatest pleasure to serve you, though I fear what this unexpected revelation means."

"Do not fret. In due time, all will make sense."

Nessa leaned in and gave Mina a kiss on the forehead; a gesture foreign to both women. Mina accepted with frightened gratitude and Nessa skated off without another word.

Barefaced, barefoot, and dressed in her simplest nightgown, she darted toward death. Unafraid and focused; today was her final day of suffering. She carried her heart in her hand, no longer feeling the need to hide it in her scepter's crystal orb.

Kentaro caught her scent as she dashed through the open fields toward the spot beneath the fence where she and Kipp used to sneak in and out. Though the old, crystal posts were reinforced with steel after she took the throne, she left the large hole under the fence as a keepsake. In recent years, she forgot the flaw in her security was even there, but tonight, she relived her glory days one last time, squeezing her adult body through the small opening. Kentaro followed.

The wet snow and dirty soil unearthed from the broken glass terrain stained her white nightgown.

Her focus was intense and the energy of the forest shifted beneath her momentum. The trees stood eerily still and animals emerged to watch their beloved queen race toward death without fear. They followed her, slowly enlarging her posse. When she reached Jökull Cliff, an army of wild creatures stood at the edge of the forest, watching her every move. Boreal bears, gelid foxes, hyperborean moose, meridional wolves, austral sheep, arctic hares, snow leopards, musk oxen, and feral penguins were among those in attendance to wish Nessa a final farewell. Appropriate, she thought, as she never truly learned how to connect with people.

They gave her space as she encroached the hill. Kentaro and Obelia followed, but stopped halfway. The animals understood this was an end of an era and though the change in power would likely end their prolonged safety, they did not fight their queen's wishes. Instead, they stood back and watched in support; aware of the heartache she was putting to rest.

"Let me live," her heart finally said, breaking their long-held silence.

"I don't want to be rebuilt."

"You never learned to love again."

Nessa shrunk as she recalled the forgotten advice she received from Baldric. She looked down at the tree-shaped stain on her palm. How could she enter heaven with a soul incapable of feeling love?

"And you heard Gaia's warning," her heart continued. *"How can you pursue the sound of life if all of you has perished? I must remain. You must leave me behind. Your death is not sealed."*

Her heart was right. Too many ends were left unfinished and if Orlan's final words were truly a message from Gaia, a complete self-shattering would likely curse her to Kólasi's abyss. She did not wish to anger Gaia.

Nessa lobbed her heart into the early morning air and watched it land in the dark ocean below. Its red glow faded as it sunk to the bottom of the sea.

Now, it was her turn. She stripped naked, leaving her soiled nightdress as the only evidence of her suicide.

With a deep breath, she fell. A single, easy step over the edge and she plummeted to the ground, shattering amongst the nameless masses. Her pieces scattered, blending into the glass remains of the countless deceased Glaziene lining the graveyard shoreline.

Once lost in life, now found in death, the bittersweet beauty of letting go set her broken heart free.

Epilogue

Mina found Lorcan in the solarium reading the final draft of Dalila's memoir. The room smelt of burnt wood and sage incense. Mina paused, afraid to disturb his peace.

Lorcan sensed her presence and waved her over. He sat in a large, ornately-carved glass chair beside a raging fire. Without a word, she handed him the sealed envelope and then left.

Lorcan hesitated when he recognized Nessa's handwriting on the front. After a moment of confused worry, he ripped it open and unfolded the letter.

Uncle Lorcan,

Calix is rebuilt. You will find him in Kipp's tomb. Though I wished to see the life return to his eyes, I could not stay; I could not face him after all that I've done, all that I've become. You were right when you once told me that his return would bring my end, but I trust that you will guide him to be the merciful king Crystet needs. He will be told horrible stories about me, I am sure, but I hope you will speak kindly of me. Tell him that no matter what he might hear, I always loved him more.

With love,
Gwynessa

Lorcan stared at the note, heart racing. He was the only surviving member of the Gunvaldsson family, the only living person left to take the throne. This was his chance to reign.

Without further hesitation, he crumpled the letter and threw it into the fire.

He then raced to Nessa's childhood bedroom, barreling through the door and locking it behind him.

Calix lay lifeless on the floor. His heart hadn't finished the fuse; his rebuild was not complete.

Lorcan laughed at Nessa's foolish mistake. A rebuild after such prolonged death took hours, if not days, for the spirit to find its way back to its vessel. Lost in purgatory, Calix was still dead; Nessa left before his soul had a chance to find its body.

Lorcan slammed his fist into the small boy's chest and yanked the heart from its glass-boned cage.

It shrieked in protest, calling to Calix on the other side, but it was too late. The boy did not navigate the maze of purgatory fast enough.

Lorcan breathed heavily, impressed with himself. He opened the music box that sat on the floor, releasing an eerie melody into the room. It reminded him of Gwyn; the small princess, forever doomed by her enormous heart. He placed Calix's squealing heart into the music box and closed the lid, silencing them both.

There would be no resurrections under his watch.

Thank you for reading *Crystet* — I hope you enjoyed the story! If you have a moment, please consider leaving a review on Amazon. All feedback is very helpful and greatly appreciated!

Amazon Author Account:

www.amazon.com/author/nicolineevans

Facebook:

www.facebook.com/nicoline.eva

Twitter:

www.twitter.com/nicolineevans

Goodreads:

www.goodreads.com/author/show/7814308.Nicoline_Evans

Instagram:

www.instagram.com/nicolinenovels

To learn more about my other novels, please visit my official author website:

www.nicolineevans.com

Made in the USA
Lexington, KY
25 November 2019